A deep chuckle sent Jessica whirling around.

Despite the familiarity of the tall man standing in the open doorway of her room, his shoulder resting negligently against the frame, Jessica felt chills of alarm. They increased as she stared into that darkly handsome face. She had seen those gray eyes darken with anger, dance with mischief and burn with desire. Never had she seen them flooding with hate . . . before now.

She began to know genuine fear. ''What are you doing in my room?'' she demanded.

Morgan barked with harsh laughter. ''Still playing the Widow Miller, all schoolmarm proper, even though you're wearing only chemise and drawers!''

He jerked away from the door frame; Jessica flinched back. ''Morgan, please . . . I don't understand. . . .''

''Well, it's like this,'' he said with a sneer. ''You've led me a merry dance, lady. I'll give you that. But the game is over, Jessie Cameron. I've come to fetch you home. . . .''

Dear Reader,

Once again, as we will every month from now on, Harlequin Historicals brings you four new historical romances for your reading pleasure.

Bronwyn Williams is back with a delightful love story that captures the joy and pain of a young girl growing to womanhood under the uneasy tutelage of a handsome whaling captain. Set in the outer banks of North Carolina, *Gideon's Fall* is a book you will want to read again and again.

And we are very pleased this month to be publishing *Stardust and Whirlwinds,* a Western by first-time author Pamela Litton. With astonishing skill, Pamela has written a heartrending tale of a refined Eastern lady and the gun-slinging drifter who becomes her protector.

With Jan McKee's *Sweet Justice* and Caryn Cameron's *Wild Lily,* this month is packed with romance and adventure. We hope you will enjoy all four titles, and we look forward to bringing you more of the same in the months to come.

Yours,
Tracy Farrell
Senior Editor

Sweet Justice

Jan McKee

Harlequin Books

TORONTO • NEW YORK • LONDON
AMSTERDAM • PARIS • SYDNEY • HAMBURG
STOCKHOLM • ATHENS • TOKYO • MILAN

Harlequin Historical first edition March 1991

ISBN 0-373-28668-6

SWEET JUSTICE

Printed in the U.S.A.

JAN MCKEE

has lived her entire life in Raytown, Missouri, a town that has its origins as a stopping point on the Santa Fe Trail. Even as a young girl, she wondered what it would have been like to live in those days, so it is no wonder that she is now an acclaimed writer of historical romance. Although this is her first book for Harlequin, she has won several awards for previous romances, including a *Romantic Times* Reviewer's Choice Award in 1988.

To Ron, again and always

Prologue

Ellsworth, Kansas, 1872

The setting sun cast a shadowy pall over the Rossiter Shipping Yards, reflecting the dark mood of the young man staring out the dust-streaked window in his older brother's office.

Beyond the empty cattle pens, across the railroad tracks, the sound of a tinny piano could be heard as the tenderloin district of this raucous cattle town started coming to life. Lanterns were being lighted within those Scragtown pleasure palaces, and soon the quiet summer evening would become flooded with a cacophony of moral turpitude as dozens of piano players pounded out their jangling, boisterous tunes. Unfortunately, it was Morgan Rossiter's intimate familiarity with the sights and sounds of Scragtown that was going to cause his defeat in this latest, and most significant, battle with his brother.

"Dammit, Zach!" Morgan finally exclaimed as he whirled to face the balding man seated behind a big desk. Zachary Rossiter's announcement had come completely out of the blue, and it had hit Morgan like a low blow. It was taking him some effort to control his emotions. "You had no right, no damn right at all to take out a mortgage on the ranch without at least discussing it with me first."

Zachary Rossiter hid his surprise over the passionate objection he'd neither expected nor considered. "On the contrary, little brother," he stated flatly as he stared up at the tall, black-haired young man looming over the desk, hardening his heart against the hurt he saw in those dark gray eyes. "I had every right to sign those papers. Rights I've earned during the past thirteen years since Ma and Pa died. But I doubt you can understand my feelings or know what it's been like trying to squeeze by from one year to the next. You've been too blasted busy playing fast and loose with cards and your women, having a gay old time getting kicked out of one school after another—schools I busted my butt to pay for, in case you've forgotten!" Zachary Rossiter came halfway out of his chair while his voice rose in volume. "And what have you done since you've been home? Hell! The most effort I've seen you expend is on establishing yourself as Scragtown's most infamous hell-raiser!"

Both brothers knew Zachary's angry charges were exaggerated, but only Zach was aware of the underlying envy that partially motivated this denigration of Morgan's character. At twenty, Morgan Rossiter was almost sinfully handsome, and he possessed a natural charm his thirty-five-year-old brother would never own. But it wasn't Morgan's dark good looks or his winning manner Zachary resented. It was the opportunities he'd been given, then squandered so carelessly, that were eating at Zach. Zachary Rossiter would have given his right arm for the advantages Morgan had treated with the same regard as he did horse manure.

"All right, Zach," Morgan said in a resigned whisper. It was an old argument, and it wouldn't do any good to remind Zach, again, that he had never wanted any part of those fancy eastern schools with their drafty rooms, rigid rules and high walls. Yes, he'd rebelled. It was either that or go stark raving mad. But neither had he expected to come home only to be treated as if he were still wearing short pants, never allowed to voice an opinion or carry any real responsibility. "So, I've not behaved like a saint." Zach's harsh snort of derision over that understatement brought a brief and rueful smile to Morgan's face. It faded, however, when he glanced at the plans for expanding the shipping yard.

"Listen, Zach," he continued urgently. "Maybe I have acted like a roaring jackass, but I am not a complete idiot... thanks to that education I received in spite of myself. Don't you see you're risking everything we have, everything Pa worked for and dreamed of, on a gamble that those Texas drovers will turn their cattle trade our way now that Abilene has been shut down by the quarantine? And it's the Triple R you are risking to cover that high stakes bet!"

Morgan's summation of the Rossiter financial circumstances was surprisingly astute, but his legitimate cause for concern was something Zachary refused to discuss or contemplate. "It's done, Morgan," he stated with sharp impatience. "And frankly, I'm not sure I understand what's behind this sudden interest...."

"No" was the soft reply. "I guess you wouldn't. You never have. Maybe because you never cared enough."

This time Zachary Rossiter would have had to be made of stone not to recognize Morgan's pain. But before he could find the words to retract his harshness, Morgan was walking away.

"Wait...." Zachary called, but the young man didn't even pause, going straight through the door to be swallowed by the encroaching darkness.

"God," Zachary muttered, his head falling into his hands, feeling a deserved shame and regret. Why hadn't he shown Morgan the figures and the cold, hard cash from today's shipment? He knew how Morgan felt about the Triple R. All the boy had ever wanted was to take up their father's dream and build the ranch into a paying operation. But Morgan had never known the hardships, the frustrations and disappointments of ranching. Zachary had protected his younger brother from suffering those heartbreaks, wanting something better for the boy. Hell! Zachary wanted something better for himself!

Morgan couldn't possibly know how the ranching business had changed in the last few years. Raising beef had become big business. Operations like the King Ranch in Texas were running upwards of sixty thousand head of cattle on eighty-four thousand acres of grasslands. And soon even the King place would seem small potatoes when compared to the ranches being started up in the vast, virgin territories of Wyoming and Montana. My god! How could Morgan hope to compete, let alone survive, with a ten thousand acre spread like the Triple R?

Yes, the gamble Zach was taking was a big one, but Morgan needed to realize that the high stakes he spoke of could result in a payoff that would allow them to buy up all those unclaimed acres north of the Triple R, and keep on buying until there wasn't a blade of grass between here and the Nebraska border that didn't belong to the Rossiters. Little brother simply didn't understand what was truly at stake here. Maybe if they could just sit down and talk—

A loud cough brought Zachary Rossiter's head out of his hands. "Morgan?" he asked hopefully.

"No, sir, Mr. Rossiter. It's Cole Hardin." The young Texan stepped out of the shadowed doorway and into the dimly lighted room. "Could I have a word with you, sir?"

Zachary tried not to show his disappointment by giving the young man a warm smile. "Sure, Hardin. What can I do for you?" He genuinely liked Hardin, who'd proved himself a cut above the usual help Zachary found in the shipping yards. Of an age somewhere just around twenty, Hardin was soft-spoken, always respectful and had a smile that could rival Morgan's for pure charm. But where Morgan's grin hinted at his bad-boy nature, Hardin's was open and so free of guile that it encouraged immediate trust.

Cole Hardin shifted from one foot to the other while he twisted the hat he held before him in his hands. "Well, I was hoping..." He glanced uneasily at the floor. "It's like this Mr. Rossiter. I need an advance on my salary and since it's only a couple of days till payday anyway..."

Zachary frowned. He should have known Hardin would be wanting to head back for Texas the minute he'd scraped enough money together. They all did, sooner or later, these young drovers who suffered the long trail, then drank or whored themselves broke within twenty-four hours of their arrival in Ellsworth. "Texas will still be there on payday, Hardin. And you've not finished your job with me yet. Those loading pens will have to be—"

"Whoa! I never said nothin' about leaving, Mr. Rossiter. Matter of fact, I need the money to take a room at Mrs. Broadie's boarding house. Only trouble is, she won't hold the place for me, and that flea trap I've been stayin' in over in Scragtown won't return the advance rent they demanded." Hardin shrugged. "You see how it is, sir. I'm kinda between a rock and a hard place unless I can get an advance on the money you owe me."

"Well, that's different. I'll admit I hated the thought of losing a hardworking young man like yourself, Cole." Zachary left his chair and walked over to the safe. "But don't get the idea I intend to make a habit of bending the rules."

"Oh, I would never think that, Mr. Rossiter," Cole assured quickly, his smile widening as the door to the safe opened. "And I really do appreciate this, Mr. Rossiter."

Zachary didn't even notice the subtle change in Hardin's tone, the excitement that was excessive for so small a favor. Unfortunately, neither did Zachary Rossiter see the flash of light reflect off the thin knife blade Hardin lifted from beneath his battered hat. There was no warning at all, only a fiery pain in his back and a moment's confusion before the floor seemed to rise up to meet him.

"Yes, sir, Mr. Rossiter, sir." Cole Hardin kicked the body of his employer aside. "I surely do appreciate the hell out of your understanding and generosity. You see, I've got plans, places to go and things awaitin'. Most especially there's this pretty little auburn-haired girl, and she has the sweetest pair of tits you ever did see. . . ."

* * *

Jessica Cameron clutched the pillowcase holding her few belongings while she paced the dirt floor of the stuffy, windowless shack she had called home this past year.

Where was Cole? He'd said he would fetch her right after sunset, and it had been fully dark for three-quarters of an hour now. Had Mr. Rossiter kept him late at the shipping yards? Had he changed his mind...?

"No!" Jessica moaned softly, vehemently denying even the possibility that Cole wouldn't keep his promise. Cole Hardin loved her; he'd said so repeatedly these past weeks. They were leaving tonight, eloping.

Jessica hugged the pillowcase, letting the happiness she felt at the thought of being Cole's wife flow through her soul, trying desperately to hold tight to that joy. But it was hard to believe those good emotions were real while the loud moans and snores of her father's drunken stupor were flooding the room.

Suddenly Jessica needed air. She felt trapped and stifled, as if she would choke to death, suffocate. Moving to the door, she grabbed the latch and threw the door open wide, blinking back tears while she gulped the clean night air. For so long her world had been only this tumbledown shack and the strong smells of whiskey and vomit and unwashed flesh. Until Cole, she'd forgotten the sweet scent of new grass, of a wildflower or how good a man's shaving soap smelled on a clean-shaved cheek. My God! Sometimes it had been hard to remember she hadn't lived every one of her scant sixteen years in a hovel directly behind a whorehouse.

"Oh, Papa," she whispered, fighting off the guilt over her intention to abandon him tonight. Not that he would miss her. In fact, it would probably take him days, maybe weeks, before he noticed he was alone... if ever. Because the simple truth was that Jack Cameron had abandoned his only daughter three years ago, the very day they'd buried her mother and brother a few miles outside of Saint Joseph, Missouri. He'd walked away from his wife's and son's graves, away from his grieving thirteen-year-old daughter, and straight into the first saloon he could find.

Essentially, the day they'd buried Nora and Daniel Cameron was the last time Jessica had seen her father. The man who'd moved her from cattle town to cattle town, picking up odd jobs now and then, was a stranger. The man sleeping on the cot inside this shed bore no resemblance to the Jack Cameron who'd been a good husband and father, a loving and generous man. The man in this shed lived only for the whiskey, worked only for the whiskey, thought about and loved only the whiskey. Jessica no longer deluded herself that a miracle would happen and he'd change back into the man he'd once been. The night he'd brought Billy Gardiner home with him, Jessica had finally accepted she had a father no more.

Leaning back against the splintered door frame, Jessica tried to pray as her mama had taught her, asking God to help her learn how to forgive. But Jessica knew, even as she prayed, that even if she was someday able to forgive, she would never forget that her papa had been willing to sell his soul, and his only living child, for the jug of whiskey Bill Gardiner carried beneath his arm.

"Oh, Cole," she moaned, knowing the beginning quivers of despair. "Where are you?"

If Cole didn't come for her, she'd die! Lord, but she'd rather be dead than endure another night like that one, living with the perpetual fear of Billy Gardiner and men like him....

"Jessie! Let's go!"

With a glad cry, Jessica ran straight into Cole's strong arms, clinging to him. Cole Hardin had saved her from Billy when she'd escaped, and he'd been her entire world since that night. "You came," she sobbed against his chest. "You came, you came...."

Impatient with this emotional display and the need to get out of Ellsworth fast, Cole started to push the girl away. But when his thumbs brushed the outer swell of her beautifully generous breasts, he hesitated for a moment, filling his palms with the ripe bounty. Lord! She was going to make a delicious little bonus. Plus, Cole would have the pleasure of breaking her in. He'd never had himself a virgin before.

At his fondling, Jessica pulled away, not yet entirely comfortable with the familiar and possessive way Cole touched her body, although he'd explained it would be his right as her husband soon enough. And it wasn't unpleasant, just strange. All that really mattered was that Cole loved her. Just to be held with loving affection and tenderness, Jessica would have gladly granted Cole anything he wanted from her. "I love you so much," she told him with feeling.

"Yeah," Cole replied, his voice gruff. Just touching her, even with the barrier of that ratty old dress between them, had him so worked up he was tempted to satisfy himself here and now. "Get your things and meet me in front of Myra Belle's. And make it quick!"

Jessica didn't understand his angry tone or why he stalked off, but right now it didn't matter. He'd come for her and she was going to start her life over, beginning right now.

Retrieving the bundle she'd dropped by the door, Jessica started to follow Cole. Then, following an impulse she didn't entirely understand, she hurried back inside the shack to kneel beside the cot where her father was sleeping off his last bottle. In the flickering light of a nearly gutted candle, Jessica looked for a last time upon those haggard and ravaged features before another impulse had her tearing at the knotted end of the pillowcase. Reaching inside, she withdrew a framed photograph, which was her most cherished possession. She didn't need to look at the images within the tarnished frame. The features of her once-happy family were imprinted forever within her heart and mind. Taken before they'd left Ohio, before the cholera had taken her mother and Daniel, this photograph was a constant reminder of what had been and what might have been had her father and mother not decided to join Uncle John in Oregon.

Jessica took one last, loving look at the photograph before she tucked it in the crook of her father's arm, right next to the whiskey bottle he still cradled as if it were a beloved object. "Goodbye, Papa," she whispered. "I'll pray for you...." With a sob, she rose to her feet and ran out of the shed.

Chapter One

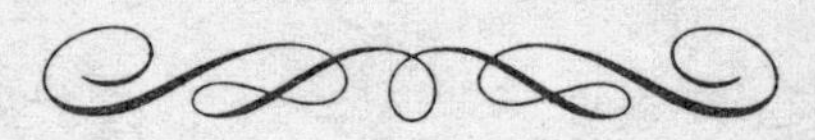

Moonshadow Valley, California, 1882

"Moonshadow, mister!"

Every muscle in Morgan Rossiter's body quivered when the stagecoach driver's bark penetrated his blessed oblivion. But it wasn't until he felt the sharp prod of a bony finger that he finally gave up and opened his eyes.

"Hey! Did you hear me? I said—" Will Fletcher stepped back from that gunmetal-hard gaze. "Sorry," he muttered, whirling away to seek the safe interior of Moonshadow's Wells Fargo office.

Without the irritation of the cranky, bandy-legged driver staring in his face, Morgan took his time waking up, moving one sore muscle at a time. That he'd actually slept nearly every mile of this last leg of a very long journey was not surprising. After traveling half a continent inside an overcrowded train compartment overflowing with immigrant families and squalling children, the bounce and sway of the stagecoach had seemed a babe's cradle. Nonetheless, Morgan felt anything but rested as he unwedged his six-foot frame from the tight confines of the coach. Draping his gun belt over his shoulder, he stepped out onto the cobbled street and retrieved his bag from where the driver had tossed it down. It didn't sweeten his disposition to note that the Wells Fargo office was at the farthest edge of town.

With a resigned groan, Morgan adjusted his black Stetson against the glare of the late-afternoon sun and started walking, noting as he went the unarguable accuracy of the Pinkerton detective's description of this unusual town.

If he hadn't known better, Morgan might have sworn he'd somehow been transported to some sleepy little hamlet in Vermont or New Hampshire. God knew that this place, with its tree-lined streets, gas lamps and brick buildings, bore scant resemblance to any former boomtown he'd ever seen. Unfortunately, Richard Burke's faithful and meticulous depiction of this community probably meant the detective had also given a pretty reliable sketch of the lady Morgan had come here to find. That knowledge wasn't particularly heartening. Morgan scowled, totally oblivious to the local populace, many of whom stopped and stared at him with mixed expressions of curiosity and alarm. Today, as it had been for the past eight years, the quest to find the young girl seen leaving Ellsworth with Cole Hardin on the night of his brother's murder was all-consuming, an obsession that dictated and directed every aspect of his existence. Of late his search for Jessie Cameron had taken on the added quality of desperation. Because unless he found Hardin's accomplice soon, the murdering bastard would go free. At least, Hardin would go free until Morgan caught up with him....

Right now, however, Cole Hardin was marking time in a Kansas penitentiary, serving a ten-year sentence for cattle rustling. But despite all his efforts, Morgan had not been successful in getting Hardin charged with Zachary's murder. Justice demanded more than an accusation of guilt to put a rope around a man's neck, no matter the certainty and credibility of the accuser. That Zach had named his killer with his last breath meant little to the law. Zachary Rossiter had been barely conscious, only seconds from death, when Morgan had returned to the office. And shock, grief, could possibly have colored and impaired Morgan's own ability to reason. That single whispered word wasn't enough for Judge Parker. He wanted corroborating evidence, witnesses. Nothing had been found on Hardin at the time of his capture to link him with the shipping yards' robbery or Zachary Rossiter's death.

But Morgan knew Judge Parker was wrong. He hadn't been with Zach in those last seconds, hadn't seen the momentary clearing of Zach's vision when he'd looked straight into his brother's tormented eyes. Zachary Rossiter had demanded justice with his dying breath, clinging to life until he heard Morgan's vow to see Hardin punished. And if it took the rest of Morgan's time on this earth, he'd see Zach's last request of him fulfilled.

With Hardin tucked away in prison, Morgan was free to concentrate on his search for Hardin's accomplice, the auburn-haired girl who'd been with him that night ten years ago, and the only witness to Zachary's murder. Of course, she'd be a woman now. Certainly Morgan didn't expect Jessie Cameron to bear much resemblance to the pretty, smiling child in that framed photograph he'd taken from her drunken father, but most days he managed to avoid the knowledge that finding Jessie Cameron carried the same odds as finding a needle in a haystack. Morgan had attempted to reduce those odds with the vast network of Pinkerton agents who'd been aiding him all these years. Even so, the results had been disappointing. God! There had been so many towns, so damn many auburn-haired women matching the Cameron girl's general description. Still, strangely enough, not once in all these years had Morgan found a possible candidate who answered to the name of Jessica... until now.

Although he cautioned himself not to put too much stock in the mere coincidence of a shared name, Morgan could not entirely overcome the anticipation that granted him a temporary resurgence of energy as he spotted the Seibert Hotel. Within that hotel he would find Jessica Miller, the widow of a local rancher, who also seemed to possess some promising gaps and question marks in regards to her background and origin. She was also of the right approximate age and coloring.

Unfortunately, that was where the positives ended and the negatives began. According to Richard Burke's report, the Widow Miller had about as much in common with the daughter of a Scragtown drunk as a saint would have with a demon. Currently she had taken up temporary residence in the hotel to aid a friend and fellow widow, Oramay Seibert, during a family crisis. There was talk, Burke reported, that Mrs. Miller was giving serious thought to the sale of her ranch, the Eldorado, and buying herself a partnership in the hotel. The Pinkerton detective had also gone on to depict a woman who was extremely well liked and respected in this community, a lady with a philanthropic nature. In fact, she was a veritable paragon of unquestionable virtue.

But then maybe, just maybe, Jessica Miller was just too damn good to be true....

On that thought, Morgan strode into the hotel, pausing just inside the door to give his eyes time to adjust to the dimness within the lobby. Seconds later, he was fighting the urge to turn on his heel and head straight back to the Wells Fargo depot before the stagecoach had a chance to pull out for the return trip to Sacramento. Only his extreme exhaustion stopped him.

Seated upon a high stool behind the registration desk, so absorbed in paperwork she was oblivious to his entry, was the most respectably virtuous-appearing woman Morgan had had the misfortune of encountering in all his thirty years of living. From the top of her tightly coiled auburn hair to what he could see of the god-awful black dress she was wearing, this female virtually redefined respectability. Worse, she was scrawny and plain to boot!

This was the woman he'd traveled half a continent, nearly killing himself in the process, to get a look at?

God! If the *lady* behind the counter was, had ever been or could even aspire to being the one and only Jessica Cameron, Morgan would happily kiss that Pinkerton detective's incompetent ass!

Morgan's raging frustration and disappointment expressed itself in an angry expulsion of breath that immediately brought her head up. She looked directly at him, and the eyes peering over wire-rimmed reading glasses perched on the sharp end of a haughty, tip-tilted nose went wide with surprise and more than just a hint of alarm.

Jessica had probably forgotten more about dangerous men than most women could imagine in their worst nightmares. And if she was to judge the dark, rough-looking stranger by first impression alone, Jessica would have vowed him to be about as dangerous as they came.

He was tall and hard muscled, as if soft living was foreign to him. The Union-blue shirt and black chino trousers he wore were of good quality but sweat stained and badly wrinkled, as if he'd been living in them for several days. Likewise, his jaw was covered with a heavy growth of black stubble. The rest of his face was obscured by the wide-brimmed Stetson he wore tipped forward on his brow, keeping his eyes and their expression hidden from her, making it impossible to determine if he was as mean and ugly on the inside as he appeared outside.

But regardless of whether he was an outlaw on the run or merely a bedraggled cowhand looking for work, Jessica found his manner intimidating. Even more so than the gun belt and holstered six-shooter he carried negligently over one broad shoulder. Outside Moonshadow, she knew, men armed themselves with the same nonchalance reserved for pulling on their pants each morning. No, it wasn't his looks or the weapon or even the old memories being stirred by his presence that she found unsettling. It was the way he stood in the doorway, unmoving and silent, his posture rigid with an almost palpable tension that was causing the hair on the back of her neck to rise. Inexplicably, surprisingly, Jessica's fear manifested itself in anger.

"Well? Are you going to stand there all day and scowl at me? Or is there something I can do for you?"

Morgan might have added shrewish to his growing list—if he hadn't seen the fear in those big eyes of hers. Her spunk impressed him, especially since she'd been staring at him as if he were some wild animal that had wandered into town. It occurred to him—rather belatedly—that he probably did look pretty much the varmint. So there was more apology than charm in the smile he gave her.

"Sorry, ma'am," he drawled softly, resettling his hat farther back on his head. "It wasn't my intent to distress you. Actually, I was just standing here waiting for my second wind to come along and hoping my knees wouldn't buckle before it arrived."

Jessica had little trouble believing he was exhausted. There was no denying the pallor underlying the sun-darkened skin or the dark circles of fatigue beneath smoky-gray eyes. Her anxiety dissipated.

"You need a room," she observed more kindly.

Morgan gave a short laugh. "Ma'am, right now I'd be happy with a pillow and a quiet corner...as long as the floor doesn't move or some poor kid doesn't start squalling because he's been too long inside a hot, airless train compartment, forced to sleep on a rock-hard bench for days and days on end..."

He was denied the opportunity to finish his haphazardly thought-out explanation. A distraction arrived in the form of two youngsters, boys of about eleven or twelve years of age. They came bursting into the lobby from a back hallway behind the staircase. That neither of them noticed his presence was immediately apparent.

"Jessie!" Patrick Seibert gasped, breathless and flushed with excitement as he charged the desk. "Mabel Harrison said there was some big, vicious-looking gunslinger headed...this way."

Oramay's son nearly strangled on the last two words of his announcement as Jessica's nearly frantic gestures finally penetrated his feverish exuberance. He turned slowly and immediately wished the floor would open and swallow him up. "Gawdamighty!" he breathed when eyes the color of black smoke and, in his mind, just as deadly, fell upon his person.

Jessica didn't know whether to laugh or cry in mortification over Patrick's embarrassing outburst. Unfortunately, much to her increasing discomfort and bewilderment, things immediately went from bad to impossible when Patrick's friend, Tommy Hughes, marched right over to the stranger, looked him up and down and then proceeded to spout, "Listen, mister! You should know we've got us a sheriff who don't tolerate your kind of trouble. So...if you're smart, you'll get outa Moonshadow fast."

Shock over Tommy's outrageous statement kept Jessica frozen and dumbfounded until she heard the stranger's bemused "Pardon me?" and saw Tommy drawing breath to repeat himself.

"I said—"

"Thomas Hughes!" Jessica cried out. She rushed around the desk, cheeks flaming, to take a firm hold of that young troublemaker's arm. "I think we've all heard quite enough out of you, young man," she stated firmly as she drew Tommy away. Patrick Seibert soon joined Tommy, and both were ordered to remove themselves to the kitchen. "And stay there," Jessica added, her voice vibrating with exasperation. "I'll want to speak with the two of you shortly."

"But Jessie," Patrick argued, his pale blue eyes pleading, "what if he *really* is a gunslinger? Ma wouldn't..."

Patrick's anxiety was genuine, not part of some fanciful bit of nonsense or one of their boyish pranks, Jessica realized. Remembering her own foolish alarm earlier, she hastened to reassure the boy. "Patrick, no self-respecting gunslinger would dare carry his gun in a manner that would make the use of that weapon awkward. The speed with which he can get his six-shooter unholstered and into his hand could mean the difference between life and death...." The look on Patrick's face plainly expressed he lacked confidence in her expertise regarding this subject. Jessica sighed and gave him a stern look. "Just trust me on this, all right?"

Patrick scowled, but he gave in. Right or wrong, Jessie was in charge around here while his mother was out at

Kathleen's. "If you say so...." he grumbled on a shrug. Kids were supposed to be seen and not heard—wasn't that the Golden Rule? "Let's go, Tommy." He gave his friend, who was even less eager to depart, a firm shove toward the hallway. "Ma made some cherry tarts this morning," he whispered as encouragement.

Jessica watched them go with a mixture of relief and dread. What on earth was she going to say to the man who'd been the victim of this embarrassing comedy of errors?

Morgan saw her chagrin but couldn't resist teasing her just a bit. "Know a genuine gunslinger when you see one, do you, ma'am?" Actually, she'd shown a surprising insight into the relationship between a gunman and his weapons. A lucky guess—or firsthand knowledge?

The deep voice filled with amusement spoke practically in her ear, sending prickles up the back of her neck. She'd not heard his approach. Turning slowly, Jessica forced herself to meet those laughing, dark gray eyes, needing to crane her neck to do so. He was even more intimidating up close, but she was relieved to see he wasn't without humor. In fact, he seemed to be taking their collective foolishness in stride, shrugging it off with a grin. "I...I don't know what got into those boys...."

Oh, yes you do, lady. You thought the very same thing when I first walked in here, Morgan thought. "Hey, they're just kids," he said, shrugging. He wasn't going to let her apologize for what had proved to be some of the most entertaining moments he'd enjoyed in quite some time. "But maybe it would be a good idea if I secured that room and cleaned myself up some before I create any more chaos...." His grin widened. "I honestly don't think I'm up to dealing with a cantankerous sheriff bent on running me out of town right now."

The idea of Earl Taylor chasing this man, or any other, out of Moonshadow was so ludicrous Jessica chuckled. If anybody was to leave, it would likely be Earl, heading fast for the safety of the hills. Oh, he was sufficiently adequate for this town's needs. Trouble around here usually was no more menacing than curtailing a group of rowdy schoolboys or handling the occasional mouthy drunk. But one look at this big, tough-looking stranger would turn Sheriff Taylor's thinning hair white.

Jessica continued to chuckle softly as she again rounded the desk and fetched the guest ledger from beneath the counter.

Morgan joined her there and absently accepted the pen she handed him, but he made no attempt to sign his name to the register she turned toward him. Hell! Right now he didn't trust himself to remember just who he was supposed to be this trip. He was too dazed by the stunning power and unexpected beauty of her smile. With the lingering echo of her sweet, melodious laughter ringing in his ears, Morgan took another long look at the woman he'd earlier dismissed as being dishwater dull.

This time he ignored the whole and examined her feature by feature. Her complexion, now warm with color, was creamy smooth and flawless, so pure it might have belonged to a babe. The hair coiled so unattractively atop her head was a particularly dark and rich shade of reddish brown. He'd already noticed how her eyes seemed to change color from one second to the next, depending upon the light and her mood, going from a greenish hue to a light golden brown in a blink. Almond-shaped and thickly lashed, they might have been exceptional were they not so impossibly large in her otherwise narrow face. Her mouth—

The smile Morgan had found so enchanting wavered beneath his bold and thorough inspection. This kind of intense scrutiny was as unsettling for Jessica as it was unprecedented. Men rarely gave the Widow Miller a second glance, let alone a third and a fourth and . . .

That she didn't appreciate his interest was being made very clear. It didn't take long for her pretty smile to sour and become a tight-lipped, prudish frown. Morgan decided the sooner he got himself into a room the better, before he alienated this lady beyond redemption. He signed the ledger. "Since I'm not certain how long I'm going to be in

Moonshadow, I'll just pay one day at a time for now—if that's agreeable?"

"Of course," Jessica responded pleasantly enough, though she was still confused and shaken by his strange behavior toward her. So much so, in fact, she didn't even think to ask his business here in this quiet community. If he was looking for steady work, he'd be disappointed, but his request to pay for his room by the day suggested that was probably his intent...and that he was possibly short of cash. "The rooms are two dollars per night," she informed him almost apologetically.

"Sounds fair to me," Morgan said, and smiled slightly at the flicker of relief he saw in her eyes.

Jessica turned and reached for one of the keys hanging on a board mounted to the wall behind the desk. She might as well let him have the best room in the hotel; he was their only guest, after all. "I'll show you upstairs, Mr. Ross."

Morgan retrieved his bag and followed her up the carved cherry staircase, listening with only half an ear while she recited a list of the services and amenities the Seibert Hotel offered. He was more interested in watching her figure—what little of it there was to watch. Nevertheless, though he was probably attaching too damn much importance on the fading memory of a mere smile, Morgan had seen enough to warrant a fresh evaluation of some earlier, possibly hasty, conclusions regarding a certain Pinkerton detective's eyesight and competence.

"I just don't understand your nonchalance about this, Jessica," Mabel Harrison exclaimed, her expression one of horrified disbelief. "Giving that man a room! Why, he could very well murder each and every one of us in our beds tonight and take everything we have...."

"Aren't you being just a slight bit dramatic, Mrs. Harrison," Jessica suggested, drawing upon the last of her patience.

"I am not!" was the indignant response from the dignified, well-dressed wife of Moonshadow's long-standing

mayor. "If anything, I'm understating the case! Good heavens, Jessica! I don't believe I've ever seen a more vicious-looking human being in my entire life. That man positively gave me the shivers!"

Mabel shuddered again for effect. Jessica choked back a laugh when the woman's enthusiasm sent several feathers flying from her outlandish hat. But beneath her amusement was an increasing irritation. Mabel Harrison was only the most recent—although hopefully the last—in a continuous succession of Moonshadow's citizens who were positively reveling in the excitement generated by Morgan Ross's arrival. Not a single one of them was genuinely alarmed, or so she hoped. It hadn't escaped Jessica's notice how everyone had managed to forestall their curiosity and concerns until the dangerous desperado was safely tucked away in his room upstairs.

"Mrs. Harrison, I assure you—"

"Oh, Jessie—" Mabel sighed wearily "—I know *you* believe that man harmless. But it's perfectly clear to me that you are entirely too naive and trusting. Which isn't at all your fault, of course. John sheltered you far too much when the two of you first arrived here in our valley. You were so very young . . . and then, just when you began to come out of your shy little shell, John's age and illness required your devotion and constant nursing. You've just never had the opportunity to be exposed to some of the harsher realities of the world . . ."

Jessica ground her teeth while Mabel continued, going on and on. Mabel Harrison wouldn't know harsh reality if it came up and gave her a hard boot in the bustle! And Jessica didn't know which of them was the worse hypocrite. The supercilious Mabel, expounding upon a subject about which she knew absolutely nothing. Or herself, the so-called sainted Widow Miller. How easily she could shock this woman speechless.

"Well!" Mabel exclaimed, pausing to draw breath. "I guess there's nothing to be done now until Earl Taylor gets back from wherever he's gotten himself off to this time—

though what earthly use that do-nothing sheriff will be, I really don't know...."

"Moonshadow hardly needs an aggressive lawman. We are a peaceful community, after all." Jessica could hardly believe she was risking Mabel's wrath to defend Earl Taylor.

"*Were* a peaceful community," Mabel corrected grimly. "You mark my words, Jessica Miller! There will be grief over that man before all is said and done!"

Obviously deciding she'd won the last word on that topic, Mabel switched to another, and suddenly she was all warmth and smiles. "Have I told you how much I admire what you are doing here for Oramay? Every night I remember poor Kathleen in my prayers. Perhaps this time she'll be able to deliver a healthy child and finally make Oramay a grandmother. How many miscarriages has that dear young woman had now? Three? Kathleen and my Theodora were in school together, you know. My Theo has been blessed with three healthy, precious little girls."

Jessica's knuckles went white as she gripped the edge of the desk and began to count slowly to ten. She told herself Mabel wasn't truly mean spirited, merely insensitive and self-absorbed. Mabel was also extremely fortunate she'd made her thoughtless comments to Jessica. Oramay wouldn't have counted; she would have vaulted over this desk and gone for Mabel's throat.

Forcibly restraining her own temper, Jessica said tightly, "Kathleen is in her eighth month, and Dr. Griffith feels confident all is well. The enforced bed rest is merely a precaution."

"I'm delighted to hear that," Mabel said pleasantly enough, but had to spoil the rare moment with another frown. "But I would personally feel so much more reassured if our youthful Dr. Griffith had more seasoning and experience."

Jessica had had all of Mabel Harrison that she could stand for one day. "You *will* excuse me, Mrs. Harrison. I've neglected my work far too long, and the hour grows late.

Please give my regards to Horace and Theodora . . . and the children." She gathered up the ledgers and receipts she'd vainly been attempting to organize. Since there wasn't a soul in Moonshadow who would believe Jessica Miller capable of being purposely rude, she got away with walking out on Mabel Harrison, leaving the mayor's wife to see herself out.

When Jessica reached the hotel's big kitchen, she sagged down upon the nearest chair and groaned. Days like this could make her long for the peaceful quiet of the Eldorado. Unfortunately, the same silence and solitude that seemed so appealing at this moment could become an unbearable torment when one endlessly lonely day stretched into another, and she walked that big, empty house over, her only companion the hollow sound of her own footsteps. And the nights—

Jessica's genuine shudder put Mabel Harrison's dramatics to shame.

Leaving the chair, she went and put the kettle on for tea, sorry now she'd sent Patrick and Tommy away. But she could hardly expect two rambunctious youngsters to cool their heels, waiting for the talk she'd intended to have with them, for heaven only knew how long while she was parleying with half the town. Besides, if the boys had lingered any longer, the cherry tarts intended for this evening's dining room menu would have been reduced by more than the six they had managed to wolf down.

Remembering the scene in the lobby with those two scamps and Morgan Ross had Jessica shaking her head and laughing silently. But since she'd quite had her fill on the subject of the hotel's recent guest, Jessica pushed those thoughts aside, finished making herself a cup of tea and settled down at the kitchen table to attempt another go at making sense out of Oramay's financial records.

As cook, housekeeper, mother, friend and hotel proprietress, Oramay Seibert was without equal. But when it came to bookkeeping, the woman was positively inept. She rarely recorded anything in the ledgers, and when she did the entries were often put in the wrong column, were illegible or both. Usually, however, she simply didn't bother, preferring to toss what receipts and invoices she managed not to lose into a shoe box. It was enough to make Jessica want to tear out her hair.

Frustrated with the impossible job, Jessica leaned back and sipped her tea. Was she making a terrible mistake in deciding to sell the ranch and joining Oramay here at the hotel? It was a question she'd asked herself countless times before. The decision to leave the Eldorado and buy a partnership in the hotel had been a painful, gut-wrenching one, and not a day passed that she didn't waver in some degree or another. Since Oramay didn't really believe she'd actually go through with the sale in any case, Jessica could have backed out of their rather casually made agreement at any time. In the end, however, Jessica always came back to the one singular and vital reason for remaining firm: until she'd come here, she had been slowly dying of loneliness. The nine months she'd lived alone on the ranch after John's death had been unbearable. She'd lost weight because she despised eating alone. Sleeping had become impossible because at night the silence screamed loudly with haunting memories and nightmares that made her dread each sunset.

Even if becoming part owner in this hotel meant financial suicide, Jessica thanked God for the day Moonshadow's youthful physician, David Griffith, had brought her and Oramay together.

With Kathleen taking to her bed for the final months of a precarious pregnancy, she needed her mother's care and support. Oramay needed someone to look after the hotel and Patrick. Jessica had needed—well, not the least of her needs was the very warmth, affection and companionship she'd found right here. Like a single flower wilting in a forgotten garden, Jessica soaked up even the smallest gesture of love as if it were life-giving rain.

She was happy here, even if there were times when her role within this family seemed too much that of a maiden aunt who'd come for a visit and then just refused to leave. Because all she'd left behind was emptiness, with more of the same assured for the future. . . .

Chapter Two

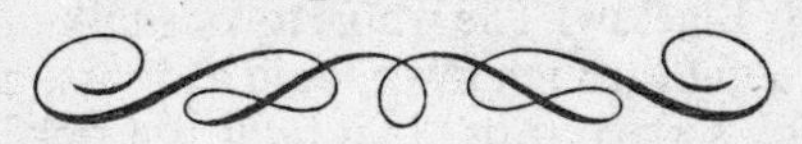

It was well after sunset when Lonnie Taylor climbed the loft ladder of the Hughes Feed and Livery to plop down in the straw beside his two friends. "What's so important that we needed a council meeting tonight? My pa will have my hide for not finishing the chores."

Tommy Hughes ignored Lonnie's grumbling. "You saw the man who came in on the stage today, didn't you?"

"Yeah, I saw him. Who didn't?"

"Your Pa?" Patrick breathed, only to get Tommy's sharp elbow in his ribs.

"Nah," Lonnie said. "Pa was out at the Muninger place all day. They've been having trouble with foxes gettin' into their henhouse. Why?"

Patrick and Tommy exchanged looks, but by prior agreement both had decided to tread softly on the subject of Sheriff Earl Taylor. "We got trouble, Lonnie," Tommy said with serious urgency. "*Big* trouble," he emphasized before tossing what he was holding close to his chest into Lonnie's lap. "Just look at that...."

The lantern hanging from the rafters didn't put out much light. Lonnie got to his feet and held the object Tommy had given him up where he could see it better, but mostly the gesture was out of courtesy. Lonnie was all too familiar with the shape and feel of Tommy's prized dime novels. The only thing unusual about this one was that it was more dog-eared and ragged than most. *"Black Bart's Revenge,"* he read slowly, quoting the title. "So?"

"'So?'" Tommy cried, leaping up to yank the book out of Lonnie's hands. "I thought you said you saw him?"

"Who?"

"Who? Him, that's who, dumb ass!" Tommy's voice was shrill as his index finger pounded the illustrated cover. "Black Bart Bigelow! The whole town's talking about him. Walked straight through town, bold as brass, before holing up at Patrick's place. Ain't that right, Patrick?"

"You bet," Patrick agreed, not about to get in the middle of the argument history told him was inevitable. Tommy and Lonnie had never agreed on anything in their lives, except that they were friends. Patrick drew his head in and scooted back when Lonnie began to chortle and slap his knee.

"Black Bart Bigelow," Lonnie snorted with a laugh. "Tommy, you're a hoot a minute! Boy, this is almost worth gettin' a lickin' over! I ain't heard anything so funny in all my born days!"

Tommy's expression turned murderous. He gave Lonnie a hard punch in the shoulder. "It ain't funny! Swear to God. Me and Patrick saw him up close, eyeball-to-eyeball. And it *was* Black Bart. He looked exactly like his picture. Dressed all in black...."

"Shirt looked dark blue to me when I saw him," Lonnie argued, sober now as he rubbed the sore place on his upper arm.

Why argue when you possessed indisputable evidence? Tommy flipped the dime novel open to read a brief passage. "'He walked with an arrogant swagger, letting all know—'"

"Seemed to me he put one foot in front of the other just like anybody else," Lonnie retorted derisively, knowing once Tommy got started reading, he'd be at it all night.

"Explain them pistols then, Mr. Know-it-all...if you can! Or are you so danged blind you didn't see they were custom-made and nickel plated, with fancy ivory grips. It's them guns, if nothing else, that would have told me who he really was, no matter what other name he's using. They're his trademark! Tell him, Patrick! You saw it right off, too!"

Patrick stifled a groan, not sure at all he wanted to go on with this. "The guns are exactly like Tommy described," he offered, hoping that would satisfy. However, Patrick could recall only one revolver, not the two guns Black Bart was infamous for packing. And the gun belt, though expensively tooled, hadn't really resembled the silver-studded one described in Tommy's book. But he couldn't argue the man looked dangerous as all get out, mean and ruthless. Then again, neither could Patrick forget how mad Jessie had been over him and Tommy spouting off. Jessica never got mad or raised her voice, but today she'd been right sharp with him. Patrick was inclined to trust Jessie's judgment over Tommy Hughes's.

"Is that all you can say?" Tommy complained disgustedly, giving Patrick a hard nudge with his foot.

Patrick looked up, but he honestly didn't know what else to add. He was, for certain, between a rock and a hard place. If he sided with Lonnie, then Tommy would pitch a fit and give him the business for weeks, months even. But if he agreed with Tommy, then Lonnie would start laughing at him, too. Still, Lonnie was always too busy with one thing or another to spend time with his friends. So, if Tommy got peeved at him, then Patrick wouldn't have anybody to talk with. He decided.

"It was Black Bart Bigelow, all right! Bigger than life and ugly to boot. And since your pa's the sheriff, I expect you to do something about this! After all, my ma and Jessie might be in danger!"

At thirteen, Lonnie was a year older than these two, and wiser. Who the hell did Patrick Seibert think he was to be handing out ultimatums? "If you really want to know what I think—I think the two of you have got beans for brains!" Lonnie whirled and started back down the ladder.

Neither Tommy nor Patrick attempted to stop their friend's leave-taking, nor would either of them ever say a word against him for it. They understood. Lonnie was afraid for his father. Good man that he was, everybody knew Earl Taylor wasn't no gunman. It was damn certain Sheriff Taylor would never be a match for Black Bart Bigelow.

"Guess we're on our own, buddy," Tommy said softly as he stared at the artist's drawing on the cover of his book.

"Yeah, guess so. . . ." Patrick sighed.

Jessie escorted Hiram Landry out of the dining room at nine o'clock, as she did every night. Hiram was always the first customer to take a table and the last to vacate.

On a weary yawn, Jessica took his coffee cup to the kitchen. "Mr. Landry's cup," she announced to the woman washing dishes, before adding it to the stack remaining to be washed.

"Is that the last of it?" Oramay Seibert asked while she lifted her arm to her damp brow and blotted it dry with the sleeve of her dress.

"Isn't it always?" Jessica returned wryly, flashing a smile toward the distinguished, white-haired gentleman standing next to Oramay with a dish towel in his hands. "I can take over the drying, Stan," she offered, not really expecting him to agree. As predicted, he waved her away.

"Find your own fun, ma'am," Stanley Turner said with a stunning grin. "This is mine. Besides, Oramay and I have developed an excellent working relationship. Haven't we, my dear?"

Despite the slight flush of color that came into her cheeks, Oramay ignored her dish dryer, choosing to pretend she hadn't heard the emphasis he'd placed on the word "relationship" or the endearment.

Stan cocked a single eyebrow. "Should I take your silence to be a slur upon my services?"

Oramay shot him a look. "Just don't you go all fumble fingered on me, Stanley Turner. I've never put much faith in a man when he's holding something breakable in his hands." Oramay didn't think she'd ever accustom herself to seeing this dignified, handsome man in his shirtsleeves, cuffs rolled to the elbows, wielding a dish towel with the same competence he applied to his law practice.

"Which only goes to prove that you've never fully appreciated my special talents, Mrs. Seibert," he shot back at her. "I'll have you know I'm very handy around the house. Bachelorhood does that for a man."

"Ha!" Oramay scoffed as she lifted her hands from the soapy water and shook them free of excess moisture. She was still clucking to herself when she went to collect the last stack of dirty dishes. "'Handy' my mother's night rail," she muttered beneath her breath. "Randy'd be more like it."

Stan's ears perked up at her grumbling. "What was that you said, my dear?"

This time Oramay's cheeks turned vivid red, the stain spreading all the way to the roots of her silver-streaked blond hair. "I wasn't talking to you, Mr. Ears," she told him, chancing a glance toward Jessica. The young woman was leaning back against the big table, biting her lip to keep from laughing, and the hot color on that usually pale face told Oramay that Jessica had heard what Stan missed. "I guess everybody went home pretty disappointed tonight when our mysterious guest didn't appear."

Jessica's back stiffened just a little. She was really very weary of this particular subject. "Which means they'll have all this night and perhaps much of tomorrow to create even more vivid fantasies about the man. Disappointed? On the contrary, they're having the time of their lives."

"From what I heard, he gave everybody plenty of cause for honest and concerned speculation. After all, it's not every day we get men of that ilk in our little town. . . ."

Jessica took a deep breath. "Oramay, that man is being judged and condemned merely on the basis of his appearance. You wouldn't look any better if you'd traveled the rails for thousands of miles squeezed into the coach section. They don't ship cattle packed in any tighter."

Stanley Turner's expression was one of interest and puzzlement. "I thought you and John traveled by steamer from

Washington Territory to San Francisco. Not that I disagree with your depiction of the railroads. I just wasn't aware you had traveled them such great distances."

"I haven't," Jessica quickly denied. "I've just heard other people recalling the experience."

This was one of the drawbacks that worried her about living here in the hotel. She would have to be constantly on her guard, watching every word. Otherwise, she'd open her mouth and the truth would come flying out. It had already happened twice today. First with the boys as she'd described gunslingers. Now with this business about train travel.

Stan Turner was still staring at her. Jessica shrugged. "It only seems logical—"

"Logical," Oramay piped in, "would have been to get more information on Morgan Ross than his name, if you ask me. Might be nice if we could go to bed tonight with a little peace of mind."

"You've let a lot of silly gossip worry you overmuch, Oramay," Jessica reassured her mildly, praying she was right. "He's an out-of-work cowhand, nothing more."

"Did he tell you that?"

"You know he didn't." Jessica tried to maintain a soft tone. Never had she seen Oramay in such an irascible mood as she was tonight. She'd claimed Kathleen was doing fine, if a little cranky over her enforced bed rest. Perhaps that was it. Mother and daughter had had a bad day together. "Oramay, I'm genuinely sorry I didn't think to question the man. I—I guess I'm not very accomplished at the hotel business."

Oramay looked shamed. "Honey, it's me who should be apologizing. And I do trust your judgment . . . completely. Besides, the only thing you're not accomplished at is being an experienced old busybody like myself."

Now both women were feeling miserable and shamed for making each other feel miserable and shamed. Jessica offered Oramay the gift of her beautiful smile. "Busybody?

Nonsense! Why, you are the soul of discretion, Mrs. Seibert."

Stanley Turner made a strangled sound and then began to cough. "Sorry," he choked out, facing Oramay's threatening stare. "Must have caught something in my throat. Probably my other foot."

"Likely so," Oramay stated. "Since that's where you've kept them most of your life."

Jessica knew they were probably good for another ten minutes of insulting each other. She decided this would be a good time to sweep the dining room floor, although it grieved her to miss the entertainment these two provided. Grabbing the broom, she exited the kitchen.

Jessica's absence was barely noticed. Oramay gave Stan a sharp poke on his firm chest, feeling a little disconcerted by the touch of hard muscle beneath her fingertip. "Watch it, Mr. Turner. Mess with me tonight, and you'll find yourself with more trouble than you can handle."

Stan captured the damp hand before she could draw it away. "Don't tempt me, my dear Oramay. That's the most enticing offer you've made me since we were both seventeen and you vowed you would marry me...pledging to make my life the living hell I so richly deserved."

Oramay jerked out of his hold when his thumb began tracing circles in her palm. What was the matter with him lately? More to the point, why was this handsome man of forty-five wasting his time with a plump widow who was about to become a grandmother? It never occurred to Oramay that the soon-to-be grandmother Stanley Turner was flirting with was only forty-five herself, and that what she considered plump would have been called beautifully full figured by any man with sense.

Stan watched her nervously pluck at the ruffles on her white apron. He knew her too well to keep pushing, for a little while, anyway. "Where's Patrick? I haven't seen him all evening."

"Spending the night with Tommy Hughes. The two of them came tearing in just after I got home and then went running back out again. Hardly saw him but a minute."

In Stan's opinion, the youngster had entirely too much freedom and not nearly enough responsibility. He was fond of the boy but saw trouble brewing from lack of attention. His mother's absence couldn't be helped, but spoiling him to make up for it wasn't good for him, either. "Did he see Moonshadow's desperado?"

"If he did, I didn't hear anything about it." She looked up at him then, thinking he really did have the nicest brown eyes. But then she'd always thought so. "Do you really think he might be dangerous?"

Stan threw his dish towel onto the table. "If you are truly worried, I could stay the night..."

He'd meant that he could sleep in Patrick's room, but as usual Oramay was trying to make something of his innocent comment. Her blue eyes flashed just as they always had; their brilliance hadn't dimmed in the least since her youth. Her temper hadn't improved, either.

"I never said any such thing! Worried? A nosy old busybody like me? For your information, Mr. Stan Turner, I've been sleeping with strangers under my roof for nearly twenty years."

"Is that so?" Stan returned with a slow grin that was blatantly roguish as he snaked an arm around a very agreeably fleshed waist. "Then perhaps you should consider putting some variety in your life by sleeping with a friend."

"Now you listen here..."

Stan Turner was tired of listening, and he knew only one way to shut that pretty mouth of Oramay's up, at least temporarily.

Out in the dining area, Jessica had heard the inevitable shouting, the argument that was as predictable and anticipated as the changing of the seasons. Stan and Oramay had been going at each other since childhood, and both seemed to enjoy every minute of their verbal sparring. Strangely enough, if either was asked to identify their best friend, both would give the other's name without hesitation. Even when Randall Seibert had been living, Stan and Oramay had exhibited a bond between them, one Randall had tolerated but never entirely appreciated.

But there was something different about this latest teasing battle. Usually when Oramay reached a certain volume and tone, Stan would prudently retreat. Jessica's broom stilled when that moment came, and she looked toward the kitchen door, anticipating to see him coming through to bid her a gruff "good evening" at any second. Instead, all hell broke loose in there.

First there was a high-pitched shriek, immediately followed by the sound of glass shattering. Then Stanley Turner began to yell, loudly and authoritatively, at the top of his lungs, and to cuss as she'd never heard him cuss before.

What on earth?

Jessica never considered her actions. She dropped the broom and ran straight for the kitchen. Her hand hit the door and shoved it open just in time to see the usually proper attorney plop down upon a chair and drag a struggling Oramay across his knees.

"This," he growled while giving her fanny two sharp whacks, "is for the pitcher you attempted to break over my head. And this," he went on as he deftly turned her over and captured her chin, "is for all the years I've waited... and wasted...."

The way Stan kissed Oramay should have set the kitchen ablaze. Lord knew, Jessica's cheeks were flaming as she backed slowly out of the doorway. It didn't occur to her that Oramay needed rescuing. Not with Oramay's arms locked firmly around Stanley's neck....

The possible ramifications of what she'd witnessed were just beginning to penetrate Jessica's shocked daze when she turned and collided with an unyielding wall of flesh and sinew.

"Whoa," Morgan exclaimed, saving her from falling when she bounced hard off his chest. "You all right, ma'am? Is there some kind of trouble here? I heard shouting...."

The voice was familiar. So was the tall, muscular form. The face, however, Jessica would not in a million years have associated with the rough-looking drifter who'd arrived earlier. The man holding her upright was clean shaved...and handsome. Remarkably handsome. Heartbreakingly handsome.

"Everything is fine, Mr. Ross," Jessica told him, extricating herself from his grasp and trying, without much success, to hide her feelings toward his transformed appearance. It wasn't fair of her, or particularly rational, but Jessica carried within her an inordinate aversion to extraordinarily handsome men. Especially ones who possessed the devil's own charm. And she instinctively knew Morgan Ross had received triple the devil's usual share of his favor. She put more distance between them than was reasonably necessary. "What you overheard was merely a small squabble between...friends. I apologize if it disturbed you."

Jessica's apology had barely left her mouth when pandemonium broke out once again in the kitchen. And it wasn't long before the chaos was brought straight out to them. Oramay came storming out of the kitchen, Stan Turner right on her heels.

"Dammit, woman! Haven't we been denying—"

There was another collision. Seeing the stranger with Jessica, Oramay stopped dead in her tracks. Stan nearly ran her over and got her sharp elbow in his ribs for the transgression.

Oramay's already flushed face went the color of overripe plums, but she recovered with admirable aplomb. With a hasty repair to her disordered hair and clothing, she looked straight at Jessica. "Don't tell me this man is the dangerous and frightful desperado that has our town in such an uproar?"

Morgan laughed.

Jessica moaned softly, wondering when she would ever entirely accustom herself to Oramay's outspokenness. She stammered her way through the introductions and then left Morgan Ross to fend for himself as she went to reclaim her broom.

"Glad to have you with us, Mr. Ross," Oramay said as she went over and shook her guest's hand. Lordy! She could understand why Jessica had acted all aflutter just now. Morgan Ross was one incredibly gorgeous male specimen. Personally, however, that knee-melting grin he was giving her was being wasted. Oramay was too sensible to let herself be dazzled silly by this heartbreaker, or any other, for that matter. Some men were just natural-born rogues, and any woman crazy enough to think they could be tamed deserved all the misery she was going to get.

"You have a very nice place here, Mrs. Seibert," Morgan complimented sincerely, his eyes roaming the attractive room. Blue-checked tableclothes and matching curtains at the windows conveyed a homey atmosphere. In fact, the entire hotel had been decorated and furnished with comfort and simplicity in mind, from the cushioned chairs and settees scattered around the lobby to the thick feather mattress and braided rug that made his room so pleasantly cozy. "Make yourself at home," the Seibert Hotel seemed to say. And the lingering smells in here made his mouth water....

Oramay heard the loud rumbling of an empty stomach. "Could I fix you a sandwich, Mr. Ross? You slept through the dinner hours, I'm afraid. But the day won't come when a guest of mine has to suffer hunger pangs."

"I couldn't trouble you...."

"Nonsense!" It was Stan Turner, not Oramay, who piped up. "Mrs. Seibert is a woman of her word. She never says anything she doesn't mean or won't stand behind with her dying breath once it's been said. Twenty... thirty years can go by, and this woman will still be holding the opinions being formed at this very moment. She's a veritable rock. As steadfast as they come."

Morgan arched a brow at the dignified, white-haired man who joined them. He was younger than Morgan had first assumed and more than a little out of sorts. It was pretty obvious that small, friendly squabble had been more a lover's spat. Oramay Seibert gave the man a look that should have raised blisters on his face.

"Mr. Ross, this *gentleman*—" she spat the word contemptuously "—is Mr. Stanley Turner, Moonshadow's resident attorney-at-law." Oramay heard the way her derisive tone had carried over to malign Stan professionally, as well, and was struck with shame. "Stan is an excellent lawyer, and this town is very lucky to have him," she added more humbly.

"You'll turn my head with such praise, my dear," Stan shot back with a grin. "Pleased to meet you, Ross. May I ask what brings you to our fair community?" Stan knew very well he'd just stolen Oramay's thunder with that question and felt positively smug.

Jessica Miller might have been a fly on the wall for all the notice anyone appeared to be giving her as she quietly swept crumbs from beneath the tables. But Morgan had not forgotten her for a second. Nor had he missed the way she'd pulled away from him earlier as if he were a leper and would contaminate her with his touch. This afternoon that kind of reaction would have been understandable. But now...

"Actually I'm here to speak with a woman by the name of Miller. A Mrs. John Miller."

Jessica's broom handle crashed to the floor.

"What a coincidence," Oramay said, looking with surprise at her suddenly pale friend.

Chapter Three

The combination of church bells and sunlight awakened Morgan, although he tried in vain to shut both out by rolling over and pulling a pillow over his head. But when his stomach came into contact with the sharp edge of a cold metal object, he gave up on sleeping. With a muttered curse, he sent the pillow flying and lifted himself off the thing gouging his belly. Not for the first time he had fallen asleep staring at the photograph of the Cameron family. It had been appropriated ten years ago, snatched from the fingers of a slobbering drunk, and it had traveled with Morgan ever since.

After all this time he didn't know why he kept dragging it out, looking at it with such rapt attention. He knew each and every one of those images within the tarnished frame as well as his own. Most particularly, Morgan had committed to memory every line, every curve and every nuance of that young girl's radiantly lovely face. The familiarity, however, did not stop him from staring at the young Jessie Cameron one more time or keep him from looking for something, anything, that would tie this child on the brink of her womanhood to the adult downstairs.

There was the smile, of course. Both possessed heartbreaking smiles. Or did they? After meeting with Jessica Miller again last night, Morgan was more than half convinced he'd dreamed the smile. In fact, Morgan had cause to wonder if Jessica Miller had ever laughed a day in her life.

Lord! Talk about a stone-faced, frigid female! Even if he hadn't imagined that beautiful smile, there were other things that didn't match up with Jessie Cameron. According to the bartender who claimed a fast friendship with Jack Cameron and an *intimate* knowledge of Cameron's daughter, the girl who'd run off with Cole Hardin had possessed a goddesslike body. A body Billy Gardiner had described in lurid, graphic detail. Even then, with his fury over his brother's murder still painfully fresh, Morgan had felt a stab of pity for that sixteen-year-old girl. Fortunately, the emotion hadn't been sufficiently affecting to linger longer than that brief moment. But he certainly couldn't make a connection between little Jessie Cameron and this woman. From what he'd seen, there were boards with more shape than the widowed Mrs. Miller.

"Damn!" Morgan spat, swinging his legs off the mattress and sitting up to rake his hands through his hair. On the basis of a thirteen-year-old photograph and descriptions provided by a remorse-filled drunk and a depraved bartender, could Morgan really believe he would know Jessie Cameron when and if he found her? Hell! All he'd really gotten out of the father was that the girl's eyes were "sorta green." Then Jack Cameron had clammed up, refusing to speak another word about his daughter, drunk or sober. Morgan knew, because he'd tried questioning the man under both conditions.

The simple truth was that Morgan had spent eight years of his life chasing after a woman with only the barest facts to go on and damn little hope in ever finding her.

His best bet in actually discovering Jessica Cameron was in the use of the Pinkerton agents he worked with. They were his eyes and ears all over this country. When they ran across an auburn-haired lady of the approximate right age, questions were cautiously asked. If the woman had generations of family around her or a history in that particular town going back further than ten years, no further investigation was necessary. But any with questionable backgrounds sent Morgan heading for the first train he could catch or whatever other mode of transportation was available to take him where he wanted to go. And while he hung around getting personally acquainted with the lady, the detectives made those background checks, verifying every tidbit of information already known and whatever else Morgan could discover. And there had been occasions when his methods of extracting that additional knowledge didn't bear close scrutiny. Neither was living with himself afterward particularly pleasant. It was a necessary evil, but one he'd never entirely resigned himself to.

Leaving the bed, Morgan walked to the washstand and splashed his face with cold water. He purposefully avoided his reflection in the shaving mirror. He already knew what he would see—weariness that went soul-deep, if he had any soul to speak of, anymore.

Cole Hardin's knife had irrevocably altered the course of Morgan's life. Zachary Rossiter hadn't been dead a week before the bank had called in the mortgage on the Triple R. The rest of Zach's creditors had come hard on the bank's heels in panic, not trusting that a twenty-year-old could fulfill the obligations of the contracts Zachary had signed. Morgan had shamelessly used the Rossiter name, playing on both his father's and Zachary's memories and reputations to dissuade the bank from demanding payment in full on the mortgage. But that had only been accomplished by letting them take eight thousand of the Triple R's ten thousand acres as an appeasement offering. He'd kept the others off his back by reminding them of a simple, basic fact of arithmetic: nothing from nothing equals nothing. And nothing was exactly what they could expect if he was forced to close down the shipping yards. Because, as Morgan had sworn repeatedly, he would damn well give those yards away before he would let any one of those greedy bastards come in and profit off Zachary's dreams.

Eventually, Ellsworth went the way of other cattle towns such as Abilene and Wichita. Railroads expanded into Texas, and those long drives to reach northern markets were no longer necessary. The Rossiter Shipping Yards died a natural death, but while they'd been in operation, Morgan Rossiter had become a rich man. Richer perhaps than Zach could have possibly ever imagined. But success and wealth had not brought him any measure of contentment or joy. It merely allowed him to continue these endless, fruitless searches for Jessica Cameron.

With most of the land forfeited, the ranch house he had managed to save had become only a place to be used as a rest stop between trains and those women with auburn hair. Morgan lived there with only a half-blind old cowhand and a shrew-tempered housekeeper for company.

Every now and then Morgan would look at the man he saw in the shaving mirror every day and ask that cold-eyed stranger a question that had yet been answered. What happens, he asked that man now, when the day finally comes and Hardin had paid for his crime against the Rossiters? What then?

Morgan turned away from both the reflection and the question. Picking up the Cameron family photograph from where he'd dropped it on the mattress, he reached for the carpetbag he'd stashed beneath the bed and put the photograph away within the hidden compartment he'd had installed in the bottom of the bag. At the same time, he also withdrew a packet of papers and a small, oval metal object.

He held the badge signifying him to be a deputy United States marshall, remembering the day Judge Isaac Parker had forced him to take the oath to uphold the law. "I'll not endorse vigilante justice, Rossiter. You wear that badge or I'll make you the sorriest son of a bitch who ever tried to take the law into his own hands. And they don't call me the hangin' judge because I've got a soft side...."

Morgan had agreed to Parker's terms, not having had any real choice in the matter. He would play by the rules, if he could, for as long as he could. Whether Hardin hanged legally or from a rope tossed over a lonely, out-of-the-way tree made no damn difference to Morgan. Just as long as Hardin hanged. Neither did he much care what happened to Jessie Cameron after she testified against her lover. That was one problem he could leave in Judge Parker's capable hands. His job was to find the bitch!

Moving to the lace-covered window, Morgan stared down at the empty street below. The church bells had ceased to ring, which meant most everybody would be seated and listening to a sermon right about now. Undoubtedly, Jessica Miller was part of that God-fearing group. He remembered his mother dragging them off to worship service every Sunday, a practice Zach had insisted on continuing up until the time Morgan had gone back east to school. Lord! It had been forever since he'd seen the inside of a church or heard a sermon.

Today he'd meet again with the Widow Miller, although she would probably not welcome his company. He didn't understand the sudden, inexplicable yet palpable dislike she'd communicated last evening. If he didn't know better, he'd swear she had taken that aversion on the mere basis of his looks. That might have made sense earlier the same day, but there was no logic in how she'd emotionally recoiled from him last night. Certainly, it made the lady interesting. Too bad she'd had that reaction prior to his mentioning her name to the attorney; afterward would have been encouraging. As things stood, however, he had his work cut out for him. Thawing that lady was going to take some real effort on his part. The challenge, if nothing else, promised to be stimulating at the very least. It was a rare woman who turned her nose up at Morgan Rossiter.

Besides, thanks to Richard Burke's advance information, Morgan was posing as a possible buyer for that ranch of hers, which meant she was going to have to deal with him. Despite her claim of uncertainty regarding selling, Morgan didn't plan to be easily discouraged. Because, unless he heard of someone else more likely to be Jessica Cameron, Morgan had nothing to lose by hanging around until Burke could complete his background check.

The midafternoon sun warmed the back of Jessica's neck as she worked diligently to clear the area around John Miller's grave of weeds and overgrowth. The job was made more taxing due to her negligence lately. And that was something she'd been taken to task for when she'd stopped by the ranch to collect her horse for the trip up here. Boone Larsen, her foreman, wasn't entirely happy over her plans to sell the Eldorado. Oh, not because he was worried about losing his job. Boone had been threatening to retire and return home to Wyoming Territory for the past three years. He'd only stayed on because he believed she needed him, both during John's lengthy illness and afterward when she had been alone; with the money John had left him, along with what he'd put aside through the years, Boone Larsen could now buy that little spread he'd always dreamed of and spend the rest of his days fishing mountain streams for fat trout.

No, if Boone had any quarrel with Jessica over the sale of the ranch, it was because he was convinced she was making the wrong choice for herself. Neither did Boone want the land sold off to someone who wouldn't be able to appreciate what he had helped build. And who knew better than Boone Larsen just how much of her heart and soul Jessica had invested in the Eldorado and the pride she felt at its unquestioning success? What he couldn't understand was that pride was a very lonely companion, and that no matter how much she loved the Eldorado, it could never fulfill her need to be loved in return.

But after what Jessica had witnessed between Oramay and Stan last evening, she now had more questions than answers about the status of her future. It had never occurred to her there might be more than friendship between those two, but the kiss she'd observed seemed to state otherwise. How could Jessica even consider attaching herself to the Seibert family if Stan Turner could offer Oramay so much more than a mere business partnership?

Jessica sat back on her heels. Her eyes went to the marble headstone. "Oh, Uncle John," she cried softly, granting him here in this isolated place the true family relationship she'd been forced to deny him in life. "What am I to do now?"

Jessica knew very well what her mother's older brother would say. He'd tell her, "Just live your days one at a time, Jessie. And remember, you've survived worse trouble than this."

A tear slid down her cheek, and Jessica used the back of her sleeve to wipe it away. Taking a deep breath, Jessica pulled off her leather gloves and tossed them atop the wide-brimmed hat she'd removed earlier. It wasn't wise to expose her pale skin to this much sunlight, but it felt so damned good....

Out here in this small graveyard adjacent to an abandoned old mining camp, Jessica often discarded some of the constraints she imposed upon herself. She made no effort now to restrain the wispy tendrils of hair that had escaped the braid coiled against the back of her neck. They whipped freely around her face, lifted on an early summer breeze scented heavily with pine. Just this much freedom was so delicious that Jessica sometimes wondered what it would be like to cast off all the outer trappings of the Widow Miller and stand naked, as God had made her, without shame or fear, beneath the purifying rays of the sun.

She actually had her fingers on the top button of her bulky riding jacket when the stallion she'd tethered nearby gave a snort of alarm. Jessica came quickly to her feet, her gaze searching. She saw no threat but took the precaution of going for the rifle Boone had thrust into her saddle scabbard. She'd just withdrawn the weapon when Morgan Ross came sauntering around the corner of an old, tumbledown building, leading a dun-colored mare of questionable breeding. When he saw the rifle being aimed at his belly, there was only the slightest hesitation in his gait before he continued.

"Afternoon, ma'am," Morgan said with a lazy half smile and a tip of his black Stetson. "You're expecting trouble, I see...."

Jessica lowered the weapon, but she didn't return it the scabbard just yet. "Bears and wolves are indigenous to this area, Mr. Ross." She noted he was wearing the gun belt he'd carried into the hotel yesterday.

"I'll keep that caution in mind."

"What are you doing out here, Mr. Ross?" Jessica knew her tone was acerbic, but away from the hotel she felt no obligation to force civility.

"Well, I could tell you it was such a pleasant day I decided to take a ride. But the truth is, I wanted to look around your ranch, so I hired this nag and asked directions in town."

"And you just *happened* to chance upon this old mining camp?"

"No, ma'am," Morgan admitted freely. "I had a visit with your foreman—a cantankerous rascal by the name of Larsen—and he told me I'd likely run across you out this way."

Jessica thrust the rifle back into its scabbard. Obviously, Morgan Ross had managed to win Boone Larsen's trust, which was no small achievement. Nevertheless, she promised that Boone would pay for this betrayal. "Mr. Ross, I'm truly sorry you've traveled so far only to learn your friend was premature in reporting that my ranch was for sale. It's something I have considered, but no firm decisions have been made...."

"I understood you perfectly last evening, Mrs. Miller," Morgan told her, looping the mangy mare's reins to the hitching post where Jessica's big black stallion was already tethered.

"Then it must have also been clear that there's little point in you looking around until I've made up my mind."

Morgan walked around the stallion, not missing how again she seemed to shrink from him. Subsequently, he turned his attentions to her horse. This was one helluva lot of animal for a woman to handle. "He's got some Arabian in him, doesn't he?" Morgan observed, running his hand over muscled hindquarters before moving to examine the animal's proud head. "What do you call him?"

"Titan," Jessica answered through tight jaws. He was also mesmerizing her horse. Titan usually kicked up a fuss around strangers. "Mr. Ross..."

Morgan turned toward her then, tipping back his hat to look directly into those unfriendly, hazel-hued eyes. "Mrs. Miller, it's not my intent to make a nuisance of myself. But neither am I going to waste your time or mine waiting around to hear a decision if the Eldorado isn't to my liking."

"And is it?"

Morgan avoided the question. "You said this was an old mining camp?"

"You are changing the subject, Mr. Ross."

"Right again, ma'am. And for good reason. You see, once upon a time there was this green cowhand who ran across a man with a horse for sale. And that horse was the prettiest little chestnut that young cowhand had ever seen. The minute he saw her, he knew he'd die if he didn't get that animal. Well—to make a long story short—that wily ol' horse trader saw that it was love at first sight and hiked the price up way beyond the poor young cowhand's reach. He lost out on the horse, but he learned to bargain with his head, not his heart."

Oh, yes...Morgan Ross certainly had the devil's own charm. Jessica shook her head slightly in chagrin, because she was very much tempted to like him. "I begin to understand why Boone Larsen was so taken with you, Mr. Ross. I assure you Boone isn't normally so quick to trust. Undoubtedly, though, he recognized a kindred spirit. I'm surprised he let you get away from him. Boone loves nothing more than to swap tall tales... for hours at a time."

Unwittingly, Morgan spoiled the inch of progress he'd made by giving her one of the smiles that had been breaking female hearts since he'd come out of short pants. And it wasn't costing him half the effort he'd feared, either. She definitely looked more appealing, younger and far less the frump today.

Jessica turned on her heel and walked away from his blatantly sensual, intentionally seductive grin. Any other woman would have probably swooned at his feet, or worse. Luckily, she was immune. One encounter with a man such as this one had cured her for life.

Morgan scowled at her retreating backside. And a very nice backside it was, too, he noticed with some surprise. The soft, well-worn fabric of her split riding skirt hugged slender hips and flared around legs that were intriguingly long. They would be sleekly muscled, as well; it took strength to handle that big stallion. Otherwise, however, there was little else to recommend about that dull brown riding costume. The jacket was bulky enough to be a castoff, one that had once belonged to the carnival's fat lady. If she had any breasts beneath that voluminous garment, they weren't discernible. But it certainly might be interesting to find out....

Damn! He couldn't seriously be considering seducing the lady? Watching the sway of her hips and the graceful way she moved on those long legs, Morgan's body emphatically answered that question for him.

By the time Jessica stopped and leaned back against the bark of a towering old oak, her conscience was nagging her. She'd judged and condemned him to suffer her prejudicial dislike simply because his parents had blessed him with extraordinary good looks. The appeal, she was certain, he'd acquired all on his own.

Looking at him now, standing way over there, uncertain and bewildered, Jessica came to a new, truly alarming conclusion. Maybe—just maybe—the reason she felt such antipathy in his company was because she wasn't nearly as invulnerable as she wanted to believe. Fortunately, she assured herself, she had nothing to worry about. Morgan Ross's charm was for the owner of the Eldorado, not Jessica herself. The story he'd told earlier had been a smoke screen. Whatever else he might be, Mr. Ross wasn't stupid enough not to want the Eldorado. And though he couldn't know it, Jessica was a pretty shrewd horse trader herself.

"Mr. Ross," she called out. "Please feel free to look around the mining camp. Sobs Hill is a piece of California history. It is also public domain. You aren't on Eldorado land here."

A peace offering? He had just decided to make a temporary retreat. "I'd like that," he answered, approaching her hesitantly. When she didn't bolt behind the tree, Morgan decided to brave another rejection. "Could I talk you into serving as my guide? Please. . . ." he added softly.

Jessica ignored the arm he offered and began walking. She wasn't prepared to grant him that much familiarity. "Gold was discovered here at Sobs Hill only a few months after color was found on the ground where Moonshadow now stands. But in contrast to the comparatively sedate manner of Moonshadow's miners, this camp quickly earned a reputation for a more typical wildness. Although Sobs Hill had only one street and a total of six constructed buildings, it boasted three saloons and two gambling houses."

Morgan suspended their leisurely stroll to ask, "That accounts for only five buildings. What was housed in the sixth?"

Jessica didn't look at him but answered him straightforwardly. "Ladies of questionable virtue, Mr. Ross."

"Sounds like home," Morgan observed wryly, watching her carefully. "Kansas cattle towns have earned their own notoriety."

"So I've heard," Jessica said without inflection, although her stomach knotted briefly at the casual reference to his state of origin. "Over here," she continued, leading him toward the back edge of the old town, "are the remains of an old sluice."

"It looks as if someone has recently cleaned up this area, even started some work on the buildings."

Jessica's expression was a little sad as she responded to his observation. "My husband was fascinated by this place and by the history of the forty-niners. He'd hoped to restore this camp as a tribute to them, but before he could finish, his health failed. I'm hoping I can find someone who will take a similar interest, even if that means hiring somebody to get the job done."

"I'm sure your husband would like that," Morgan offered. The sorrow in her eyes was genuine. So was the affection. "Sobs Hill...Moonshadow," he reflected, changing the topic. "Unusual names. Is there any rhyme or reason behind them?"

Jessica felt her cheeks heating, but she didn't avoid the question. "Actually, Sobs Hill is a modification of what the miners originally called their camp. You see, the ladies belonging to our local chapter of the historical society found it a bit disconcerting every time the subject of this camp came up. The literal, actual name is SOB Hill, referring, of course, to the male offspring of a female dog."

Morgan threw back his head and laughed. "I can understand why those ladies might have balked. Does Moonshadow have an equally colorful origin?"

"No, thank heaven. But in this case, I believe showing will be easier than telling."

Morgan followed her over the rotting boards of what had once been a sluice box and into the tall pines just behind the camp. They traveled a narrow path but one that had been kept clear of overgrowth. It sloped upward gradually at first, then the trail grew steeper until Morgan could see blue sky above the needle-covered branches.

At the edge of a sharp rise, Jessica turned back and asked, "You aren't one of those people who gets dizzy from heights, are you?"

Morgan honestly didn't know, having never been atop anything taller than a barn loft. "I assume we're about to find out, ma'am," he answered as she grabbed hold of an exposed tree root and pulled herself up the incline, adding a final caution for him to step carefully.

The ridge of ground was narrow but solid, and Jessica felt completely comfortable here in this familiar place overlooking the entirety of the Moonshadow Valley. In the distance, beneath the cloudless sky, the jagged, snowcapped peaks of the Sierra Nevada could be seen. Today there wasn't even the hint of a haze to shadow their breathtaking splendor. On days like this one, they looked so close it seemed as if she had only to extend her hand—

"My God!"

The reverent exclamation that burst in her ear was identical, an echo of her own reaction to this scenic wonder eight years ago. "The tallest mountain over there is called Moon Mountain, though no one living remembers how it came to be named. At sunrise, Moon Mountain casts its shadow over the valley. Hence, you see below the Moonshadow Valley...or so I've been told."

"My God!" Morgan couldn't stop himself from repeating. He was unaware, at this moment, of anything beyond the view before him. But the stark magnificence of the mountains was only a small part of his awe. Equally impressive were the seemingly endless meadows, the livestock grazing upon variegated grasses.

Jessica twisted her body to catch his expression but found much, much more than the approval and wonder she'd anticipated. In those dark eyes she recognized a yearning so great it was almost painful to behold, and when he sensed her gaze and lowered his own to hers, Jessica felt a jolt of something inside herself that defied explanation. Uncomfortable with the feeling, she looked away quickly before cautiously starting to inch around Morgan Ross's tall form. He made no effort to stop her. In fact, he seemed quite willing to assist in allowing her to pass safely behind him. Neither did he seem particularly inclined to give up his view at present.

"I'll meet you back at the horses," she told him.

Morgan only nodded, his brows nearly meeting as he tried to make some sense out of what had just happened. When he'd looked into her eyes, it had felt as if some unseen fist had given him a punch in the gut.

Before she'd taken more than a few steps back down the path, Jessica turned back to the man silhouetted against the sky. "Mr. Ross," she said just loud enough to be heard. "You are extremely lucky I'm not some crafty old horse trader."

There was real humor and warmth in her jest. He was indeed fortunate he wasn't a serious buyer for this land. Because what he must have just revealed would have proved a monumental mistake at the bargaining table. But anyone seeing this view might be tempted to throw caution to the wind and his hard-earned money after it. Undoubtedly, that punch in his gut had been from the devil, reminding him to keep to business and to forget that all this was out of his reach.

Or was it? Maybe he'd found the answer to that question of *what then?* Maybe this valley, or a piece of it, could be the future he'd never dared consider before. Damn, but it was a tempting thought!

Morgan had no idea how long he'd lingered before starting back. He found Jessica Miller waiting for him near the horses when he walked out of the camp. "That, Mrs. Miller, was a dirty trick. And you've more horse trader in you than I care to acknowledge."

"Perhaps one or two of my foreman's stories might have influenced me, after all."

"Oh! Speaking of Larsen. He had a message for you, a rather cryptic one. He said to tell you that at least this one—meaning myself—wasn't no danged woodchuck."

This time there was no controlling her smile or the unaffected laughter. "Woodchuck," she explained, "was Boone's affectionate, if somewhat disgruntled, nickname for my late husband. Before we moved here, John had been a lumberman by trade and a carpenter by preference. Boone's message is a compliment, Mr. Ross. It means he considers you to be a true-blue cattleman down to your bones. In Boone's eyes that puts you squarely on the right side of the Lord."

"Lumber," he muttered unevenly, having trouble concentrating on what she was saying. He was too engrossed by the tiny dimple that had appeared at the corner of her mouth when she laughed. He hadn't noticed it yesterday. Wasn't there the slightest hint of such an indention on Jessie Cameron's smiling face? "I wasn't aware of any sawmills in this area."

"There aren't any," Jessica corrected. "We were originally from the Northwest."

"Exactly where in the Northwest?" Morgan prodded.

"Washington Territory," Jessica told him as she untethered Titan and swung up into the saddle with practiced ease. "We should start back, Mr. Ross. I promised Mrs. Seibert I would help her with some paperwork she keeps trying to avoid." No matter what, Jessica would see Oramay's accounts put to rights.

"She told me this was her day to rest and do as she pleased."

"That's true. Sundays are reserved for her son." Jessica was already turning Titan in the direction of the ranch. "Are you coming?"

Was he imagining things, or had her sudden anxiousness to leave come at the same moment as his questions about her personal history? The friendly smile had disappeared, as well. "No. I think I'll stick around here for a while and enjoy the scenery. Don't look for me back at the ranch. I'll head straight to town from here and spare that nag I'm riding the extra miles. I'm not sure she'll make it, otherwise."

Jessica looked toward the swaybacked mare and frowned. "She is pitiful," she agreed. "You know, I'm surprised David Hughes would keep such a sorry excuse for horseflesh in his stable, let alone let her be ridden."

Morgan shrugged. "The boy—Tommy, I think his name is—said she was all they had available, that every other animal had been spoken for." He could see Jessica didn't quite believe that story. Neither had Morgan, but he'd taken the nag rather than argue.

"Well, I'll leave you to enjoy Sobs Hill then, Mr. Ross."

"And if I don't return by midnight, send out a rescue party," he added jokingly. Her response was a nod and a quick word of farewell. Then she whirled the stallion around and galloped off. Watching the expert way she rode and handled the big Arabian, Morgan, who was a pretty fair horseman himself, had cause to admire the widow's expertise and confidence with such a spirited animal. She looked more the old-gray-mare-and-buggy type and acted it more times than not. That thought had Morgan staring out at the retreating figure. Was that the answer to the puzzle of Jessica Miller? Could it be that the respectable, sedate, above-reproach image she presented was just a well-practiced act?

Morgan wandered to the overgrown graveyard. The marble tombstone confirmed what he already knew, but somehow seeing the dates deeply etched into the stone made the age discrepancy between John Miller and his young wife more profane. Morgan estimated that Miller would have been in his mid- to late fifties when he'd taken his bride of sixteen or seventeen to his bed, and it disgusted him.

"What could you offer her besides security, old man?" he said aloud. "Did you give her a place to hide in exchange for an occasional night between those strong, smooth thighs?"

He winced at his own crudity. Unfortunately, although he would like very much to believe there had been something vile and irregular about the Millers' marriage, what he had learned about the couple seemed to indicate there'd been a genuine and loving devotion between them.

Wasn't it entirely possible that Jessica Miller was exactly what she seemed—a complex human being who wasn't altogether one thing or another? Making her over to suit his needs and purposes was the danger he'd been fighting from the first. He couldn't afford to lose his objectivity now. There wasn't time to waste on proving an innocent woman to be someone she wasn't.

At least his instincts were functioning properly. He'd let the widow ride off without him, when normally he would have stuck to her with the tenacity of a bad habit. But this particular lady would need special handling, since it was obvious she wasn't going to fall easily beneath the spell of his so-called fatal charm. He rather admired her for that, as well, Morgan acknowledged with a self-mocking grin.

Well, he'd learned a few things that might aid Burke and save the detective and himself some of the time that had become so precious. John Miller had been a lumberman and/or a carpenter. That much had the ring of truth, so the story they were from the Northwest was probably also valid. But it was a big territory, far too large for just one man to cover. Morgan would authorize the additional funds for the extra men Richard Burke would need to start scouring the lumber camps and mill towns up and down the Pacific Northwest. The sooner this was resolved the better, before this valley could finish weaving its spell on him, before he found himself wishing and wanting things he'd not considered since the night of his brother's death.

Such were Morgan's thoughts as he approached the swayback mare and prepared to mount, too distracted to notice the slight give in the saddle when he slipped his foot into the stirrup.

A second later, Morgan Rossiter was flat on his butt, still holding on to the saddle while the nag that had previously refused to produce a gait faster than a slow trot went racing off into the woods.

"Son of a bitch!"

Chapter Four

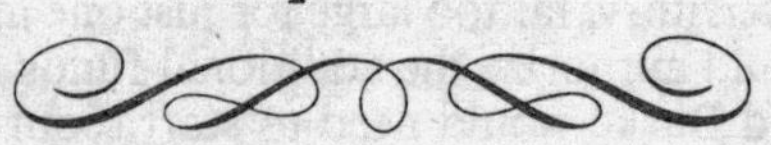

"Let me show you what I'm talking about, Oramay," Jessica said as she produced an invoice for a shipment of strawberries from a Sacramento firm. "Compared to Randall's ledgers of two years ago, you are now paying more than double—"

"So? Prices go up, don't they?" Oramay snapped a little peevishly. She hated book work of any kind, because she'd always been so abysmally bad with figures. Having Jessica insistently point out her failures was not sweetening an already less than pleasant mood.

Jessica sighed wearily, trying very hard to be patient, for they needed to resolve these matters. Unfortunately, Oramay was being extremely uncooperative and growing increasingly snappish.

"Yes, Oramay. Prices go up. However, since there have only been slight increases overall from your other suppliers—"

"Maybe it was a bad couple of years for strawberries!" Oramay knew she was being unreasonable. Jessica was only trying to help. "I'm sorry, honey. I know you think this is real important, and I'm sure it is. But I simply don't have the energy to worry over whether I'm being cheated a few pennies here and there. The price of strawberries isn't high on my list of priorities right now."

Jessica watched Oramay bounce out of her chair and go to the oven to check the cookies she'd suddenly taken a notion to bake. Already there were enough oatmeal cookies cooling on the table and packed away in tins to feed half the state. She'd lived here long enough to know Oramay always baked to excess whenever she was deeply disturbed. Since Jessica had asked several times and been reassured several times that Kathleen and Patrick were not the source of her agitation, there could only be one other cause: Stanley Turner. It was a subject they'd both been avoiding.

"Oramay," Jessica said gently, "about Stan..."

Oramay nearly dropped the batch of cookies she'd just taken from the oven. "What's that bothersome attorney have to do with anything?" she snapped, slamming the oven door shut with a ringing vengeance. "Except to make it his life's purpose to irritate me into an early grave. The man's been a thorn in my side since he began yanking on my pigtails out in the school yard when the teacher wasn't looking. He never did get caught, though I spent more than my share of time with my nose in a corner paying for trouble he started. Always Mr. Perfect. Bah!"

Jessica fought a smile. "Didn't you tell me Stan was your first beau?"

"And nearly my last!" Oramay shot back, flopping back down into her chair. "He botched my first kiss so badly it nearly soured me on kissing for life." This time she chuckled a little.

On a deep breath, Jessica leaned forward slightly and said, "And has he improved his technique since those days?"

Oramay's face flushed crimson, and she fidgeted nervously with her hands, but she didn't avoid the topic. "Saw that, did you? I suspected as much when you said you might not be selling the ranch with Ross last night. Well, don't make too much of it."

"Oramay," Jessica said softly, covering those wringing hands with one of her own, "I'm not the one to worry about here. The question is how much you and Stan made of it. And it seemed to me neither of you were taking that kiss lightly."

"It doesn't matter, Jessie. It would never work. We're too different. He was always the smart one, while I just barely got by. Stan wanted to go out into the big world and become a lawyer. All I wanted was a home and family and never to leave Moonshadow. He got what he wanted. We both did. And I've never regretted the decision I made back then. Randall Seibert was the best and most loving husband a woman could ever want. I adored him. We hardly ever disagreed. In fact, come to think of it, the only arguments we had were usually about Stan Turner."

"That was then, Oramay. What about now?" Knowing Oramay as she did, Jessica knew the woman thrived on disagreements—friendly ones, at least. She suspected that between Randall Seibert and Stanley Turner, Oramay had enjoyed the best of two worlds. Randall had provided the gentle security and peace Oramay felt was needed for a good home and family. But Stan had returned to Moonshadow, and through him Oramay was granted the spice that prevented her harmonious world from slipping into tedium. "You're still a young woman...."

Jessica should have known better than to offer that particular argument, because Oramay immediately threw it right back in her face.

"Look who's talking! A girl half my age who's vowed she will never marry again more times than I care to count."

It was Jessica's turn to make light of the subject. "What man would have a scrawny, plain woman like me?" she stated with a smile that was not self-pitying.

Oramay countered by grabbing Jessica's chin. "Any worth his salt, that's who! And maybe if you'd eat more than a bird's diet there'd be some pretty flesh on those bones."

"What is it they say about silk purses and sows' ears...?"

"Balderdash! That's what I say! Do you think I'm stone-blind, girl? I see—"

"Oramay...please...."

The look of pleading in those big hazel eyes couldn't be resisted. Oramay had known that Jessie Miller carried painful secrets inside of her since the first time she'd looked into those haunted young eyes eight years ago. She also knew that someday, when the time was right, Jessica would tell her what they were.

With a frustrated sigh, Oramay sat back in her chair. "All right. I'll keep my opinions to myself. In fact, let's make us a deal. I won't nag you about that crazy vow—which I don't expect you to keep, anyhow, knowing your love for children and people in general—if you don't worry me about Stan Turner, or these papers, until after Kathleen's baby is born."

"You drive a hard bargain, Mrs. Seibert. Or should I say a dirty bargain, since it's mostly blackmail you're using. But I agree. We'll have no more man talk."

"Speaking of men," Oramay chirped, snapping her fingers, "what do you think of Morgan Ross? Strictly as a buyer for the Eldorado, that is. Of course, we can't discuss what a prime specimen of manhood that young man is or how just looking at him starts a woman's toes curling and her heart to pounding." Oramay laughed, then noticed that Jessica didn't seem to share in her amusement. Instead, she looked worried. "Honey, what's wrong? Did that man do or say something he shouldn't?"

Jessica told Oramay about the sorry horse Morgan Ross had ridden to the old mining camp. "I just realized how late it's getting and that I haven't seen him. Have you?"

"Not likely, since we've been together for the past three hours. Maybe he got sidetracked by something or somebody here in town. Or could be he changed his mind and went back to the Eldorado for another chat with Boone."

"You're probably right," Jessica agreed, already reaching for the papers strewn across the table, carefully packing them away. At least they were in some kind of order, she thought ruefully. "Let me help you get this cookie mess cleared away."

Thirty minutes later, Oramay looked at Jessica just as the young woman took yet another glance at the clock. "Why don't you roust Patrick out of his room and send him down to the livery to check on that horse. If the animal made it back, it's a good bet Mr. Ross is around here someplace."

"Yes. I think that's a good idea. After all, he isn't familiar with the area. And I'd feel responsible for leaving him out there...."

"Sure, honey. I understand," Oramay concurred evenly, keeping the smugness out of her voice and off her face as Jessica left the kitchen. Morgan Ross hadn't impressed her as the helpless type. So why was Jessie fretting over him like a mother worrying over her lost lamb? Lord knew, if Morgan Ross couldn't awaken the sleeping woman inside Jessica Miller, there was no hope for the girl. John had been a good man; Oramay had been fond of him. His young wife had obviously adored her aging husband. Still, there were just some aspects of marriage better accomplished by the young and healthy. John Miller had been neither.

Jessica found Patrick sprawled across his bed reading a book. Or, more accurately, Patrick was engrossed in one of those dreadful dime novels his mother had quite plainly forbidden. At her entry, the forbidden book was immediately stuffed beneath a pillow. Jessica suspected she'd just found the source of Patrick and Tommy's nonsense yesterday.

"Hiya, Jessie."

She opened her mouth to scold him about the book but again lost heart. The novels were basically harmless and so plainly exaggerated that even Patrick couldn't take them too seriously. She would speak to him about it later. He really shouldn't go against his mother's wishes.

Seeing that she was making the youngster nervous, Jessica managed a small smile. "Patrick, would you do me a favor and run down to the livery? Mr. Ross hasn't returned to the hotel. He acquired a horse from Mr. Hughes this morning, a dun-colored mare—"

"I know the one," Patrick said quickly, getting up off his bed. "You want me to see if it's back yet."

"That's about it. But please don't stay and talk with Tommy into the night this time. Your mother would worry."

"Yeah. All right," he agreed grudgingly.

When he would have darted past her, Jessica blocked his path. "You look pale, Patrick. Are you feeling well?" She put her hand on his brow.

"Aw, Jessie! Don't fuss!" Patrick complained with a roll of his eyes.

She stepped back with a muttered apology. There certainly was a rampant case of irritability going around. Either that or she was managing successfully to set everyone around her on edge today.

Patrick found Tommy Hughes sitting in one of the empty stalls in his family's livery. Between his legs, tongue lolling out with delirious contentment, was the shaggy, mixed-breed mutt nobody in town would claim, although just about everyone took a turn at feeding the homeless dog. In between snips with the scissors he was using to cut large chunks of matted fur from the animal's back and belly, Tommy would pause and scratch his own flesh.

"Danged fleas are going to eat me alive!"

"Tommy," Patrick groaned impatiently, "what am I gonna tell Jessie?"

"Tell her you didn't find nobody around."

"Then she'll just come down here herself. And when she sees Flossie back in her stall—"

"Gawdamighty! Do I have to do your thinkin' for you, too?" Tommy wailed with scorn. "Fib and tell her we ain't seen hide nor hair of Ross or Flossie." Not for anything would Tommy let Patrick see his own worries and fears. This morning, when he'd purposely taken a saddle needing repair from his pa's tack room and put it on Flossie's back for the gunslinger, those extra cuts he'd put in the riggings had seemed a grand idea. But that had been before he'd had all day to consider the possible consequences of his impulsive actions. Tommy could only pray Black Bart wouldn't notice that the cinches had been sliced. The whole idea was for this to appear an accident or, at worst, just carelessness by some kid not watching closely enough to notice the saddle was unsafe.

Patrick counted to ten twice and was still angry at the tone Tommy had used with him. "It's come to me that maybe I've already let you do too much of my thinking for me, Thomas Hughes. Hell's bells! That Ross fellow didn't look a damn thing like Black Bart this morning!"

Tommy shrugged. "So he cleaned up some. Probably just to throw everybody off the scent after all the commotion and gossip yesterday. He ain't stupid, you know." Another clump of flea-infested dog hair went into a glass jar nearby. Black Bart Bigelow or not, Morgan Ross was *somebody* other than what he claimed. Tommy was sure of it. "Besides, he told me himself he was from Kansas," he went on vehemently, as if that fact alone was proof positive Morgan Ross was up to no good.

Patrick squatted and began picking at the straw beneath his feet. "Listen...I ain't so sure about this anymore. What if he took a bad tumble off Flossie and is out there bad hurt...or worse."

"Shoot," Tommy scoffed. "Flossie don't move fast enough to do any real damage. Lord knows I've taken enough tumbles off her myself to know. And ain't makin' him uncomfortable our plan? Make him wish he'd never stepped foot in Moonshadow? Well, them feet he came into town on yesterday is gonna be wearing blisters tonight."

Patrick still looked dubious, so Tommy gave the mutt a shove and came to his feet as the dog went rolling. "Blast it, Pat! Didn't you read *The Cheating Heart* like I told you?" At Patrick's grumbled admission that he had, Tommy let go with an exasperated snort. "Well? Don't you see it, then? He's here in Moonshadow to swindle Jessie Miller outa her ranch just like he did that poor, dumb widow back in Kansas. You just watch. He'll start sidling up to Jessie, and before you know it, she'll be makin' goo-goo eyes at him. Then, when he's got his thieving hands on the Eldorado, he'll start on the rest of the valley. Only we ain't got no lawman like Wes Hardy to run him out of our town."

"But—"

"But nothin'! It's up to us, Pat. We've got to aggrivate him into showing his true colors so Jessie won't fall for his smooth act. At least we've got to try," Tommy said earnestly, managing to reinforce his own convictions while he worked to turn Patrick back to enthusiastic cooperation.

Patrick wasn't sure what worried him most: that Tommy could be right about Morgan Ross being Black Bart Bigelow or that he could be dead wrong. "All right," he finally conceded. "We'll do things your way for a time. But if it looks like this ain't workin', I want your agreement—right now!—that we'll get help, even if that means going all the way to Sacramento for it. Plus, I won't start telling outright lies to my ma or Jessie Miller. I'm going back to the hotel and tell the truth, that Flossie came back without her rider," Patrick stated in a manner that told Tommy he didn't intend to argue. More than his concern over fibbing, Patrick didn't like the idea of leaving an injured man out there, Black Bart or not.

Tommy was not accustomed to Patrick taking a stand. His first impulse was to bully his usually submissive friend back into line, but he thought better of it. This was too important and he needed Patrick's cooperation. "All right, Pat. But would it *exactly* be a lie if you didn't mention how long Flossie's been back in her stall?"

"Guess not," Patrick mumbled, surprised that Tommy hadn't torn into him. Maybe being so flea-bit had affected his brain? "What the blazes do you want with that mutt and a jar of dog hair?" he finally asked.

Tommy Hughes grinned from ear to ear. "Just listen and I'll tell you. . . ."

Twenty minutes after Patrick returned from the livery, Jessica was preparing to climb into Oramay's buggy.

"Jessie, I still say you've got no business out on the road alone at this hour of the night," Oramay continued to protest, even as Jessica was settling herself upon the seat and taking up the reins. "Honey, please let me send for Sheriff Taylor. . . ."

"Earl Taylor couldn't find his backside in the dark with both hands," Jessica stated with an uncharacteristic brashness that brought a shocked gasp from Oramay Seibert. "Well, it's true," she defended on a laugh. "Besides, Boone would have my hide if I dragged Earl along. The last time those two did any tracking together, Boone threatened he'd purposely lose Earl if he ever got another chance." Seeing that Oramay was determined to worry about her brought a surge of warm affection. "I'll be fine," she reassured, patting the six-shooter on the seat beside her. "I have a gun, and I know how to use it. Plus, there's a nearly full moon up there. You just promise me that you'll send for Stan should Kathleen need you. Otherwise, I'll be back around dawn . . . hopefully with our missing guest."

"Lordy," Oramay breathed. "I do hope that young man isn't bad hurt. . . ."

"So do I, Oramay," Jessica returned with a sincerity that surprised her, although she immediately told herself that she would feel the same for any human being in trouble.

As Jessica had predicted, the trip to the Eldorado was made without incident. But when she pulled the horse up in front of the bunkhouse, Jessica was puzzled to find the lights ablaze. She had just climbed out of the buggy when one of the cowhands, a young man in his early twenties by the name of Bobby Callahan, came stumbling out of the bunkhouse, carrying a bucket. But he didn't make it two steps from the door before dropping to his knees, where he began to retch violently.

Jessica rushed to his side. "My God, Bobby," she cried, alarmed by the terrible spasms wracking his young body. "Boone!" she screamed when Bobby groaned and slumped heavily against her. "Boone! Charlie!" With relief she heard the screen door slam shut behind her, and then strong arms were hauling Bobby to his feet.

"Well, my young friend. I see you didn't escape this, after all."

The velvety, deep drawl brought Jessica's head up with a snap. "Ross," she said with surprise. "What are you . . . ? I thought you were . . ."

Morgan didn't take the time to explain his presence or the reason for it. "Could you fetch us some fresh water, ma'am?" he said with a nod toward the discarded bucket. "And I hope to God you've got a strong stomach. If not, stay the hell out of the bunkhouse."

Jessica watched Morgan Ross half carry, half drag Bobby inside, but she didn't question the reason behind his request for water. Within minutes she'd filled the bucket from the pump and was inside the bunkhouse, seeing for herself. All four of the Eldorado's hands, including Boone Larsen, were doubled over on their bunks, alternately moaning and hanging their heads over the sides. Beside each man was a pot or a pail to receive the foul contents of his stomach. Jessica felt her own insides begin to revolt at the terrible odor. "Dear heaven," she whispered, reaching behind her to find the wall, bracing herself until she managed to control the involuntary response.

"Lady," a voice growled in her ear. "I told you to stay outside if . . ."

Jessica took a deep breath and blinked her watery eyes, drawing herself up to look into a handsome face wearing mixed expressions of concern and annoyance. "I'll be fine," she told Morgan Ross firmly. "What's going on here? What happened?"

"Damned if I know," Morgan answered, again feeling a surge of admiration for the way she'd pulled herself together. The stench in here would put a buffalo down. "But I have my suspicions this has something to do with that pot of stew over there on the cookstove. Bobby was the last to eat and the last to sicken. Except for that fellow over there. Seems he's been in his bunk most of the day."

Jessica's gaze moved in the direction of Ross's pointing finger. "That's Charlie Mitchell. He's the cook."

Because Charlie was the only unconscious man, Jessica went to him first, fearing his condition to be the most critical. "Did you get hold of some bad meat, Charlie?" she asked softly, worriedly, bending over the man's bunk as she placed her hand atop his brow. His skin was moist but cool. He didn't seem to be in any pain, nor was there any pail beside his bunk. When she went to press lightly on his stomach, Charlie expelled his breath in a loud grunt. Jessica jerked upright, and her voice was strained as she turned to the man standing behind her. "Would you please bring me that bucket of water, Mr. Ross."

Morgan quickly complied, then watched in stunned amazement when she took up the bucket and threw the entire contents straight into the prone man's face.

"He's not sick—he's drunk!" Jessica announced as Charlie came up off the bunk, spitting and sputtering, only to lose his footing and fall back, striking his head on the wall behind him.

Jessica ignored his grumbled curses and walked to the stove at the far end of the room. What she found in the big pot caused her to grimace. Lifting the ladle, she sniffed the greasy, unappetizing contents, noting a strange odor, but not the sour, spoiled one she might have expected. By chance, her gaze passed over the shelf above the stove, and her heart nearly stopped beating. Sitting side by side were two boxes of frighteningly similar shape and packaging. One contained salt, the other a common brand of rat poison.

"Dear God," she whispered.

Her hand trembled as she took the poison off the shelf and carried it back to the cook. Shoving the box in his face, her calm control shattered. "You've poisoned them!" she shrieked. "You put rat poison in the stew because you were too damned drunk to see the label on the box! Rat poison instead of salt! But God watches after drunks and fools, doesn't he? You passed out before you could eat any of your own deadly—"

"Whoa, there," Morgan intoned soothingly. He took her by the shoulders and drew her back before she could follow her apparent intention of stuffing the box down the bleary-eyed man's throat. "You can tear him apart later. I'll even help. But right now we've got some seriously sick men to deal with."

Jessica shuddered, but his words penetrated the red fog of her murderous fury. "They need a doctor," she croaked. "Soon...."

"I'll take your rig."

"No!" Jessica's fingers dug into muscular forearms. "Send Charlie. He knows where Doc Griffith lives."

"Ma'am, I doubt he can see—"

"Then stick his head under the pump until his vision clears," she snapped back. "I need somebody here steady on his feet to help me with these men. We have to get that poison out of them." On that, Jessica went back to the stove and began adding handfuls of salt to the tepid coffee she found there. "I'll need some more water, Mr. Ross. Quickly, please...."

She didn't hear his response or see him haul Charlie Miller outside and all but throw the rapidly sobering cook into the buggy. Jessica was only aware of his return and of the strong hands that gently lifted Boone Larsen while she poured warm, salted coffee down her desperately ill old friend's throat.

It seemed an eternity passed while Morgan and Jessica moved from bunk to bunk, forcing down liquids that induced violent spasms of vomiting. Although she often thanked him for his help, Morgan knew she was barely aware of his presence. Only once did she look straight into his face, and that was to wonder if Charlie had made it to town.

"I told him I'd break every bone in his body if he didn't," Morgan told her, expecting the sincerity of his threat to cause shock or distaste. Instead, she only nodded approvingly before kneeling to offer comfort to the man heaving up his guts.

The physician's eventual arrival brought only a modicum of relief. Within his bag he carried more liquids and substances needing to be administered. Griffith, Morgan noticed, was a young man, tall and blond, confident and attractive. He worked with Jessica Miller with the ease and quiet compatibility of long and familiar association. That the doctor had a special fondness for the widow was evidenced by the frequency with which he would take her arm or rest a hand upon her shoulder as they traveled between sick cowhands. And the lady did not seem at all distressed by the contact, accepting the doctor's touch as if it were an everyday thing.

Morgan couldn't help but remember the way she'd avoided taking his offered arm this afternoon, or the many times tonight when she'd visibly recoiled from even the most accidental brushings of their bodies. At the time he had taken her by the shoulders, Morgan had assumed her shudder to be one of high emotion. Later, he'd not been so sure. Granted, they were essentially strangers, but her aversion to him struck Morgan as extreme. He had concluded that Jessica Miller found any man's touch repulsive, which certainly would have explained her choice in husbands. But that had been prior to seeing how cozy the widow was with her dead husband's physician. Perhaps the sainted Mrs. Miller wasn't so virtuous, respectable or frigid, after all. And just maybe her relationship with the young and virile Dr. Griffith explained how a healthy young woman had managed to content herself in what must have been a sterile marriage those final years. What Morgan couldn't explain, however, was his own rather perplexing reaction to these possible answers to the riddle of Jessica Miller. There was no chance he could be feeling disappointment, let alone jealousy.

If Jessica could have read Morgan Ross's mind, she would first have been astounded he could have such thoughts about her and David Griffith. Her second reaction would have been to laugh until her sides split. David was blissfully married to his childhood sweetheart and had only recently discovered Melanie was pregnant with their first child. Like most of the residents in this valley, the Griffiths had been adopted into Jessica's far-reaching family constellation; their baby would become another foster niece or nephew to fill the empty spaces within a heart that had more to give than she could ever dream of receiving. But where David's hand on her shoulder or arm went unnoticed, much as the touch of a brother or cousin would have, Jessica could have recounted each and every instance she had come into contact with Morgan Ross with vivid and alarming clarity.

Even now, with him clear across the room, Jessica felt his presence, heard that resonant voice as he administered care with a quiet steadiness that inspired confidence. These men were nothing to him. He could have refused her when she'd asked him to stay, could have left on a borrowed horse anytime since David's arrival. She had suggested he do just that, but he'd elected to stay and help. And every time she saw him extend a kindness to these men who were strangers, Jessica felt something inside of her grow warm and soft, and she knew a dangerous yearning to feel those strong and gentle hands....

"Jess," David was saying, giving her shoulder a little shake. Apparently her mind had been drifting. "I think we've got this under control now. Why don't you go up to the house, put some coffee on and put your feet up for a while. Ross and I can handle things here."

Jessica argued but soon realized she was wasting her breath. Both men were adamant. "Only an hour," she reminded sternly on her way out. "I will be back in an hour."

Chapter Five

Jessica turned her face away from the light, only to jerk upright in the chair seconds later, coming awake to full sunlight. "Damn!" she mumbled, forcing her cramped muscles to function as she uncurled her twisted limbs. She remembered making the coffee and flopping down in this chair with a cup. Everything after that was just a blank. "Damn those men!"

Jessica flew out of the house and ran the distance to the bunkhouse. David's buggy was nowhere in sight, and she was furious with him for going off without waking her, for letting her sleep in the first place.

When she entered the bunkhouse, she found her cowhands asleep and Charlie Mitchell on his knees, scrubbing the floor. The pails that had been beside each bunk were gone, and the room smelled of lye and vinegar.

"Mornin', Mrs. Miller," Charlie said uneasily, his eyes downcast.

Jessica ignored him, feeling no sympathy for him despite his humbled voice and shamefaced expression. To Charlie's credit, she supposed, he'd at least been man enough to return with David, although he must have known he would find no favor here. Unfortunately, the memory of his drunken negligence and the near tragedy it had caused was too fresh for Jessica to feel kindly disposed toward the man. Still, he was the only person awake and capable of answering questions.

"Did the doctor leave instructions?" she asked brusquely.

"Imagine so, ma'am. But you'll have t' ask that fellow out in the barn. He didn't tell me nothin' except to rid the stench outa here and to take care o' them puke pails."

An appropriate job, Jessica thought with approval, though hearing that Morgan Ross still remained was both puzzling and unsettling. Why hadn't he awakened her and hitched a ride back to town with David?

Suddenly Jessica realized just how late it was. "Oh, my God!" she muttered under her breath, remembering her promise to be back at the hotel around dawn. Surely David had stopped by to report her situation here. If so, Jessica hoped Oramay wouldn't be stubborn and would ask Stan Turner to look after Patrick. Of course, she might take her son to Kathleen's, which would be good for all of them. Jessica couldn't worry about that now. She had four unconscious, sick men to look after and their duties to perform. The stock would need to be fed.

"You can find me in the barn, Charlie. I want to be fetched the very minute any one of these men begin to stir."

"Yes, ma'am," Charlie replied with hangdog humility. He had a lot of genuine respect for the boss lady, even if she was a real pain on the subject of a man's drinking. Still, this time, maybe, it could be the lady had a justifiable bone to pick.

When Jessica reached the barn, she discovered that the horses had already been taken care of. They'd been turned out into the paddock, their stalls cleaned and sweetened with fresh hay. A further search led her to the man she assumed was responsible for those chores. She found Morgan Ross sound asleep in the stuffy tack room.

He was stretched out on an old blanket with a saddle beneath his head and his arms flung back. His long legs were spread wide, and one knee was slightly bent. There would have been an almost childlike abandon in the way he was sprawled, but for the fact that there was little boyish innocence to be found in the totally mature and virile form on display.

His shirttails had pulled free of his trousers, and the black cloth had ridden up, revealing smooth, darkly bronzed skin. A wide line of silky, dark hair bisected his flat abdomen and swirled around the navel set deep in a hard-muscled belly.

Dear God! If she'd accidentally stumbled across a sleeping cougar, Jessica would not have felt more vulnerable or have been more shaken. Neither could she deny the compelling magnificence of this inherently sexual male animal.

As if offering proof of her wayward thoughts, Morgan Ross stretched and shifted in his sleep. Sleek muscles tautened when his hips arched slightly off the blanket, drawing her helpless gaze to his powerful thighs and the undeniable potency of his sex.

Suddenly the soft cloth binding her breasts began to tighten painfully. Her skin felt too hot, as if she were burning up from the inside out. She became aware of deep pulses within her body that she'd not known existed.

On a choked sob, Jessica began to back out of the room, wishing she could run yet knowing her watery knees would not have let her get very far. Had it been only yesterday she'd silently accused this man of trying to charm her with an intentional and practiced sensuality? How unfairly judgmental she'd been. Morgan Ross didn't need to work at being sensual. Sound asleep and oblivious to his audience, Morgan Ross was making a joke out of everything Jessica had come to believe about herself. And the acknowledgment frightened her, giving her the impetus to turn and flee the private devils of an insane and impossible yearning, never knowing she had escaped just in time.

"God!" Morgan spat on an explosion of trapped breath, rolling up to stare at the now-empty doorway. "What in the hell is going on here?" he mumbled, feeling angry and disgusted with himself. He also felt painfully aroused and as frustrated as hell!

When she'd walked into the tack room, Morgan had been only half-asleep but lucid enough to know he was too foggy to deal rationally with Jessica Miller and the ongoing, unresolved debate she invariably instigated within him. Last night he'd been eager to accuse her of an adulterous relationship with the good doctor. But after she'd gone to the house, he'd been forced to listen while Griffith all but waxed poetic about his perfectly beautiful, perfectly perfect little wife—occasionally interspersed with glowing superlatives regarding his respectful admiration for the grieving young Widow Miller. Morgan had had to privately concede he had been mistaken. Hell! After some of the things Griffith recounted concerning her devoted care to her dying husband, Morgan had been prepared to nominate the lady for sainthood himself!

Of course, that had been before she'd stood over his prone form and proceeded to scald him with the banked heat radiating from those big, big eyes of hers. In fact, she'd been so caught up and involved with her ogling, she hadn't seen him open his eyes to do a little ogling of his own....

The tight knot she usually made of her hair was all askew this morning, with long, thick ribbons of titian flame falling across her shoulders. Color suffused her cheeks as she looked at him, drawing his own gaze to her mouth. Her lower lip was unnaturally full, reddened, reminding him how many times he'd watched her worry that lip last night with her small, pretty teeth. She was all mussed, tousled and disheveled—and more appealing than he had already imagined was possible. More, the naked and tortured emotion he'd seen on her face, the painful loneliness he sensed, had moved him, touched him. Dammit! It had inflamed him.

Morgan had closed his eyes upon the unexpected fierceness of his arousal. But even with his eyes closed he could still see her, could hear again that strangled little sound she made and knew exactly where her gaze was fixed. Morgan had wanted to drag her down to him, wanted to soothe her swollen lip with the stroke of his tongue before tugging it to even lusher fullness with gentle nips. He could almost feel the silky texture of her hair falling into his hands. God! He'd broken out in a cold sweat just imagining the velvet softness of her strong thighs and the moist, hot core of her sex....

In another second, if she had lingered one second longer, Morgan knew he would have acted out the insane fantasy for real and without a single thought to the possible consequences. All reason and logic had been disconnected by the hard and swollen throbbing between his legs. Luckily, the involuntary jerking of his hips had scared her off. Otherwise—

"Damn!" Morgan growled, coming to his feet, grabbing up the blanket with the intention of folding it neatly. Instead, he balled it in his fists and flung it across the airless room.

He couldn't remember the last time he'd so totally lost control over himself. Oh, admittedly he had felt little twinges of desire for some of those other auburn-haired ladies through the years. One or two of them had been temptingly beautiful and more than willing to welcome him into their beds. Only once, in the very early days of his search for Jessie Cameron, had he made the mistake of becoming physically intimate with one of the candidates. But that experience had left such a foul taste in his mouth he'd vowed never again to go so far. Subsequently, he'd used the allure he had for women to seduce their confidences, to encourage their secrets and, hopefully, to expose their lies. But he drew the line at using their bodies in the process. It was a small concession to his conscience, he knew. Still, he'd had little difficulty in resisting temptation . . . until now.

Surprisingly, despite his profligate youth—or maybe *because* he'd been such a hell-raiser, Morgan acknowledged wryly—he had mellowed quite a bit in his sexual practices through the years. Of course, more than a few folks might take exception to his claim if they accompanied him on one of his trips to Kansas City, where he spent several days visiting a certain parlor house and its madam. But Morgan had learned to appreciate a little genuine friendship and affection accompanying sex. Temple Tyler provided that and more. She was also wickedly inventive, exciting and completely insatiable. Temple spoiled him for the indifferent and unsatisfying services provided by ordinary harlots. Neither was Morgan interested in accepting the invitations offered by supposedly decent women; they usually wanted more than a night or two of pleasure.

Unfortunately, none of this helped him understand nor did it seem to apply to his inexplicable reactions to Jessica Miller. It didn't make any damned sense at all!

Morgan didn't realize he already possessed the answer to his perplexing and elusive puzzle. It had been blazing out at him from the expressive depths of a lonely woman's eyes; the same soul-deep emptiness he so diligently avoided in his shaving mirror every morning.

For Jessica to claim that the incident in the tack room had left her shaken would have been the understatement of her lifetime.

Using the rails of the paddock fence to support her still-quaking body, Jessica was stroking Titan's proud nose with a very shaky hand. Right now she was convinced that some cruel and sadistic force had been let loose within her world—one that had brought Morgan Ross into this valley for the sheer purpose of taking Jessica Miller down a peg or two... with the descent leading straight to hell.

"Well, it's not going to happen, will it, Titan?" she murmured against the animal's warm neck. "Because I've already spent my time in hell, and a return visit has absolutely no appeal. So," she stated more forcefully, her voice stronger with the determination beginning to take hold, "we will just have to tell ol' Satan what he can do with his invitation...."

It was all nonsense, of course. Jessica was perfectly aware that if there were any devils at work here, they had their origin within herself. But it made her feel better to confront the issue head-on while avoiding the blame at the same time. Besides, right now, with the shock of her feelings and the vivid images of their source, she simply wasn't capable of being entirely rational. And she definitely wasn't in any shape to coolly stand aside from those emotions, pick them apart and put them in some manageable perspective. Later, perhaps....

She heard Charlie calling her name at the same moment Titan lost interest in being petted, especially since his affection apparently wasn't going to be rewarded with an apple or the cubes of sugar she usually brought with her. As the stallion whirled away and went racing across the enclosed pasture, Jessica caught her breath. This happened every time she watched the magnificent animal, saw the beauty and power. Now she told herself this feeling was very much akin to what she'd felt in the tack room. She only prayed the self-deception would help her get through the rest of the day with Morgan Ross.

Walking across the yard, Jessica turned her attention to the buildings that were the lifeblood of the Eldorado. By Texas or Montana standards, this was a relatively small operation, although profitable. With the comparatively moderate California climate, Jessica didn't suffer losses due to blizzards or hard drought. She didn't have to run massive herds to counteract high death rates. There were problems, losses, naturally. Some years were better than others. But Jessica took great pride in the knowledge that she'd never failed to make some gain in the Eldorado's coffers, even if those earnings were small on occasion.

Because her Uncle John had supervised the construction of the buildings, they were built to stand the test of time and weather. The rustic look, however, had been all Jessica's idea. She had wanted to keep to the rugged ideal of the frontier and keep faith with the natural beauty around them. Moonshadow had its own quaint and unique attraction with its look of a transplanted eastern village, but Jessica had preferred that the Eldorado reflect its true western setting. For the most part her uncle had agreed with her ideas wholeheartedly. Their only conflict had arisen when he'd shown her the plans for the main house. The two-story frame house had been such an obvious reproduction of the old Ohio farmhouse where they'd both been born that Jessica had not been able to be objective. Luckily, John Miller had quickly seen that while he wanted to recapture cherished memories of his childhood, Jessica would only suffer from reminders of how her entire life had been shattered after she had left that house.

So all the buildings except the two big barns had been constructed of logs, including the house. John's skills and talents were reflected in the size of those structures, with a little help from the huge California pines that were so abundant hereabouts. But the rough-hewn look stopped at the front door of both the bunkhouse and the main house. Inside, beautifully paneled walls and gleaming hardwood floors were further testaments to John Miller's cleverness and craftsmanship. And as Jessica stepped into the bunkhouse now, she was struck anew by the respect and pride the cowhands took in their pleasant quarters. In fact, the sparkling cleanliness in here led Jessica to think Charlie was attempting to scrub away any and all traces of his drunken actions. But, if the murderous glare he was getting from the man sitting up in his bunk was any indication, Charlie wasn't ever going to be allowed to forget his drunken sins.

Jessica moved to Boone Larsen's side. "How do you feel?"

"Like I been kicked, trampled and savaged by a whole goddamn herd of rampaging cows!" Boone barked, his gravelly Texas twang sounding even harsher than usual as it emerged from a painfully raw throat. "What's your excuse, missy?"

"Pardon me?"

"You look redder 'n fire, girl," he announced, grabbing her hand. "Feel hotter than a pistol, too. Since you didn't eat that witches' brew Charlie tried to kill us with—"

"I'm perfectly fine. I was just enjoying the morning sunshine and must have picked up some color," Jessica told him, privately cursing this man who saw too blasted much. She would have to be very careful around Morgan Ross for Boone not to guess the real problem. Only Boone Larsen and Oramay Seibert had ever really looked beyond the guise that was Jessica Miller. That they saw more of the real Jessica was one of the reasons she adored them both; however, it created problems for her, as well. "And don't start fussing with me...unless you want some of your own medicine. I might decide to wonder just who it was who turned a blind eye while Charlie brought that whiskey onto the ranch, disobeying the no liquor of any kind, for any occasion—"

"Missy, I done heard that rule quoted till my old head hurts. Don't need to hear it repeated. You just never wanted to understand that a man's got to relax once in a while and forget his troubles."

"No! I'll never accept that stupid rationalization, Boone Larsen!" Jessica snapped, her hazel eyes blazing green. "Alcohol destroys people, turns them into creatures not even those who love them would recognize and causes good men to make tragic mistakes. Last night, I believe, was proof positive of that. And..." She paused to draw a breath for control, knowing this was a subject that could send her into a rage quicker than any other. "And if there is ever another single drop of liquor brought onto the Eldorado while I'm still the owner, that person will find himself fired without references. *Do I make myself clear?*"

Charlie grumbled something that might have been his agreement or might not have been before he shuffled off to the far side of the bunkhouse. Jessica only hoped he took her threat to heart, mostly for his sake. She meant every word.

"No need to get in an uproar, missy," Boone cautioned softly. "Charlie there knows he done wrong and was man enough to fess up to his mistake. It won't happen again. You have *my* word on it."

Boone had learned almost nothing about the lives of this young woman or her dead husband prior to the day he'd first met them. He'd heard about some greenhorns needing to be nursemaided into learning the ranching business and had chanced they would be so ignorant they'd take on an old scalawag like himself. They had, and he'd minded his manners. Which meant not being nosy, even if his curiosity killed him. But he'd picked up enough tidbits through the years to make some guesses. And if Boone Larsen had been a gambling man, he would have bet every dollar of that nice little nest egg John Miller had bequested to him that the Millers were hiding something. Just what, or how serious, he couldn't say, and frankly, didn't much care anymore. Useless as a rancher he might have been, but Boone had liked and respected poor John. And he came as close to loving this confounded female as possible for an old scalawag. If Boone Larsen had held still long enough in his younger days to produce offspring, he would have been proud to call one like Jessica daughter. Only trouble he'd ever had with her was regarding a cowhand's occasional need to get roostered. She could be a real hard-nosed shrew when it came to liquor. But then he strongly suspected she had damn good cause for her feelings....

There was such patient affection in his rheumy eyes, Jessica was humbled by it. He'd nearly died and here she was all but yelling at him before he even had his strength back. "I'm sorry," she whispered, seeing the paleness beneath his darkly weathered skin, the weariness he wouldn't have admitted for anything. She wanted to smooth back the sweat-matted yellowish-white hair from his brow, but she didn't dare. Displays of affection embarrassed Boone, although she always suspected he secretly didn't hate them nearly as much as he claimed. "But you gave me such a scare...."

Boone surprised her to tears by voluntarily taking her hand and giving it a little pat. "Missy, I—"

Whatever Boone was about to say was interrupted by the creaking of the screen door. Morgan Ross stepped inside, preventing Boone from making some asinine sugary statement he'd later regret. "You still here, Ross?" he croaked, his throat tight for more reason than just sickness. "Couldn't they find you a horse last night? Or did you just decide to squat on the place until the boss lady makes up her mind whether to sell or not?"

Morgan's gaze flickered to the widow briefly. She still looked attractively mussed, but that was where the resemblance between the woman he'd seen in the tack room and this lady ended. Although her eyes met his squarely, Morgan might have been a stick of wood for all the response he saw there. He would have expected, at the very least, a little pinkening of her cheeks. He began to wonder just how much of a fantasy he'd had out there in the barn....

Boone was afraid Jessica was going to crush his fingers, and just because this smooth-talking, good-looking son of a gun had walked into the bunkhouse. And that fellow wasn't exactly looking at her as if she were somebody's maiden aunt, neither, which meant Ross had more sense than most. Boone felt inclined to chuckle but restrained himself on the notion. "You going to sell him the Eldorado, missy?" Boone barked when the quiet between those two began to make *him* fidgety.

"I haven't decided if I want to buy."

"I haven't had an opportunity to consider—"

They both spoke at once. Jessica shrugged slightly. "It's fair to say no decisions have been made." Only years and years of an enforced control that by now had become second nature kept Jessica from heeding the impulse to flee those steady, stormy eyes. Despite his lazy stance and smile, Morgan Ross's eyes were not quiet. She looked away only to realize she still held Boone's hand with the tenacious force of a vise. She released him and saw his mouth quirk knowingly.

"You know," she said quickly in an effort to cover the blunder, "I came out here with the intention of rescuing Mr. Ross, believing him lost or injured. Instead, he rescued me until Dr. Griffith arrived. What happened that your horse came back without you?" She had to look at him then.

Morgan snorted in derision. "Calling that lump of crow bait a horse is being generous, ma'am." He then repeated an abbreviated version of the story he'd told Larsen the previous evening, before all hell had broken loose here. "My guess is the kid didn't notice or realize how worn those cinches were. Unfortunately, the nag chose the moment to remember past glories and galloped for home."

Jessica frowned. Tommy Hughes had been helping out in the livery since he'd been tall enough to saddle a horse by standing on a stool. Plus, his father wouldn't risk the fine reputation of his business with the use of inferior equipment. "I'm very glad you weren't hurt," she said sincerely.

"And I'm flattered by your concern, Mrs. Miller," Morgan said very softly.

He really was a master at sending a woman's pulses racing, Jessica decided again with renewed irritation. Morgan Ross might come by his sensual appeal naturally, but that didn't mean he didn't exploit what nature had granted to the very limit. "Did Dr. Griffith leave any instructions on the care of these men?" The change of subject was intentional, though Jessica was further distressed that it hadn't been the first question out of her mouth. Why had she concerned herself about Morgan Ross? Obviously, he was healthier than any human being had a right to be.

Morgan knew he'd displeased her somehow. Once again, this woman's shifts in moods put him off balance. "He felt the poisoning was minimal and would cause no lasting difficulties beyond some weakness for a day or so. He recommended rest and a light, mostly liquid diet for today and said he'd be back later this afternoon to check on them."

Boone had groaned when he heard the part about the diet. "I suppose it'd be a waste of breath to ask Doc's orders be ignored. A thick steak with two or three eggs on the side—"

"Don't even think it," Jessica reproved teasingly before turning toward the cook. "Charlie..."

"Already got a hen stewing, Mrs. Miller. Knew that much myself without hearin' it from the doctor. You want I should fix you and Mr. Ross there some breakfast?"

Although Jessica was certain there was no danger now from eating Charlie's cooking, the idea was still sufficient to spoil her appetite. The look on Morgan Ross's face told her he shared the same opinion. "Thank you, but I wouldn't want to take you away from your work, Charlie. I can fix something for Mr. Ross and myself at the house." She would have rather shared a meal with a real wolf. On the other hand, after all his help it would have been churlish not to repay him with at least this much. Neither did she think he would fall upon her like some ravening beast the moment they were alone. He wasn't the pouncing kind. He didn't need to be. All Morgan Ross had to do was set out his enticing lures.

"Thank you, ma'am," Morgan returned gratefully, pressing his empty stomach, talking low so only she and Larsen could hear. "It's still vivid in my mind how close I came to accepting a bowl of that stew last night."

"Well, I'll get started then," Jessica said, moving away from the bunk. "I will let you know when I get the food on the table."

"That's fine, ma'am. It will also give me a chance to wash up some." And get myself straightened out, Morgan added silently, watching that stiff back as she exited.

Had Jessica Miller been the one to slice those cinches? It seemed unlikely. Still, *someone* had taken a knife to that leather. Just who or when or why was something Morgan hadn't figured out yet. But there were only three places where it could have happened: at the livery, here on the Eldorado when he'd first arrived yesterday and out at that old mining camp when he'd been left alone on that ridge.

Chapter Six

The rolling pin hit the biscuit dough with a vehement thump. "There is fresh coffee on the stove, Mr. Ross," Jessica told the man leaning negligently against her kitchen wall, not once looking up from the flour-coated surface of the table. "You'll find the cups over on the sideboard behind me, along with fresh cream and the sugar. Just help yourself."

Thump, thump, thump went the rolling pin.

Jessica didn't see Morgan Ross's puzzled frown over the excessive zeal with which she was attacking the lump of dough. But she definitely heard the sound of his booted feet on her kitchen floor and his deep, mellow voice matching her own honey-tongued congeniality asking, "Might I pour a cup for you while I'm at it, ma'am?"

"No, I don't think so. But thank you, anyway."

Thump, thump, thump!

Why hadn't he waited until she had his meal on the table—as she had most clearly requested—instead of sauntering in here straight from washing up to make a nuisance of himself! He made her so nervous with those dark, watchful eyes and that damnable roguish grin. Not that he would ever guess her distress, thank heaven. Jessica was far too disciplined to wear her emotions on her sleeve. Plus, she would rather drop dead on this spot than suffer either his amusement or pity because the poor, hapless Widow Miller was all aflutter over the devilishly good-looking man prancing around her kitchen—especially when he didn't even have the common decency to fasten his shirt up properly!

"Is there anything I can do to help, Mrs. Miller?"

Whack!

For a second Jessica could only stare dumfounded at the dough she'd just cleaved in half. Recovering quickly, she whirled around and strategically placed herself in front of the embarrassing disaster she'd just made of the biscuits. "No! I mean... thank you, but I can manage. Besides, you are a guest—"

"I'm also a fair cook," Morgan informed her, wondering what she found so fascinating on the wall behind his head, since her gaze seemed to be stuck there. "And since I haven't eaten anything since about noon yesterday, I'm also a desperately hungry man more than willing to do whatever is necessary to put some grub in my empty stomach."

"Well... in that case..."

Soon Morgan was cutting off slices of ham and laying them in the skillet to fry while Jessica surreptitiously began rekneading the biscuit dough. This time the rolling pin was employed with a feather-light touch, although the urge to pound *something*—mainly herself—was stronger than before. But she was also doing her very best to make Morgan Ross the scapegoat for her irascible mood. It would be so much simpler if she could cast him the villain here. So what if three neglected buttons could hardly be considered a flagrant display of masculine, hair-roughed chest? That was a moot point since Jessica had already seen quite enough of Mr. Ross's virile form to last her several lifetimes. And so what if his early arrival and offer to help was perfectly understandable, even practical? Jessica needed Morgan Ross underfoot in here the way Eve had needed an apple! Her kitchen was too small for the two of them.

Damnation! Jessica silently cursed when she nearly fell over the man while carrying her biscuits to the oven. The world was too small with Morgan Ross in it!

"Oh! I'm sorry, Mr. Ross. Did I step on your foot?"

The oven door closed with a slam.

"If you did, I doubt a wispy little thing like yourself could do much damage, Mrs. Miller."

It actually hurt Jessica's facial muscles when she attempted to smile at the ludicrous comment. The translation of his words was so clearly "skinny female." Flirting and paying insincere compliments was probably second nature to a man like Morgan Ross, but Jessica couldn't help feeling mocked nonetheless. She'd fallen for winning smiles and pretty words once before, and it had been one time too many.

"Yes," she finally stated stiffly. "Well... I'll just clean up my flour mess on the table. Then I'll be free to relieve you of your duties."

"There's no need—"

"You can relax in the parlor with your coffee while I finish preparing breakfast. I'm certain you must be exhausted."

Despite the affable tone and manner, Morgan could see by the determined set of her chin that his protests would be ignored. In fact, for all intent and purpose, he was being ignored. She refused to look directly at him. He supposed he should be encouraged by her avoidance, since it probably meant she hadn't been as unaffected by the episode this morning as she wanted him to believe. Wasn't the whole purpose of this latest charade to wear down the lady's defenses, cozy up to her so she'd bare her soul just for a taste of the unspoken promises he had no intention of keeping? Unfortunately, looking at her now, Morgan had an inkling Jessica Miller might have more defenses than he had time to blast through.

The meticulously groomed widow was back in residence, looking starched from head to toe, regardless of the wrinkled condition of her dress. Morgan suspected that if it were possible, she'd have pressed any sign of disorder in her person away by sheer force of will. Even as he watched, she was removing all traces of biscuit makings with the frenzied speed of a whirligig, sending up clouds of flour in her wake.

Despite her vigor, not even a single hair had loosened from those restricting pins. There was a perverse little devil inside Morgan that fairly itched to wreak havoc on all that perfection. He wanted the woman who'd ogled him in the barn. That lady had ignited a fire in him the like of which he'd never before known, sorely tempting him to toss out all his wise and conscience-sparing restrictions. But reality dictated he could not afford to let emotions get in the way of his judgment. Because when his brains weren't being controlled by the area of his anatomy south of his belt, Morgan realized Jessica Miller's confounding and increasingly ambiguous nature was more than just an intriguing stimulant to his baser instincts. She was arousing his suspicions, as well.

Jessica worked the indoor pump John had cleverly installed along with the fine porcelain sink. Water gushed over her trembling hands while she cleaned all traces of dough from her fingers. With Morgan Ross hovering over her, watching every move, she felt like a hen locked in the chicken house with a wily fox. Luckily, enough of her usual good sense had returned to remind Jessica that this particular fox was more interested in the chicken yard. The scrawny bird was merely taking up the space he wanted to claim his own. It *should* have been a welcome realization....

"There!" she exclaimed, drying her hands. "Now you can relax in the parlor." She was in motion, grabbing up his now-tepid coffee, dumping it out, refilling the cup and leading him out of the kitchen with a stubborn and cheerful manipulation Oramay Seibert would have admired. That he followed without argument was a restorative to Jessica's lost control.

Somehow Morgan sensed her satisfaction in having him pad along behind her like an obedient lapdog. He had noticed that she was accustomed to being in charge of both herself and situations. Usually she wasn't quite this pushy or obvious about it, but it was the one unwavering trait to her personality he had seen. Unfortunately for the lady, it was a characteristic they shared. And also unfortunately, whenever that peculiarity manifested itself in Jessica Miller's nature, it produced the same effect in Morgan as waving a red flag at a bull.

"I apologize for the disorder and dust, Mr. Ross," Jessica stated as she took him through the dining room, frowning at her beautiful mahogany table and china closet, whose lustrous wood finishes had been dulled by neglect.

Morgan barely glanced at the room. Hell! She didn't give him time to see more than a blur of furniture as they raced out of the dining room, across a long hall and into the parlor. His immediate impression of this huge log house, soon confirmed by the room they'd just entered, was of space and light and furnishings that provided both elegance and comfort.

While Jessica stripped sheets from sofas and chairs, Morgan was deciding the widow had a rare good taste—especially in this day where silly knickknacks cluttered every available space and popular furniture overwhelmed itself with ornate carvings and impossible shapes that would challenge a contortionist's comfort. There was no clutter in this room. Actually, except for decorative oil lanterns, which had a practical use, and one or two scenic pictures upon the wall, the room was bare of bric-a-brac. Morgan was eyeing the long sofa, with its inviting yellow brocade upholstery and matching throw pillows—he was also wondering what Mrs. Miller might do if he dragged her down on that cool, smooth surface—when he spotted the singular personally significant object in the room. Atop the carved shelf of the mantel was a framed photograph. Morgan didn't hesitate to satisfy his curiosity. He regretted the impulse a second later.

"Is this a portrait of you and your father?" he asked in a voice not recognizable as his own. The elderly, white-haired man standing beside a young woman, who couldn't have been more than twenty years of age, had much the same effect on Morgan's stomach as Charlie's rat poison.

Jessica was accustomed to the mistake and the customary reaction of disgust that went along with it. She didn't blink an eye when she answered. "No. That's John . . . my husband. Mrs. Seibert bullied us into visiting a traveling photographer when he passed through Moonshadow several years ago. It was during one of our election day celebrations, I believe. As you can see, neither of us look too thrilled over the experience. However, I'm grateful to have it now."

The emotional catch in her voice at the end was genuine. As real as the tender sadness he saw on her face. Once again, Morgan was forced to concede that the bond of love between Jessica Miller and her aged husband had existed, even if it was beyond his comprehension. Even if he wanted to rage at the thought of her wasting her youth and passion on a man who had to be more than triple her age. But at the same time that his gut churned, Morgan found enough objectivity and presence of mind to notice that, although five or six years must have passed, Jessica Miller had not changed in any essential way. The wife had been just as seemingly colorless and unassuming as the widow, with her taste in clothing equally abominable. Maybe worse then than now. At least her widowed state gave her some excuse to look as unattractive as possible.

Jessica was tempted to snatch the photograph from his hand. His curiosity and scrutiny of the images within the frame was somehow more disturbing and intolerable than any of the many others she'd endured in the past. And despite his unreadable expression, Jessica could feel his condemnation.

She squared her shoulders and lifted her chin. "John Miller was a wonderful man. The finest human being I've ever known or hope to know in my lifetime."

"I'm sure he was," Morgan agreed flatly, eager to return the offensive family portrait to the mantel. Oh, yes, the lady had certainly adored her aged husband. Morgan had no doubt about that. What he doubted, however, was just *how* Jessica Miller had loved the late John Miller. As a surrogate father? A companion? Because Morgan could not believe she'd ever known the white-hot passion of a lover's embrace from that old man. And he felt damned certain she'd never looked upon her husband with the unabashed yearning he'd seen in her eyes this morning.

"How long since your husband's death, Mrs. Miller?"

"It will be a year next month," Jessica informed him, still bristling at herself for the defensive tone she'd taken earlier. Never before had she felt compelled to justify her affection or relationship regarding the man everyone believed to have been her husband.

"Your period of mourning is about to come to an end, then," Morgan observed, though he'd be hanged if he knew the reason behind the asinine statement. The lady didn't think much of it either, if her stiff-lipped response was any indication.

"I will *never* stop grieving for John, Mr. Ross. Now, if you'll please excuse me, I have breakfast to prepare."

No thought or planning went into Morgan's impulsive move to block her hasty retreat. God knew, he'd never intended to touch her. But it seemed his left hand had a will of its own when it reached out and took a firm hold of her arm as she passed by, pulling her back around. "I'm sorry. That was an extremely callous remark."

The apology came out flat, even to his own ears. Probably because there was no sincerity in him. The firm conviction in her voice when she'd vowed that unending lament of John Miller had infuriated him. She was only in her mid-twenties, for God's sake! Not some dried-up old stick with little choice but to bury herself alive in a perpetual state of widowed limbo. The proof of her youth was in the supple and resilient flesh beneath his fingers, not at all the skin and bone he'd expected.

Jessica stood still, accepting both his unwanted regret and his equally unwelcome grip on her arm, until she felt his hand move in a gliding manner that had little to do with restraint. "No offense taken, Mr. Ross," she said with a composure on the verge of shattering. It nearly did shatter when the little move she made to extricate herself proved ineffectual. "I really must..."

Morgan saw the flash of panic in her eyes when his hand slid up her arm and over her shoulder. There was resistance in every muscle and line of her body as his fingers lightly captured her chin.

"W-what do you think you are doing?" Jessica's heart was pounding so violently she barely heard his response.

"Just a minute, ma'am," Morgan said softly, huskily, again rocked to his core by the inexorable effect this woman produced within him. "You have flour all over your face."

The brush of his callused fingers across her cheeks created a maelstrom of emotions and sensations within Jessica. She felt icy chills and heated tremors. Part of the room was spinning violently while the solid form of the man before her seemed the only stability on this merry-go-round she was riding. She felt the compulsion to grab hold of him and cling tightly until the world righted itself once again. Only it never would, she accepted. Never again would anything be quite the same, because in less than forty-eight hours of meeting Morgan Ross, her very existence had been upended and spun off its foundation for all time to come. And she despised him not one whit less than she despised herself for destroying so quickly and easily what it had taken her years to build.

"There," Morgan finally said with effort, allowing a final stroke across the trembling softness of her lips. God! Her skin had the feel of the richest satin. If the exposed areas of her body felt this good, then the flesh hidden, protected from sun and wind would feel—

Morgan cleared his throat and forced himself to step back. "You're free of all traces of flour now."

Jessica hadn't realized she'd closed her eyes until it became necessary to open them. Because she didn't dare lift her gaze for fear of what it might reveal, Jessica found her eyes riveted on the open throat of his shirt and the silky, dark hair exposed there. Yes, the serpent had invaded paradise....

Gathering what little dignity he'd left her, Jessica muttered something about the ham burning and fled the devil on wobbly legs.

Hear that, Rossiter, Morgan chided himself as he watched her leave the parlor. The sound you are now hearing is the chink, chink, chink of stone and mortar.

"Damn!" he rasped, whirling back to the mantel, where the portrait of John and Jessica Miller stood to taunt his stupidity. He doubted dynamite would blast through the lady's shored-up defenses now.

Once again he lifted the framed portrait, forcing himself to study the more youthful image of Jessica Miller for similarities with that other Jessica—the one in the photo now in his possession. He found none. If by some increasingly remote chance the widow had ever been that pretty, laughing, glowingly healthy young girl, then life had certainly stripped her of more than just flesh.

Suddenly, eight years' worth of weariness and frustration seemed to catch up with Morgan. He'd get that telegram off to Burke the minute he returned to Moonshadow, although his surveillance of the Widow Miller had given him little hope of anything coming of it. One thing was certain, however: he'd consider himself lucky to get the time of day from Jessica now. Certainly, pressuring her for some kind of answer about this ranch wasn't going to work anymore. As things stood now, she would probably tell him the place wasn't for sale just to get rid of him.

But why? Why did the lady behave as if acknowledging the powerful attraction between them was tantamount to a fate worse than death? Was the desire he awakened within her—the passion all his instincts told him existed—so terrible a thing? Was she really so devoted to her dead husband's memory that she would disavow any chance for a normal future and content herself with the sexless existence of an old maid?

It didn't make sense to Morgan, was beyond his comprehension that any woman would purposely freeze her emotions and deny nature. But then he was hardly in a position to argue her decisions, was he? Since he'd walk out of her life in a few weeks or less, it wasn't any of his goddamn business how Jessica Miller chose to live her life. He'd move on when Burke's background report confirmed the woman's story. There would be another town and yet another auburn-haired woman—

Morgan sank down into the soft cushion of the chair nearest the hearth and closed his eyes. Would there be another town? He wasn't sure anymore. Maybe he would just go home and wait...wait until the day Cole Hardin stepped out from behind those protected prison walls.

Jessica dumped the charred biscuits and started all over again. There was something rather soothingly familiar in the act, symbolic even. She was an expert at rising from the ashes to begin again. The trouble was, she just didn't know how many times she could survive going up in flames. And there was no denying she felt singed from head to toe right now.

Damn Morgan Ross!

Damn all smooth-talking, wickedly handsome men! And damn her for being vulnerable to them!

Not for a minute did Jessica believe Morgan Ross was interested in more than the Eldorado. Men like him wanted pretty faces and womanly bodies. They wanted perfection. Anything less repelled them. Subsequently, Ross must want her ranch with a ruthless determination if he'd stoop to seduction in order to soften her up for the sale. Either that or the tale he'd told last evening about an inheritance from a long-lost relative was as phony as the smoldering desire she'd seen in those stormy, dark eyes. Maybe he, too, thought the prize of the Eldorado sufficiently worthwhile to suffer the widow in the bargain.

"Your period of mourning is about to come to an end," he'd said. Funny, but those were nearly the exact words Earl Taylor had used only a few weeks ago when escorting her home from church.

"John will be dead a year soon, Jessie," Earl had reminded just before he'd begun to fidget with the high starched collar on his shirt. Jessica had thought then how odd it had been for Earl to get all dressed up in a suit, even for church. Usually his only concession to altering his appearance was the addition of a string tie to those standard blue shirts on Sundays. But even so, Jessica had nearly been bowled over by what followed.

"It ain't easy livin' alone, I can tell you. My wife's been gone nearly ten years now. And raisin' Lonnie all by myself gets harder every year, with him growin' so fast and all. It ain't good for a boy to grow up without his ma to teach him the finer, gentler things. And without a good woman at his side, a man tends to lose his ambition.

"You take me, for instance. I always wanted to be a rancher, to make something of myself...have something to leave behind for my boy. But the heart just went outa me when I lost my Margie. So I'm livin' in that little place behind the jail, collecting a salary that's next to piddlin' and pretty much just driftin' along from one year to the next...."

The way Earl had looked at her then told Jessica he'd halfway expected to see tears of sympathy sparkling in her eyes over his sad, sad tale. His face had gone florid at her level, dry-eyed stare. He'd started hemming and hawing, his paunchy body squirming within the tight suit of clothes. "Well...it come to me the other day, when I heard you was thinkin' of selling the Eldorado and going into business with Oramay..."

Jessica had thought she understood him then, and she'd smiled gently at Sheriff Taylor. "You want to purchase the ranch," she said, knowing full well Earl Taylor could never have saved up enough of his earnings to even make a down payment. Still, she didn't want to hurt his pride. "Why don't you talk to Stan, Earl. He'll be handling all the financial details."

"No!" he'd all but shouted. "That is... Ah, hell, Jessie, you know I ain't got that kind of money!" Even then,

Jessica hadn't anticipated what came next. "What I was thinkin'," he'd gone on with surprising directness, "is that you and me, both being alone now, could maybe get hitched. Then you'd have a man to run your ranch so you wouldn't have to give it up, and Lonnie would get himself a mother. He's real fond of you, you know. Matter of fact, I don't know many kids who don't think Jessie Miller is just about the best thing there is."

"And what about you, Earl?" Jessica had felt compelled to ask. "Beyond the ranch you've always wanted, what would you be getting out of this deal...should I agree to your proposal?"

Earl Taylor had not been able to come up with a satisfactory response. "I'd be content enough," he said finally. "I'm not a demanding man, Jessie. One trip a year to Sacramento is usually more than enough—if you catch my meaning."

Oh, she'd caught his meaning well enough. In plain words, he would have no trouble avoiding her bed and might not even give up his yearly visit to Sacramento. To gain the Eldorado, Earl Taylor would sacrifice himself to a marriage of convenience. More, he genuinely had believed the Widow Miller would jump at the opportunity he offered, would even be grateful.

She'd turned him down flat and had continued back to the hotel unescorted, leaving Earl Taylor with his mouth agape.

Poor Earl. He would never understand why she hadn't agreed to be his wife. After all, Jessie Miller surely couldn't expect that a better offer would come along, especially if she went ahead and sold off her most attractive asset, the Eldorado. Which, of course, Jessica now realized was exactly what she must do. Either that or continue to leave herself wide open for repeated difficulties with men who would covet the ranch, if not the owner.

She would tell Morgan Ross the ranch was his...if he could meet her price. Then she would turn the entire matter over to Stanley Turner, distance herself from the details of the sale and go on about the business of being the poor Widow Miller for the remainder of her natural life.

Whack!

Through a flood of tears, Jessica stared down at the second batch of biscuits she'd pulverized today. "Damn," she muttered, not really sure if she cursed herself or the man who had brought this turmoil into her life. Prior to forty-eight hours past, Jessica had been reasonably content, resigned to the only future that fate and her youthful foolishness had decreed for her. Only occasionally did she allow herself to indulge in rebellious resentment or rail because of the unfairness of it all. Making the best of what was, she tried not to think about what might have been and made no attempt to avoid the unalterable reality that controlled and directed her very existence, ruled her every decision and dictated the impossible yearnings of her heart. Because ten years ago next month, Jessica had sealed her own destiny when she'd stood before a Coffeyville, Kansas, preacher, binding herself forever to a young cowhand with the face of an angel and the devil's own soul.

Chapter Seven

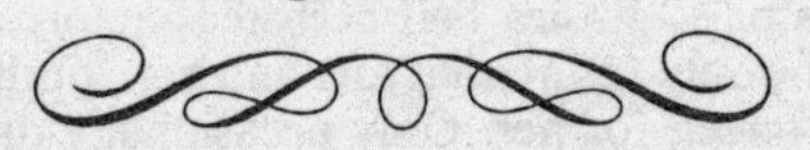

"I'll drop you at the hotel and then return Mrs. Seibert's horse and buggy to the livery. I wanted to have a word with Hughes about his saddle, in any case...."

"That will be just fine, Mr. Ross," Jessica returned with the same pleasant grin-and-bear-it civility she'd forced throughout this interminable day. Actually, her disposition was edging up to the mean and ugly side of shrewish as they entered the outskirts of Moonshadow. Miles of being jostled repeatedly against Morgan Ross hadn't— "Oh!"

Once again, Morgan rescued the recalcitrant Mrs. Miller from a tumble off the buggy seat. Since it wasn't the first near mishap but the third, maybe even the fourth, he was prepared this time. Grabbing a handful of skirt, Morgan hauled her back to safety. And once again, the minute their bodies came into contact, the foolhardy female immediately scooted back over to the very edge of the seat.

"Thank you," Jessica mumbled, getting a firmer grip on the precarious perch beneath her hips. She glanced at Morgan Ross only to catch him with a smirky grin on his too-handsome face. Damn him, anyway! she fumed silently. If she did end up sprawled in the street, it would be all his fault! He was taking up far more than his share of space, having plopped himself down nearer the middle than the left side, where he belonged! Plus, if he'd taken the horse she'd offered and returned to town earlier... But no, he couldn't possibly leave, wouldn't have dreamed of abandoning her to manage those sick and recovering men alone.

"Pardon me, ma'am? Did you say something?"

Dear Lord! Had she really been grumbling aloud? "I...I was just thinking how glad I am that the past twenty-four hours are over and done with."

"I'm sure you are," Morgan replied, thinking that was the most honest thing she'd said to him yet. Because he hadn't bought for a minute all that phony affability she'd been dishing up to him all day. "I know you're also relieved about what David had to say regarding their recovery."

David? How chummy he'd become with the young doctor in so short a time. Not to mention the way Charlie had snapped to attention at his slightest word or how Bobby had followed at this heels like some adoring young pup. And Boone! Boone Larsen was the most difficult man she knew to win over, yet he and Ross had spent most of the day swapping tall tales and attempting to outcuss each other like two boyhood chums.

For all anyone had noticed, Jessica might have been a fly on the wall. The cowhands had accepted Morgan Ross as one of their own, soliciting his advice and opinions on topics they would never have broached with the lady boss. Not that she truly had any burning desire to sit down and chaw over the most painless and efficient methods of castration.

Attempting to distance herself from personal, sometimes childish, emotions, Jessica forced herself to acknowledge that Morgan Ross was the perfect buyer for the Eldorado. She needed only to listen to snatches of those bull sessions or watch while he worked alongside Bobby this afternoon when the stubborn boy refused to stay abed, to recognize that Ross was a rancher to his bones. In that respect, at least, he was a man after her own heart—

"Mrs. Miller?"

"What?"

A moment of confusion was followed by the disgruntled realization that the buggy had probably been resting in front of the hotel for several minutes while she'd been preoccupied with her thoughts.

"Oh! We're here, I see. . . ." she said stupidly, again winning herself another smirking grin from the man who'd let her sit here like a dazed lump, likely thinking she was so enamored of his company she couldn't bear to give it up!

Morgan wasn't at all surprised to see her all but jump from the buggy before he could get his leg out to give her assistance. He knew he'd committed the ultimate, unpardonable trespass when he'd touched her this morning. It was a sin he knew he would repeat when the time was right. Only next time, Morgan would make damned certain he gave the lady something to really holler about.

On that thought and with a nasty chuckle, Morgan snapped the reins and turned the horse toward the livery.

"Arrogant scoundrel! Thinks he is God's living gift—"

"What on earth are you grumbling about, Jessie Miller?"

Oh, wonderful! Mabel Harrison was all she needed to round off her day and her temper. "Mabel," she cooed with feigned warmth, turning toward the overdressed woman in pink silk, who was just coming out of the empty dining room. "A bit early for dinner, isn't it?" Jessica glanced at the clock, confirming that it was not yet six. She still had thirty minutes before they began serving customers.

Mabel Harrison puffed up like an overstuffed bird at the suggestion that the mayor's wife would stoop to dining with the common rabble in a public place, especially when everyone knew what a delicate digestive system she possessed. "Actually, my dear, I came to speak with you. Preferably in private," she added, lowering her perfectly modulated voice to a perfectly modulated whisper.

Jessica looked around the lobby. "We're quite alone here, Mabel."

"What about *that man?* Won't he be coming in soon?"

"Mr. Ross is delivering Oramay's buggy to the livery. We have a few minutes, which is about all I can spare. . . ."

"All right, Jessica. If you insist, though if someone overhears this conversation, then let the blame be on your head, not mine."

"Goodness, Mabel. This sounds serious." Obviously, Mabel had a juicy bit of gossip she was just dying to share. Jessica could never understand why she always insisted on whispering the very news she would soon spread all over town.

"Oh, my dear," Mabel wailed as she approached. "I'm certain you don't realize—you're such an innocent—but people do talk . . . and the most innocuous things can get so blown out of proportion."

Jessica was really getting annoyed. "Please get to the point . . ."

Mabel seemed not to notice the sharp edge in Jessica's tone. She did, however, respond to the prompting. Moving closer, she put her hand on the young widow's shoulder and gave her a concerned smile. "Jessica, I'm sure everything was quite aboveboard—" The soft, impatient sound Jessica Miller made had Mabel rushing on ahead without all the preamble. "My dear, you really should be more cautious about the company you keep. More specifically, you shouldn't put yourself in a position that might encourage speculation about your relationship with *that man.* You are a widow, a woman alone and unprotected, frankly vulnerable. And when everyone knows you've spent the night alone and unchaperoned with a handsome rogue like—Good heavens, Jessica! What are you laughing about? A woman's reputation is a serious thing, and yours, my dear, is in jeopardy right now."

Jessica was nearly howling with laughter; subsequently, she missed anything beyond her possibly licentious night with *that man!* "Oh, Mabel," she said with a sigh, wiping amused tears from her cheeks. "That's the loveliest compliment I've ever received." She gave the dumbfounded woman a warm hug. "Thank you," she managed before walking off, still chuckling, and certain she'd just taken the wind right out of Mabel Harrison's gossipy sails. There wasn't any fun in spreading nasty rumors when the victim of that talebearing thought it was a kindness.

As Jessica expected, she found Oramay in the kitchen, pounding a piece of steak with a vehemence that seemed very familiar. Before Jessica could speak, Oramay looked up and started to put on a bright smile. Then she saw the moisture in her friend's eyes and assumed it to be tears of hurt.

"You ran into Mabel Harrison, didn't you?" Oramay spat, not waiting to hear Jessica's reply. The girl's tears and shaking shoulders were enough to send her into a rage. "Oh! I'll serve that nasty-minded, barb-tongued, gossipy old bat her own liver! Told her when she came in here, prancing and whispering, rolling her eyes, that I'd rip her tongue out if I heard a single breath of that ridiculous hogwash—"

"Oramay...stop...." Jessica couldn't stand any more. Her stomach hurt, and watching Oramay storm around the room, waving that meat mallet in defense of Jessica's maligned virtue... "Please...." she gasped.

Oramay stopped and stared, arms akimbo. "You're not crying, Jessie Miller," she accused sternly. "You are laughing! Well, maybe you can find some humor in this right now, but it won't be so danged funny when your good name is being bandied about and you see folks whispering behind your back just because Mabel's got her nose out of joint for some reason or another. What did you do or say to set her off against you, anyhow?"

"I defended Morgan Ross when she would have set up a committee to run him out of town within an hour of his arrival. *And* I wouldn't stand still while she verbally flogged Earl Taylor and accused him of incompetence. Plus," Jessica added a little sheepishly, "I essentially yawned in her face when she launched into another tiresome trumpeting about the virtues of Theodora and the grandchildren."

"Is that all?" Oramay queried with a disbelieving shake of her head. "Lordy, girl. When you go looking for trouble, you don't go for half measures, do you? In one session you gave Mabel enough guff to keep her craw outa shape for a year." Then a beatific smile appeared. "Honey, I'm proud of you. I didn't know you had it in you. Question is, now that you've lit the fire, can you stand the heat?"

"There won't be any heat to stand, Oramay," Jessica told her friend with a matter-of-fact grin. "You see, I told Mabel that I considered her concern for my reputation and virtue to be just about the loveliest compliment I'd ever received...right after I laughed in her face."

"Took the starch right out of her bustle, did you? Well, maybe this time. But Mabel's not likely to forget."

"It won't do her any good to hold a grudge, Oramay. Because I won't give her any ammunition to use against me. This was Mabel's one-in-a-million opportunity."

Oramay frowned slightly. "I'm almost sorry to hear that. Matter of fact, mad as that dressed-up old bat made me with her insinuations, guess I was sort of half hoping there might be *something* of the truth in that gossip she was about to start spreading about. I mean...well...he is a good-looking devil...." She shrugged. "But I suppose you're going to tell me he was also a perfect gentleman?"

Jessica refused to dignify that question with a response. Instead, she gave Oramay a reproving stare, one that was immediately spoiled by the heated flush that rushed into her cheeks. "I...I should clean up and change out of this dress," she said, heading for the water pump to avoid those raised eyebrows and the feverish interest in Oramay's eyes. "I was glad to hear from David that Melanie was able to spend the day with Kathleen. I was concerned that since I had the buggy you'd be stranded..." As she rattled on, Jessica worked the pump furiously, filling the water pitcher she'd grabbed to overflowing.

"Jess-ie...." Oramay had followed the flustered young woman to the sink and was hovering at her shoulder. "You can't blush like that and then just leave me wondering. What happened?"

Knowing she'd never have a minute's peace, Jessica protected herself. "Certainly nothing nearly as exciting as what

I witnessed here in this kitchen two nights ago. How is Stan, by the way?"

"You know, I always thought you were such a sweet and gentle little thing. Timid, even. But you've got a nasty streak right upside that stubborn streak, Jessie Miller." Oramay backed away a few paces. "And I'd prefer not to discuss Mr. Stanley Turner, if you don't mind."

"Are you two still arguing?"

"I wasn't aware we ever stopped for a single minute these past thirty or so years. But he's gone too danged far this time," Oramay huffed and began to grumble. "Tellin' me how to run my business, lead my life and raise my son..." She began to shake with anger. "Said Patrick was a lazy do-nothing, spoiled rotten, and that he needed a father's firm hand before he was ruined entirely by two females who let him get by with murder because he was the only man in their lives."

Although she was equally guilty of indulging Patrick, Jessica thought Stan might just have a valid point. "I'm sure he meant well, Oramay. He said those things because he cares...."

Oramay sniffed derisively. "You wouldn't be so quick to defend Mr. Turner if you could have heard what he said about me taking you into the business and encouraging you to become a dried-up, cranky old biddy before your time. Said we were both heading that way, when what we really needed—" Oramay hesitated before going on, her expression chagrined and indignant all at once. "Well, to phrase it more delicately than he did, Mr. Turner's suggestion was we'd both be happier if there was some man tossing his trousers over the bedpost every night."

Although Jessica enjoyed Oramay's rare discomfiture while she attempted to reword what must have been an extremely blunt suggestion, she wasn't so amused by Stanley Turner's gall at including herself in those opinions. If Jessica chose to become a "dried-up, cranky old biddy," it was none of Stanley Turner's damned business. And she would tell him so at the first opportunity! However, the situation between Stan and Oramay was an entirely different thing.

"Oramay," Jessica began carefully, "it's pretty obvious that Stan wants and desires to make you his wife. Granted, his wording—"

"Hogwash!" Oramay spat, though her chin began to quiver slightly. "Oh, he's made his *desires* perfectly clear, all right! But not a word was said about marriage. Never—not once, when we were young, or now—has Stanley Turner offered me anything more permanent than a romp between the sheets."

Jessica had trouble believing that accusation. "Surely you misunderstood. Or maybe Stan has had trouble expressing himself."

Oramay shook her head, fighting tears now. "Our golden-tongued attorney at a loss for words? You know better, Jessie. No. What Stan Turner has is an itch in his pants, and now that I'm a middle-aged woman past childbearing, he's decided my services would be more convenient than having to make all those frequent trips to Sacramento and San Francisco. Though one part of him might still be too lively for his own good, the rest is undoubtedly having trouble keeping up."

"Oramay, you're not thinking sensibly," Jessica argued. "A discreet affair in this town would be impossible. Not while Mabel Harrison is playing watchdog to our morals."

"Oh, you'd be surprised at the well-kept secrets some folks in this town have hidden in dark closets," Oramay announced cryptically, remembering all too vividly, painfully, that night long, long ago when she'd gone looking for Stan during a harvest party out at the Muningers'...and found him in the barn, bare assed between Mabel's not so lily-white thighs. "There're also ways of dealing with Mabel Harrison's big mouth...."

Oramay couldn't know the nerve she'd struck in her reference to well-kept secrets. She struck another when she whispered, "Can you even imagine the hurt of catching the man you love with another woman?" Realizing she'd said too much, she cleared her throat loudly. "What I mean is, I've always known Stan had other women, probably more than his fair share, with him being so danged handsome and virile. And I don't believe for one minute he'd be satisfied to give up all that variety for this aging body of mine—married or not."

"Maybe that's a question you need to ask him straight out," Jessica suggested gently, realizing now there was a great deal more to the story of Stan Turner and Oramay Seibert than she might ever have guessed. And a goodly number of well-kept secrets, as well.

"Maybe I would do that—if he hadn't taken off for San Francisco first thing this morning on another of his so-called business trips. Though I'd be willing to wager this hotel that his *business* wears silk underwear, and damned little else!"

For Oramay's sake, and her own, Jessica wasn't at all happy to hear Stan was out of town. "How long will he be gone?"

Oramay shrugged. "He usually stays a week, sometimes longer."

Since Jessica had been planning to dump the problem of Morgan Ross and the ranch in Stan's lap, she ground her teeth in frustration. "Well," she attempted more lightly, "from one confirmed old biddy to another, I think men are more trouble than they're worth."

"Damn right!" Oramay agreed promptly, which seemed to put a finish to this conversation.

Picking up the pitcher of water she'd pumped earlier, Jessica said, "I'm going to clean up now."

On leaden legs, she went to her room and sighed heavily the minute the door closed behind her. Her head had begun to throb from too little sleep and far too much emotional turmoil. Before she'd taken two steps into Kathleen's old room, Jessica was already yanking the pins from her tightly bound hair. In less than ten minutes, she would just have to put it back up again, but she couldn't resist shaking it out and rubbing her aching scalp. The relief was almost immediate, the sense of freedom almost too alluring.

Because this room had once belonged to a very young and pretty girl, the decor reflected its previous inhabitant. The wallpaper was patterned with tiny daisies and small yellow tea roses. Tiered lace curtains covered the single window, which Jessica opened immediately to dispel the stuffy, trapped heat. The sleigh bed, with its pretty sunburst quilt, was a temptation she was hard-pressed to resist. It was going to be a long evening before she would be allowed to rest on the downy mattress.

She took a clean black dress from the wardrobe and laid out fresh underclothing before stripping down to the skin. The water she poured into the washbasin was straight from the well and close to icy. Still, it felt wonderful as the cloth moved across her sticky, heated flesh. Her nose wrinkled slightly over the scented soap Oramay always put in here. It was a nice gesture, but an extravagance Jessica would have forgone on her own, just as she avoided pretty clothing, mirrors and anything else remotely associated with feminine vanity.

But she wasn't feeling at all herself tonight. Everything seemed out of kilter. The wet cloth that had been so soothing moments before began to feel abrasive, irritating, as it moved over her naked flesh, encouraging her to make quick work of her ablutions. Unfortunately, those annoying sensations were aggravated by the brisk toweling she gave herself. She clenched her teeth against them, discovering, to her dismay, how disturbingly similar they were to those she'd experienced this morning when she'd looked down upon a healthy, virile male form and felt . . . what?

"Too damn much," Jessica mumbled angrily as she threw the towel down and turned toward the bed, only to be ambushed by the full-length pedestal mirror lurking in the corner. The sight of her own reflection was usually something Jessica avoided with determined diligence. For once, however, she faced the stranger who existed only in the looking glass. Of course, Jessica knew that the reflected image was her own. She just felt no connection to the woman in the mirror. It was as if that person was an old, not very well-known acquaintance, and someone she'd not liked very well in the bargain. But honesty compelled her to admit that no man breathing would ever look upon this woman and dismiss her startling physical appeal.

She was still not typically beautiful, but like this, naked, with her unbound hair spilling over her shoulders and halfway down her back, features usually exaggerated by a severe hairstyle lost their enforced sharpness. Large oval eyes now took on a slightly exotic cast. Her mouth suddenly appeared fuller, more sensual, even sultry. It was a face that now complemented the frankly voluptuous breasts and slender body. And it was a body that could easily be declared the standard for every carnal fantasy imagined by any male over the age of twelve. Which, of course, was precisely why Jessica went to such drastic extremes to cover, bind and camouflage herself from those undesirable thoughts and attentions. At least she'd believed them to be undesired until Morgan Ross had come storming into her tranquil existence.

Jessica whirled away from the mirror, confused and alarmed. She was obviously losing her mind. Either that, or she'd forgotten that beyond satisfying her desperate need for any kind of love and affection, she'd found little else to celebrate in regard to the marriage bed. Even that small reward had not survived long. Not after the perfect body Cole had so admired began to swell with the child conceived in the early weeks of their marriage. Cole had turned away from her entirely then, giving nothing and showing only his disgust for her misshapen form.

Oh, yes, Jessica knew firsthand the terrible agony of sharing the man you loved with another woman. She'd been nearly six months pregnant with her husband's child when Cole Hardin had thrown her out of their bed, replacing his wife with the skinny whore he'd brought home....

It was close to midnight when Morgan fell across his bed and considered himself lucky to have made it through the night without busting somebody. At the same time he was furious with himself over the underlying cause of the short fuse he'd barely kept from exploding all evening.

Running across Sheriff Earl Taylor at the livery had seemed a stroke of good fortune. He'd also enjoyed the Hughes kid's squirming when he and the potbellied sheriff had come face-to-face for the first time. This was the man who would have run him out of town? Morgan had been hard-pressed not to laugh his ass off when he'd remembered how Tommy Hughes had threatened him with the sheriff's ferocity in dealing with desperadoes. Hell! If a genuine outlaw had come to town, Earl Taylor would have probably headed for the hills with his tail tucked between those stout, fortune-hunting legs of his.

"Bastard!" Morgan spat in the darkness, absently reaching beneath him to scratch an itchy spot.

Despite his amusement over the sheriff's less than intimidating reality, Morgan had determined Taylor might very well be a good source of information about the residents in this valley; most lawmen knew more about the people they were sworn to protect than those citizens were comfortable with. So he had offered to stand Earl a drink or two at the saloon. But except for some confusion over whether the Millers had moved here from Oregon or the Washington Territory, all Earl Taylor could tell Morgan about Jessica Miller was that she was "a frigid, stupid female, who'd rather lose her ranch than accept an honest and sincere offer of marriage."

"Sincere, my ass!"

Morgan had wanted to knock Earl Taylor's teeth down his throat while he'd loudly bewailed, for all and sundry to hear and comment upon, his thwarted courtship of the widow. And as the liquor flowed, the disparaging comments and slurs upon Jessica Miller's good name became even more insulting, the raucous laughter louder, and Morgan's temper got shorter and shorter.

"Jackasses!"

It didn't help his black mood any that he'd nearly had to sit on his hands not to defend her honor or that he deserved to have his own butt kicked for even giving a damn over what was said or thought about the lady. She was nothing to him! He felt sorry for her, was all.

Yeah, right! said a sarcastic voice inside him. Any pitiable female will make your blood go hot and your sex go brick hard! Happens every time!

Morgan squirmed. There was an increasingly uncomfortable stinging sensation spreading head to toe across the back of him, as if millions of tiny critters were chewing on him with the intent of eating him alive.

"What the—" Morgan exclaimed, jumping out of bed when that clawing itch spread to his groin.

Chapter Eight

One full week after discovering that a nest of fleas had taken over his mattress, Morgan Rossiter was standing in the middle of the second room he'd been given, cussing a blue streak over the package supposedly containing his laundry.

Except for the buttonless shirt he'd just removed from the top of the bundle, not one single item belonged to him or even closely resembled wearing apparel. And where the hell were the buttons on *this* shirt? They'd been there when the laundry had gone out.

"More bad luck, I suppose," he grumbled. Already he'd had more than a bellyful of ill fortune, starting with the saddle that had left him stranded up on Sobs Hill.

Doorknobs amazingly came off in his hand, leaving him trapped both in this room and the bath. Wardrobe doors that opened easily one day practically had to be torn from their hinges the next. Windows he could have sworn were closed when he departed in the morning were found open at night, inviting a swarm of mean-tempered hornets, along with some painful stings.

Although every one of these annoying but basically innocuous incidents could be explained logically or tossed off to an unusual run of bad luck, Morgan had his doubts. Could so much misfortune befall a single person in such a short period of time without human assistance? He didn't think so, but proving that suspicion was another matter entirely.

Dressed in the only pair of trousers left to him and wearing the buttonless shirt, Morgan slammed out of the room, taking the bundle of sheets and towels Patrick had delivered. He wanted a word with this hotel's acting manager. In fact, he wanted one hell of a lot more than a word or two from that increasingly aloof female.

Behind the registration desk, again attempting to sort through Oramay's chaotic records, Jessica heard him stomping down the stairs. Hoping he'd go straight through the lobby on his way to breakfast, she made a point of not looking up from her work.

"Mrs. Miller," Morgan attempted calmly, even as he tossed the unwrapped laundry atop the desk with sufficient force to send her papers flying. "It would seem the laundry has mistakenly thrown my things and the hotel's together. If I could look through the other bundles that were delivered today for my clothing..."

Jessica's head came up, but her gaze never got beyond the ribbon of bare chest exposed by his open shirt. Her eyes seemed to freeze there, her throat going dry. She'd always thought a man's chest hair to be wiry in texture. But his looked as if it would feel silky....

As the bottom started to drop out of her stomach, Jessica jerked upright to look straight into those less than friendly, turbulent eyes. "There were no other bundles, Mr. Ross. All the hotel's laundry is delivered on Friday. Mr. Chin was asked to rush your wash as a special favor to the hotel."

"Well, it would seem your Mr. Chin made a mistake, because all that I received was this shirt." Morgan waved the edges at her, exposing more of himself in the process. "The rest, as you can clearly see, are towels and sheets. Added to that, the buttons that were affixed to this shirt when it was sent out are now missing."

"Yes, I do see," Jessica said in a small voice. "Well...uh...I'll send Patrick over right away. As soon as he gets back, that is," she added, suddenly remembering that Patrick had gone out immediately after he'd taken what he believed to be Mr. Ross's laundry upstairs to him.

"Do you know how long Patrick might be?" From Morgan's experience, the boy was almost never around more than a minute here or there. "I haven't had breakfast, and I can't very well go out like this."

Again he flopped his shirt to one side, only this time he didn't miss how her eyes widened a little before she jerked them away, her lips pursing reprovingly.

"Surely you have another shirt, Mr. Ross," Jessica snapped, not bothering to keep the sharp edge out of her tone for once. How dare he flaunt himself before her like this, half-dressed, with his bare chest hanging out, as if it were an everyday occurrence? Then he had the nerve to be concerned he wasn't attired decently for Moonshadow's streets! How the devil did he think it would look should someone come striding through the lobby door right now?

At any other time, Morgan might have cheered her waspishness, preferring it to that infuriatingly polite facade. Any emotional response was better than that distant courtesy. Today, however, he was annoyed to the teeth by all the so-called mishaps he'd unfortunately been suffering. Neither did he think that the inadequate and rather nonchalant explanations she had produced were sufficient. Since she had made clear her preference for keeping him at arm's length, Morgan wouldn't be at all surprised if these unfortunate incidents were manufactured just to keep him so irritated that his resulting ill humor would give her the excuse to maintain her remoteness. She might as well have been wearing Don't Touch Me Again signs across that uninspiring flat chest of hers.

Anger spurred him as he stepped back a few paces from the desk and put his hands on his hips beneath the open edges of his shirt, baring nearly his entire chest and torso in the process. "Have you forgotten, ma'am?" he drawled slowly. "Last evening you dumped an entire bowl of stew all over me."

When he looked down at the brownish stain clearly visible across the front of his trousers, Jessica's eyes automatically, stupidly and helplessly followed. She realized her mistake, but it wasn't the first she had made since his arrival, of which the chief one was not trusting her instincts from the start. This man was dangerous. He might not be a killer, but a bullet straight through the heart would be a kindness by comparison. Because if any woman allowed herself to love this man without being loved fully in return, she would begin to die slowly, painfully, until her spirit eventually withered and her heart ceased to beat from lonely despair. Jessica knew then that she couldn't sell the Eldorado to Morgan Ross. The cost and the risk to her own heart and spirit would be greater than all the coin on earth could buy. There could be no deal between them, no compromise. Morgan Ross could not stay in this valley.

If Morgan's intent had been to disconcert the lady with his brazen exhibition, the plan backfired. Hell! It blew up in his face when he felt her eyes moving over him. At that moment, something happened that he'd not suffered since his first infatuation with the wife of a professor, when he had gotten hard every time that pretty lady had smiled at him: he embarrassed himself.

Although she was trembling inside, Jessica forced herself to look up, fully expecting to see a knowing smile on Ross's outrageously handsome, arrogant face. She was so prepared for one of those taunting grins, in fact, that she overlooked the faint stain of color creeping up his darkly tanned neck before he quickly adjusted his stance and his shirttails and stepped back up to the counter. Neither did she notice the perplexed expression on his face. Self-preservation was ruling all her senses.

"Yes, I remember my clumsiness, Mr. Ross," she told him, her voice strained but growing stronger with every determined minute. "I'm just grateful that when I tripped over Patrick, I was carrying little Billy Martin's uneaten dinner. I shudder to think what grievous, perhaps disabling, injury might have been done had that stew been straight off the stove and boiling hot."

Every word she uttered emphatically and clearly warned him that he could either start minding his manners and cease any future lewd displays, or begin guarding his privates against serious damage. While he could admire the point she'd scored, Morgan also resented that cool, unblushing, unmoved delivery. His embarrassment faded.

"I guess we were both fortunate, Mrs. Miller. If memory serves, you didn't exactly escape unscathed...."

Though his reminder brought the blush he'd wanted from her, Jessica's present color couldn't touch the crimson hue her face had worn the previous night. In her vain attempt to spare Morgan Ross the dousing he'd received anyway, Jessica had gone headlong into his lap. The force of her landing and their combined weights had sent the chair over backward. Morgan had ended up flat on his back with Jessica sprawled atop him—every blasted lean and hard-muscled inch of him!—in a puddle of stew.

"Yes... well..."

Her remembered mortification had Morgan laughing anew. What she'd lamented, he had enjoyed to the fullest. "It was a show this town will long remember, you'll have to admit."

Jessica was not pacified by the remembrance of being made a laughingstock for this town's amusement. Seeing the prim and proper Jessica Miller looking the fool was going to be the highlight of the month. Well, at least Oramay had gotten a moment of fun out of the incident. She'd been so down-in-the-mouth lately that Jessica could console herself that some good had been served, after all. And really, if she'd not been a participant, Jessica probably would have found the scene funny, as well, especially their comedic efforts to get up off the slick floor, sliding and falling, while their backsides became as stew soiled as their fronts.

Morgan saw the quirking of her lips and suspected she, too, was mentally reliving the ludicrous moments. He very much wanted to see that beautiful smile again. She had been downright miserly with her smiles these past days. Or at least he'd not been on the receiving end of them. He wasn't going to be so blessed this time, either. Just at the moment that he was certain she was losing the battle to maintain her rigid, humorless expression, Patrick Seibert came meandering back into the lobby.

At the boy's surprisingly adult and decidedly censorious glare regarding his manner of dress before the lady, Morgan determined it was time to excuse himself. Young Patrick, he'd noted several times, was very protective, even possessive, in regard to Jessica Miller. If he got his back up now, Morgan might never see his clothing again.

On his way upstairs, Morgan looked back just in time to see Jessica Miller smile gently at the youngster, favoring him with a loving hug before she sent him back out again.

Lady, you're not nearly the sour cold fish you would like me to believe. And I might have to prove that to you before I take my leave of this valley.

Morgan wasn't aware, as he continued to his room, that he had already begun to accept another failure in his search for Jessie Cameron. Neither had he yet admitted to himself that his continuing stay in Moonshadow had very little to do with any anticipated detective's report, although he'd gone through the motions of wiring Richard Burke the inconsequential bits of information he had managed to learn. At this moment, Morgan wasn't thinking beyond the day when he, much like Joshua at Jericho, caused Jessica Miller's fortified walls to come tumbling down.

"I'm flat running out of ideas, Patrick," Tommy Hughes was saying worriedly as he retrieved Black Bart's missing clothing from where he'd hidden them behind a hay bale in the livery stable's loft. "What are we gonna do? Stan Turner ain't gonna stay in San Francisco forever...."

"Maybe Bart won't have the money to buy Jessie's place," Patrick offered hopefully.

"And maybe after the last bank job he pulled, Bart's got enough stashed away to buy the ranch twice, along with most everything else in this valley. Or maybe he don't really intend to buy it at all, like I said in the first place. Is he still pussyfootin' around the widow?"

"Yeah. He's trying, anyway. Though Jessie don't seem too taken with him, despite all his efforts."

Patrick scowled when he recalled Black Bart standing before Jessie this morning with his shirt hanging open, sticking his bare, hairy chest right in her face. From things his ma had learned him about proper behavior between ladies and gentleman, Black Bart should have gotten his face slapped silly. Instead, Jessie hadn't seem outraged at all, which worried Patrick quite a lot. He was old enough to start appreciating more manly things, like a glimpse of a bare ankle and the way Laurie Callahan had begun filling out her dresses in the front. Did girls feel the same about muscles and hairy chests? The way his sister looked at Luke when he washed up seemed to indicate they did. In fact, Kathy had all but eaten up Luke's bare torso with her eyes. Maybe Bart had been trying to entice some of that feeling out of Jessie this morning, get her to notice him in a really intimate way and then move in on her for the kill.

"I ain't gonna let him do it!" Patrick grumbled vehemently.

"Do what?"

"Just never you mind," Patrick snapped angrily, retreating from a subject he wasn't about to discuss. Neither was he willing to admit to thoughts that would only make him suffer one of Tommy's endless ribbings.

"Maybe we ought to poison him like what happened out at the Eldorado...."

"No!" Patrick exclaimed, setting his jaw against even entertaining such a crazy idea.

"We could just make him a *little* sick," Tommy modified.

"We'll think of something else," Patrick insisted stubbornly, wondering, not for the first time, if Tommy Hughes was right in the head.

Agreeing to meet Tommy in the loft after supper that evening, Patrick headed back to the hotel with Black Bart's clothing under his arm, saying a prayer that Jessie wouldn't speak with Mr. Chin about this, wondering what story he could tell her if she did.

Patrick heard the sounds of a galloping horse coming up the street behind him and turned to see who might be in such an all-fired hurry. "Lordamighty, it's Luke," Patrick breathed just as his sister's husband raced by him. Afraid of what Luke's urgency meant, Patrick started running, following his brother-in-law's trail all the way to Dr. Griffith's house.

Jessica had never cooked for more than ten people in her entire life, and then she'd had the help of the bunkhouse cook to prepare the Eldorado's annual Christmas dinner. Still, after assisting Oramay all these months, she had truly believed that with a simplified menu, she could manage the small number of regular customers who patronized the hotel's dining room through the week. She could have closed the dining room—loss of income was a minor consideration—but Jessica knew she needed to keep occupied so as not to worry herself into a frenzy about Kathleen's premature labor.

What she hadn't counted upon or considered however, was that her own anxiety would be shared by this entire community, most of whom had decided to congregate in the dining room to wait out the long vigil that had begun this morning. Though Jessica might love them for caring so much, she also wanted to wring each and every one of their shortsighted necks for choosing tonight of all nights to have someone else do their cooking for them. On top of everything else, she couldn't even count on Patrick's help. Once again, he'd disappeared on her.

"Jessie, when you get a minute, we could sure use some more coffee over here—"

"Honey, did you forget that pie I ordered?"

"My dear, I really hate to complain, but this chicken is just a tiny bit overcooked for my taste...."

That last brought Jessica to a halt as she rushed by the crowded tables. Glancing down at the source of Mabel Harrison's complaint, which was browned only a slight shade darker than Oramay's golden-hued perfection, Jessica gave the mayor's wife an impatient glare and then proceeded to whisk the woman's plate out from under her nose. "Well, we can't have that, can we?" she snapped with a tight smile. "I'll bring you another serving...the minute it's ready."

At a small table near the kitchen, Morgan Rossiter watched the whirlwind that was Jessica Miller, damning these inconsiderate idiots who couldn't see she was practically running herself into the ground trying to keep up with cooking and serving them all at once. He would have thought at least one of these women might have realized her difficulty and could have at least offered to help. And where was that damned kid? He had assumed the boy had gone out to his sister's place with the doctor, but after hearing Jessica ask after him several times, Morgan was ready to go looking for the lazy, thoughtless brat. The exchange between the frazzled widow and the snooty mayor's wife made him want to cheer.

"Good for you," he commended as she dashed by his table and pushed the door to the kitchen open with her shoulder while skillfully handling an armload of plates. But Morgan's admiration of her plate-handling skills was premature. A second later he heard a loud crash and an alarmed cry...and smelled the smoke.

Jessica's mind went blank. She froze where she stood, her eyes wide and frightened as she watched flames shoot up from the skillet and black smoke begin to fill the room. She was barely aware of the dark form who pushed her aside and lunged toward the stove.

The heavy smoke stung Morgan's eyes and choked his throat, but somehow he managed to locate the salt and a heavy cast-iron lid. Within seconds the grease fire was extinguished and he was removing the skillet from the stove. Jessica Miller still hadn't moved, although she appeared to be coming out of her terrified daze as she began to cough and gasp. Grabbing her arm, Morgan drew her toward the door leading to the alley and out into the clean summer air. He filled his own lungs with several cleansing breaths before turning to the woman slumped against the stone wall. She was shaking like a leaf in high wind.

"Are you all right, Mrs. Miller?"

Jessica nodded once, then covered her face and burst into tears. "I—I could have—burned the—hotel down...."

"But you didn't," Morgan said gently, surprised by both her inaction inside and the emotional display now. After watching her handle the emergency at the Eldorado last week, he wouldn't have thought this lady could be fazed by something as commonplace as a kitchen fire. "Hey," he repeated, reaching out to touch her, then drawing his hand back again, repeating the hesitant process several times with an uncertainty that was foreign to him. Morgan didn't handle a woman's tears very well, especially when they were genuine and not any part of female manipulation. This kind of crying, heartfelt and sincere, got to him every time. And because it was so unexpected and seemingly out of character for this particular lady, Morgan was affected more profoundly than usual.

"Hey, it's all right," he told her, unable to stand this anymore, drawing her into his arms. That instant of resistance he felt was ignored as he gathered her close to his chest. "I got the fire put out in time. No damage was done. I don't even imagine the folks in the dining room are aware of any problem. Listen," he whispered against her ear. "I don't hear any shouts or screams of panic. Do you?"

Jessica felt that warm breath rush against her ear and waft its way into her soul. Just for a moment, she told herself, just for a minuscule moment, I'll let him hold me. But those moments stretched as she gave in to the compelling lure of strength combined with tenderness, the soothing music of a heartbeat....

It was Morgan who broke the embrace. Not because he wanted to let her go, more because having her in his arms and sensing her vulnerability right now made holding her this way too great a temptation. Or so he told himself, side-stepping those other mystifying emotions he preferred not to acknowledge, let alone define.

Jessica felt his withdrawal before she was gently pushed away. Her hands clenched into fists to keep herself from grabbing hold of his shirt; she so much wanted to cling to him for a little while longer. Nonetheless, she conquered those seductive impulses and drew herself together. "Th-thank you, Mr. Ross. For both your quick action and your kindness. I...I don't know what happened to me in there. I'm usually not so helpless in a crisis."

She was still a little shaken, but otherwise Jessica Miller was again herself—calm, controlled and distantly polite. Morgan had cause to regret his earlier insane chivalry. He should have taken advantage while he had the opportunity. "You've had a lot on your mind today," he offered lamely.

"Yes. I'm very concerned about Mrs. Seibert's daughter. The baby is coming too soon...."

Her voice broke, and Morgan suspected he'd found the underlying reason for both her paralysis a little while ago and the storm of tears. She was a great deal more than concerned about her friend's daughter. Earlier he had thought her drawn expression was the result of overwork and harassment. Now he saw it was really frantic worry. "Everything will be fine, I'm sure," he reassured, although it was meaningless. Morgan was anything but an authority on childbirth.

Jessica offered him a weak smile even as fresh tears threatened and chills of dread spread throughout her body in spite of the warm night. She shook off those negative thoughts, clinging to Melanie Griffith's confidence earlier that evening. Apparently David had had some recent suspicions that a miscalculation might have been made in Kathleen's favor regarding her due date. "I pray you're right, Mr. Ross. Oh, dear sweet Lord . . . how I pray you are right."

Morgan had never heard a more heartfelt prayer in his life, and it affected him profoundly. Clearing his tight throat, he looked into the kitchen. "Most of the smoke has cleared out, now. Do you want to brave that crowd again?"

Straightening her shoulders, Jessica took a deep breath, this time for courage and strength. "I suppose I don't have any choice," she said as they stepped back inside, emitting a small groan at the sight of the charred chicken.

"Not necessarily. I could clear this place out. . . ."

Jessica waved his suggestion off, reaching for another of Oramay's collection of huge skillets. "I'd rather keep busy. Otherwise, I'll just sit and stew." His laugh drew her attention, and it didn't take her long to guess the reason for his humorous grimace. "Poor choice of words, huh?" Her chuckle, however, became a gasp of surprise when she watched him reach for Oramay's apron and don it with casual nonchalance. "What are you doing?"

"Well since I'm not much of a cook, I thought I'd work out there. It can't be that difficult to take orders and serve food." Morgan ignored the wide-eyed astonishment while he straightened the ruffles on each side of the bib. "How do I look?"

Wonderful! Silly! Laughably ludicrous! Absolutely wonderful! "Y-you can't mean to go out there in that?"

Morgan cocked an eyebrow at her. "Why not? Isn't it my color?"

His foolishness lightened her heavy heart and warmed the worried chill from her bones. It also made her want to cry again. On a gulp of feeling, Jessica said, "Mr. Pervis is waiting for a slice of apple pie. And just about everyone has asked for a refill of coffee."

Her glowing smile of gratitude had more brilliance than a hearth fire on a cold day and was more satisfying than a swig of good Kentucky bourbon. But even more heartwarming was the sound of her laughter when he presented his backside and drolly asked, "Is my bow straight?"

Even as Jessica laughed at his tomfoolery, she was also acknowledging that only Morgan Ross could wear ruffles and bows and manage to accentuate, not diminish, his masculinity. There wouldn't be a woman in the dining room who would be able to drag her eyes from the sight of those streamers trailing over taut buttocks and leanly muscled thighs.

"Well?" he asked.

She dragged her gaze from that rather intriguing view. He was watching her over his shoulder, wearing a teasing grin more appealing than any of the more flagrantly seductive and carnal ones she'd seen. "It's an attention getter, that's certain," she teased back, unable entirely to believe he intended to go through with this silliness. He proved otherwise when he stepped to the door, a coffeepot in one hand and Mr. Pervis's pie in the other.

"Anything you'd like me to tell a certain lady out there who's going to get damned hungry before a chicken dinner suitable to her exalted palate can be served?"

"Nothing that would be suitable for polite company, Mr. Ross."

This time it was Morgan who laughed, genuinely and heartily, as he put his shoulder to the door and walked out into the dining room.

Chapter Nine

It was nearly midnight before Morgan was finally able to hang up his apron. Which happened to be two hours past the last stubborn straggler in the dining room and after more dirty dishes than he'd care to see again in his lifetime.

With a weary sigh, he leaned back against the kitchen wall and silently watched Jessica Miller as she obstinately attempted to gouge and scrape the charred remains of a chicken out of a heavy cast-iron skillet. It was a useless exercise, but Morgan didn't waste the breath to repeat an earlier observation that the skillet was beyond salvage. Still...

"Why don't you give that a rest and get off your feet for a few minutes."

"I'm fine, Mr. Ross."

The hell you are!

The camaraderie they'd shared so briefly had not survived the lady's increasing anxiety and worry over the fate of Mrs. Seibert's daughter and unborn grandchild. Deep frown lines marred her smooth brow, and Morgan didn't know why her bottom lip wasn't a bloody mess by now. The way she kept gnawing at it, that possibility seemed imminent.

At least the mystery of young Patrick's whereabouts had been solved, affording her some relief. According to Tommy Hughes, who'd taken his good sweet time delivering the message entrusted to him, Patrick had taken one of the livery stable's horses and had ridden out to his sister's place sometime this afternoon.

Morgan suspected that Jessica might have followed the boy had she been informed of his actions earlier. Thinking she was needed here to look after Patrick had kept her in town when she'd have been far better off smack in the thick of things. Like himself, Jessica Miller wasn't the kind who took sitting back and waiting well. Even if she had no real control over what was happening, just being on hand and close by would have spared her some of the misery she now suffered. And she was suffering. To the point where he couldn't stand back and watch any longer.

Morgan had to search through practically every cupboard before he found what he was looking for. Uncorking the bottle of sherry, he poured a healthy swallow into one of his freshly washed glasses and carried it over to the table where she worked.

"Lady, you need a rest," he told her, forestalling any argument on her part by taking her by the shoulders and forcing her to sit down. Then he wrapped her hand around the glass. "Drink that. It will do you good."

Jessica's stunned compliance as she brought the glass to her lips lasted no longer than it took for the fumes to reach her nose. The smell was sufficient to send her reeling off the chair. "I never touch strong spirits, Mr. Ross."

"Make an exception this time," Morgan said calmly, pushing her back down. When she set her mouth firmly and averted her face in a childish display of defiance, Morgan chuckled. "Come on. Take your medicine. You'll feel better." When she continued to resist, he squatted beside her. "We can do this easy, honey. Or we can do it hard. But the end result will be you swigging down this sherry. Now be a good girl and drink up. Please," he tacked on softly as an afterthought.

Jessica turned her head and glared at him. "I'll throw it back up again," she warned.

Morgan reached for a bowl sitting in the middle of the table and placed it in her lap. "No more excuses. Now drink!"

She did, draining the contents in a single gulp. Her eyes closed as a look of nausea crossed her face, but within minutes it was obvious the sherry was going to stay down. Jessica shuddered from head to toe. "God! That's awful! How could anyone drink themselves into oblivion on such vile, disgusting..." She shook all over again.

"Do I hear the squawkings of a temperance champion? I suppose you're also one of those addled females who believes women should get the vote?"

Responding to his teasing, Jessica eyed him menacingly. "Are you attempting to rile me, Mr. Ross?"

His left eyebrow lifted slightly. "Are you getting riled, ma'am?"

Suddenly, Jessica wasn't so sure she trusted his tone or that devilish glint in his eyes. "Mr. Ross—"

"Speaking of topics for annoyance... I'm going to start getting more than a little provoked myself if you don't stop calling me Mr. Ross. My name is Morgan."

"I... I don't think..."

"Lady," Morgan growled softly, "I just spent the better part of an evening prancing around in a frilly apron for your sake, enduring snickers, not to mention the aspersions cast upon my manhood. I'd say our being on a first-name basis is the least of what's due me for that sacrifice. Don't you agree, Jessica?"

Surely it was the liquor, not the way he spoke her name, that caused Jessica to feel so warm and light-headed. "Why did you?" she asked quietly.

Her thoughtful, curious expression made Morgan uncomfortable. He shrugged. "You needed help. And rescuing pretty damsels in distress is a particular specialty of mine," he finished on a grin that was anything but modest.

Yes, Jessica could well imagine the number of specialties he could claim when it came to women. Strangely enough, though, she was disappointed in his glib, flirtatious reply, disheartened that he'd fallen back on his roguish charm. Which was ridiculous, of course.

"Well," she said with a ghost of a smile as she left the chair and returned to her skillet. "I'm very grateful for your assistance... Morgan."

"Why do you do that?"

Jessica's skin tingled when she realized he stood directly behind her. "Do what?" she queried nonchalantly, picking up the wooden spatula. But before she had a chance to use it, it was being taken from her and tossed aside. And Jessica was once again being manhandled.

"Stop it!" Morgan spat, pulling her back around to face him. "And don't try insulting my intelligence by claiming you don't know what I'm getting at. You know exactly. It's too deliberate. You know what you remind me of? A gopher who pops her head up out of a hole now and again. But the minute the sun gets too warm or the air too fresh... or somebody gets too close, it retreats."

Jessica wished to God she had a hole to hide in. Unfortunately, she had to brazen this out. "A gopher. Well, that's undoubtedly a more apt comparison than 'pretty damsel.' You, Morgan, on the other hand, look the very epitome of the handsome prince. Meaning no disrespect to you, Morgan, but why on earth would you care if this simple, not very attractive gopher ducked her head and pulled the hole in after her?" Jessica forced herself to look directly into his eyes, forestalling any disavowal he might have made by rushing on. "I would much prefer your honest friendship and respect to a meaningless flirtation peppered with empty and insincere compliments. Now, I realize most women seem to expect, even demand, such treatment, deserving or not. But the truth is, it makes me uncomfortable. Probably because I'm unaccustomed..."

Morgan might have laughed had it not been so patently obvious she believed every word of this nonsense. But he'd listened to her spin out this garbage long enough. "Lady, since you've been married and can hardly claim maidenly innocence, I must assume you need those glasses I saw you wearing that first day worse than I was beginning to believe. Because you would have had to be blind this morning not to see the hard evidence of how sincerely I'm attracted to you."

When Jessica gasped and attempted to turn away from his purposely crude and graphically descriptive argument, he captured her face between his hands. "You wanted honesty, Jessica? Well, there it is. A man can't fake or pretend that kind of reaction to a woman."

Despite his hold on her, Jessica managed to shake her head in denial. "But I'm not even—"

Morgan anticipated what she was going to say. "Pretty? No, Jessica. I'll agree with you there. You aren't commonly pretty. There's more to you than merely a few pleasantly arranged features. And don't ask me to explain exactly what those mysterious qualities are. I can't. God knows I've tried often enough to explain them to myself with no success. But there is one thing I can tell you without qualification. Since I was a randy youth of fourteen, no woman has affected me the way you do."

"No!" Jessica spat breathlessly, refusing to believe him, afraid to believe him. Her fingers tore at his wrists. "I don't know what your game is, or what you truly want..."

Her frenzied panic really shouldn't have surprised him, but it did. It also awakened a tenderness in Morgan he'd never felt before. He wrapped her in his arms until she stopped struggling and sagged against him with a defeated moan. "For a woman who claims to value truth, you sure do kick up a ruckus against hearing it," he said gently while brushing his lips across her damp brow. "Maybe showing would be more convincing than telling...."

When Jessica felt his mouth moving across her cheek, she stiffened again. "You're crazy. This is...insane."

"Could be," Morgan muttered against a mouth that was firmly closed and set against him. He moved his attentions to that incredibly silky place just beneath her ear. "But I don't know a better way to prove or disprove this argument to both our satisfaction." He softly nipped the delicate curve of her jaw before tracing the shape of her ear with his tongue. She began to tremble. In pleasure or fear? Morgan was afraid to find out which. "Don't be frightened, Jess. I'm only going to kiss you. Nothing more."

"And what I want makes no difference, does it? Just like the sherry, you're going to force this on me, no matter how repugnant—"

Morgan lifted his head at that and scowled down at her. He wasn't accustomed to having his kisses compared to bitter medicine. Despite her words, she made no effort to move away. Her cheeks were flushed with warm color. Moving his hand up her back, Morgan entwined his fingers in the heavy knot of hair at the nape of her neck, pulling her head back until he was looking directly into her face. He saw anger in those big eyes of hers, not disgust. "God, but you're obstinate," he whispered, unable to stop a smile of admiration. "And the sooner you give me your mouth, the quicker this horrible experience will be over and done with. Because I am going to kiss you, Jessica Miller. With or without your cooperation."

"Damn you! Don't—"

He caught her angry words within his mouth, pressing the advantage her outburst had granted him. There was nothing tentative or coaxing in the way he kissed her. Morgan claimed, invaded and demanded what he knew would not be granted freely. He wasn't about to let this woman close herself off to him again, not until he'd found and tasted her passion.

Jessica stiffened at the first bold stroke of his tongue, a helpless shriek dying in her throat. She expected to suffer a repulsive rape of her mouth; instead, he teased wickedly, almost playfully, with a lazy and unhurried assurance that sent waves of sensation coursing throughout her entire body. He'd said she wasn't a virginal innocent. That was true enough. Her body had known a man's possession. But any stirrings of youthful passion had not survived the reality of Cole Hardin's true character. That part of Jessica had died from his many cruelties. Or so she'd believed... until Morgan Ross had come storming into her life.

Oh! This man was a devil! God knew he could kiss like the very devil, consuming her will, damning her soul to eternal hell with these slow, soul-devouring kisses.

Morgan groaned when her lips softened and parted even farther for him. That sweet, almost timid, response set him on fire. But it wasn't enough. He buried both hands in her hair, only to be frustrated by the number of pins confining the heavy silk. He withdrew to begin mounting a new attack. "Don't fight me, Jess," he said between soft nibbles of her pouty lower lip. "Don't fight yourself." His mouth trailed to her pointed little chin and below, finding the wildly fluttering pulse of her neck.

Even as she began to tremble from the dark and forbidden desires starting to overwhelm her reason, she attempted to deny him. "No," she whispered raggedly.

"Yes!" Morgan breathed, returning to take her mouth again and again, alternately fierce and gentle, giving and withholding, until her lips were as reaching and as desperate as his own. "Oh, lady," he growled, shifting against her while his tongue wet her mouth from corner to corner. "You've needed a good kissing for a long time, haven't you?" He wasn't even aware of the deep tenderness in his own voice before he ceased his tormenting and gave her what they both wanted.

Jessica's head fell back wantonly. She forgot where she was, who she was. There was nothing beyond this man holding her. Even as he took, he was also demanding that she give. And Jessica had stored more loving inside her than ten lifetimes and ten million kisses such as this one could ever begin to use up.

Morgan had thought to tear down her walls, but he'd never dreamed she would come apart in his arms this way...or that her sweet hunger would have the power to make him want to possess her beyond reason. Their kisses were becoming carnal, explosive. Almost of their own volition, Morgan's hands left her hair to curve around her hips, bringing her up hard against him in an attempt to assuage that fiery, throbbing ache.

Jessica cried out at the contact, the shock of that most intimate caress jolting her out of her sensual haze. She tore her mouth from his. "No...please," she rasped, pressing her forehead to his chest while she gasped for breath and prayed for a return to sanity.

It took effort, but Morgan somehow managed to get his raging desire under control. Still, he wouldn't let her go, keeping her tight against him. "Tell me now how unattractive and unappealing you are, Jessica Miller," he said huskily, his own breathing none too steady yet. "Because if I get any more sincere than I am right now..." He let his voice trail off as he moved against her one more time, making his point and nearly killing himself in the process. "God!" he spat through clenched teeth.

Had Jessica been able to recognize his misery, she wouldn't have been able to muster sympathy. Her own suffering was too great. She wanted to die from it. And even more, she wanted to kill Morgan Ross for destroying, in the space of minutes, the person it had taken her nine difficult and determined years to forge and become. Tonight he'd shown her just how little she'd grown away from that desperately lonely, affection-starved young girl. She was still very much little Jessie Cameron, so famished for any kind of human warmth and loving that she would latch on to the first passerby offering to take her in his arms. God! How she despised herself, despised him, for the shattering of her illusions.

"Let me go!" Jessica commanded, shoving at his immovable chest. "Damn you! Let me go!"

Too late, Morgan realized he should have anticipated both her fury toward himself and the self-loathing he saw too clearly on her now-pale face. "Just listen to me a minute," he demanded softly, refusing to let her run away from this, though he did put more distance between them. "The whole point of this was to prove you're a flesh-and-blood woman with needs and desires. *And desirable!* Dammit, Jessica.

You deserve better than this loveless existence as the perpetual widow."

"And you're the savior appointed to save me from such a fate, I suppose?" she spat back sarcastically, furiously. Unlike the girl she'd once been, Jessica had at least learned to stand up and fight for herself under John and Boone's tutelage. Because maybe if Jessie Cameron had fought her father's drinking from the start, Jack Cameron wouldn't have died from his weakness. And maybe if she'd killed Cole Hardin as he'd deserved—

"Or...have I misjudged you, Mr. Ross?" she asked, peering up into his darkly handsome face. "Can I expect an avowal of love and an offer of marriage to be forthcoming? Will you now drop down on your knee with a proposal?" The stunned and cornered expression he wore was sufficient answer. "No, I thought not," she sniffed with cold contempt. "Well, then, as I see things, all that's been proven this evening is that you, Morgan Ross, are an unprincipled scoundrel. One who recognized my emotional vulnerability tonight and thought to alleviate some of his boredom."

Her charges were a little too close to truth for comfort. "And you loved every minute of it!" he accused in an attempt to defend his indefensible position. But he would not have lost control of his temper or pushed this argument further had she not made a production of drawing the back of her hand across her mouth as if to wipe away all traces of his tainted kisses. Her eyes, brilliantly green with scornful disdain, challenged and provoked.

There was no calculation in Morgan's actions this time when he hauled her up against him and pinned the arms that would have flailed at him behind her back. "You really shouldn't have done that, Jessica. Now I'm just going to have to prove my point all over ag—"

Morgan never got the chance to do anything more than grunt with surprise as something heavy landed squarely in the middle of his back with enough force to knock the breath right out of him and cause him to release Jessica.

"You dirty, low-down, stinkin' outlaw bastard!" Patrick Seibert shrieked as his forearm locked around the gunslinger's neck. "I'll carve your gizzard for puttin' hands on our Jessie!"

Jessica gasped, her face flooding with shame as she watched Patrick Seibert defend her honor with all the outraged fury his ninety-pound, twelve-year-old strength could muster. How much had he seen, had he heard? Enough to spur this attack, obviously. "Patrick!" she shouted, more alarmed now than embarrassed as Morgan Ross tried to shake the boy loose. "You'll get hurt! Turn loose of him!"

If Morgan could have breathed, he would have made some disparaging comment regarding her assumption that this tenacious little bastard would come out on the losing end of this struggle. But between the blow to his back and the kid's choke hold— Lord! He needed air!

"You'll never get your thievin', murderin' paws on the Eldorado or anything else around here, either, Black Bart Bigelow!"

Out of necessity, Morgan reached and grabbed a handful of pale blond hair. The youngster yelped in pain but didn't turn him loose, as he'd hoped. Instead, Patrick lifted one of the legs he'd wrapped around Morgan's thigh and drove his booted heel straight back in a bruising blow. At that, Morgan resigned himself to hurting the boy. His only other option was letting himself be strangled until he passed out.

He'd just grabbed hold of the kid's shirt with the intent of throwing him over his head, when two things happened simultaneously. A wall of icy water hit him squarely in the face, and a new voice was introduced to this fiasco.

"Good gawdamighty! What in tarnation...?" Oramay Seibert hollered before marching over to forcibly pull her son off Morgan Ross's back. "What in the name of heaven is going on here?" she demanded, hauling Patrick away by his belt. She looked pointedly at the flustered young woman holding an empty water bucket in her hand.

"I...I..." Jessica sputtered before whirling away with a mortified groan.

"Mr. Ross? Are you all right?"

On his knees, Morgan was bent over and gasping, water running in rivulets from his drenched hair. He could only nod.

"Well, somebody better start explaining, and mighty damn fast! After the kind of day I've just experienced—"

Jessica jerked as if every muscle in her body had just been pulled by an invisible cord. "Kathleen," she cried urgently, her fearful gaze going to Oramay. Dear heaven! How could she have forgotten Kathleen, even for a single minute?

Oramay saw Jessica's distress and immediately put her mind at rest with a beatific smile. "The Lord granted us a double blessing today, Jessie. Kathleen gave birth to healthy twins. A boy and a girl."

"Thank God," Jessica breathed, sagging with relief. "I'm so—"

"He was maulin' Jessie!" Patrick pointed an accusing finger straight at the man just now getting to his feet. "The bastard had her up against the table, and he was . . . he was all over her like a . . . like a . . ." Unable to think of any way to describe what he'd seen, Patrick just threw up his hands. "He was just all over her, Ma! And he ain't who he says he is, neither!"

Oramay's brows shot skyward. One look at Jessica's livid, and clearly mortified, expression seemed to confirm Patrick's charges. Morgan Ross didn't look any too comfortable, either. "Well?" she queried with pointed interest, her gaze moving from one to the other. Sadly, it appeared neither Jessica nor Ross showed any willingness to satisfy her galloping curiosity. Oramay frowned her disappointment, though she flashed Jessica a silent warning that this topic was not yet exhausted. "Well, perhaps we'd all be served by a good, restorative night's sleep. Patrick—"

"Ma! Didn't you hear nothin' I said? That man there is a fraud, not at all who he claims he is." Patrick had the momentary satisfaction of seeing the gunslinger stiffen with unease. "He's an outlaw, a cold-blooded killer and bank robber. And he's come to Moonshadow with the intent of cheatin' Jessica outa the Eldorado, just like he did that poor widow woman back in Wichita, Kansas, a year or so back. But you ain't gonna get away with it this time, Bigelow! We're onto you here!"

Oramay grabbed her son's shoulders. "Patrick Seibert, I believe you've taken leave of your senses. Where on earth did you come up with such a wild and crazy story? Good heavens, son...."

Patrick shook off his mother's restraining hold. "I got proof! I'll show you!" He whirled and raced out of the kitchen, leaving the adults staring after him in bewilderment.

From his room, he collected the four books Tommy had lent him. But the cover drawing on one brought Patrick up short. It showed Black Bart standing over a downed and bleeding man, with the smoking revolver still in his hand. Bart was grinning while his victim was obviously pleading for his life. Patrick began to shake with fear. Dear God! Bigelow could kill the lot of them, with only Tommy Hughes left to tell the story.

Patrick made a detour to his mother's room and found his father's old pistol. It was unloaded, and Patrick didn't know where his mother kept the bullets—if she had any around in the first place—but maybe Bigelow wouldn't know the difference.

The noisy chatter in the kitchen came to an abrupt halt when Patrick marched in, pointed the gun at Ross and threw the books on the kitchen table. "There!" he stated smugly, ignoring his mother's gasp of alarm.

Oramay was furious. "Patrick, you give me that pistol this very minute...or I'll tan your hide until..."

Closest to the table, Jessica picked up one of the dime novels, remembering the night she'd caught Patrick reading. Perusing the tattered and obviously well-read copy of *The Cheating Heart,* Jessica observed drolly, "There is a slight resemblance between Mr. Ross and this Bigelow fellow. Of course, you wouldn't see it now, Oramay. Without the whiskers and all cleaned up—"

"Mrs. Miller—"

"See there, Ma! Jessie sees it, too, 'cause she was here that first day. . . ."

"Maybe you should go fetch Sheriff Taylor, Patrick," Jessica suggested with feigned alarm while she also examined copies of *Black Bart's Revenge* and *The Left-Handed Gun.* It was this last that caught her attention.

"Jessica!" Oramay couldn't believe the young woman could be taking any of this nonsense seriously. "Don't you dare encourage—"

"That's right, Jessie," Patrick jumped in eagerly. "Earl Taylor ain't no match for Bart Bigelow. Me and Tommy decided that from the first. Knew we'd have to take care of this on our own. Only nothin' seemed to discourage him," the boy wailed on a sigh. He shot a hostile glance toward the tall outlaw, who was just standing there with a stupid expression on his face and wet from head to toe. "Too bad you didn't break your damned neck when that saddle came off Flossie!" He remembered the gun and waved it menacingly.

Morgan flinched and let go with an expressive curse. "God! Be careful with that thing. It could go off!"

Jessica felt her stomach knot while Oramay cried out her own frightened concern over Patrick's careless handling of the weapon. She cursed herself for the stupidity of her comments to Patrick a few moments ago. But just briefly, the image of Morgan Ross spending a day or two in Moonshadow's tiny, hot jail had held an undeniable appeal. Not that she would have ever allowed this silliness to go so far. However, having the sadistic pleasure of seeing him squirm briefly was one thing. Getting him killed by an overzealous, overly imaginative youngster was another altogether. She had to put an end to this . . . and now.

"Patrick," she said with steady calm, "I want you to give me the pistol and then go fetch Sheriff Taylor. I'll guard Mr. Ross—Black Bart, I mean—until you get back."

"But . . ."

"I'm a crack shot, Patrick. Better than most men, actually. Boone made certain I was proficient with firearms years ago." She approached the boy cautiously, not wanting to make him any more nervous. Thankfully, Oramay had wisely chosen not to interfere. "He won't get away. I promise. But we could tie him up now, if that would reassure you."

Obviously, Jessica was convincing, because Morgan's face was dark with fury and his eyes were as hard and cold as the metal of the gun Patrick reluctantly placed in her steady hand.

With a sigh of relief, Jessica immediately checked the gun, only to discover it wasn't loaded. Without warning, she sent it sailing, throwing it to Morgan. Actually, she hurled it at his head. But he caught it nevertheless, in a quick, defensive motion that spared his skill and proved her supposition. "As you can see, Patrick, Mr. Ross is right-handed," she announced matter-of-factly, paying little mind to the disgruntled man glaring daggers at her. "And according to one of those books, your Black Bart Bigelow is most definitely left-handed."

Patrick wasn't inclined to be swayed by her deduction. "He learned to use his left hand because he took a minié ball in the right shoulder during the war and lost partial use of that arm. But he can still shoot—"

"Could I have a towel, please?" Morgan requested dryly as he thrust the empty revolver into his belt. When the towel came sailing at him, too, Morgan made damn sure he caught it with the proper hand. Then he proceeded to leisurely mop his face and hair before his eyes swept the occupants in the room and he began to recite, "Yep, I'll never forget that day at Bull Run when we charged Beauregard's forces—"

"Oh, would you shut up!" Jessica snapped. "If you were at Bull Run, then it must have been as a nine-year-old water boy!"

Morgan just grinned and shrugged.

"Black Bart fought with the South," Patrick argued, then frowned, scratching his head. "Somethin' ain't right here. Bart was young, but he weren't no kid...."

"What's wrong, Patrick," Jessica said patiently, "is that you've made a mistake. The Civil War ended seventeen years ago. And Mr. Ross can't possibly be more than five or six years older than myself. Which means he'd have been far too young to serve, even if either army would have had him," she added caustically.

"Then if he ain't Black Bart, and if he's not here to cheat you outa the ranch, then why was he trying to kiss you?"

Oramay stifled a startled laugh.

Jessica's face turned purple.

Morgan answered the boy. "Maybe because your Jessie is the most kissable woman I've come across in many a year."

A rather profound and pregnant silence followed, with everyone suddenly becoming fascinated by the pattern on the kitchen towels or the textures in the wood grain of the table.

Finally, Oramay cleared her throat. "Goodness. This has been quite a day."

"Ma, I—"

"Not another word out of you, young man," Oramay scolded. "You've caused quite enough trouble. Though I'm not at all sure I've yet to comprehend the enormity of this Black Bart farce you've created. But I will. You can count on that, son. In fact, you and Thomas Hughes are going to have a great deal of explaining to do tomorrow. For now, however, you're to go to your room and you are to stay there until I fetch you. Is that understood?"

"Yes, ma'am," Patrick said woodenly, turning to leave.

"Just a minute, Patrick," Morgan requested firmly. "The saddle cinches—you and the Hughes boy were responsible for that mishap?" The youngster hesitated, then nodded his guilt. "And those other incidents? The fleas in my bed, the doorknobs—"

"Yeah," Patrick inserted hastily, not particularly eager to have an entire list of his sins recounted in front of his mother. "We took the pass key Ma and Jessie keep under the registration desk." He glanced at his mother. "I'm real sorry about that mattress, Ma. I never thought it would have to be burned...."

"Go to bed, Patrick!" Oramay ordered again with an appalled shake of her head. "Lordamercy," she breathed tiredly when he'd gone. "I apologize for my son, Mr. Ross."

"No real harm was done, Mrs. Seibert. As a matter of fact, this situation has its amusing aspects."

"You're too kind." The smile she gave him faded when she saw Jessica move to the alley door and step outside, as if to escape any possibility of being drawn into conversation. Or more likely to avoid any chance of further contact with this man. Oramay would have given just about anything to know what had really gone on here tonight but was realistically resigning herself to settling for the barest, dullest facts—if she got that lucky.

Morgan had also taken note of Jessica's withdrawal from the kitchen. She was on the run again. His first impulse was to go after her and—what? Just what in the hell would chasing after her prove? Except perhaps that he was even more of an unprincipled bastard than she already believed him to be. If only the lady knew that in the process of breaching her defenses tonight, his own had taken quite a shaking....

Not even an icy bucket of water or the kid who'd landed squarely in the middle of his back seemed to have much effect upon the powerful feelings Jessica stirred within him. Feelings that had nothing whatsoever to do with the quest that had brought him to Moonshadow in the first place. And after tonight Morgan could no longer delude himself that there was even a remote possibility Jessica Miller was anything other than the very real and genuinely unimpeachable person she claimed.

Had he ever truly believed her to be otherwise? Everything Morgan had learned about Jessica, had witnessed with his own eyes and felt deep inside his gut, confirmed she was not the woman he sought. He needed no Pinkerton investigation to reinforce that certainty. Wasn't it time—past time—to admit that his continued presence in Moonshadow was unnecessary? That the anticipated detective's report had become nothing more than an excuse, a self-deceptive justification for lingering here in this valley, close to the woman who'd captured his fancy to such an extent that he questioned his reason where she was concerned? For the first time since Zach's death, Morgan had allowed himself to be sidetracked. Morgan realized it was time to do some running himself, preferably all the way back to Kansas, before he created more excuses and justifications.

"Mr. Ross, hadn't you better get out of those wet clothes?"

The extent of how completely the subject of Jessica Miller absorbed him was proved by his surprise at hearing Oramay Seibert's voice. The thought that she'd been there all the time, watching him wrangle with himself, was damned unsettling. "Pardon me?" he asked, having no idea what she'd said to him.

"Your clothes—they're soaked. I'm afraid you'll catch a chill if you don't get dry soon."

Though phrased as a suggestion, Mrs. Seibert's tone had the definite ring of command. Morgan, too, was being sent to his room. With a small, wry smile that told her he knew what she was about, he let himself be escorted from the kitchen.

When they arrived at the staircase in the lobby, Oramay placed a detaining hand upon Morgan Ross's arm. "Mr. Ross, Jessica Miller is undoubtedly one of the finest young women I've ever been blessed to know. She deserves better than to be toyed with."

Morgan didn't pretend to misunderstand. "Yes, she does," he concurred softly, sincerely, gazing down into her kind, worried blue eyes. "I'll be leaving Moonshadow when the weekly stagecoach comes in from Sacramento, Mrs. Seibert."

Oramay's disappointment showed in her voice. "Then you've decided against purchasing the Eldorado and becoming a resident in our valley?"

"I'm afraid so." On impulse, Morgan leaned down and gave her a kiss on her cheek. "Congratulations on the healthy birth of your grandchildren."

"Thank you, Mr. Ross." The unexpected affectionate gesture nearly left Oramay speechless.

"Good night, Mrs. Seibert."

Oramay watched him ascend the stairs until he was no longer in sight, more confused and curious about what had happened here tonight than before. There had been something in Ross's eyes when she'd confronted him about Jessica that made Oramay believe the man genuinely cared about the girl. That Jessica had not been herself since Morgan Ross first appeared in town was inarguable. Nonetheless, those two young'uns were obviously determined nothing would ever come of the sparks they set off between each other. Why was it, Oramay wondered, folks were often so blamed foolish when it came to taking a chance on loving?

Realizing the subject she pondered was hitting a little close to home for comfort, Oramay took herself off to bed, grumbling and mumbling every step.

In his own room, Patrick Seibert was stretched out across his mattress while he plotted every sort of vengeance he could imagine against Tommy Hughes, blaming him entirely for the trouble they were both in now.

His nasty plans were soon interrupted when the ceiling trembled and shook on the heels of a crashing thud. "Oops," Patrick muttered, grimacing ruefully when a muffled but distinct roar of frustrated fury came from that room above. In the excitement, Patrick had forgotten all about those bed slats he and Tommy had weakened the other day.

Chapter Ten

Tommy Hughes nearly killed himself trying to get to the buggy to offer Jessica assistance. "Afternoon, Mrs. Miller," he said breathlessly, fairly oozing with polite friendliness. Tommy was not the most popular person now with the folks at the hotel, and he was eager to make amends. "Hot day, ain't it? Is everything all right out at the Tanners'?"

"Everything is fine, Tommy," Jessica returned, hoping her selective response would satisfy. The new and reformed Tommy Hughes, with his ingratiating manner, really wasn't any more likable than the sullen, troublemaking one. Still, she gave him credit for the efforts he was making.

"You and Mrs. Seibert are sure giving this ol' horse and buggy a workout. With you going out to Kathleen's every morning and Patrick and his ma takin' off afternoons, I hardly have time to unhitch, groom and feed this mare 'fore she's trottin' off down the road again."

"Yes...well, I really don't have the time to chat, Tommy. Just do the best you can with the animal for now. Luke will see she's taken care of tonight."

"Yes'm. I surely will. You have a good evening."

The boy looked so earnest and anxious to please that Jessica couldn't withhold a warm smile as she took her leave from him. Seeing his face light up over such a small gesture of mellowing brought a wave of guilt.

When she had put the length of a block between herself and the livery, Jessica felt the strange sensation of being watched. But any unease was immediately alleviated when she looked back and saw that Tommy was still staring after her, wearing a bemused expression on his young face. With another smile and a slight wave, Jessica continued on toward the hotel, thinking it really wasn't fair of them to lay the entire blame for the Black Bart episode at Tommy's feet. Granted, he might have been the mastermind and driving force behind the boys' mischief, but Patrick had certainly been a most willing and faithful accomplice. And Tommy had suffered the greatest punishment. Not only had he and Patrick been forbidden each other's company for the remainder of the summer, but Tommy's entire collection of dime novels had been confiscated and destroyed.

In fact, Patrick seemed more than content with the new arrangement, for it allowed him his mother's exclusive attention during the day. He even appeared to eagerly anticipate spending the late afternoons and evenings at his sister's, actually showing signs of becoming a doting uncle toward the twins.

All in all, Jessica reflected, things were working out very well. Oh, there were a few problems. Like the necessity of keeping the dining room closed until Kathleen was on her feet again. And though Luke never complained, he was the one losing sleep, getting up with the twins in the middle of the night. Then, of course, there were those long and tense hours when Jessica found herself alone in the hotel with Morgan Ross. Not that it had been a problem. In fact, she rarely saw him. It was as if that night in the kitchen had never happened....

Tommy Hughes basked in the splendor of Jessica Miller's smile, probably more affected than most because they so rarely were directed his way. It scattered his wits, making him forget something he'd intended to tell her. But by the time it came to mind, she was halfway down the street.

"Dang!" he griped. "I was going to tell her about that fellow who rode into town today." Not that it really mattered, Tommy decided, going back to his work. She'd find out the hotel had another guest from Mrs. Seibert soon enough.

From the saloon, Morgan watched Jessica Miller walking toward the hotel. When she paused suddenly and began to look around, he quickly pulled back into the shadowed interior of the doorway, staying out of sight. Even all the way over here, he could feel the gut-twisting power of that smile she flashed the boy.

"That's her, isn't it?"

"Yep," Morgan answered the man speaking just behind his left shoulder. "The sainted Widow Miller in the flesh."

Burke winced at the young man's caustic, guttural tone. Neither was he reassured when Rossiter tossed down another shot of whiskey and then immediately thrust the empty glass into Burke's face.

"Get me another, will you?"

Burke hesitated. "Hadn't you better start easing up on that stuff?"

In Morgan's opinion, he'd not had nearly enough. "You just concern yourself with anticipating that fat bonus you've earned."

The insulting tone tempted Burke to tell Rossiter what he could do with his damned bonus. But Richard Burke wasn't a stupid man. He took the shot glass with a careless shrug. "It's your party, Rossiter. But you won't be enjoying it much if you're flat on your back and passed out cold from overindulgence."

Burke also didn't mention his growing apprehension that they might not get the Cameron woman out of town alive, let alone to Fort Smith, Arkansas. Rossiter was in such a black mood, Burke didn't trust the younger man not to strangle her on impulse. He'd sure as hell never see any bonus if Rossiter hanged for murder.

Morgan watched the Pinkerton detective's placid face, wondering what emotions were hidden behind it. Burke's unassuming and innocuous appearance and manner were what made him so effective in his work. He looked, dressed and acted more a whiskey drummer or dry goods salesman than one of the renowned and infamous Pinkerton agents. He was good, one of the best, or so he was quick to claim. Morgan could hardly argue. He had the proof of the man's abilities. Burke had accomplished what legions of men just like him could not: he'd found Jessica Cameron.

"Don't worry, Burke. I'm merely celebrating the end of a long search. I have no intention of doing anything stupid after all this time."

Obviously relieved, Burke moved off. Morgan turned back and braced his right shoulder against the door frame. He stared out at the street but saw nothing. Jessica Miller—no! Jessie Cameron—was beyond his vision. But not beyond reach, by God. Not beyond reach!

"Damn!" he spat beneath his breath. She'd really played him for a prize fool. Suckered him good with that so very respectable and above reproach act. Then she'd finished him off with her breathtaking smile and wiped the floor with him when she'd come apart with such sweet fire as he'd kissed her....

Morgan ground his teeth. He'd been so certain that Jessica Miller couldn't possibly be the woman he sought. She was too good and fine, caring and giving and loving. He'd admired her for so many reasons, including the contempt she seemed to hold for his fatal charm. And when it came to her looks, he had meant every damn word of what he had said to her that night in the kitchen. No woman before her had ever stirred such a confounding hotbed of emotions.

God! He'd been within a fatal breath of falling in love with the deceitful bitch!

Luckily, Burke's timely arrival had spared him from making an even greater jackass of himself. Otherwise, he might have succumbed to the impulse of offering the lady a full confession of his identity before throwing himself upon her saintly mercy.

"Might have been interesting to see her reaction, though," Morgan murmured with a derisive laugh. He gulped down the shot of whiskey he couldn't remember

Burke handing him. Nosiree, Morgan Rossiter hadn't begun to start some real serious drinking yet. Not by a damn long shot!

"Like I was saying, I put that Burke fellow in room four, right next to Mr. Ross," Oramay was telling Jessica. Oramay had been talking nonstop since Jessica walked into the lobby, hardly taking a single breath between topics. Which was just as well; Jessica wasn't much in a mood for chitchat, in any case.

"And would you believe that man hadn't been in his room a full hour before he'd managed to smash his washbasin and pitcher to smithereens? Patrick and I must have been up there the better part of the afternoon, mopping water and picking up tiny shards of porcelain. I suspect he was throwing a fit over the dining room being closed. Said he was looking forward to my superb cooking. Then he climbed up the wall like a monkey and began to dance upside down on the ceiling."

"What?"

Oramay pursed her lips and tweaked Jessica's nose. "You haven't heard half what I've been saying, Jessie Miller. Matter of fact, you've been walking around in a mope since the night the twins were born. Maybe you ought to tell me just what went on here...."

"Oramay, please. As I've told you before, Patrick misunderstood. I was worried about Kathleen. Mr. Ross was trying to comfort me. That's all."

"Then why'd he make that statement about you being kissable?"

Jessica threw up her hands in frustration. "How would I know the workings of that man's mind? Possibly he wanted to get back at me for siding with Patrick, even briefly, over his resemblance to Black Bart. That artist's drawing wasn't particularly flattering, you know."

Oramay didn't bother to hide her expression of disbelief. "So you're not at all upset by his leaving tomorrow? He really is, you know—leaving, I mean. Settled up his bill and everything."

"Of course I'm upset. Now I have to look for another buyer for the Eldorado."

Oramay knew when she'd run herself into a brick wall. "Well, I don't have the time to argue this issue right now. I've got to get out to Kathleen's before the sun sets." Turning, she bellowed for Patrick. "How were my sweet babies today?"

The minutes until Patrick presented himself were spent in discussing the twins' progress. Although apparently healthy, the infant boy and girl were smaller than the average newborn. Happily, they seemed to be thriving, Jessica reported to their concerned grandmother.

"Kathy tells me you're a natural-born mother, Jessie. Maybe you ought to consider children of your own."

It simply was impossible for Oramay to keep her busybody tendencies under control for very long. Jessica sighed. "I just might do that, Oramay. In fact, I'll grab the first man who walks through the door and drag him off."

If she thought to shock Oramay off this topic, she failed. "Oh, no, you mustn't do that, honey. Goodness! What if it was old Charlie Mitchell who hobbled in to pay a surprise visit? Nope, if it's breeding you have in mind, then you'll be needing the services of a healthy and randy young stallion—Jessie Miller! Where are you running off to in such an all-fired hurry?"

Already halfway down the hall, Jessica shouted back over her shoulder, "To my room. For some peace and quiet!"

When she was out of Oramay's sight, Jessica ran for her room, wanting to avoid any chance of accidentally meeting Patrick. As it was, the door had hardly closed behind her when Oramay called her son again and Jessica heard Patrick depart his own room next door.

At this narrow escape, Jessica sagged back against the wall and covered her face. But it wasn't the heat of embarrassment her palms encountered; it was the wetness of tears. She hadn't dared let Oramay see them. The woman would not have ever let up on her if she had. And what explanation for them could Jessica have given?

That Oramay's teasing had struck too closely upon the forbidden yearnings and desires she'd been battling for days....

It was mostly being with the babies, Jessica fervently told herself. Caring for them, cuddling them close and smelling their sweet newborn scent had fully awakened her never entirely suppressed longing for another child, a family of her own. At times, when she held one of the twins, Jessica's breasts would ache and feel swollen, so strong was the instinct to suckle and nourish. She'd been denied the wonder of feeling the hungry tuggings of an avid little mouth at her nipples, drawing sustenance from her body. All she'd ever known was the agony of waiting for nature to accept there was no living child to need what it had provided in such bountiful supply.

When a choked sob escaped her throat, Jessica pushed herself away from the wall and swiped at the moisture on her face. "This is the road to madness," she chided hoarsely. "Just as thinking about what might have been with Morgan is madness. More so...."

With a small screech over her inability to curb her own willful thoughts, Jessica marched over to the window and threw it open, drawing in deep gulps of air that was only slightly more refreshing than the trapped, stale atmosphere within the small room. The next priority was to shed herself of a dress that smelled of sour milk and babies' breath.

There was an almost mad desperation in the way she tore off her clothing, jerking her dress over her head, uncaring of the hairpins that were torn free. But in the end it was no use. She was fighting a losing battle. Finally, she gave up the struggle and sank down onto the vanity. Pressing the detested black dress to her nose, she let herself cry. Not the hard, wracking sobs that might have given her some genuine relief. She was too fearful she might shatter like Mr. Burke's washbasin if she really let go. Instead, she cried softly, silently, releasing just enough of her misery so she might get through this evening. So she could get up again tomorrow and put Jessica Miller's steadfast and serene expression back on for another day—and then another, and another, until eventually it became easy and natural for her again. Until she could forget the man who'd so forcefully reminded her that she was a flesh-and-blood woman. Perhaps more flesh and blood than she might have ever dreamed or imagined....

The emotional outpouring was brief. She wouldn't allow it to be more. Rising, she released the ties and fastenings on her petticoats and bustle, stepping out of them when they pooled at her feet. Tucking the tousled strands of hair that had loosened from their moorings behind her ears, Jessica started for her own washbasin to remove all traces of baby odors and tears. Only then did she notice the dull gleam of an object propped on her pillow. Due to the alley beyond her window and the lateness of the afternoon, the light was bad, making it difficult to see the object clearly.

She frowned slightly in puzzlement. Had Patrick or Oramay brought her a small token of some kind, either to cheer her up or in gratitude for the time she was spending with Kathleen's new family? If so, why was her stomach knotting in that familiar way that always bespoke or warned of something unpleasant?

She rounded the bed slowly. The pain in her midsection seemed to grow with every step closer. And even before her fingers touched the dulled and tarnished frame, she knew.

The images frozen in time were as beloved and familiar as if she'd just seen them yesterday, and the vivid memory of the last time she had seen them catapulted her into the past. Papa was snoring in his drunken stupor in the shack, his breath reeking of whiskey. God! She could smell it still. How she despised that disgusting odor! But how could it be so strong? Only in nightmares—

A deep chuckle sent her whirling around, nearly falling when legs she hadn't realized were trembling almost refused to move at all.

Despite the familiarity of the tall man standing in the open doorway of her room, his shoulder resting negligently against the frame, Jessica felt chills of alarm. They increased as she stared into that darkly handsome face. She had seen those gray eyes darken with anger, dance with mischief and burn hot with desire. Never had she seen them flooding with hate . . . before now.

The mouth that had tried to seduce her with slow, lazily sensual smiles and even more stirring kisses, was now twisted and distorted into a shape abhorrently cruel.

But when the strong, nauseating smell of whiskey lingered, warning it was not a product of her imagination, Jessica began to know genuine fear. "What are you doing in my room, Ross?" she demanded, surprising herself with the strength of her voice.

Morgan barked with harsh laughter. "Still playing the Widow Miller, all schoolmarm proper, even though you're only wearing chemise and drawers!"

He jerked away from the door frame; Jessica flinched back. "Morgan . . . please . . . I don't understand . . ."

"Well, it's like this," Morgan sneered with cold pleasantry. "You've led me a merry dance, lady. I'll give you that. But the game's over, Jessie Cameron. I've come to fetch you home, so to speak."

The Cameron family photograph slipped from suddenly icy fingers. Her eyes fluttered shut and she reeled physically from the reality of a nightmare come true.

Cole Hardin had sent him after her!

Never dreaming Cole would be content denying himself the pleasure of his own dirty work, Jessica had never anticipated this, was having difficulty accepting it still. Morgan Ross acting as Cole Hardin's henchman? No! It wasn't possible. . . . *I've come to fetch you home. . . .*

At the sound of her door being forcibly closed and the bolt being thrown, her eyes flew open. Morgan was advancing toward her. She cried out softly, backing away from him, but her shoulders came up flush with the wall before she'd taken two full steps. Her heart pounded more violently the closer he came. She felt trapped, a helpless creature being stalked. Once she'd likened Morgan's sinewy grace and beauty to that of a powerful cougar, and she had found him magnificent. Now there was only danger and menace in that magnificence.

"Morgan, I— You're mistaken. I don't know... I—I'm not..."

Morgan snarled as he flattened both palms against the wall on either side of her head. "My only mistake, *lady*—" he made the word "lady" sound a filthy malediction "—was in not recognizing you for a lying, deceitful bitch from the first!" When she would have averted her face from his whiskey-laden breath, he barked, "Look at me, damn you!"

Jessica obeyed. She searched those hard, unrelenting features for any hint of the man who'd played nurse to a bunch of sick cowhands or the clowning cavalier who had so nonchalantly worn a ruffled apron with a laughing disregard for his masculine image. What she found was loathing, pure and absolute. At least she knew then that Cole Hardin had never sent him to fetch her. The kind of hatred she saw in Morgan's face couldn't be bought and paid for at any price. Whatever the reason, his grudge against her was personal. Deeply and horribly personal.

"Why?" she croaked in a strained whisper. "What have I ever done...?"

Morgan's mouth curled. "I guess you are at a disadvantage, aren't you, *Miss Cameron?* And we have never really been properly introduced."

"Morgan... don't...." Instinctively, she was afraid of hearing what he would tell her.

"Oh, the Morgan part is right enough. But the last name isn't Ross, Miss Cameron. It's Rossiter." His tone was almost conversational, so the only excuse she had for flinching and crying out at the sound of his real name was recognition. "Ah, I see you do remember. Don't you, Miss Cameron?"

Don't lie to me now, Jessica, something inside Morgan was pleading. For God's sake—for the sake of my soul and yours!—don't lie to me now!

When she remained silent, Morgan brought his face closer to hers. "Answer me, damn you!" he grated. "You recognize the Rossiter name and where you first heard it. Isn't that right?"

"Yes. . . ." was the pained response.

"Do you also remember the ten thousand dollars your lover, Cole Hardin, took from the Ellsworth shipping yards office before the two of you skipped town?"

"Yes. . . ."

"And my brother—the man who owned and operated those yards—do you also remember him? Can you describe the look on his face when Cole Hardin planted a knife in his spine?"

"No!" Jessica cried in horrified denial, her hands coming up from her sides to clutch his shirtfront. "Oh, no, Morgan," she moaned sickly. "Oh, God! I never knew—"

"Shut up!"

"But you must believe me," Jessica begged, close to sobbing. "I didn't know about your brother. I'd never have kept quiet if—"

Morgan erupted. He jerked her away from the wall. "Shut your lying mouth!" With every word he gave her a hard, furious shake. Hairpins flew. Her hair tumbled free and flew around her face, buffeted upon the violent storm of his enraged fury. Then, as quickly as it had begun, it was over.

The only sound now in the room was ragged, uneven breathing.

The death grip Jessica had maintained upon Morgan's shirt during his violent outburst had pulled buttons free of their fastenings. Looking at that bared strip of hair-roughened skin, never had she wanted anything so much as to press her cheek against that warm flesh and wish these past minutes away.

Morgan was staring down at a woman he'd never before seen. Her hair had tumbled wildly around her face and shoulders, softening and adding beauty to features that her previous stark hairstyle had made seem harsh and bony. But even that incomparable and rare loveliness paled in significance when Morgan's gaze trailed a streamer of rich auburn silk to the gaping bodice of her chemise. What he found there had him hissing between his teeth.

Jessica saw the muscles of his chest grow taut before she heard that explosive expulsion of air. Her gaze darted to his, and she knew instantly just where he was looking. She began to struggle once more against the hands still holding firm to her shoulders.

Morgan's grip tightened even more cruelly. "Take it off!" he commanded gruffly. The obvious purpose of that wide band of cloth circling her chest had immediately become the cursed symbol of her treachery and deceit, the physical evidence to the enormity of the deception she'd perpetuated all these years.

As hard as she fought, Jessica was no match for his superior strength and agility. Every move she made was easily countered. When she would have clawed his face, Morgan quickly captured her hands and shackled them behind her back. Her bare, kicking feet were effectively curtailed when he simply thrust his legs between her own and pinned her against the wall again, using the leverage of his hips to keep here there, feet dangling several inches off the floor. And this time, while she gasped for air, Morgan wasn't even breathing hard.

The explicitly sexual way their hips were joined brought about a strictly involuntary reaction in Morgan that the lady immediately noticed. Her eyes all but rolled back in her head on a strangled sob. Morgan could have told her he wouldn't have her now if she were the last woman on the last day and she was offered up to him as a parting gift from the gods. That's what he could have told her—if his own body wasn't making a damned liar out of him. He dropped her and stepped back, glad to see she was sufficiently cowed to stay where he left her, trembling and frightened right out of her wits. Damn!

"Remove the binder, Jessica," Morgan again demanded, anger and stubbornness refusing to allow him to relent. "I want to see what you've been hiding beneath that sackcloth and ashes pose all this time." She surprised him by being equally bullheaded, shaking her head furiously in denial. "Lady, this issue isn't up for debate or vote. You'll either remove that damned thing, or I will. Your hands or mine is about the only choice you've got here."

Helpless tears filled Jessica's eyes as she hung her head and resigned herself to the shame and humiliation of giving in to his demand. She could only pray he'd be satisfied with stripping her entirely of dignity. She didn't think she'd survive what very well might follow.

Swallowing hard and biting her lip to control its quivering, she reached up beneath her chemise. With a firm tug, the cloth swathing her chest was drawn down until it pooled uselessly at her waist. With her last reserve of pride, she forced her eyes to remain open and on his face.

Morgan couldn't prevent a harsh "God!" as he watched the once shapeless bodice of her chemise fill to the point of nearly overflowing. Two exquisitely formed breasts—high, firm and generously full—spilled free, swelling above the rounded neckline of a now woefully inadequate undergarment. Only the pouty crests of her nipples remained elusively, tantalizingly hidden—just barely—beneath the straining edges of her chemise. Although Morgan had never measured a woman's desirability by the size or shape of her breasts, he knew with a lamentable certainty that from this day forward, every woman he encountered would be measured by Jessica Cameron's standard and would be judged wanting. For this, if nothing else, he could despise her.

"My, my," he sneered, wanting to lash out. Wanting even more to touch. "You are just chock-full of surprises, aren't you, lady?"

Chapter Eleven

Morgan stripped the quilt from her bed and threw it to her, noting her shock and relief even as she was busily wrapping herself from neck to toe. She'd expected he would rape her, Morgan realized with some shock of his own. A bitter taste filled his mouth.

"You're safe from physical abuse... of any kind," Morgan told her gruffly. "Despite any erroneous impressions I might have already given to the contrary."

Jessica fought the impulse to break out in hysterical laughter. Erroneous impressions? There was no mistaking the bruises on her arms, and elsewhere, from their struggle. Her neck was already aching and going stiff from the shaking she'd gotten. Just what did he consider abusive? Did being cursed at, accused of foul deeds and being degraded beyond all bearing count for nothing?

Since she looked anything but reassured, Morgan moved to the opposite side of the room, putting a safe distance between himself and that delectable body. Because the view from her window offered little in the way of distraction, Morgan couldn't prevent his gaze from wandering back to her. What he saw made him grimace wryly. While his head had been turned, a spark of insurgence had been trying to take fire within her. Obviously, being swathed in cloth was making her feel brave again. It couldn't be allowed. Another tussle might very well get out of hand.

"You'll be safe, that is, *if* you don't start spouting lies again. Now, for someone with your gift of spinning tales, I know that will be difficult, but you'd damn well better try. . . ."

Jessica nodded and averted her face from his warning, though she knew his demands for truth weren't worth a dollop of horse manure. Nothing short of a full confession that she'd been involved in the robbery and his brother's murder would satisfy. And that was something Jessica could not, would not, give him.

Dear Lord! What was she going to do? How could she force him to listen to her, make him understand her inadvertent and essentially innocent participation in Cole Hardin's crimes? His mind was already closed against her. She wouldn't get two truthful words past her lips before he came springing across that bed with murder blazing out of his eyes. But she had to do something!

Making a decision, she drew a shaky breath. "This quilt is hot. May I fetch my dressing gown from the wardrobe?"

Since his own shirt was sticking damply to his heated skin in this stuffy room, Morgan couldn't justify being nasty enough to deny her reasonable request. Besides, the sooner she put that mouth-watering body of hers under wraps, the better he might be able to start thinking straight.

"All right," he agreed gruffly, fixing his attention upon the brick wall beyond the window. He hoped to God her so-called dressing gown would reflect the Widow Miller's frumpy tastes. Hell! Who was he kidding? A nun's habit wouldn't erase the vision of her now. The trip to Fort Smith, and all those miles in such intimate contact, promised to be living—

"Morgan, I swear to you, I had nothing whatsoever to do with either the robbery or your brother's murder."

The softly spoken declaration brought Morgan whirling around, his thinly held restraint snapping again. "Listen, damn you! I've—" The angry tirade was snatched right out of his throat. Morgan could only gape silently. Not only had the lady availed herself of the covering of a simple cotton wrapper, but she'd added the more effective and deadly shield of a six-shooter, as well. And that revolver was pointed straight at his belly. "What the...?"

"Please stay right where you are," Jessica cautioned as firmly as possible, since he was again glaring at her with murderous intent. "Unlike Patrick's gun the other night, this revolver is fully loaded."

Morgan believed her. The reference to the incident three nights past also had him recalling her claim to proficiency with firearms. He could believe that, too. She wasn't handling that gun like a novice. Damn! How could he have been so stupid not to search this room for a weapon when he'd left the photograph earlier? "Lady, you should know that my Sacramento friend, Richard Burke, is a Pinkerton agent. And right now he's stationed in the lobby. I don't think you really want to risk drawing his attention by firing off a shot."

"And I don't think you want to gamble on your friend being able to break down the door *you* bolted before I can pull this trigger, Morgan," Jessica told him with more bravado than she truly felt.

Morgan conceded her point with a grim nod. "You declare your innocence in one murder and then threaten my life with the very next breath. Pardon me if I find some contradiction there."

"I won't let you hurt me, Morgan. No matter what you *think* I've done. Neither will I be terrorized into making a confession just so you can exact more vengeance, inflict further abuse and feel justified in the process." Jessica thought she saw a momentary shadowing of guilt, maybe even a flicker of self-reproach, in Morgan's eyes, but couldn't be certain. If so, the emotions were quickly controlled. He just continued to stare at her. Somehow she found this obdurate silence even more intimidating.

"I am innocent, Morgan," she went on, not understanding the compulsion that drove her. Yes, she was afraid of his temper, of his superior strength and of the terrible punishments and hurt he could inflict. But she was driven by more than fear; she fervently wanted him to believe in her innocence. The contempt in his eyes was killing her.

When Morgan hooked his thumbs in the waistband of his trousers and leaned back against the window, she took his more relaxed posture as a hopeful sign he might now give her a fair hearing. "I knew nothing about your brother until you told me just a little while ago. In fact, I didn't know Cole had robbed the shipping office until several days after we'd left Ellsworth. One of the pouches he'd taken from your safe fell out of his saddlebags. And when I asked him about it, Cole didn't even attempt to whitewash the theft. But he never, never, said anything about a killing. I wouldn't—"

"Yes, I know. You wouldn't have kept quiet about murder," Morgan interrupted, not bothering to hide his skepticism. "But even if I were willing to give you the benefit of the doubt regarding your knowledge of my brother's murder—and I'm not yet convinced by any means—that doesn't explain why you kept quiet about the robbery. Does it?"

I was a bride of less than twenty-four hours, confused and trying desperately to convince myself that the man I'd just married wasn't some awful monster, she cried silently. You see, he'd hurt me so dreadfully the night before....

"You look distressed, Jessica. Could that gun be getting a bit heavy? Or are you simply having trouble manufacturing lies on such short notice?"

Jessica knew then she'd never be able to risk exposing the true horror and shame of that time with Cole to Morgan's mocking scorn. He would rip her soul to shreds with the information. "Cole convinced me the authorities would never believe I hadn't been involved, that I would go to prison...."

"Poor hapless little Jessica," Morgan jeered. "That's not the whole story, though, is it? Ten thousand dollars was...is...a lot of money. Enough to carry you a long way from Scragtown. Wouldn't you have struck a bargain with the devil himself if it meant never having to go back to that stinking shack, or any other place like it...?"

"Cole Hardin *was* the devil!" Jessica hissed while her eyes implored Morgan to understand something he, as a man, was incapable of comprehending.

"Then why did you protect him?" Morgan snapped back.

"I was barely sixteen years old, Morgan," Jessica told him, her voice vibrating with emotion. "Just sixteen and terrified that if I didn't get away from Scragtown soon I'd end up working in Myra Belle Watson's bordello, instead of just living behind it. Cole Hardin claimed he loved me, though I know now he never did. I was alone and frightened most of the time. My father...my father was sick...." She fought not to cry, despairing as she looked for any sign of humanity in Morgan's stony countenance. But when he began to clap his hands together, loudly, slowly, in a travesty of applause, she lost hope. The fight went out of her. She lowered the revolver and offered him no resistance when he came and removed it from her icy fingers.

"Bravo!" he exclaimed, his voice colder than ever as he thrust the revolver into his belt. "That was a flawless performance, Miss Cameron. The perfect blend of drama and pathos to tear at the heartstrings. I found it particularly stirring when you came close to tears. Those short, jerky little gasps that set your breasts aquiver were inspired. However, poignant and effective though that dramatic ploy was, I can't say I'd recommend a repeat performance for a judge or jury."

"A performance?" Jessica protested weakly before painfully accepting Morgan's determination to believe the worst of her. "Yes," she went on sadly, "I suppose that is how you would see this."

Her bleak, dispirited manner brought none of the satisfaction Morgan had anticipated all these years. Instead of savoring sweet victory, he tasted only a galling bitterness. Neither was he particularly proud of the intentional verbal cruelty he'd inflicted just now. But it had been necessary. He didn't dare reveal the grudging compassion he'd always felt for that hapless Scragtown girl. Jessica was far too clever not to turn those sympathetic feelings to her own advantage. Twisting his guts—not to mention the hell she could play with his wits—into hard knots of conflicting emotions was this lady's particular specialty. That she still possessed that power in spite of everything infuriated him. He wanted to hurt her for it. Wanted to punish her for spoiling this moment. Damn the bitch! *He still wanted her!*

"How else could I see it?" he drawled unpleasantly, his fingertips toying with the carelessly belted tie of her wrapper, ignoring her rigid tension and the renewed alarm in her big eyes. "With the evidence of what a skillful little actress you are right before my eyes." A slight tug loosened the garment. It parted to reveal her mouth-watering perfection. "It must have been distressing to keep all that beauty under wraps. To have admiring glances pass you by, all the while knowing that, with a simple adjustment of cloth, you could have every man in this valley on his knees and begging...."

Jessica slapped away his hand before he could touch her and quickly gathered the dressing gown tightly around her again. She no longer feared his physical reprisals. He was far too adept at making her bleed with his razor-sharp tongue. Right now Jessica believed his fists couldn't possibly be more hurtful.

"If I'd wanted to be a whore, Morgan," she told him quietly, "I could have stayed in Scragtown and let my father sell me to Billy Gardiner for the jug of whiskey he carried under his arm."

She couldn't have found a more effective method to shut Morgan up if her response had been calculated. Billy Gardiner's disgustingly graphic depictions of the young Jessie Cameron had made Morgan want to bash his repulsive face in back then. He felt no differently now.

On an expelled breath, Morgan raked his fingers through his hair. "This is getting us nowhere," he grated harshly. "The fact is, lady, I don't give a damn how you came to be with Hardin. My only interest is in getting you to Fort Smith and hearing you recount your story about the money and Hardin's confession to the robbery. As to your involvement—I'll let Judge Parker determine your fate. Hardin's the one I want, because it was Hardin's name my brother whispered as he died...."

Morgan's jaw clenched. He could still see Zach there on the floor before the open safe. Could feel the warm stickiness of his brother's blood soaking through his clothing and the helpless despair of knowing the last words spoken between them had been angry and hurtful ones. He had gone back to the office to apologize, hoping they could begin mending the rift that had grown up between them. That he'd come too late was something he would never forgive himself for. And the only atonement he could make would be with Hardin's blood.

The anguish Jessica saw in his eyes was so profound she felt it deep within herself. Perhaps because she understood what he was feeling so well. This they shared, the emptiness and pain of irrevocable loss...and a mutual hatred for the man responsible.

"Morgan," she said gently, reaching out to offer solace. "I'm so deeply sorry—"

He flinched away with disgust. "Keep your damned condolences! All I want from you is the testimony that will prove Hardin was there in the office that night. Your story will confirm that Zach's dying words weren't wild, aimless ravings. My brother spent his final breath to name his killer and, by God, I'm going to see that bastard hang for what he did! And you're going to help me fashion the noose. If you cooperate fully, freely, I can promise you a fair trial. But if you cross me—"

"When do we leave, Mr. Rossiter?" Jessica broke in calmly. She neither needed nor was she interested in hearing either his promises or threats. Jessica had her own scores to settle with Cole Hardin. Ones that, in her mind, anyway, superseded even the grievous loss of a brother. Today, when she'd thought Morgan to have been sent by Cole, she had come face-to-face with her greatest fear...and her greatest shame: the cowardice that had allowed Cole Hardin to live. God only knew how many others like herself and Rossiter had suffered because she had lacked the guts to kill him years ago.

Morgan dismissed the heated resolve burning brightly in her eyes as just another cunning act. On a short, disbelieving laugh, he said, "What new game is this? No more protestations of innocence or hypocritical offers of sympathy? Suddenly, after all this time, you're all fired up to do your duty as an honest citizen?"

Jessica refused to allow him to goad or wound her further. Her chin lifted. "If you'd told me what you wanted in the first place, instead of storming in here, mean-drunk and raging, as if you meant to tear me limb from limb, we both could have been spared a lot of unnecessary unpleasantness."

"'Unpleasant'?" Morgan said with a soft menace. "Lady, I will happily redefine that word for you if this proves to be just another of your lies. Because if you somehow manage to wiggle your way out of this and Hardin walks away from prison a free man a year from now—"

"Prison? What are you talking about?"

Morgan smirked. "That's right. You wouldn't know about your former lover's misfortune. You were already in Oregon with *Uncle John,* preparing for the grand charade, when Hardin was rounded up by Indian police, along with two other scum, while attempting to rustle some scurvy reservation cows in the Indian territory. The Choctaw took them to Fort Smith. Unfortunately, I was unsuccessful in persuading Judge Parker to charge Hardin with murder, despite my brother's dying words." His forbidding expression spoke volumes regarding the fury and frustration he'd experienced butting heads with the autocratic judge. "But at least the son of a bitch has spent the better part of the past nine years locked up in Leavenworth, sweating out a ten-year sentence and knowing I'm outside searching for the woman who can give Parker the proof he demanded. And I've made damn certain Hardin never had the opportunity to forget the name Rossiter. I see to it he gets regular reminders...."

While delivering this bit of news, Morgan watched Jessica carefully, gauging her reaction. Once again, though, the lady proved herself to be a master of the unexpected.

Jessica Cameron's mouth began to curve slowly upward in what could only be described as a triumphant smile.

"Damn, but you are a sadistic bitch," Morgan observed dryly.

Jessica sobered. "Perhaps I am, Mr. Rossiter," she retorted more sharply than she had previously dared. She had finally reached the limits of her tolerance. "Perhaps I am indeed each and every one of those disagreeable and insulting things you've called me today...and more. Or maybe I'm none of them. Either way, why should you care? All you're interested in—or so you've repeatedly insisted—is my cooperation in testifying against Cole Hardin. Well, I'm giving it to you, fully and freely. In plain words, I will most happily accompany you to Fort Smith. Whether you choose to believe me or not, however, is something over which I have no control."

"Why?" Morgan queried, genuinely curious now. That smile had some significance, and he wanted to know the reason behind it. "Why 'most happily'?"

The answer was one that Jessica could never voice, but she spoke it now in her thoughts. Because though Cole Hardin robbed you of a beloved brother, he took from me something even more infinitely precious: my child.

She turned her face away from Morgan's probing gray eyes, now alight with something other than contempt. "I have my reasons," she said with a soft finality that announced her withdrawal from any further discussion of this topic—or any other, for that matter. She refused to participate any longer in her own victimization.

Morgan persisted in demanding answers for several more minutes, but he gradually realized arguing with the wall would be just about as effective...and productive. Besides, the whiskey he'd guzzled earlier was starting to punish him now with the merciless headache he almost invariably suffered from overindulging, which was rarely, for that very reason. And since the pain only aggravated an already foul disposition, Morgan didn't entirely trust himself to keep even minimal control over his temper.

"We leave Moonshadow tomorrow, when the stage pulls out at noon. In the meantime..." Morgan went and gathered up every article of clothing he could find, not that it took him very long. For a woman with some financial means, this lady had damn few dresses...and all of them were hideous.

"What are you doing?" Jessica demanded when he opened the door and threw her things out into the hallway.

"I'm betting that you won't be tempted to climb out that window, either to escape or summon aid, if it means exposing your secret identity to all and sundry. I'll take that dressing gown, as well."

"No!" Jessica said vehemently, clutching the garment to her, backing away from his advancing threat. "You will not! You are going too far!"

Morgan stopped and rubbed the back of his neck. "Listen," he stated tiredly. "We've been through this before. I'll have it my way—and you know it. So, be a good girl and give me the dressing gown willingly and, as a reward, I'll let you keep a modicum of modesty by not demanding the chemise and drawers, as well...."

He'd made himself perfectly clear. She had a choice between near naked and stripped to the skin. Jessica tore off the wrapper and threw it at him.

Morgan balled it up and stuffed it inside his open shirt, wishing now he'd let her keep the damned thing. Looking at her made his mouth water and his hands itch. On a muttered curse, he stalked to the door, pausing there briefly. "By the way, just in case you start entertaining second thoughts about cooperating or decide to call the local cavalry to your rescue..." Morgan reached into the breast pocket of his shirt for the shiny oval disk he'd forgotten until just now. "So there's no misunderstanding about my authority to take you back to Fort Smith..." He tossed the marshal's badge so it landed practically at her feet. "There's a legal warrant that goes along with that, too."

While she stared down at the badge of a United States deputy marshal, Morgan opened the door.

"Officially stated, Jessica Cameron—you're under arrest."

It was very close to midnight when an exhausted Oramay and a sleepy Patrick returned to the hotel. With a huge yawn, Patrick kissed his mother's cheek and went straight to his room. Oramay lingered in the lobby only long enough to extinguish the gas lamps that had been left burning in anticipation of their late arrival.

She considered checking in with Jessica before retiring but dismissed the idea, deciding they both needed sleep more than a late-night talk.

Oramay had just walked past Jessica's room when she noted the light coming from beneath the hallway door to the kitchen. "Now, who left...?"

The door opened and Morgan Ross stood there, wearing a very serious, and therefore alarming, expression. "Mr. Ross? Is something wrong?"

Morgan tried to manage a reassuring smile for her sake, but failed. "Could I speak with you privately, Mrs. Seibert...?"

Oramay followed him into the kitchen.

Twenty minutes later, her face pale and her blue eyes pained, Oramay rose from the kitchen chair. "I want to see her."

Although the request was softly made, there was no mistaking the undertone of steel in Oramay Seibert's voice.

"Maybe in the morning...."

"*Now,* Rossiter. Right this very minute."

Oramay didn't await his permission. She whirled on her heel and marched straight out of the kitchen. A few feet short of Jessica's room, Richard Burke materialized from seemingly out of nowhere to block her path. Oramay didn't bother with the Pinkerton man. She stopped and looked back at Morgan Rossiter. It was a battle of strong wills, but in the end there had never really been a contest. Morgan relented. "Let her pass, Burke."

Every muscle in Jessica's body tensed at the distinctive click that preceded the opening of her door. She grabbed up her quilt covering and scrambled off the bed, but the quilt slid from her fingers when Oramay stepped into the room.

Jessica was so glad and relieved to see Oramay that she entirely forgot her altered appearance and state of undress, both so clearly manifested by the soft glow of the bedside lantern. But she was immediately reminded when her friend's eyes went wide with shock and her jaw dropped open with gaping astonishment. Shame and dread flooded Jessica then, and she lowered her head and braced herself for the condemnation that was sure to follow.

Surprise temporarily robbed Oramay of both her wits and the ability to speak.

"Lordy, Jessie," she breathed at last. "I always did think you were pretty. But now I can see that the outside is every bit as sweet and beautiful as the inside. And it's a darned shame that stupid jackass of a U.S. marshal can't see it, too."

Jessica lifted her gaze slowly, afraid to believe what she was hearing, until she saw the unqualified affection in Oramay's eyes. Hope blossomed, although she still didn't dare give it free reign. "But you don't know what I've done, don't know how I've—"

"I know *you,* honey. And that's all I need to know," Oramay said firmly, gathering Jessica into her arms to hug her tightly.

Jessica hung on for dear life as the first harsh sob erupted. Then the woman who'd learned to control and ration tears with the frugal restraint of a tightwad safeguarding his money, opened the floodgates and let the anguish pour freely from her soul.

Neither woman was aware of the man who observed them from the darkened shadows of the hallway. Nor did they notice when he stepped inside just far enough to take hold of the doorknob and pull the door closed, granting them their privacy.

Unfortunately, Morgan was unsuccessful in shutting out the sound of those heartrending sobs that threatened to turn him inside out.

Chapter Twelve

The eastbound train was nearly two full days out of Sacramento before Morgan reluctantly allowed the faint possibility that Jessica Cameron's cooperation might actually be genuine—though her motives for such ready compliance escaped him, which also made them highly suspect in his opinion. Richard Burke, however, hadn't agreed there was even the slightest cause for suspicion. In fact, the detective had become so convinced of Jessica's sincerity that he'd dismissed himself from further involvement. The lady didn't need a guard to get her to Fort Smith, Burke insisted, when an escort would serve just as well. And surely a U.S. Deputy Marshal could handle looking after one lone, unresisting little female.

Morgan glanced across the private railroad car that the Pinkerton agency had so generously provided to where Jessica was seated, quiet and pensive, staring out at the encroaching darkness beyond the window. She spent most of her time there, he'd noticed, with her gaze fixed upon the landscape rushing past. At least that was how she occupied her time when he was present. He now understood the full meaning of the term *cold shoulder*.

With a frown, Morgan reached for the silver coffee service and poured himself a second cup. His mouth tightened even more when he saw again her plate of food and how little of it she'd eaten. "Are you brooding, Miss Cameron? Is that why you've had so little appetite these past days? Were you expecting some last-minute legal maneuver or rescue attempt from your friends back in Moonshadow?"

"I'm not brooding, Mr. Rossiter...over anything," was her coolly dispassionate response. "Besides, if you will remember, Mrs. Seibert promised not to summon aid or attempt anything rash—"

"Only to spare you the public humiliation I threatened if she tried."

"Yes, there was that, too." There was no point in telling him that she had begged for Oramay's silence hours before he'd made his nasty threats and warnings. Oramay had wanted to stall somehow until Stanley Turner could be summoned home, but Jessica feared a violent confrontation between Rossiter and the town if anyone tried to stop him from putting her on that stagecoach. Actually, she and the marshal had been in complete accord regarding a quiet and uneventful departure, though he would never credit her for it. Just as she, at the time, would never have believed he would deny himself the satisfaction of parading her around Moonshadow, denouncing and vilifying her to all and sundry, for any reason.

Morgan sipped his coffee and admitted privately that though getting Jessica out of Moonshadow had proved relatively painless—if he discounted the ear-blistering heat of Oramay Seibert's fiery tongue-lashings—he'd not trusted the woman to keep her word longer than it took the dust from the stagecoach to settle. Mrs. Seibert didn't need to call upon the entire town to save Jessica from what she considered an outrageous and wrongheaded injustice. A quiet trip out to the Eldorado would have been sufficient to have Boone Larsen, and probably the Eldorado cowhands as well, come gunning after them. And to protect his Jessie, Larsen wouldn't have hesitated to put a bullet squarely between Morgan's eyes, U.S. marshal or not.

Ordinarily such unquestioning loyalty, especially from people of Mrs. Seibert and Larsen's caliber, would have encouraged Morgan to at least reconsider some of his more unyielding opinions. But not in this case. The lady was all too clearly the quintessential actress. As the Widow Miller, from dress to manner, she'd been entirely believable. So much so that Morgan had questioned his own sanity because of the unbelievably strong attraction he'd felt for such a basically unprepossessing female. Obviously, his instincts had recognized what the eye couldn't perceive: that beneath that sackcloth and ashes pose was the most sensually appealing woman he'd ever encountered. And he wasn't even sure why that was. Oh, there was her undeniably luscious body. But it wasn't altogether that. Nor was she classically beautiful or commonly pretty. She simply had the sultry look of a born seductress, a woman who would burn you alive with the fire and passion that looking at her inspired. Yet...there was also an innocence and elegance about her that was totally at variance with the other. It was a devastatingly dangerous combination for a man's peace of mind.

Looking toward her again, Morgan couldn't prevent the self-deprecating smirk of someone who'd discovered himself the brunt of his own joke. Determined Jessica would not capture Judge Parker's sympathy with her Widow Miller facade, Morgan had gone on a most unusual shopping expedition during their brief time in Sacramento. And he'd been particular about the choices he made. He had scoured Sacramento for the most outrageous costumes he could find, fully intending Jessica to look nothing less than a garish tart when he was done.

He'd failed miserably.

The dress she wore now with its plaid taffeta skirt draperies and plum-colored jacket, was the worst of what he'd thought a bad lot. Though not visible now, the bustled skirt sported an absolutely gargantuan bow above the most excessive riot of ruffles and flounces and ribbons he'd ever seen...anywhere. The cream-colored silk bodice might have been sedate enough, if not for the diamond-shaped lace insert placed squarely between her breasts, revealing in the open-worked design the bounteous swell of flesh and the shadowy cleft in between. And the wide-open lapels of the jacket served only to frame that enticing display.

Yep! That dress had been *exactly* what he'd been looking for. Made even more perfect when an alarmed salesgirl had blushingly confided it had been designed upon the specifications of a local lady with questionable morals, who'd fallen upon hard times before she could pick up the dress.

But despite the garish colors and scandalously extravagant styling, Jessica wore this dress with the confidence and assurance of a woman born to wealth and breeding, as if she belonged to that elite society who thumbed their noses at convention and prevailing trends, choosing instead to determine for themselves what would soon become next year's rage.

And she looked beautiful!

Morgan's slight smile faded. If he'd come back with crimson satin adorned with feathers and cut to the navel, she would probably have ended up looking like a goddamn queen.

Needing some outlet for his suddenly surly disposition, Morgan jumped upon the subject of her birdlike appetite. She was already bordering upon being too slender. If she kept picking at her food this way, there wouldn't be enough left of her to face Judge Parker by the time they reached Fort Smith.

"Is there something wrong with the food, Miss Cameron?" he asked softly. If it was her plan to make herself sick—

The hint of concern she thought she heard in his voice was so extraordinary that Jessica foolishly allowed herself a second's hope he might be softening. The notion was immediately dispelled by the unrelenting contempt she'd grown accustomed to seeing in his eyes. "The food is fine," she told him, once again turning her face back to her study of the darkness, wishing she'd spared herself the disappointment... and the pain.

"Then why aren't you eating?" Morgan persisted.

God! As if he didn't know— "Could you enjoy food or have much appetite in my circumstances, Mr. Rossiter? This is not exactly a pleasure trip...."

He conceded her point even as he was absorbing the wretched misery he'd seen so briefly on her face. So she was miserable? What the hell did she expect? His sympathy? "If you and your uncle had had the good sense to abandon the old family name, I'd have been making this trip back alone," Morgan reminded her nastily, knowing Burke had already filled her in on all the details of how easily the connection between John Miller of Oregon and the family he'd left behind back in Ohio had been made. Or the people who remembered John Miller's grief when he'd received word of his sister's death en route to join him, and his worry when his brother-in-law and only surviving niece had never been heard from again. And those same folks had a great deal to say about crazy ol' John's disappearance some years later, in the company of a young girl.

"That was your only mistake, you know," Morgan continued to taunt. "Otherwise..." It didn't please him to acknowledge, even to himself, that he'd been so completely taken in by her act that he would have left Moonshadow never knowing the very woman he sought had been within his grasp—quite literally on at least one occasion.

"Uncle John feared he was too old to start answering to any name but the one he'd been called by for nearly sixty years. He was concerned he would slip up and draw suspicion." She smiled sadly. "Funny, but I never knew—not until the Pinkerton man told me—that he often would speak of his former home in Oregon, completely forgetting we had told everyone our former home was in the Washington Territory. It's strange no one in Moonshadow ever remarked to me about the discrepancy...."

"They probably thought him a doddering old fool."

Though Morgan's comment was made casually, Jessica took exception to it nonetheless. He could malign her character to his hateful heart's content, but she would not silently tolerate any insults directed toward John Miller. She swiveled around to face Morgan fully, holding the arms of the blue velvet chair to keep herself from coming out of it altogether.

"John Miller was nothing of the kind! He was a good and decent man, who didn't take easily to spinning lies. Every untruth he ever told was for my sake, to protect me. On his own, Uncle John wouldn't have known how to lie if his very life depended upon it! So, call me what you will—rip my character to minute shreds—*but leave my uncle out of this!*"

Even without those hazel eyes flashing green with justifiable outrage, Morgan wasn't so hardheaded that he didn't know when he had hit his own all-time low for despicable. Taking jabs at dead men was scraping the bottom of the barrel. "You are absolutely right, Miss Cameron," he said with a sincerity that had her blinking with astonishment. "My remark about your uncle was uncalled-for... and regrettable. I apologize."

As much as Jessica wanted to set him straight, she wasn't sure his apology was worth it when he put his coffee aside and came to his feet a second later. When he refastened his shirt collar and straightened his loosened tie, her stomach began to knot.

"I'm going to the smoking car for a while," Morgan announced as he pulled on his discarded suit coat, mentally grumbling over the constraining clothing. The simple shirts and trousers he'd worn in Moonshadow had been— With a slight wince he determined it would be best to forget everything about that valley, including all the feelings that had been awakened there.

"You don't smoke, Morgan."

The quiet statement, along with her use of his given name, caused him to pause on his way to the door. What was this? Except for meals and to sleep—and damned little of it, too—Morgan spent most of his time in the smoking car choking to death on the smoke of other men's bad habits. By her own actions and words he wasn't fit company, so surely she couldn't be asking him to stay. "There's usually a card game going on," he stated on a shrug.

"How nice for you." This time Jessica couldn't keep the sarcasm out of her voice, waspishly hoping he would lose that fancy shirt he was wearing. But underlying that wish was another: that he wouldn't go at all. For as difficult as the ever-present tension and his barely restrained hostility was, the hours she was locked in here alone were even worse.

Morgan had been very clear when he'd laid down the rules for this trip. Lucky though they were to have hooked up with the weekly Hotel Express and all the comforts and conveniences this ultraluxurious train offered, Jessica wasn't to leave this comfortable compartment, even to take her meals in the dining car. Despite all the pleasant outer trappings, she was his prisoner. Even allowing her the benefit of the doubt on her sincerity in regards to cooperation, it didn't change the facts or alter that warrant bearing her name.

Morgan turned and looked at her fully. She came slowly to her feet. Neither spoke for several seconds. Finally, Morgan broke the silence. "What is it you want, Jessica?"

Jessica hesitantly bit down upon her lower lip, having no idea how provocative he found that innocent little trait. "A walk...through the train." She saw the anger in his eyes and rushed on before he could speak. "Or just some time out on the platform . . . for some air."

Only a monster would deny her the last. "Come on," he said somewhat gruffly. The gratitude lighting her face made him feel that he really was a monster. She hurried past him, as if fearful he might change his mind.

It was much windier on the open platform between cars than Jessica had expected; its surprising force nearly took her breath away. It was cooler, as well. The temperature inside had been on the warm side and stuffy. She rested her hip against the safety rail and crossed her arms against the chill.

"Too much for you?" Morgan asked when he followed her outside. There was enough moon for him to see that she was trembling slightly. The rush of air, as the train traveled rapidly through the night, was tearing at her hair, whipping soft wisps about her face.

"No!" Jessica disclaimed vehemently, forcing her teeth not to chatter. It really wasn't cold, just cool and refreshing. "It's wonderful. Thank you."

Although there'd been occasions where he'd had to accept it graciously, guilt was not an emotion Morgan relished. He especially didn't care for it being dished up in double portions, all in the space of a single hour. "We're in the desert now. The nights will be very cool and the days probably very hot." Making polite conversation seemed a small amends to offer her.

"What?" Jessica shouted back at him, having caught only every other word between the repetitive clacking of the wheels and the wind. She was also forced to use both hands to keep her hair out of her eyes and mouth.

Morgan stepped closer, preparing to repeat his words. At that moment she raised her hands, her breasts lifting with the same motion. The chilly night air had turned her nipples to tight, hard peaks that not even two layers of cloth could veil adequately. Morgan wished he could blame the weather for the hard swelling of his own body, but it damn certain didn't have anything to do with the cold.

Jessica was entranced by the stars above them. Strange how they seemed to remain constant and still while the earth below rushed beneath her feet at a dizzying pace. The sky was so clear it might have been a dark crystal shot through with diamonds. She moved a few more inches away from the wall of the railroad car, tilting her head farther back as she went, letting the balustrade around the small vestibule absorb more of her weight. The train had been moving smoothly over the stretch of desert, so the jolt of the brief rough patch of track caught her unaware. With a cry of alarm she made a desperate grab for the railing, but her fingers had only brushed the cool metal when strong arms went around her and she was hauled hard up against Morgan's body.

Morgan was mentally cursing himself for being twenty kinds of a careless fool for not realizing how far back she'd been leaning over the rail while he'd been ogling the mouth-watering thrust of her nipples. Now those hardened tips were stabbing him in the chest, contrasting with the softness of the rest of her. He continued to curse himself but he also began cursing at her, as well.

"Dammit, woman! Don't you have any better sense than to hang back over a rail like that? I should have known better than to give you an inch, knowing you'd do some stupid, goddamn thing to keep from going through with your bargain." Part of Morgan's brain accepted he was being unreasonable and irrational, but her near miss had scared him and her nearness was setting him on fire. That neither was intentional on her part just didn't seem to matter at the moment.

A little shaken herself, Jessica gripped those solid shoulders, hanging on tightly, even as her own temper took spark at the unfair accusations he was all but spitting into her face. "You're right, Marshal!" she yelled back at him. "Flinging myself from a moving train in the dead of night, in the middle of the desert, is ten million times more preferable than suffering your hateful disposition for the next thousand miles! And I sure as blazes never bargained to receive the brunt of your revenge—"

Because she spoke too much truth, Morgan had to silence her. "Shut up!" he spat, grabbing a handful of that hair lashing him around the face and neck. The vibrations coming from the wood beneath their feet were moving up his body and hers, creating sensations the like of which he'd never known. Her mouth opened in protest at the sharp tug on her scalp, and whatever reason he might have been clinging to went to hell with the rest of him. He took her mouth with the resigned surrender of a man who already knows his soul is lost and has no reason to give a damn anymore.

In those first seconds while his lips crushed and his tongue plundered, Jessica could only respond with stunned shock. Then came the anger and outrage.

She pressed the heels of her hands hard against his chest; strangled sounds of complaint issued from her throat. How dare he! But when she twisted in an attempt to free herself, the moan that came from him was so helplessly despairing that Jessica knew instantly this was no hateful punishment but a passion beyond his ability to control. That this strong-willed man could be made helpless for want of her created within Jessica a sense of power and a terrible tenderness all at once. There was also her own need to escape, to run from the harsh reality ahead and to stave off the isolation and loneliness within the comforting strength of his arms.

Morgan was lost in the taste of her. When her arms entwined around his neck and her full, soft lips turned giving and warm, her tongue no longer evading but seeking, he shuddered from the fierce, wild need that stole whatever sanity was left in him. Mindless instinct had his fingers working the buttons running the length of her back, but there were so many. He wanted to feel satiny flesh, not silk and taffeta. Even more, he wanted to be buried deep and full within her before reason had a chance to threaten a return. Had they been anywhere other than on this small, rocking platform, Morgan would have put her down and found his way beneath those frustrating layers of clothing.

Only moments before, Jessica had been willing, had believed she wanted to give this man all of herself, but his feverish urgency began to alarm her and cool the awakening stirrings within. Though she knew better than to ask for love, she needed more than a quick animal coupling that would satisfy nothing other than his lust. Neither was she so desperate as to settle for anything less than a modicum of human warmth and kindness. She wanted at least what he had given her that night in Oramay's kitchen. That there could be more went beyond her experience and comprehension. Tearing her mouth from his, she prepared to fight him with all her strength.

To her regret, as misfortune would have it, Morgan's frustration with cloth and limited space had penetrated the red haze of an insane desire. And with typical male perversity, Morgan shifted the blame for his own weaknesses and failings squarely upon Jessica's shoulders. God forbid he should take responsibility for his own desires!

His eyes were nearly black as he glared down at her. "As you've discovered, *lady,*" he grated in a voice thickened by the force still pounding through him, "I can be seduced—anytime, anywhere. But I won't be swayed. The only thing you'll gain is this...." Morgan dragged her hand down between them and crudely emphasized his warning by pressing her palm firmly against the hard flesh straining to burst free of his trousers. "So, if your game is to bargain your body in exchange for freedom, be advised it won't work!"

"Game?" Jessica croaked, breaking free of him. She shook with the rage and hurt of his unjust judgment of her, just another in an increasingly long list of such charges. "If that is indeed my game, what's yours, Marshal Rossiter? What kind of man would allow himself to be seduced—anytime and anywhere—by the very woman he believes involved in his own brother's murder? But one moment ago you would have yanked up my skirts and taken me... right here... against this very wall... with all the conscience and family loyalty of a rutting stag in season! How would your brother feel about you copulating like an animal with his murderer's whore? Would he be proud?"

Her adder's tongue had struck a vein, and Morgan retaliated in kind, without thinking. "And how would you feel if I told you your sainted Uncle John, on his own and for his own reasons, lied through his teeth when he told you your father was dead?"

"My father *is* dead," Jessica insisted even while she was backing away from him, her hands coming up as if to ward off some expected blow. "Uncle John got a letter years ago...."

"A letter that conveniently came just weeks before your arrival in Oregon. One that you never saw. But there wasn't any letter, Jessica. And no kindhearted Ellsworth matron to nurse your father through his last days, either. Because as of one month ago, Jack Cameron was hale and hearty and living happily on a prosperous farm just outside Ellsworth...with his wife and their two young sons!"

Jessica reeled. With the wind gusting around her, she suddenly couldn't seem to draw air into her lungs. Her head began to spin and her legs buckled. She was only half-aware of being carried back inside and of the steady stream of verbal self-flagellation coming from the man who lowered her gently into a chair. But the smell of brandy beneath her nose brought her around quickly enough. She shoved it away.

Morgan didn't argue with her this time. He just set the glass aside, feeling every kind of heel possible. "Listen, Jess, I know your uncle only meant the best—"

"Go away!" she whispered, turning her face away from him so he wouldn't see the tears. "Please...just leave me alone...."

Sparing her himself was the very least he could do for her. "We'll talk about this again in the morning." He left, not bothering to padlock the door behind him.

Jessica sat stone-still, staring fixedly at the brandy snifter he'd left on the table beside the chair. So...Papa was alive and well, living happily with his new family. Part of Jessica rejoiced at the news, but a bitter part couldn't forget how he'd been the last time she had seen him. Obviously, he'd straightened himself out and found something to love and treasure more than the whiskey—a reason to live. She hadn't been able to do that for him. Her only value in his eyes had been as an object of trade for his beloved whiskey.

Almost absently Jessica found her fingers curling around the brandy snifter, lifting it from the table. An ugly laugh left her mouth as she lifted the glass in toast. "To you Papa, and to your new life." She tossed the liquid down her throat, closing her eyes against the fiery path it took. It did take some of the chill from her soul.

Also on the table was the bottle Morgan had poured from. Jessica reached for that, too, and refilled her glass, hoisting it again. "And to my stepmother and new brothers." This time it didn't burn so terribly going down.

After the third glass, she lost count. But somewhere before the bottle was finally empty, she softly cried, "Oh, Papa, why couldn't you have loved me?"

Chapter Thirteen

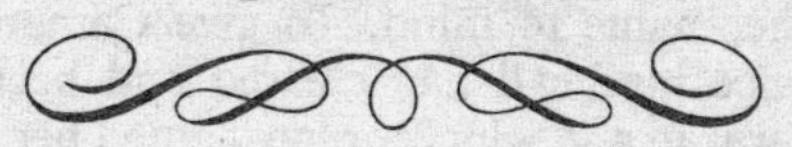

Morgan looked in on the sleeping woman he'd had to put to bed when he returned. She'd not had a very restful night despite the brandy she had consumed. She had tossed and turned and muttered, sometimes jerking violently. Then she would quiet for a time before the process would start all over again. He'd kept watch throughout the night, fearing she had made herself truly ill. But each time he'd checked for fever, her brow had been cool, if somewhat clammy to the touch. He noted that once more she had kicked off the sheet. This time he didn't bother to cover her up again, since it was nearing noon and getting hotter than hell in here. The realization that some of the heat he felt was being caused by the sight of her barely clad form only made him grimace with total self-disgust.

Her aim had been perfect last night when she had hurled those charges at him. And because she had drawn blood, he'd struck back. Well, he'd wanted to hurt her. Clearly, he'd been successful. He knew very well Jessica's aversion to liquor of any kind and also the reason underlying that strong prejudice.

Damn Jack Cameron anyway! If John Miller had fibbed about Cameron's death, it was undoubtedly to protect his niece, just as she'd said, from any further abuse and neglect from that sotted excuse for a father she'd been cursed with. Miller had probably logically assumed his brother-in-law was indeed dead from what Jessica must have told him about his dissipated life. And he would have been—had Morgan not come searching for that auburn-haired girl.

God! He didn't think he would ever entirely forget the god-awful stench in that shack where he had found Jack Cameron. And the filth. Or the number of days it had taken—weeks, actually—to purge the bastard's whiskey-soaked brain sufficiently to recall that he had a daughter, let alone call her name to mind. To give Cameron his due, however, once his head had cleared and he realized the trouble she was in and why Morgan wanted her so urgently, ten thousand horses couldn't have dragged any information out of the man. It was damn certain he never mentioned any relatives in Oregon, and some detective back in Ohio had done some pretty damn slipshod work in not finding out about Mrs. Cameron's older brother, gone West.

Jessica deserved to know that her father had protected her with his silence all these years. She should hear the story of the time Morgan, in his frustration, had quite sincerely threatened to beat the information out of Jack Cameron.

"Do your best, young man," Cameron had replied. "Somebody should have beaten the living hell out of me three years ago. So, start pounding away, for all the good it will accomplish. The least I owe my Jessie now is my silence. Just try not to kill me. Dying would be too easy. My torment will be living with myself sober, so I can't escape the shame and guilt of what I've done."

Jack Cameron had been true to his word. To Morgan's knowledge, he'd not taken another drink in all these years. Jessica needed to hear that...and more. First and foremost, she needed to hear Morgan admit aloud what a first-class son of a bitch he'd been last night. He hadn't appreciated hearing the unvarnished truth of his own weaknesses and failings. And like a spoiled brat, he had thrown a tantrum and inflicted his thin-skinned fury on the unfortunate person who'd dared point out his imperfections.

"And why can't you answer her question, Rossiter?" he asked himself savagely. "What kind of man are you, indeed? You do covet this woman—so much it hurts, inside and out. How is that possible if you truly believe her guilty of all you've charged her with?" His voice was hushed as he continued to gaze down at this sleeping beauty. "And who are you, Jessie Cameron? The innocent bystander, the accidental participant you claim? Or the reigning, uncontested queen of fraud and deception?"

The dream always began pleasantly enough, with a little girl skipping and twirling through a big field of ripening wheat. In her hand, swinging as she went, was a small basket she was carrying out to her papa. When she saw him, she waved excitedly in greeting. How fine and handsome he was with his russet hair catching the warm sunlight. When he extended his arms to her in welcome, she began to run.

It was always then that the dream began to change. The once-sunny sky began to darken, going so murky it was hard to see the man she was rushing to meet. The wind turned cold, making her long for the warmth of his arms. And when she saw them within reach, the little girl hurled herself at him with a glad cry that became a wail of hurt when he backhanded her away while jerking her basket out of her hand at the same time. Only it wasn't a basket anymore, but a slender bottle filled with amber-colored liquid.

Then, as if he'd been swallowed up by the swirling fog, her papa was gone and she was totally alone. The wheat field was no more. In fact, in all directions there was only endless emptiness and a silence so profound it was terrifying. She felt trapped by it, walled in, as if she were being buried alive in a place smaller than a coffin and grayer than death itself. She began to run in circles, going around and around, trying to escape this nothingness; fear and panic were her only companions, her pounding heart the only sound.

And then she heard the faint, muted sound of a baby's cry....

* * *

Jessica jerked herself awake on a strangled scream that never really materialized in a throat more parched than the desert itself. The groan that followed when she attempted to lift her head off the pillow was very much the same. A great many kinds of physical aftereffects commonly followed her nightmare, but never before had she experienced this blinding pain. She made another attempt to rise, rolling her body nearer the edge of the mattress, thinking to climb out on her hands and knees if necessary. Unfortunately, all she succeeded in doing was rolling herself right off the bed, landing facedown on the floor, where she lay still, crying from a misery the like of which she'd never known.

Having heard the soft thud, Morgan found her prostrate atop the blue-and-gold patterned carpet. As gently as he could, he lifted her and sat her upright on the bed again, drawing the sheet around her shoulders.

Jessica was suffering too greatly to remember, let alone care, about the terrible scene between them. She just looked at him in mute agony and rasped, "Am I dying?"

Having more than a passing acquaintance with what she was going through, Morgan smiled gently. "Undoubtedly that would be a blessing of sorts. But, no, I'm afraid you'll live to remember, with regret, the nasty kick that comes out of a bottle of brandy. Do you think you can sit up there by yourself for a minute or two?"

Jessica attempted a nod and pitched forward. Morgan caught her and held her steady while he stacked and fluffed pillows, resettling her more securely against them. Her eyes fluttered shut and were still closed when he returned with a glass of water and two headache powders he'd begged off a kindly looking woman in the dining car this morning. "You haven't passed out on me again, have you?" he asked. The negative croak he received in reply was the only sign of life in her. Morgan mixed the powders and held the glass to her lips.

It tasted awful but at least it was cool and wet. However, holding her head upright even that long was excruciating.

She fell back against the pillows again. "My God," she whispered, "how did my father survive this day after day?"

Morgan heard a deeper pain in her voice. "I doubt even he has the answer to that, Jess," he responded gently while his fingers began to smooth over her brow in a sweeping motion, changing the rhythm with his thumbs as they worked over the bridge of her nose. Even more than attempting to ease the ache, he wanted to keep those haunting eyes closed while he spoke. "I'm sorrier than hell for last night, Jess," he said with a humbleness she couldn't possibly begin to appreciate, because she couldn't possibly know how unfamiliar he was with humility. "My actions all around were inexcusable, so I won't even try to justify them. Except to say the truth hurts."

"Apology accepted, Morgan," Jessica said wearily, though an apology wasn't what she wanted. She wanted him to believe her. Unfortunately, without revealing in entirety the whole shameful and painful truth of her past, she was asking him to believe on trust alone.

"About what I told you regarding your father... You should know—"

"He's alive and happy. Yes, it was a shock to hear, but I'm glad you told me. Yesterday, I didn't think I had a single living relative on this earth. Today I know I still have a father, a new stepmother and two younger brothers. That's hardly bad news, is it?"

Despite her attempt to cover it, Morgan heard the hurt in her voice that went deeper than the misery pounding through her skull. "You don't understand—" he pressed.

She cut him off, opening her bloodshot eyes to gaze at him pleadingly. "Please," she whispered. "I'm not up to this right now. Besides, your voice is so *loud*."

Morgan knew she was evading a subject she had no intention of discussing...now or ever. It only confirmed that the wounds concerning her father went deep and were still pretty raw. She also wanted to avoid him and what had happened between them last night. Not that he blamed her. "Does my rubbing your brow bother you... in any way?"

Jessica knew what he was asking, only she didn't have the answer. His touch, by all rights, should sicken her, but it didn't. She took the comfort as a starving child would accept any kind of sustenance. Beggars could hardly be choosy. And with the aborted version of her dream still haunting the edges of her befuddled consciousness, Jessica needed his touch. "It feels good," she admitted, giving herself up to the pleasure as she'd not done before.

It felt pretty good to Morgan, too—to his everlasting damnation. She had the most wonderful skin. He could have run his fingers and hands over her satiny flesh without cessation, into eternity, and never have tired of the feel of her.

Desire, distrust and a myriad of other emotions he couldn't begin to sort out were doing battle within him. And for the first time in many years, Morgan Rossiter wasn't in charge. All he could do was stand on the sidelines and await the outcome, helpless against the dictates of fate.

When she once again slipped into deep and seemingly peaceful slumber, Morgan left her. Going out onto the platform, he suffered the scorching sun and heat for a time. Then, on impulse, he went and removed the padlock from the door. Putting all his strength behind the throw, he hurled it out into the desolate Utah plains.

Two hours later, Jessica bolted upright in bed, the sound of her own bloodcurdling scream echoing in her ears. Burying her face in her hands and drawing up her knees, she began to sob while tremors quaked through her from head to toe.

"What the—" Morgan rasped as he charged through the curtain. "What is it? Are you ill?" he demanded in alarm. Her only response was a furious shake of her head. "Nightmare, then?"

"Yes," Jessica sobbed while she began to take deep breaths to calm herself. This time she'd experienced the full and complete horror, in all its clarity and terrifying realism. Clearly, the news of her father coupled with the brandy's effect and her ever-increasing apprehension regarding what lay ahead for her at journey's end, had regenerated the beasts hiding in the shadowy darkness of the corners of her mind.

Morgan pressed a washcloth into her hands. "Here, wash your face with this. Then, if you possibly can, you should get up and try to eat something. Do you think you can manage that?"

Jessica nodded on a deeply drawn breath.

"Good," he said in the overly cheerful tone of an adult talking to a sickly child. He fetched her wrapper and placed it across her knees. "Don't try doing anything so strenuous as dressing." When Jessica gave him a suspicious, sidelong look, he held up his hands. "You see before you a reformed man, determined to behave himself."

If it kills you, Jessica thought ruefully. But she also agreed that trying to get herself into one of the outlandish costumes he'd purchased, with all their buttons and bows and gewgaws, was more than she could handle at the moment.

Ten minutes later she emerged from behind the curtain, a little wobbly in the knees, but she managed to cross the room to the small walnut dining table on her own.

Morgan noticed her only attempt at repairing her appearance had been to fashion her tangled hair into a single, thick braid that hung down the middle of her back. "You'll feel better with some food in your stomach," he assured her, even as he watched her face turn slightly green as he uncovered a plate of cold meats, fresh fruit and a light roll. Pouring her a glass of chilled lemonade, he passed it across the table. "Start with a few sips of this."

His solicitous manner was a welcome improvement, but Jessica couldn't help but regard it guardedly. The sweet-tart beverage was refreshing, washing away any remaining residue of overindulgence, soothing her throat. With caution she nibbled on some cold sliced turkey, growing braver with every bite, surprising herself with how hungry she was.

Seeing the wry grin on his face as she gobbled up her food, Jessica shifted on her chair uneasily. "It's very warm, isn't it?"

"It's hotter than hades," Morgan amended. "But if we opened windows, the dust would cover everything and everyone within seconds. Earlier I arranged for a tub to be brought in so you might bathe. I'll go now and let the porter know you're ready."

He was nicer about it, but autocratic as usual, leaving before she had a chance to refuse or thank him for his thoughtfulness. Soon there was a procession of railroad employees marching in and out of the compartment, tidying, changing bed linens and filling a moderate-size brass tub with lukewarm water. When all was done to his satisfaction, Morgan draped his jacket over his arm and prepared to leave.

"If you are feeling well enough, I thought we'd dine in the dining car this evening."

Jessica's gaze flew to his, her eyes wide with surprise... and warm pleasure, as well. "Do you mean it?"

Morgan was uncomfortable with her childlike wonder and gratitude. It made him want to take her in his arms and hold her tight. No desire or hot passion, just tenderness. That scared the hell out of him. "I'll be back to collect you about six o'clock."

She didn't notice his slight gruffness, though she did take note of his subtle way of letting her know she was guaranteed privacy for these next few hours. For once, her stomach didn't knot with dread. "Thank you. I'll be ready."

She was hip-deep in the restorative, tepid water of the bath before she realized she'd not heard the infamous sound of the padlock snapping shut, though she didn't question that the door was securely locked. But with a chiding scowl she banished such distressing thoughts. She wasn't going to allow any unpleasantness to spoil the present pleasure and the relief from nightmares and worries it brought—momentarily, at least.

The lilac-scented soap pleased her senses, and she spread the rich lather from head to toe, luxuriating in the indulgence. For so long she'd denied herself such feminine pampering, and she refused to feel sinful for it now. Oramay would be right proud of her for making this small concession.

Dear heaven! How she was going to miss that woman! The thought sent a pang of renewed pain coursing through her.

Well, so much for tranquility, she thought with a sad smile. Within minutes she was rinsed of soap and standing beside the tub, her head and body wrapped with soft and absorbent towels.

Actually, despite her concern over how Oramay was managing now with the hotel, Kathleen and the twins and Patrick, thinking of Oramay was actually one of the more pleasant ways to occupy her mind. She was homesick for them all already. Since yesterday, their importance in her life seemed even more significant. A family—a true family—was made up of people who could count upon one another during the good times and the bad. Especially the bad. Oramay's ready acceptance, the nonjudgmental way she'd listened to Jessica's story and her unwavering faith in both Jessica's character and innocence in spite of it all, was the true stuff upon which the foundations of families were made.

And Jessica had made very certain her true family in Moonshadow would not suffer for the sins of her past should things not work out as well as Oramay seemed to believe they would. With the written instructions Jessica had sent Stanley Turner, Oramay's bank account would by now have become a little fatter. Jessica had taken the precaution after John's death of giving Stan her power of attorney, so she'd left it to him and Boone to determine if the Eldorado should be sold right away or continue as it was for the time being. But she had also told Stan that should her absence from Moonshadow last more than a year, then he should sell the ranch and divide the proceeds as she'd broken them down for him, among her extended family of friends and neighbors. The list, she'd discovered with pleased surprise, was longer than she might have ever hoped or dreamed.

While Jessica busied her hands drying and working the tangles from her thick, long hair, her thoughts obstinately kept straying to less-pleasant topics. She wished she could share, even in small measure, Oramay Seibert's fierce confidence that no judge with a "brain bigger than a walnut" would hold her responsible for crimes committed without her knowledge.

"Oh, you'll get a stern lecture," Oramay had stated, crediting her years of listening to Stan run on and on about the law for her expertise. "He'll dress you down for your crime of omission, but he's not going to slap you in prison for being too young and ignorant to know any better. And too afraid of that bastard...." Oramay had added softly with a hug.

Jessica dashed away the tears threatening to spill. How could she convince a strange judge when Morgan didn't even want to give her the benefit of the doubt? And regardless of that problem, she also had Cole Hardin to face again. She dreaded and feared that most of all. Firstly, because if anything went wrong, if her credibility was rejected by a jury...

That brought a good hard shudder, with another to follow on its heels. Because it was also Cole Hardin who possessed the most potentially damaging information against her: the question of just what exactly had happened to the stolen money Cole had stashed away on that isolated farm.

If Morgan Rossiter had been present at that moment, he would have seen an exact replica of the puzzling smile he'd seen when he'd told Jessica of Cole's imprisonment. And if he knew the reason behind that smile, he just might do a little smiling himself—if he could bring himself to believe the outlandish tale, that was.

Cole wouldn't believe it, not in a million years. It would be beyond his limited comprehension, and he had more reason to know her motives and state of mind than anyone.

So how could Jessica expect Morgan, or anyone else, to accept even the remote possibility of *anyone* being able to use nearly ten thousand dollars for fire kindling? But that was exactly what she'd done. She had fed the fire with Cole's ill-gotten gains... and she'd enjoyed every minute of watching it burn! That gratification was tenfold now. Because the only reason Cole would have been rustling scurvy reservation cattle was to buy his next meal! Jessica, though she'd been thousands of miles away, had put Cole Hardin in prison, and he knew it. He would also kill her for it if he got the opportunity.

The money was the primary reason she'd taken on a new identity and appearance all those years ago. She'd had to hide from the threat of Cole Hardin's revenge. He would never have come after his wayward wife, but the wayward wife he believed had the money he'd stolen...

She might very well need more than Stanley Turner's legal services before this was all over. If Cole got out of jail, she might need the intervention of a miracle to keep her alive.

Chapter Fourteen

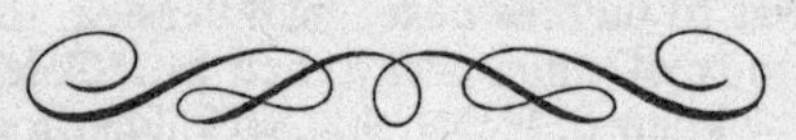

The elegant dining car was everything Jessica had anticipated and more. Brass kerosene lanterns, mounted within the inlaid paneling between velvet-curtained windows, were casting a soft, romantic glow. A clerestory roof gave the impression of space where there was actually very little. And, of course, only the finest linens, china and tableware were in use.

So why then was she wishing she'd never come?

Jessica continued her study of the patterned ceiling and tried not to squirm in her chartreuse silk dress, while every ounce of her self-discipline was brought to fore to keep her hands from covering her exposed upper chest. But she was acutely aware of the number of times she kept fussing with the black ruching there. Common sense told her the square-cut neckline was fashionably modest, but Jessica was unaccustomed to exhibiting *any* flesh other than her hands and face. And if she wasn't on display, why was every man in the room gawking at her?

Morgan swirled the wine inside the glass he held and watched her fidget, his mouth quirking in an attempt to restrain a smile. At first he'd been perplexed by her nervousness, until he'd noticed how her hands automatically rose to the neckline of her dress as every gentleman passed by. Or the way she would suddenly become fascinated with the ceiling when she caught someone quite openly admiring her special beauty. The attention she was receiving had its effect on Morgan, as well. He was alternately smug and contentious enough to bust a few gaping jaws all at once. However, if she didn't come to accept her admirers, the evening would be spoiled for her.

"They are only staring because you look so lovely this evening, Jessica. Exceptionally lovely," he added.

His low, softly uttered compliment caused her stomach to contract strangely. She lowered her gaze to his and suffered another funny little quaking inside. Tonight those gray eyes were the color of smoke. The thick, dark smoke usually seen rising above raging hot fires. "I... I'm not accustomed... I'm not sure I like being so... *noticed.*"

Yes, he supposed it had been a good long while since the world had seen the genuine Jessica. But that was a subject not for consideration tonight. "I see you made a few alterations to your dress."

"That I did," she replied in a way that dared him to challenge her right to remove the horrendous profusion of bows and tassels. Unfortunately, there hadn't been anything she could do about the tiers of silk fringe running from the snug dropped waist to the floor. The fringe undulated in a most ridiculous and irksome manner when she walked. "I borrowed your razor to make the adjustments. I hope you don't mind."

"Not at all," Morgan said politely. Privately, he was kicking himself for being so careless as to leave his razor where she might find it. Then again, since she'd told him, he thought he could assume she wasn't planning to cut his throat while he slept anytime soon. "Besides, I can't argue with the improvements," he went on. "If I remember correctly, that particular dress was a little—well, it seemed..."

"Ridiculous?" she supplied archly. "Excessively ornamental? Bordering on horrid? And more suited for the bearded lady performing in a carnival sideshow?"

Morgan's grin didn't hold a single ounce of guilt. In fact, it was more admiring for the clever and plucky way she'd taken him to task for her outrageous wardrobe. Every single costume had something outlandish about it, such as the fringe on this one. However, Morgan had once again found himself hoisted with his own petard when he'd walked behind her through the train compartments earlier. What that fringe did when she moved, and the thoughts it inspired, were enough to make one particular man reconsider his intelligence. And though the greenish-yellow hue of the dress wasn't the most flattering for her pale complexion, it brought out the green in her hazel eyes in a way that made up, in spades, for any negatives. Though he was hard-pressed to claim that translucent square of satiny-looking flesh exposed by the low-cut bodice a negative under any circumstance.

Jessica began to squirm under Morgan's appreciative stare, which was far more unsettling than any other in this room. She fussed with the wispy tendrils of hair tickling her bare neck. His gaze followed. She studied the burgundy-colored velvet curtains, only to give him the advantage of her profile. But when his eyes rested upon her mouth, Jessica suddenly realized that, in her agitation, she'd begun chewing her bottom lip as she always did in uncomfortable situations.

She wasn't the only uncomfortable one. Morgan's rebellious thoughts were causing him to wonder what might have been. Things could have turned out so very differently, if Jack Cameron had been then the man he was now. Morgan might have met this woman under other circumstances. Their paths might have crossed as she strolled one of Ellsworth's streets, a pretty young girl catching a young man's appreciative eye.

Some of the tension between them was relieved when their dinner arrived. The sirloin tips smothered in a fine French sauce gave them something to converse about. But when their meal had been consumed, her coffee and Morgan's port served, an awkward silence once again rose between them.

Morgan lifted the carafe their waiter had left and saw how she followed the movement. "Are you certain you wouldn't like the waiter to bring you a glass and join me?" The face she made was so uninhibited and expressively comical that Morgan laughed aloud.

She liked the sound of it, rich and deep and genuine. Tonight he'd once again been Morgan the Charming, but without the affected seductive smiles and roguish looks. In fact, she found his natural charm even more appealing, yet not one whit less devastatingly sensual. "I wouldn't dream of breaking my vow of abstinence. I'm afraid the misery far outweighs the benefits."

He knew she was talking about the wine, but he was wondering if the same opinion might be applied to many other of life's pleasures, in her case. Otherwise, how could she have lived a virtual nun's existence all those years in Moonshadow? It wasn't only sex. Jessica, from what little he knew, had rarely allowed herself to participate in fun or excitement of any kind.

Because of her aversion to spirited beverages, Morgan only allowed himself another sip or two before he placed his napkin atop the table. "Would you like to see more of the train before we return to our compartment?"

And prance by every passenger with her skirt jiggling provocatively? Jessica thought. No, definitely not! Claiming fatigue, she thanked him kindly for the evening. It had been wonderful—too wonderful—making the reality of their true relationship and the circumstances more painful. If not for Cole Hardin, they might have been friends. As it was, they couldn't even converse for the number of unpleasant and taboo subjects hindering any possible discourse.

Those harsh truths were even more emphatically driven home when they stepped onto the vestibule of the private car and Jessica noticed the absence of the padlock. She turned and looked up at Morgan in bewilderment but with a dawning hope. Too much hope.

The expression in her eyes made Morgan regret that insane impulse earlier in the day. It was unfair to let her believe anything had essentially changed between them. His cruelty had been unnecessary, and tonight had been his way of offering what amends he could, but he couldn't allow her to think it might have meant more. "The lock broke earlier today. I'll be getting another when the train stops in Cheyenne tomorrow."

Jessica's face fell, but she recovered quickly. Her expression was sad when she said, "I only wish you could believe me just a little. But that's asking a great deal, I realize. Good night, Morgan."

On that she walked straight through the compartment to take refuge in the privacy of her sleeping quarters. She didn't need to hear the silence beyond the curtain to know he'd once again taken himself off to the smoking car.

She prepared herself for bed, even going so far as to make up the bed setter out in the parlor so Morgan would be spared that chore when he returned, which would be very late, she knew.

Then Jessica propped her back against the pillows and stared fixedly ahead, refusing to allow her eyelids to droop, pinching herself hard every time they did. She had no intention of sleeping any part of this night, because she knew what awaited her in the shadows of her dreams.

Morgan had been back a good hour, lying on his back in the bed she'd thoughtfully made up for him. His arms were crossed behind his head, and his knees were drawn up so his feet wouldn't dangle off the end. He was also grinding his teeth against the unwanted desire crawling through his belly. Wanting Jessica, unfortunately, was a malady he was just going to have to suffer, because there apparently was no cure—at least none...

He frowned when he heard those first faint mumblings and incoherent groans that told him she was having another bad dream. He was already reaching for his trousers when her scream—so chilling and terrible it brought gooseflesh—rent the air.

Jessica was sitting up, her arms clutched tightly around her legs, her face pressed against her knees, when he entered, still struggling with the buttons of his trousers. But the sound of her gasping sobs and the sight of her quaking form wiped all traces of triviality from Morgan's mind. "Dear God, Jess," he breathed with soft concern, reaching out and laying his hand upon one trembling shoulder. At the touch, she sprang like a cat, leaping off the bed to attach herself to his neck in a hold that was nothing short of strangling. Of their own volition his arms encircled her slenderness.

She couldn't clutch Morgan hard enough or get close enough to his strength and warmth. It was so cold where she'd come from, so lifeless and dead. And he was so alive and vital and real. She could feel his heart beating, knew the rise and fall of his chest and heard the soft, deep sounds of his comforting words. She never wanted it to end....

Morgan knew he'd better put a stop to this soon before comfort turned into something else altogether. It wasn't very noble of him, but the feel of her beneath that too-thin layer of her night rail was creating some pretty profound changes in his lower body. He cursed that willful part of himself even as he tried to adopt a fatherly role.

"There now," he soothed, patting her back. "It's all right. You'll be fine now." Gently, he attempted to pull her arms from his neck. But not yet ready to give up his comfort, Jessica instead pressed even closer, reaching higher, so that her face was buried against his throat and he was fitted more intimately to the softness between her thighs.

Morgan groaned with the effort it was costing him not to lower his hands to her hips and bring her even closer. With a supreme exercise of will, he used his superior strength to force her, as gently as he could, away from him, lowering her until she was once again sitting on the mattress. He kept hold of her shoulders but made sure there was a full arm's length between them as he asked, "Better now? Do you think you'll be able to sleep, or do you want me to sit beside you for a little while?" That last concession wasn't a wise one, he knew. But those big, haunting eyes, so filled with fear and the bright sparkle of tears, wouldn't let him just turn on his heel and walk out. "Why don't you lie back . . . ?"

Jessica resisted the slight pressure on her shoulders. "I need you to hold me, Morgan," she said quietly, earnestly. "Will you hold me?"

He looked at her a very long time before he said, "I can't do that, Jess. Because if I crawl into that bed with you, I won't be able to stop myself from giving you much more than comfort. I'm sorry, but that's the way it is."

He would have turned and left her then, but Jessica caught his hand and drew it to her breast. "Stay with me, Morgan. Please." She simply could not face the rest of this night alone.

The soft fullness of her filling his palm very nearly broke his resolve. "Listen, I know I said it hatefully before, but . . ."

She came up on her knees and with her free hand drew his head down. His stiff-necked determination to be honorable didn't make it easy for her. "I know," she whispered against his mouth. "It won't change anything. I accept that, Morgan. Stay. . . ." Her lips roamed his cheek and jaw, playing the seductress but having no real idea how to go about it.

If he'd known her quandary, Morgan could have told her she was doing just fine. The butterfly brushings of her lips on his face, the brief passes she made over his mouth, were teasing him to distraction. With the hand he had kept clenched at his side, he took a fistful of her thick, silken hair and pulled her head back. For the sake of his own conscience, he made one final effort, though it was an essentially empty one, for his thumb was already tracing circles around the crest of her breast. "Be very sure, Jessica."

Her imploring "Please" was never fully uttered. Morgan's kiss was taking the very breath from her lungs while his hand was molding, shaping and reshaping the contours of her breast.

Though he wasn't hurting her, Jessica couldn't stop herself from anticipating the moment when his touch would turn rough and she'd know that cruel squeezing. Something of her tension must have alerted Morgan. He lifted his head and his hand fell away.

Morgan searched her face but didn't see any real fear, only a cautioning uncertainty. The words "rutting stag in season" came back to haunt him then. The way he'd been devouring her mouth must have brought that unfortunate incident to her mind, as well. He cupped his hands gently around her face and then proceeded to reassure her in a manner more eloquent than mere words. His kisses became soft, teasing, as he gentled the apprehension right out of her. All the while, though, he was fighting the terrible urgency of having wanted her for too long. He'd not had to struggle this much for control since he had been an overanxious kid and literally too full of himself to even consider seriously his partner's pleasure.

Jessica reveled in his tenderness, and when his fingers began working the drawstring neck of her night rail, she felt only a small twinge of unease as the gown began to slide down over her shoulders. But she couldn't stop her eyes from drifting shut when the fabric pooled at her waist, baring her upper body to his gaze.

Morgan felt his breath catch. He'd known she was perfect, but he hadn't dreamed how perfect. The only light came from a lantern in the other room, so the exact color of her nipples was difficult to determine. He only knew they were pale and small with a natural poutiness that begged for the touch of a man's mouth. He didn't deny them or himself but bent to taste and savor, first one and then the other, using only his tongue and concentrating only on the hardening centers.

Jessica's eyes flew open at the first wet touch, and something stirred within her, a feeling so strong it was frightening. In defense her hands went to his head, tangling in his thick hair to draw him away. Instead, she could only hold on tightly when those swirling, lapping strokes discontinued and her nipple was drawn into his mouth. Jessica gasped at the sensation, feeling that gentle tugging deep within her. She wanted to give herself over to that deep pleasure, but the nightmare still lingered too strongly and the association made with his rhythmic suckling denied her any joy she might have found in this.

"Kiss me, Morgan," she demanded.

"I am," he insisted as his mouth moved to partake of the ignored breast, getting only a brief, tantalizing taste before her demand—uttered with harsh urgency—forced him to abandon one delicious bounty for another.

This time Morgan kissed her the way he wanted, deeply, his tongue searching, stroking, until she sighed and began kissing him back with a need as powerful as his own. With a groan, he pulled her hard up against him, lifting her off the bed so her gown went slithering down over her hips. He filled his hands with the tight, soft bottom that had first captured his fancy. His palms slid down to her thighs. God! They were just as he'd imagined them, silky and strong. Every inch of her was satin. No woman should have skin that felt this good! No child over the age of five had skin like this!

As before, Jessica lost herself in the skill of his kiss. The devil wouldn't have to come begging for souls if he could kiss like this! She liked it so much, Jessica was almost able to ignore the thick bulge pressing against her belly or the way his hands were manipulating her hips and legs so that he could fit himself more snugly, intimately, between her thighs.

Morgan was so aroused he thought he might burst before he got inside of her. It never occurred to him that her passion might be less than his own. Not after the way she'd been kissing him. She'd been a long time without a man, after all.

Lowering her to the bed, Morgan made quick work of his trousers, pausing only long enough to let his heated gaze roam every breathtaking inch of her. But when his gaze came to rest on those lustrous auburn curls at the juncture of her thighs, Morgan knew he had to have her now or die.

Jessica experienced a moment of uncertainty and dread when she saw him in his full naked and aroused glory. And she trembled when he spread her legs and moved between them. The length of him, hard and full, against her thigh made her realize the enormity of what she'd started here. There would be pain, and possibly even a child.

Her eyes went to his face, and she knew it was too late. His expression was hard and taut with need . . . and he was beautiful. All of him was beautiful, from his strong shoulders to the hard muscles of his hair-roughened chest. And a child of this man would be equally strong and vital.

This time when Jessica felt his mouth at her breasts, she gave herself up to the feeling. It was insane these thoughts she was having, but they were overpowering as she felt the primeval urge to mate, to reproduce. She wanted back what had been so cruelly denied her. If it was God's will . . .

She welcomed that probing between her legs, including the pain when he drove himself deep.

Morgan, however, knew only shock as he went absolutely still and stared down at her in mute disbelief. She'd not been anywhere near ready to receive him, and certainly not the way he'd taken her. Even considering the virginal tightness of her lengthy abstinence, his entry should have been easier. "God, Jess! Why didn't you say something? There was no reason for me to hurt you." When he would have withdrawn, those legs he'd dreamed about locked him tightly in place. "I can make it better, Jess. Let me. . . ." She undulated her hips and Morgan nearly lost his head.

"It's all right," Jessica whispered, rising against him again . . . and again. "It's so much better now." And it was. "Please, Morgan. . . ."

Morgan allowed himself to believe her claim, though he tempered his strength and his thrusts. But soon his control began to waver. He was lost, irretrievably lost, in a pleasure so great that he couldn't hold back. He fell into that deep, dark pit from which there was no return. . . .

Later, Morgan held her in his arms, stroking her gently, while she curled herself tightly against him like a warm kitten. But despite her contentment now, he knew damned well she'd gotten no pleasure from their lovemaking. In fact, he strongly suspected she'd not truly wanted to make love at all. "Why?" he whispered. "You didn't really want this. Why did you force it to happen?"

Jessica stiffened. "I wasn't holding a gun to your head, Morgan."

She would have rolled away from him, but he pulled her back. "All right, so maybe 'force' isn't exactly the right word. But you wanted me in your bed badly enough to pull me back when I would have left you."

"But I didn't want you to leave me. I needed you... needed this."

"And I set the rules when I said I wouldn't be able to stop at giving you just comfort," he acknowledged regretfully. "Well, I certainly got one helluva lot more than I gave...."

Jessica's head came up off his shoulder. "No!" She silenced him by pressing her fingers over his mouth. "You are wrong about that. You were gentle and tender with me. It mattered when you inadvertently hurt me. Oh, Morgan, half despising me, you gave me more than anyone professing love ever has." Her voice broke on the last. "You don't understand...."

No, he didn't. Not entirely. But he was beginning to, and the insight had him drawing her close again. "Sh," he soothed softly. "Just go to sleep."

"Will you stay with me?" she asked, and once again her voice was very small and childlike.

"I'll stay," he said against her hair.

Morgan stayed awake for a long time after she dozed off. Her sleep was peaceful, and the way she clung to him was heartrending.

He heard Oramay Seibert's voice inside his head. *You will only answer the riddle of who Jessie Cameron truly is when you look into your own heart—and open that damned closed mind!*

Chapter Fifteen

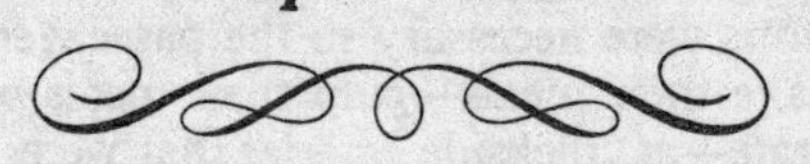

The morning after Jessica had shared her body in exchange for Morgan's comforting, she had taken one look at his brooding expression and had read his thoughts as clearly as if he'd spoken them aloud.

"It has occurred to you," she said softly, "that the nightmares and what happened last night are possibly part of some new deception of mine, another elaborate and convincing performance to soften you up. Isn't that what you're thinking, Morgan? Aren't you wondering if you haven't been duped once again?"

He had looked at her for a very long time, long enough for Jessica to clearly recognize the turmoil and doubt he was struggling with. Then he'd pulled on his coat and had gone to the door, waiting until the very last moment to give her an answer. "I don't know, Jessica," he'd said quietly, not turning around. "I honest to God don't know...."

That had been three days ago. Three difficult and perplexing and taxing days as they continued their journey toward Fort Smith, Arkansas, and not nearly in the same comfort as before reaching Cheyenne.

Jessica had assumed they would continue on with the Hotel Express at least as far as Omaha before beginning the many transfers that would eventually carry them south through Missouri. So she had admittedly been confused when, in Cheyenne, the private car had been uncoupled and then reattached to a train heading for Denver. In Denver another transfer had been made so they were now traveling on the tracks belonging to the Kansas Pacific Railroad. And in nearly the same amount of time it had taken them to cross the vast areas of Nevada, Utah Territory, and most of the Wyoming Territory, they were now crawling across Kansas, slowly and miserably.

Because this train didn't have the luxury of a dining car, frequent stops were necessary so the passengers could depart and take their meals—gulp their meals was actually more accurate—at trackside eateries that were, at best, little better than slop houses, with poor food and poorer service. From the most dignified matron to ordinary cowhand, passengers screamed for service, and more than once Jessica had witnessed physical altercations over food a discriminating pig wouldn't have touched. It would have taken the wisdom of Solomon to straighten out the pandemonium and chaos. She and Morgan, of course, had been spared such treatment and indignity. Since crossing the border into Kansas, Morgan had strapped on his gun belt and pinned on his U.S. deputy marshal's badge. And if these signs of authority were insufficient to gain immediate service or calm a recalcitrant fellow passenger, one of his granite-hard glares got the desired results. Jessica might have been impressed, even amused, by all this if the reemergence of Morgan's gun belt and badge hadn't been a very visible reminder that she was his prisoner. As was the distantly courteous manner he had adopted toward her.

Still, to give Marshal Rossiter his due, when her nightmares came, so did he. Without a word, he would slide into bed beside her and draw her into his arms, and he would remain there until sometime before dawn, rising before she awakened. But he'd never again touched her in a manner even remotely sexual, nor did he show signs of having any inclinations in that direction. It was as if his one encounter had effected a permanent cure. When once he'd claimed she could seduce him anytime, anywhere, just the opposite now applied. Jessica doubted she could entice him if she danced before him stark naked.

She was surprised and disturbed to find how much his physical disinterest hurt, especially considering all she'd wanted from him in the first place was comforting—wasn't it? She couldn't possibly, actually, desire their physical union for its own sake—could she?

She had only to shift her body slightly now and raise upon one arm to look down into the sleeping face of the man causing her such quandary. To say that he was a pleasure to gaze upon was a given, but one she could never entirely accustom herself to from one day to the next. Each time she looked at him, she felt anew the power of his male beauty. If anything, her response to him grew stronger with familiarity instead of diminishing. And since, for once, she had awakened before him, she had the rare opportunity to look to her heart's content. But it distressed her to see that, even in sleep, his handsome face wore the strain of these past days.

Was it any wonder he was exhausted? Especially after being jarred awake night after night by her banshee wails and screams. Oddly enough, he'd made no complaint in either word or manner. He just came to her without hesitation and without question. That he had no curiosity regarding the nature and source of those dreams that interrupted his rest was something Jessica found odd. If their roles were reversed... But then he had his doubts about the authenticity of her nightmares. Why bother to ask about something you didn't believe in in the first place? Still...he came. Perhaps, in this at least, she was being given the benefit of the doubt. And she thanked God for it!

She also knew it was a mistake to become so dependent upon him this way, but she was. So much so that the thought of separating from him after they reached Fort Smith caused such anguish she began to hope this trip, as terrible as it was, would never end. Jessica felt a child again, clutching her beloved rag doll in the night to keep the bogeyman away.

But she wasn't a child, and the very possibility that Morgan had become someone beloved—

No! She could not love this man; she had known from the first how disastrous loving him would prove and was even more certain of it now. Even if there had been no Cole Hardin in her past and no Fort Smith in her future, loving Morgan Rossiter would be insane.

Why did she care? He would tire of her quickly enough in any case. And if she was truly honest with herself, even Cole's repudiation of her had brought as much relief as hurt. To be spared those nightly crude and sometimes painful gropings, and the even less-pleasant moments that followed, had not been a hardship.

So what explanation could she give herself for the inexplicable sensations she was experiencing while she watched Morgan sleep? What insanity possessed her that she could actually wish him awake so he might reach for her again? Even stranger was what looking at his magnificent torso did to her insides. And this compulsion to touch? She wanted to caress him, to move her hands over that hair-roughened skin and feel the silky prickle of it against her palms, then explore the muscular firmness beneath. And the small raised nubs of his nipples were giving birth to all sorts of wild imaginings, especially when she thought of how he'd used his tongue—

With a soft groan Jessica rolled back onto her pillow and flung her arms over a face that was flaming hot, as were some other parts of her body she preferred not to consider.

Dear Lord, what was happening to her?

Morgan had admittedly been somewhat concerned about Jessica's reaction to his decision that they should detour their journey to Fort Smith by way of Ellsworth, but when she'd said nothing about their switching trains in Cheyenne, he had assumed— Hell! He didn't know exactly what he'd assumed beyond the fact he was spared any argument over the subject. Spared until now, that was. Because she sure the devil was kicking up one helluva fuss about it now!

"You know you're being irrational, don't you?" he asked for at least the tenth time. "Especially since the train that brought us this far is already five miles down the track on its way to Salina! This private car isn't going anywhere until the next train comes through, which won't be until three days from now."

"Fine," she stated mulishly, trying not to cry over the mean trick he'd played on her. "I'll wait right here until it arrives!"

Morgan blew out his breath and rubbed his brow. "Jessica, you know damned well I'll carry you out of here over my shoulder if necessary. So, why don't you—"

"Why?" she rasped. "Why did you bring me here? My God! This is the last place on earth I'd want to see again! Or is that it? Have I been brought back to the scene of my supposed crimes so I might come to terms with my sins and confess them freely? That's it, isn't it? I'm to purge myself here, where it all began."

There was some truth in what she was saying, so Morgan was at a loss to deny her suppositions entirely. "We can discuss the reasons when you are more rational . . . and in a less-public place. Unless you'd prefer all and sundry to know exactly who you are and that you've come home. . . ."

Morgan's pointed use of the word "home" worked as nothing else had. She paled, and all defiance went out of her. But it gave him no satisfaction. "Nobody needs to know anything more than that Morgan Rossiter has returned from one of his trips and that he's brought a beautiful woman along with him."

"And I suppose that's so commonplace not a soul would think it curious?" she snapped back.

"Common enough," Morgan answered honestly. "Believe me, around here they'd only get curious if I started acting like some paragon of virtue. My reputation as a hell-raiser was firmly established in this town long, long ago. I could lead a parade of women to my place and nobody would give it a second thought."

Was that news supposed to make her feel better? She felt even more miserable than before after hearing him come right out and admit what a womanizer he was and would probably always be. But then, hadn't she always known?

Jessica swallowed another threatened wave of tears. "I don't want to see my father, Morgan. Not yet... not now."

Agreeing to that was easy enough. He wasn't sure Jack Cameron deserved the peace of mind of knowing his daughter was alive. "As I said, let's make a quiet departure, and no one will even take notice. I promise." He extended his hand. "Now, Jessica. Before curiosity over this private railroad car starts drawing a crowd?"

"Our things?"

"I'll send someone for them later. They'll be safe enough once folks know who they belong to."

With a nod, Jessica straightened the plum-colored jacket to her plaid traveling costume—that was the only name she could give it—and lifted her chin. She did not, however, accept the hand he offered, but stepped around him and departed the compartment on her own. A crowd had indeed been gathering, but it was made up of children and one slightly bent older gentleman. Jessica wondered briefly if either of her half brothers might be present in the group but saw no russet-haired boys wearing the stamp of her father's face. When Morgan came up behind her and placed a steadying hand on her waist, she looked back at him, the question in her eyes before they went to the children again.

"No, Jess. They're not here." At least Morgan didn't think either of the Cameron boys were present. He'd never paid that much mind to them to be absolutely certain. "Shall we go?" he said softly in her ear. In a louder tone he greeted the elderly gentleman. "Hello there, Mr. Blake."

"That there fancy car belong to you now, Rossiter?" Blake returned, not even giving Rossiter's new lady a glance.

"Not yet, Blake. You could say I've been trying it on for size."

The old man chortled behind his hand. "Hee! Hee! Don't you always?"

Suddenly Jessica knew Mr. Blake was not referring to the railroad car any longer, though he still hadn't looked her way. Her head came up just a little higher, her back a little straighter as Morgan ushered them around the small group, warning the children to keep away from the car as they went. Jessica hadn't seen the angry glare Morgan had thrown at Blake at his comment, nor did she see the way the old man stood gaping and scratching his head as they walked away. Neither of them would ever have dreamed that by nightfall it would be all over Ellsworth that Morgan Rossiter had brought home a *real* lady this time, one who might mean more to him than his usual sort of guest.

"Don't get all stiff-necked over that old buzzard, Jessica," Morgan cautioned, seeing the mask of prim respectability once more descending over her face.

Jessica gave him a tight smile. "Of course not." She'd already been tried on for size and rejected. So why should she care if that old buzzard had assumed further trial fittings were in the plans?

Actually, Jessica was grateful to old Mr. Blake for taking her mind off this so-called homecoming. It gave her something distracting to stew over while Morgan arranged for a buggy at the livery stable and she stood alone and unprotected on Ellsworth's streets. Not that she would have ever recognized them as such. The buildings had been given much more than a new coat of paint. Vice and corruption had been swept out of the doors, as well. It was just a quiet, peaceful little Kansas town now. She began to relax a little, some of the knots in her stomach loosening. There were no bad memories here, just buildings and people and dust. Mostly dust.

But there was a bad moment or two when Morgan turned the buggy toward the area of the stockyards . . . and Scragtown. He pulled the horse up to a slow walk as they passed the Rossiter yards. Or at least where the Rossiter yards had once been.

"It's gone," Jessica exclaimed softly in dismay. "Not a single cattle pen or loading area left."

"And good riddance," Morgan answered with an emphatic scowl that left no question to his feelings regarding the business that had made him a wealthy man. Then the buggy was speeding through what had once been Ellsworth's den of iniquity, not giving Jessica more than a few seconds' opportunity to note, let alone appreciate, the radical changes. She sure as hell wouldn't find Myra Belle Watson or her parlor house any longer. On the same ground where a whorehouse had once stood to tempt men's souls was Ellsworth's new Methodist church. Morgan never failed to chuckle at the irony of it all as he passed by. Not today, however. Today Morgan was sourly reflecting upon all those despised years he'd spent salvaging and building another man's dreams at the expense of his own. And at the moment those thoughts weren't conducive to feeling particularly kindly toward the lady sharing his buggy.

Having been informed by the talkative Richard Burke that Morgan Rossiter was a wealthy man, Jessica was understandably surprised by the unremarkable simplicity of his home. The house was two stories and only moderate in size. By comparison the buildings beyond dwarfed the structure, typical of a rancher's priorities of putting the sheltering of his stock above his own comforts. "You really are a rancher," Jessica stated as Morgan lifted her out of the buggy.

"Not by your standards," Morgan said with a coldness that had been absent from his tone for many days. "What you see here is the mere outer trappings of what was *once* a ranch. Oh, I dabble in breeding horses. There's enough land left for that. And I also keep a few cows around for memory's sake. But so damn few they're practically pets."

Considering his obvious bitterness, the question Jessica asked wasn't wise. "What happened, Morgan?"

He'd been looking toward the house, but his head snapped back around. "Cole Hardin happened! Before my brother was murdered he'd put a mortgage against the ranch in order to finance the expansion of his yards. But when he died, the bank didn't look too kindly upon a twenty-year-old with not much more to recommend him than his experience at sowing wild oats. They called in that mortgage before Zach was cold in his grave. I considered myself lucky to save the house and the piddling two thousand acres they left me after they had settled for the greatest part of our ranges. Settled...ha!" he barked harshly. "They made a tidy profit selling that land off piecemeal to any farmer with ready cash in his pocket and a plow in his wagon."

Jessica knew well how ranchers felt about plows...and farmers. They were all right, necessary, even—just as long as they were somewhere else! Without thinking, she said, "If the ranch meant so much to you, Morgan, why didn't you offer them the shipping yards you so obviously despised, instead?"

Her softly spoken, perfectly reasonable observation washed over his temper like a bucket of ice water. It was a damn good question. Unfortunately, it gave rise to a good many more as Morgan stared down into the face that had started him wondering about a great many things he'd never considered before. "Let's get out of this hot sun."

Though he made the suggestion, neither took a single step. Jessica was looking up into Morgan's eyes, not understanding what had just happened or why the expression there had suddenly gone from hard anger to something she dared not call tenderness. But the icy hostility was gone. "Will you tell me now why we came here? What purpose—"

"For starters, I could use a hot bath and a meal that I'm not worried I'll have to kill somebody over. And speaking of food—"

Morgan was interrupted by a "Harrumph!" loud enough to wake the dead. Jessica heard him mutter a curse so shocking she colored, but when he turned toward the woman who'd come out onto the porch, his expression was benign. Maybe too benign. Because, by contrast, the corpulent old woman with the iron-gray hair and bulldog-mean face was staring daggers at them both.

"Mrs. Burnes," Morgan said by way of greeting as he took Jessica's arm and drew her along to the house with him, stopping just shy of his housekeeper. "I've returned, and I've brought company." The statement was said as if it were a challenge.

Mrs. Burnes looked him over and then put her evil eye on Jessica, snorting slightly in disdain. "Well, don't expect me to have everything all shipshape just 'cause you dropped in from out of the sky, Rossiter. You know how I feel about surprises, so if the place and what we got in the larder ain't to your liking, it's your own darned fault!" On that she turned and marched back into the house.

"My housekeeper," Morgan explained, looking more chagrined and off balance than Jessica had ever seen him. "I sort of inherited her along with the house. She worked for Zach. Was devoted to him, in fact. Catered to his every whim. Unfortunately, as must be apparent, Ethel Burnes never quite took to me in the same way. Probably because of all those sleepless nights I caused my elder brother in my misspent youth."

"But why do you put up with her, then?"

Morgan scratched the back of his neck, and his mouth twisted into a rueful grin. "You want the truth? Well, the truth is that old harridan scares the bejesus outa me. Always has. Besides, after Zach died she made no move to leave, and I never figured out how to retire her without fearing she'd burn this house down around my ears on her way out the door."

"You aren't serious. You can't be serious...."

"Only half-serious," Morgan conceded. "But don't let her worry you. Ethel is probably packing a bag right now. Whenever I bring guests home—of any kind—she gets a sudden urge to go visit her sister. Says I don't pay her enough to cook and clean up after extra."

"And do you? Pay her enough, I mean?"

"One helluva lot more than she's worth, as you'll shortly discover."

What Jessica discovered in those next minutes was that Ethel Burnes should never have been paid at all. If anything, Ethel owed Morgan rent on the house she obviously claimed and treated as her own. While Morgan went in search of the nasty old witch, Jessica stood with her mouth agape in a parlor so untidy and cluttered it bordered upon the ludicrous. There was at least an inch-thick layer of dust atop every surface. Empty bonbon boxes and old newspapers were strewn everywhere. Jessica found several empty and half-empty glasses, all of them now growing a healthy crop of mold. There were plates with chicken bones, and the rug was covered with such a profusion of crumbs—

"She cleans up when she knows I'm coming," Morgan offered with a shrug, though he couldn't completely hide his grimace over the state of his own parlor. "We'll just avoid this room—pretend it isn't here. The kitchen's in pretty good shape. And Ethel knows better than to go anywhere near my room with her untidiness."

"Untidy? This is an absolute disgrace, Morgan! It's . . . it's . . . criminal! This room hasn't seen a dust rag or a polishing—"

Morgan took her firmly by the arms and drew her toward the stairs. "And it's not your worry, Jess. While I'm making arrangements for Ethel's holiday to her sister's and for Shorty to fetch our things, why don't you relax up here . . . ?"

Jessica let him push her along, climbing the stairs ahead of him. It wasn't her house, after all. If Morgan wanted to ignore that filth downstairs, it was none of her business to question! As far as that woman was concerned—Jessica turned around midstep. "You shouldn't pay that old bat, Morgan! You ought to fire her!"

Their positioning on the staircase was unfortunate. He stood two steps below, which put his gaze squarely on a level with that diamond patch of lace showing between the open lapels of her plum-colored jacket. The clear sight of the flesh beneath reminded Morgan he still didn't know the color of her nipples. He was half-mad with wanting to know the color of her nipples! God! He was dying from the want of her, worse now than ever before, because he couldn't forget how tightly her body had enwrapped him or how sweet she'd tasted or how he'd not had nearly enough of that particular delight. She had nearly killed him this morning when he'd opened his eyes to find her looking at him in a manner that went far beyond mere curiosity.

Jessica saw where his gaze had fixed, and her breath caught on the sudden, fierce quaking deep within her belly. Could he still desire *her?* Or would any pretty pair of breasts have caught his rapt attention? Cole had taught her it was entirely possible for a man to love—be obsessed by, actually—parts of a woman's body without giving a damn about the rest of her in any way. And Jessica Cameron refused to ever again be considered just a pair of "tits."

Morgan was within a blink of burying his face in that lacy scrap of cloth when Jessica whirled back around and, unless he was mistaken, stomped up the staircase in an angry huff. He stared after her, wondering how he was going to survive another night of not touching her when she so clearly wanted nothing from him but his comforting. This morning must have been wishful thinking on his part. Maybe she'd actually been disgusted with the sight of his bare, hairy chest!

"Rossiter!" Ethel's jarring voice snapped Morgan out of his trancelike state. "Shorty's got the buckboard hitched up, and I'm headed for Hattie's. Just you remember that whatever mess you make, you clean up!"

Morgan growled. Fire her? He'd like to slit the old bitch's throat! Why the hell had he put up with her all these years? Out of some obligation to Zach? Some penance? In a sudden moment of insight, he wondered if he couldn't sum up the entirety of his existence, his whole reason for being, as a living penance to the memory of Zachary Rossiter!

He glanced above him and saw Jessica standing there and wondered: was she the last sacrifice? Did Zach's memory demand one final and ultimate offering? Would they only be square when Morgan surrendered his very heart and soul?

Chapter Sixteen

Even if there had been no other distractions, Jessica's intermittent and increasingly frequent bouts of restlessness would have kept Morgan awake. The plan, of course, had been to start out the night with her in the hopes they might both get an uninterrupted night's rest. Unfortunately, on Morgan's part, there was damned little chance of being able to close his eyes and relax while he was gnashing his teeth over the persistent and painful throbbing in his loins.

"So much for brilliant ideas," he whispered consolingly as she tossed in the throes of yet another nightmare, patting her with gentle reassurance until she began to settle down again. "Being here with you is driving me mad. Stark raving mad." The words he used didn't seem to matter, only the tone, so he could let off some of his frustration by telling her all the things he wouldn't and couldn't say when she was awake. "Why is it I'm cursed with wanting you of all the women on this earth? Above all women...."

He felt the tension leave her body and heard her contented sigh, but this time he couldn't seem to force his hand to withdraw from her shoulder, or drag his gaze away from the perfect breasts beneath her night rail, moving in gentle rhythm to the rise and fall of her deep, slumberous breathing. What color? his mind tormented while yet another appendage he seemed to have no control over slid down over her arm to cradle one of those soft yet wonderously full mounds. His wayward thumb began to skim back and forth atop the crest until it peaked and hardened beneath the light manipulation.

Another of his brilliant ideas had been to keep the lantern glowing just enough so the room wasn't cast into total darkness, hoping the light, coupled with his constant presence, would keep her nightly horrors at bay. But now all he could think about was the transparency of cotton when wet, and if he was very careful and used his tongue so very gently—

Jessica moaned and stirred.

With a harsh groan, Morgan rolled himself completely off the bed and away from temptation. To say he was disgusted with himself would have been the grandest understatement ever made. God knew, if she awakened and saw him as he was now—buck naked and fully aroused—it would probably scare the life out of her. But even the slight constriction of his drawers had been beyond bearing, so he'd shucked them off in the false hope of getting some relief. Besides, with the sheet covering him, she would never be the wiser. Certainly, she'd been oblivious of his condition all the other nights, clothed or otherwise. Of course, Morgan had been careful to maintain her ignorance, twisting his hips away so he could make damned certain she didn't inadvertently come into contact with that willful part of himself he didn't trust for a minute.

Take her! it demanded incessantly. So what if it would only be in trade for the comfort she needs? If she's willing to make such a bad bargain, who are you to argue, or care?

Unfortunately, despite the perpetual urging coming from down below, Morgan did care. He had hurt her that one time, and it bothered him. But what bothered him more was her ready acceptance of the unnecessary pain, as if she had expected nothing else, was even grateful the pain hadn't been worse. She'd even said as much.

Half despising me, you gave me more than anyone professing love ever has.

That statement nagged at him. Lord! If the treatment she'd received at his hands could be considered a kindness, then the other men she had known must have been real sons of bitches. Or was there only one other son of a bitch, besides himself, who'd touched her sexually? Had Hardin been her only other lover? Was it Cole Hardin who'd taught her to expect pain in lovemaking as if it were a given? Certainly it didn't take a great deal of reasoning or perception to assume that someone capable of coolly putting a knife in a man's back wouldn't prove to be a particularly gentle or unselfish lover.

All Morgan really knew for certain was that he'd rather cut the damned thing off before he would risk hurting her again! Because while he might be a prize-winning son of a bitch himself in a thousand other ways, he drew the line at forcing himself upon women. Especially a woman who'd given him a kind of pleasure unlike anything he'd ever before experienced or was likely to experience again in his lifetime.

Lost within his own selfish miseries, Morgan missed seeing and hearing those first warning signals that Jessica's nightmare had begun once again. She was thrashing wildly by the time he returned to the bed. This time words and gentle pats were useless. He gave up. Draping the sheet discreetly over himself, he gave her shoulder a hard shake. "Jessica! Wake up, honey. Wake up and look at me!"

She jerked upright, wailing, "Papa! Papa, don't leave me!"

Morgan brushed back the hair that had fallen over her face. Her soft crying told him she was awake even before her tear-filled eyes met his gaze and she croaked, "It didn't work, did it?"

"I'm sorry," he said with genuine compassion. Her distress was unarguably real. An act didn't come with an unnatural sheen of perspiration or a coldness of flesh in the middle of a hot summer night. "Maybe if you would talk about it. Tell me—"

She shook her head vehemently. "No! I tried that with Uncle John years ago. It didn't work then and it wouldn't help now. Nothing does when they start up again." She smiled at him sadly. "Not even you can slay my dragons, Morgan. But thank you for trying." In her gratitude, and not realizing his problem Jessica had turned toward him so she could cup her palm around his face in a gesture to accompany her words. She never expected him to turn his head and press a kiss into her palm that shot shivers of delight straight up her arm. Or that her fingers might want to linger and explore the texture of his beard stubble and the firmness of his jaw.

Morgan told himself not to make too much of her touch, but when her hand stayed to bestow a gentle caress, the more reasonable part of himself started listening to other things. "Maybe not all your dragons, but there're one or two we could try working on."

Since he'd awakened her before she could experience the more terrifying aspects of her dream, Jessica had recovered quickly. Nevertheless, she wasn't sure of his meaning. "Like what? I don't quite know what you mean."

That didn't surprise him. She was still so innocent in so many ways. "You can start by explaining what you meant the other night when you said I'd given you more, half despising you, than anyone professing love."

Jessica averted her face and brought her knees up, pressing her cheek against them. "I told you," she whispered uneasily. "You were gentle with me."

"Meaning, I assume, that Hardin was not gentle." Morgan had to work hard to keep the fury out of his voice, especially when her slight nod confirmed what he'd already guessed. "To what degree, Jessica?" he persisted gently, giving her fingers an encouraging squeeze. "How badly did he hurt you?"

Jessica wanted to evade his questions, but his deep voice, the way he was holding her hand, seemed to compel her to answer. On a shaky breath, she said, "The first time... I thought I would die, it was so terrible. After that—" she shrugged "—it was never exactly pleasant, but he never hurt me that way again. What really hurt," she went on, unable to stop now that the dam had opened, "what hurt most was that he never seemed to care how I felt, or if I felt, or—and this may sound crazy—if I was really there at all."

Morgan wanted so badly to take her into his arms and hold her that he shook with the effort to keep a safe distance. With his free hand he again drew her hair back from the face she wouldn't let him see. "What if I swore to you that there never had to be pain, Jess?" he said very softly. "Would you believe me if I told you it could be even better than painless? That there can be incredible pleasure, not just for a man, but for a woman, as well? So much pleasure...." Morgan was within a heartbeat of taking her by the shoulders and drawing her down beneath him when the voice of reason intruded once again. *Watch out, Rossiter,* it cautioned vehemently. *As hot as you are, you're damned close to making a promise you might not be able to keep!*

Jessica's breath was trapped somewhere between her breast and belly as she felt the warmth of his breath upon her neck and that compellingly deep voice telling her of delights and pleasures unimaginable. She felt the heat of his body so close at her back, and her heart skipped several beats while her stomach fluttered in anticipation of his touch. But it never came, and she wanted to sob out her disappointment when he retreated and left her to face the cold, grim reality that she would likely die never knowing those pleasures he spoke of. Years of self-denial saved her the mortification of begging. She lifted her face from her knees and turned it to where Morgan now rested, his back propped up against the brass rail of his bed.

"Oh, I'm quite sure you are right about there being some enjoyment to be shared between men and women. Otherwise, mankind would not have flourished. And, of course, all creatures are born with the instinct to mate."

A rumbling sound erupted from Morgan's throat, one Jessica immediately recognized as exasperation, but she was still too late to save herself from being hauled into his arms and positioned astraddle his lap. And a very shocking and telling lap it was, too.

"Morgan!"

"You are the only damned woman I know—" he was scowling straight into those saucer-big eyes "—who would strike up a hypothetical discussion with me about sex in my own bed, in the middle of the damned night, and not have any damned idea what the conversation was all about in the first damned place!"

"As far as I could tell, Mr. Rossiter, you were merely making abstract reassurances, much as a casual passerby might console a child who'd run afoul of a mean-tempered dog by assuring her that not all dogs were inclined to bite!"

They glared at each other for several minutes. Then Morgan's mouth began to curl into a grin so frankly carnal and suggestive that Jessica felt the shock of it jolting all through her body, and most particularly in that place where they were so intimately joined with only the sheet between them. Her night rail was bunched high up around her thighs.

"Well, you sure as hell are no child, Jessie Cameron," Morgan told her as his heated gaze scorched more than 90 percent of the woman he desired more than any other he'd ever known. "And it's damned certain there's nothing hypothetical, abstract or casual about that part of me you're cuddling between your thighs." Her hot flush of color and the shy ducking of her head at his frankness only made her more endearing. She would really be shocked if she knew the effort he was putting into holding perfectly still or how irritating the sheet between them was becoming. Cradling her face gently, Morgan lifted her gaze back to his own, needing to see those big eyes of hers. "No sense mincing words, Jess. I want you... badly. I've been this way for the better part of three days."

"You could have... I wouldn't..."

Morgan frowned at her. "That's what I was afraid of. That you'd *let* me have you as some sort of payment for keeping your nightmares at bay. But I want more than just the use of your body, Jess. And I want to give you something more than the cold-blooded lovemaking you had with Hardin. First, however, I needed to know how deeply that unfeeling bastard scarred you. If it is even possible for you to respond normally now to a man."

"And is it possible?"

Her hesitant, almost fearful query brought out a tenderness in him so profound it was frightening. Morgan ached to give her the answer she wanted. Instead, he gave her all he could—his honesty. "I don't know, Jess. I think so. I hope so. But..."

"I'll never know until we try," she finished for him as the love she'd rejected and denied and fought against so long came flooding in upon her with stunning force. She loved him. Right or wrong, for better or for worse, she loved this man. And it made her want to be all the woman she was capable of being for him.

"Oh, I think we can do better than try," Morgan said as he brought her face to his and nipped lightly at her pouty lower lip. Her slight intake of breath brought a smile. "You like kissing me, don't you, Jess?"

"Yes," Jessica admitted, freely offering more of her mouth to the play of his teeth and tongue. He bit gently, then soothed the imaginary hurt with little licks until her lips were moist and swollen and she grew frustrated with his teasing and tried to tell him so with the sound she made deep in her throat.

"You know what you want, Jess. Take it!"

Jessica did. She threaded her fingers into his thick black hair and fused their mouths together, and when he continued to withhold what she wanted, Jessica went seeking on her own.

When her small tongue penetrated the rim of his lips, Morgan drew it the rest of the way in, and groans burst from them both. His hands slid down over her shoulders and back and found their way beneath the bunched cloth of her night rail. He filled his palms with the soft swell of her bottom and began rocking her upon his aching flesh until even that slight friction became an agony. All the while their mouths were taking and partaking with an increasing fervor that was becoming increasingly explosive.

"Whoa," Morgan breathed, tearing their mouths apart, letting his head loll back against the top of the brass rail. Jessica misinterpreted, thinking she'd done something wrong. Morgan caught her defeated expression and breathed a harsh curse. "I'm too excited, Jess. I want to take it slow, but there's another part of me with other ideas. Especially when it's so damn close to what it wants. Maybe too damn close...." He started to lift her off of him, but she clamped her legs tight. "Jess?"

"I...I like it here, Morgan," she said, blushing.

"Did you like it when I rubbed you against me?" he returned huskily, repeating the motion.

"Yes...." Oh, yes!

Her responsiveness was as unexpected as it was pleasing. "Lift your arms over your head, honey."

His use of the endearment sent a thrill of pleasure through Jessica. But she panicked momentarily when he began drawing her nightgown up over her body. Her arms fell to her sides, trapping the cloth that had only risen as far as her belly. "Extinguish the lamp, Morgan."

Even if he hadn't heard the anxiety in her voice, Morgan could see the way she had clamped her teeth down on her bottom lip. He levered himself up and challenged her for the right of privilege, giving no quarter until it was he who nibbled on her pretty mouth. "I want to see you, Jess. All over."

"Please," she whispered, though in truth it was hard to remember now why having the light out was so important.

"Nope. Won't do, sugar. Now lift those pretty arms for me. That's my girl...." The gown came over her head and was sent flying. "Peach." Morgan sighed in gratification, his thumbs already busy skating over the pale perfection. "The palest, sweetest color of peach I've ever seen."

Too late, Jessica recalled the primary reason underlying her modesty. She was afraid his sharp eyes would notice the faint lines marring her stomach, the ones that gave indisputable evidence she'd once been with child. But Morgan gave her little time to worry over it, because he was already stealing her ability to think at all. His fingers were toying with her nipples, molding them, plucking at them until it seemed they were fairly begging to be taken into his mouth, the hard centers reaching, extending. Jessica arched her back, more than meeting him halfway. When she felt the wet glide of his tongue, she shuddered all over with the pleasure he was bringing her. And when he began drawing gently upon her, she held his head and offered herself up to him fully. "Oh...." Her cry was heartfelt.

When Morgan again had to take a breather to curb and calm the wildfire desire that just tasting her perfection had brought him, he saw there were tears running down her cheeks. That curbed him fast enough. "God, Jess! Did I hurt you?"

"Oh, no. It was...it was so very...good," she sobbed, falling against him, rubbing his whiskered cheek with her own. "Whatever happens, I'll have this—"

Morgan took her mouth fiercely, not letting her talk of something he didn't want to think about, refused to consider. There was the here and now. That's all! She was here, and he wanted her now!

Jessica was being flooded with sensations she'd never before felt, would never have dreamed existed, though her repressed sensuality had given her hints now and again. Her breasts were nuzzled and teased by the tickle of his chest hair. The little pulses she'd felt below were now throbbing as if with an independent life of their own. And when he roughly tugged the sheet out from between them, pressing her hard against the hot, silken-hard length of him, she groaned loudly.

The sound she made mingled with Morgan's own when he felt her dampness and heat and that incredible softness unlike any other on earth. "Move like I showed you, Jess. The way you liked before," he uttered in a guttural tone that betrayed how close he was to exploding. Using his hands, Morgan spread her legs even wider so that they were in even closer contact. The look on her face, a combination of wide-eyed dismay and rapt sensual bliss, told Morgan she'd discovered for herself the source of a woman's delight as she undulated against him in a way that had him gnashing his teeth again. Only now it was a sweet agony he welcomed.

When Jessica's breathing began to quicken, Morgan knew it was time. He wanted to take her this second, just this way, with her riding him to her glory. But her inexperience and the strangeness of the position might cause an awkwardness that could ruin this for her. Subsequently, Morgan took a firm hold of her hips and rolled her beneath him, guiding himself into the tight and welcoming warmth in one smooth, hard thrust.

"No pain, Jess," he explained at her little surprised gasp. "Now let's see what we can do about the pleasure...." God give me strength! he added silently as she adjusted herself beneath him and his head nearly came off his shoulders.

Jessica knew he was a part of her, seated deeply. She could feel the internal walls of her body stretching to accommodate his fullness. She was filled up with him! And there was no pain! She could have cried out with joy. It didn't matter that she instinctively knew there wouldn't be the glory he seemed to want for her. Nothing mattered but that he was deep inside, and she could love him without restraint.

If Morgan had looked down into her face at that moment, he would have seen the love she held for him glowing out of her big hazel eyes. But he was engaged in a battle with himself, and he was losing. She felt too damned good, velvet heat gloving him tightly. Too tightly. One thrust and it would be over!

When Jessica felt him withdraw, she cried out her protest. The sound became strangled joy a second later. He was stroking her with the head of his aroused shaft, gliding over that sensitive, pleasure-giving spot she'd discovered when she had rocked upon him. Something was building inside her, something wonderful and frightening all at once.

"Morgan!"

"Sh, sweetheart. It's all right. Don't be afraid."

Jessica clutched his shoulders as a fiery heat licked at her, and the tension coiled tighter and tighter. "Oh!"

When she cried out and arched up against him, Morgan thrust himself deeply within her tight sheath again. He groaned when he felt the waves of her pleasure undulating around him, ebbing and flowing, drawing him deeper and deeper into the very essence of her until, upon a primeval shout, he released the very essence of himself, bestowing upon her all that he was and everything he had ever dreamed of becoming....

Morgan stood in the doorway of his parlor, though he would never have recognized the room as his own. Clutter had been cleared away; tabletops gleamed as they hadn't in years. The glass panes in the wide open windows glistened beneath a bright midday sun. And standing upon a chair at the end of the room, straining up to dust the top shelf of his bookcase, was the hardworking little fairy who'd come in while he slept to turn chaos into neat and tidy order.

Placing the boots he'd been carrying down softly upon the recently mopped floor, Morgan crossed the room silently on his bare feet, absently wondering as he went how she'd managed to get the carpet out on her own. He also was trying to figure out where the devil she'd dug up those old clothes of his she was wearing. God knew they'd seen better days. And yet they had never been luckier, Morgan decided, envying the baggy trousers and shirt touching her wondrous skin. But for the bare feet peeping out from beneath the rolled cuffs of his pants, Morgan also determined his clothes were doing too fine a job at covering up all that ripe and luscious female perfection. With a mischievous smile spreading across his face, Morgan waited until she was standing on the tips of those bare toes before he made his presence known to her.

"Just what in the hell do you think you're doing, woman!"

The unexpected angry bark accomplished just what Morgan intended. Jessica jumped nearly three feet, screamed and tumbled right into his arms. Holding her firmly by the waist, Morgan had to laugh when he saw her urchin's face, dirt smudged and a little on the pale side right now. With her hair hidden beneath a square of printed calico she'd found somewhere, she looked a ragtag charwoman...and more beautiful than anything he'd ever dreamed. "Now I see where all the dust in here went. Most of it's on your face, sweet," he told her somewhat huskily. The feel of her all along his front was reigniting a desire he began to fear would never be quenched.

Jessica felt the change in him, too, her startled eyes going even wider. But that he could still want her so urgently after last night, especially with her looking the ragamuffin, made her heart swell with joy and took most of the bite out of her scolding.

"You nearly scared the very life out of me, Rossiter!"

Morgan hoped she would never know how finding her gone had scared the life out of him, as well. Particularly when he'd seen no sign of her belongings or clothing. Of course, he hadn't bothered to search beyond the obvious. He had just jerked on his trousers, pulled on a shirt—not even bothering with the buttons—and grabbed up his boots. He felt ashamed of himself now, but not so much that it kept him from adjusting his hold so his arms formed a shelf beneath her hips, forcing her long legs to wrap around his waist. The strangled little sound she made turned his smile of mischief into one of pure wicked, lusty male delight.

"You've been a busy little bee, I see," he muttered against the clean spot he found on her chin.

Jessica's head rolled back to give him greater access to the delicious spot he'd found beneath her jaw. "Since it seemed you were planning to sleep the day away, I had to find *something* to keep me occupied." Did her voice sound as strained in his ears as it did in her own?

"Well, I'm definitely awake now. All of me. Wide-awake and raring to go...." he said naughtily.

"Good! I could use your help with the rug Shorty helped me drag out earlier."

He repaid her sauciness by releasing her hips and forging his way beneath the voluminous shirt she wore. His breath caught when he encountered nothing but smooth, satiny flesh. Morgan scowled. "Don't tell me you were prancing around Shorty with nothing on under this shirt?"

His jealous growl brought a delighted smile to Jessica's face. Undoubtedly Morgan would really be upset to know she wasn't wearing any drawers, either, since they were drying on the clothesline outside beside her chemise and night rail. And since Shorty had been the very one to show her where she might find the clothesline— Jessica chuckled. "You know very well that grandfatherly old cowhand can't see farther than the end of his own nose."

"Shorty's old—he's not dead!" Morgan barked, though he was starting to feel ridiculous. This kind of possessiveness was new to him. He'd never given a hoot before if any of the women he brought here pranced around in even less. It was also damned certain none of them would have dreamed of cleaning the parlor, no matter what god-awful condition Ethel had left the room in before taking off in her usual huff.

"And you are very sweet to keep him around and on the payroll," Jessica said with genuine admiration as she linked her fingers behind Morgan's neck and extended her arms so she could better see that heartwarmingly fierce expression.

"Shorty has been around since I was a kid," Morgan returned in a voice that surely belonged to someone else. When she'd leaned back it had brought her lower body into even more solid contact with his own. Any genuine fire that might have been in his temper immediately resettled itself in the area of his loins.

"He's devoted to you," Jessica said softly, just beginning to realize what she'd done by altering her position. Not yet comfortable with these new feelings Morgan ignited within her body, Jessica attempted to distract him from the desire she saw in those darkening gray eyes. "Shorty also told me what a young hellion you were." Actually, Shorty had been more inclined to spend his time maligning the elder

Rossiter brother. Jessica admitted she wasn't very impressed by the image of an autocratic, self-absorbed and generally narrow-minded Zachary Rossiter. Of course, she allowed a great deal for Shorty's obvious bias and favoritism toward Morgan.

Morgan had lost total interest in the subject of Shorty Parker. All his attention was focused upon the soft swells of womanly flesh pressing against worn blue cotton. "Unbutton your shirt, Jess."

"What? You can't be serious, Morgan. Not here in the parlor. Shorty could walk back in at any moment. It's broad daylight. Anybody might see...."

Morgan's response was to stride to the parlor doors and pull them shut, latching them securely. Then, ignoring Jessica's giggling, halfhearted protests, he went to the windows. When the heavy lace panels of the curtains were snugly drawn together, Morgan looked at Jessica again. "Better now?"

In her most prim and proper manner, Jessica looked up into that wickedly handsome face wearing that wicked, wicked grin. "Morgan, with the draperies closed, it is going to get hotter than hades in here."

The smile he gave her then as his hands went to the buttons of her shirt was nothing short of depraved. "Damned right it will," he agreed, spreading the cloth and filling his hands with her ripe perfection. "So hot it just may burn you alive, sweet."

The entire day was magical, as if someone had woven a spell around the old ranch house that set it apart from the rest of the world. Time held its breath. There was no past or future. Only the moments Jessica and Morgan spent together existed.

He helped her with the parlor carpet, beating the dust from its dull pattern until the colors became vivid again. Then they brought it in together and rolled it out upon the clean floor. Morgan made love to her there, taking her again with a hungry urgency that belied they'd ever made love only an hour or so before in the same room, on an uncarpeted floor.

When the sun began to set in the sky, they shared the kitchen chores, working together to prepare their supper, ending up in a playful tussle over which of them looked best in Ethel's apron. The silly dispute was quickly settled, and forgotten, when a tug of war brought Jessica tumbling onto Morgan's lap. And there, upon a kitchen chair, Morgan determined that Jessica looked best in nothing at all.

After an extremely cold meal, Morgan filled his big bathtub for Jessica and then joined her in it, using his soapy hands to wash and explore every beautiful inch of her until she was breathless and more than eager to return the favor. When desire reached a fever pitch, he quickly dried them both and carried her to his bed. There he prolonged the sweet agony until she went wild beneath him, inhibitions gone, as she demanded what only he could give her and, in the taking, returned more than Morgan had ever dreamed of receiving.

But when the clock began to chime the midnight hour, the enchantment was shattered by a softly spoken question uttered in the calm stillness of a summer's night.

"Why did you stay with him, Jess? He was a confessed thief and a heartless bastard by your own account. But it took you nearly eight months to leave him. I need to understand the hold he had over you...." Feeling the tension in her, Morgan pulled her closer. "Don't be afraid, Jess. Tell me...."

Not be afraid? Jessica had never been so terrified in all her life or more certain the answer Morgan demanded was the last he expected...or wanted to hear. Let it go, my love, she silently pleaded. Just for tonight. Give me this one last night....

"Jessica?"

Choking back a sob, Jessica lifted her head from his chest. Hot tears burned in her eyes. Her throat ached with the longing to lie. But because she loved this man, Jessica gave him the truth.

"He was...is...my husband. Cole Hardin and I were married in Coffeyville two days after leaving Ellsworth."

The darkness spared Jessica from actually seeing the revulsion on Morgan's face, but the sudden rigidity of his body, before he rolled away from her and left the bed, was sufficiently eloquent. "Morgan, please...."

"Tell me again how shocked and horrified you were at the discovery of those money pouches in Hardin's saddlebags. But obviously that wasn't sufficiently off-putting to keep you from joining Cole Hardin in the bonds of holy matrimony."

"No, Morgan! It wasn't like that. Let me explain—"

"Lady, I'm not interested."

The coldly spoken words were followed immediately by the firm sound of the door closing behind Morgan. Knowing how useless it would be to go after him, Jessica fell back onto the bed. Oddly enough, the tears she expected didn't come. There was only a terrible emptiness. The curse of Cole Hardin just went on and on....

"Bonds of holy matrimony," she whispered, nearly strangling as she said those words, remembering what a travesty her so-called wedding day had been.

She knew now, of course, that Cole never had any real intention of marrying her. But neither had he anticipated the scene Jessica had made in the lobby of that Coffeyville hotel, speaking up loudly to demand separate rooms when he would have let the desk clerk believe them man and wife already. No, Cole Hardin could never have expected his stupid, docile and naively adoring little Jessie to be so obstinately determined to protect her virtue. Neither could he afford to be the subject of too much curious attention, particularly when the town marshal just happened to be one of the witnesses to the spectacle Jessica was making.

Subsequently, with all the charm he drew upon so easily, Cole quickly became all sheepish grins and boyishly guilty embarrassment. The men who'd been present to witness the ruckus guffawed and winked; the women easily forgave the handsome young rogue when he asked directions to the nearest preacher. Only Jessica had seen that momentary flash of cold fury in his eyes, but she had discounted it. She had still been too caught up in the spell of Cole Hardin's breathtaking smiles. Later she would have cause to remember that warning as she learned firsthand the price for thwarting Cole Hardin's plans and desires. But first there had been the wedding and a hastily thrown together celebration in the saloon adjacent the hotel. Then the newlyweds had retired to their room, where Cole, fortified by whiskey, had immediately claimed his husbandly rights...raping his bride with a brutality that had left her stunned and aching for days afterward. Somehow, after that, the shock of learning she'd married a thief had paled by comparison.

Not for the first time Jessica wished she had kept her mouth shut in that Coffeyville hotel and escaped the unholy, cursed alliance she'd made that day.

Drawing the pillow that still bore Morgan's scent close to her body, Jessica wrapped herself around it and waited for sunrise. There would be no dreams this night. Her painfully dry eyes never closed.

Chapter Seventeen

Shorty Parker wasn't as blind as everybody seemed to think. Oh, things were a bit fuzzy beyond the tips of his fingers. And if somebody was coming down the road, they'd be in the yard before he had any idea who they might be, but he could damn well see good enough to know anybody with sense would keep their distance from Morgan Rossiter today. But Shorty never had claimed to have much sense. Besides, being a half-blind, crippled old codger who happened to have known this young rooster since Morgan was just a tyke, Shorty had the advantage. Nevertheless, it paid to be cautious when you were about to stick your nose into the business of an ugly-tempered man with an ax in his hand.

"'Bout time you decided to chop down that dead ol' cottonwood," Shorty observed loud enough to be heard over the rhythmic thunks of the ax blade as it sliced into dead timber. "Tree's been an eyesore since it got struck by lightning three summers past. Yep! 'Bout damn time."

Morgan paused long enough to swipe at the sweat running down into his eyes with the back of his shirtsleeve, though it did him little good. The blue chambray shirt he wore was soaked through. So was the kerchief he'd tied around his forehead two hours ago. He was being blinded by the salty moisture running in rivulets over his heated face.

Shorty ambled up and offered Morgan his own handkerchief, which the younger man eyed suspiciously. "It's clean," the old cowhand grumbled.

"By whose standards?" Morgan snapped back with unnecessary curtness. "Sorry, Shorty. Guess I'm not fit company today."

"That why you all of a sudden took a notion to chop down that tree? You and your lady have a lovers' spat?"

Morgan balled the square of cloth he'd been wiping his face with into his fist. A foul curse preceded a vehement denial. "She's not my lady, and we aren't—" He snarled at Shorty's disbelieving expression and jammed the old cowhand's kerchief into his pocket. "She's nothing to me," he insisted, once again taking a firm grip of the ax handle.

Shorty backed away a few steps, but he didn't back off the subject. "Well now...that's a damn shame. And here I was thinkin' you'd finally been hit by Cupid's arrow. God knows that little missy sure is a cut and a half above any other female you've dragged in here over the years. Yep, I saw right off she was somethin' pretty special...."

Morgan buried the ax in the tree with a blow so powerful that the handle splintered, driving a jagged spear of wood deep into the palm of his right hand. "Goddammit!" he roared as blood began to gush.

Shorty quickly fished his handkerchief out of Morgan's pocket and bound the wound tightly. It didn't take long for the cloth to turn bright red. "Damn, but you're bleeding like a stuck hog. Does it hurt?"

"Hell yes, it hurts!" Morgan growled between clenched teeth.

"Let's get you to the house."

"No!"

Shorty rocked back on his heels and scowled up at Morgan. "You plannin' on just standin' here and bleedin' to death, then? Or do I gotta knock you over the head and carry you into the house?"

At a height of barely five feet four inches, Shorty Parker's claim might have been humorous if Morgan hadn't known the old buzzard meant every word, even if it meant breaking his own back in the bargain. With more grumbled curses, Morgan started walking, leaving a trail of blood behind him. With some relief he found the kitchen deserted of Jessica's unwanted presence. And by the time Shorty limped into the house behind him, Morgan was already seated at the table with his hand wrapped in one of Ethel's dishcloths. It too, though, was soaked through in seconds.

Shorty filled a basin with cool water and brought it to the table. "Let me have a look at that." Holding Morgan's hand over the basin, Shorty flushed the wound with water and then bent low over it.

"Damn, Shorty! Don't stick your nose in it!"

"Well, I gotta see how bad—"

"Let me have a look, Mr. Parker."

Morgan went rigid when Jessica gently nudged Shorty aside and took a firm hold of his wrist. "Shorty can take care of this!" he barked.

Jessica ignored him. "How did this happen?" She directed her query to the shortsighted, aging cowhand, who still hovered nearby.

"Ax handle splintered."

Jessica winced slightly. "I will need some clean linens and something to disinfect the area."

Nothing in her manner or tone betrayed the sick roiling in her stomach at the sight of the deep, jagged puncture still oozing a steady stream of blood, turning the water in the basin red. Nothing, that is, if one discounted her chalky-white complexion. Funny, she'd never been squeamish before.

When Shorty limped off to locate the items she'd requested, Jessica chanced a glance at Morgan, then wished she hadn't. The cold disdain in his eyes nearly devastated her. Though it was really no less than she had expected, Jessica felt betrayed by his condemnation, nonetheless. "After I get the bleeding under control, you really should have a physician take a look at this. There might be wood fragments embedded—"

"Just bandage the damn thing and spare me the Saint Jessica routine, Mrs. Hardin!"

His harshness tore into her with cruel force, but she refused to buckle. "Are you certain you want to risk my tainted touch? Aren't you fearful your hand will be contaminated to the point of rot, along with other valued parts of your anatomy already overexposed—"

"Believe me, *lady,*" Morgan sneered, coming halfway off the chair, "if I'd known you were married to that bastard, I would have cut it off before—"

A loud, timely cough stifled Morgan's crude declaration. Shorty approached the table. "Found some pillow shams and a bottle of brandy. Will that do, missy?"

"Excellent, Shorty. Thank you," Jessica said in a strangled whisper, unable to look at the older man for fear of what he'd overheard.

Morgan, however, was on the receiving end of a blistering glare from his old friend. He fully expected to add a bloodied nose to his list of injuries. Instead, Shorty grumbled something about chores and stomped out of the house.

While Jessica ripped the pillow shams into strips, Morgan ground his teeth. How many times had this woman made a fool of him? Wouldn't she be gratified to learn that for all his wild and wicked ways, Morgan had maintained at least one unsullied virtue...until now. Never, not once, had he committed the transgression of adultery.

He scowled up at her, noticing she'd finally gotten around to attiring herself in the third dress he'd purchased in Sacramento. Undoubtedly, the timing had finally been appropriate for her to don that inappropriately girlish spotted pink muslin, with its short puffed sleeves and profusion of ruffles. And somehow she managed to look every bit as young, vulnerable and innocent as a naive sixteen-year-old. It was such an obvious ploy, Morgan wanted to wring her deceitful neck!

"You never had any real intention of testifying, did you, Mrs. Hardin? Not only were you already protected against self-incrimination, but you also had your secret safeguard of being able to claim a wife's privilege. No wonder you were so damned cooperative," he sneered. "Because all along you knew there was no legal power on earth that could compel you to give evidence against yourself... or your beloved husband. I assume—"

"Oh, yes! Please do *assume* to your heart's content, Morgan!" Jessica hissed as she firmly pressed a folded square of linen to his wound, paying no attention to his harsh rasp of pain. "How comforting it must be for you to be so all-wise and all-knowing! The great, omnipotent Morgan Rossiter! He has no need to question or listen...."

"Lady, I don't give a—" Morgan was halfway off his chair again when she flooded his palm with the brandy. His knees buckled under the fiery agony. He clenched his teeth with the effort not to scream. His spinning head fell back against the wall on a groan. A cold sweat broke out upon his face while he repeatedly swallowed the hot bile rising in his throat.

Although Jessica had admittedly been hurt and angry over his harsh and unfair judgment, the sight of his suffering brought tears to her eyes. In spite of everything, she loved this intransigent hothead. With more gentleness than he deserved, Jessica carefully bandaged his hand and lowered it to the tabletop. "That's the best I can do, I'm afraid. You really should see a..."

Morgan's eyes opened, and though they were still glazed with pain, there was enough rancor in their depths to cause her to go pale. "You enjoyed that, didn't you?" he rasped while nausea and dizziness continued to assault him in unrelenting waves.

"No," Jessica said sadly, her bottom lip quivering. "But how typical of you to make that assumption," She removed the bloody basin from the table. Wetting another pillow sham with fresh, cool water, she returned to him. "Here... wipe your face with this. It will make you feel better."

Morgan gave an ugly bark of laughter. "You are really something, lady. Well, let me tell you—"

"Not this time, Morgan!" Jessica cut him off heatedly. "This time you are going to listen for a change!"

"Like hell—" He shot up off the chair. Too quickly. There was a sudden roaring in his ears, and the next thing he knew his backside was planted on wood once again, and a wet cloth was being applied to his face.

"You are so damned determined to think the worst of me that I don't know why I should bother to set you straight," Jessica was saying, though it seemed as if her voice were coming to him through a long, hollow tunnel. "While it might be true that there is no legal power that could force me to give evidence against a husband, neither is there any authority—short of heaven or my death—that will keep me out of Fort Smith and off that witness stand. If you can believe nothing else about me, Morgan, believe this. *I will testify against Cole Hardin!* Not because of you or for you. For myself! For my own reasons!"

Morgan's vision cleared just in time to catch her before she could walk away. With his uninjured hand, he captured Jessica's wrist. "Why? Tell me...."

This time it was Jessica who laughed in disbelief. "I seem to remember hearing words to that effect before, Morgan. 'Tell me,' you said. 'Don't be afraid,' you assured." A sob broke free, along with the tears she could no longer hold back. They fell freely down her face. "So I...I trusted you. And how...how did you reward my trust, Morgan?" Jessica began to tremble visibly as she fought to keep from falling apart altogether, knowing she was losing the battle. "You...you recoiled from me as if...as if I were something filthy...vile...."

Her voice was barely a ragged whisper at the last, but Morgan heard and felt each and every word. They ripped into him with a cutting force that made the throbbing in his hand pale by comparison. "Jess," he croaked, but when she pulled away from his grasp, Morgan made no effort to stop her. He let her go and felt a strange burning in his own eyes when she ran sobbing from the kitchen. With a mumbled curse he reached for the brandy decanter, grumbling even more when he discovered it was nearly empty. He was still staring at the lead crystal when Shorty Parker stepped back into the kitchen. The expression on the old cowhand's face was nothing short of murderous.

Morgan glared right back at the old busybody. "I suppose you stood outside the door and listened to every goddamn word!" he accused.

"I did," was Shorty's curt response. "And I ain't gonna apologize for it, neither!"

Morgan waited for Shorty to elaborate on what he'd overheard, but his old friend said nothing; he just continued to give Morgan that squint-eyed, withering glare. Finally, it began to grate on Morgan's nerves. "Just what the hell are you staring at?"

Shorty took a few steps closer, his eyes narrowing even more. "Well, if I could see clearer, I imagine I'd be lookin' at one of the most pitiful, dumbest, hardheaded and asinine jackasses the Lord ever suffered to walk this earth. What's worse is, you damn well know it, too!"

On that Shorty Parker stomped out of the house, leaving Morgan to stew in the juices of his own mule-headed shortcomings.

Morgan tossed and turned on the narrow parlor sofa. Between the deafening thunderstorm going on outside and a hand that was throbbing like a son of a bitch, Morgan consigned another night's sleep to a lost cause. Not that his thoughts would have given him any peace, regardless. He couldn't stop thinking about the woman who'd barricaded herself in his room. Neither could he begin to count the number of times he'd started toward those stairs only to change his mind. Instead, he'd had Shorty check on her a couple of times, including the delivery of her supper tray, only to feel guilty for making that old man climb those stairs on his painful joints. That he couldn't force himself to face her seemed to indicate his reluctant agreement with Shorty's assessment of his character.

Had he been too quick in condemning her? Eager, even? Perhaps deep down he had wanted to find some reason—any excuse—to repudiate Jessica. Otherwise, he might just have had to come to terms with the fact that his feelings for her went beyond desire, were so powerful, in fact, that they threatened his ability to carry out and complete his crusade for justice.

"God!" Morgan grumbled, shifting again, accidently thumping his injured hand against his thigh. The pain nearly took his breath away. Maybe he should consider having a doctor take a look at it after they reached Fort Smith.

I can be seduced. But I won't be swayed.

His own words, spoken so hatefully days ago, came back to haunt him. But dammit! What were his options? Give it up and let Hardin get off scot-free? Forget the past ten years? Could he live with himself if he did? And if he could believe Jessica, she wanted—

A loud clap of thunder following a blinding flash of lightning brought Morgan into a sitting position. He didn't know how long he sat there, bent forward with his arms resting upon his thighs, when he realized that the sound of rain splattering noisily upon a wood surface was coming from the hall. Obviously, the gusting wind had blown the front door open.

Getting up, he padded on bare feet through the puddle of water that extended several feet into the house. Driving rain struck his face and chest and wet the front of his trousers as he reached out to close the door. Then another bright flash illuminated the yard, and what he saw in that brief moment sent him bounding out into the storm. Beneath the wind-tossed branches of a tall oak tree, Jessica was kneeling, tearing at the rain-soaked earth with her bare hands.

"Jessica! What in the name of God—" Morgan attempted to haul her to her feet. She shook him off with a snarl that was nothing short of feral, immediately going back to her digging, scooping up handful after handful of mud. Her demented frenzy turned his blood to ice. He watched in horrified dismay until a snapping crack of lightning reminded him of the danger. Bending down, he wrapped his arms firmly around her. "Come on, Jess," he said more gently. "We've got to get—"

He found he was grappling with a ferocious wildcat. With only one good hand it was impossible to hold her, let alone drag her back to the house. And her screams—those terrible, blood-chilling wails of her nightmares—just kept going on . . . and on. . . .

In desperation, Morgan hooked his leg behind her knees and sent her sprawling. Following her down, he pinned her beneath him. "Jessica!" he yelled as she tried to buck him off, barely averting his face in time to avoid being clawed. Despite the excruciating pain it caused him, he used both hands to pin her wrists above her head. "Dammit, Jess!" he yelled through gritted teeth. "Don't make me hit you! We have to get back inside!"

"The baby. . . ." she wailed miserably. "Can't you hear him crying? Oh, please. We have to get him out. . . ."

The sky lighted up again and Morgan saw her eyes for the first time. Though they were wide open, the expression he saw there caused his flesh to crawl. He knew then that Jessica wasn't here with him, beneath this tree in the middle of a thunderstorm, but still in that shadowy world of her nightmare. "Sh, honey. We'll get the baby. Come on, Jessica, love. I'll help you find him. . . ."

Her struggles ceased instantly, and when Morgan stood and offered his hand, she gave him hers with an unhesitating faith that nearly tore the heart right out of him.

Not wanting to take the chance she might balk again, Morgan swung her up into his arms and carried her back to the house, murmuring his reassuring lies every step. Leaving the front door open, he headed straight up the stairs, not putting her down until they were safe inside his bedroom. Kicking the door shut behind him, he sat her gently down on his bed and quickly moved to light the lantern. When he looked back at her, she was bent over nearly double, clutching her middle, while hard shudders wracked her body. Something told him that Jessica was no longer fully captive of her living nightmare and was, in some part at least, cognizant of her surroundings.

Morgan wasted little time gathering up towels and quilts. "Let's get you out of this soaked nightgown," he said softly, cautiously pulling her to her feet. Though she continued to tremble violently, Morgan was deeply concerned over her docile, almost childlike compliance. He removed her gown and quickly fashioned a haphazard turban around her dripping hair.

With another towel he blotted the moisture from her colorless face. The terrible vacuous look was gone from her beautiful eyes, but they still held a disquieting haunted quality that gave him no comfort. But there was no time to puzzle or question now. He needed to get her dry and warm as quickly as possible.

She was completely submissive and unresisting as he moved the towel over her body, doing the best he could to remove the crusted mud from her fingers. He worked rapidly, only pausing briefly when he brought the absorbent cloth to the area of her belly. Yesterday, Morgan would have sworn he knew every inch of Jessica's body. He would have been wrong. There on the pale, taut surface of her stomach he found the faint, practically indiscernible lines crisscrossing her satiny flesh. Even an ignorant jackass such as himself recognized the meaning of those marks, where, at one time, her skin had been stretched to accommodate the child she'd carried within her womb.

The baby Jessica had been tearing up the earth to find had been her own.

"Dear heaven," Morgan whispered with a pained grimace before he reached for one of the quilts. He draped it around her slumped shoulders and wrapped her up securely before shucking out of his own rain-soaked trousers. He passed a towel over his own hair and body and then gathered Jessica into his arms. Again there was no resistance as he drew her down onto the bed with him and carefully cradled her on his lap. Her lack of animation was beginning to scare the hell out of him, which was why he was so surprised when she began to talk, her voice little more than a weak, lifeless monotone at first.

"We were living on a small farm in the Indian Territory. It was very isolated, remote from any towns or neighbors—or so Cole had me believe. When we needed supplies, he would ride off and be gone for days and days. I never left that farm in all the months we were together.

"Though I tried to tell myself we weren't unlike other newly married couples, adjusting to each other, I knew deep down it wasn't true. So when I began to suspect I might be pregnant, I very cautiously broached the subject of children with Cole. His response was so hateful that I was afraid to tell him about the baby for fear he'd hurt me and cause a miscarriage. So I kept silent and endured his gripes about my getting fat. I was nearly five months along when he looked—really looked—at me one day and realized I was carrying his child. The expression of disgust on his face couldn't have been more terrible if I'd been eaten up with leprosy. Then he began to rage at me like a madman. I really believe he might have killed me if I hadn't gotten hold of his revolver." Jessica's voice broke then with the first show of emotion she'd exhibited since Morgan had carried her back into the house. And it was hatred he heard then.

"I should have killed him," she spat vehemently, her body going rigid. "I've regretted not shooting him every day of my life since. But I... I couldn't make myself pull the trigger, though I didn't hand over the gun. I must have scared him some, because he immediately went out and saddled his horse and rode away. He stayed away nearly a month this time. When he finally came back, he brought a female companion with him. A whore by the name of Mercy. Unfortunately, the woman's character didn't match her name. Merciless would have been more appropriate....

"I became Mercy's unpaid drudge, having to wait on her hand and foot, tolerating her insults, being forced to turn a blind eye and a deaf ear while she and Cole..."

Again Jessica's voice faltered on a shudder. Morgan just held her tighter. "You don't need to elaborate, Jess. I get the picture."

"I really didn't care what Cole did by then or who he was doing it with, just as long as he left me alone. All I cared about was my unborn child's safety. You see, the one time I dared balk at one of Mercy's demands, Cole backhanded me clear across the room."

The rage that seared through Morgan was greater than anything he'd felt before in his entire life, including those moments when he had held his dying brother and first heard the name Hardin. Only for Jessica's sake did he maintain rigid control over his impulses to curse the bastard into perdition, for fear his outburst might threaten her ability to continue a story that very much needed telling. He touched her gently and softly urged her to continue.

"After about a month, Mercy began to get bored with tormenting me. She began to whine and wheedle for Cole to take her someplace where they could have some real fun. The weather was already very cold, and I'm sure the idea of being trapped there until spring held very little appeal for Mercy. Ironically, Cole didn't seem too taken with the idea. I think he was a little afraid to leave the haven of the nations. And now I know why...."

Jessica took a deep breath, and when she began to speak again, her voice was thicker, as if each word had to be forced. "That's why I was so shocked when I awakened one overcast morning to find them both gone. Even as horrible as Cole had been, I couldn't quite accept he would really go off and leave me pregnant and completely alone. I kept telling myself there was plenty of time, that Cole would come back before—" Jessica shuddered. "But a week passed, and then another. I stopped counting days. Soon it became difficult to carry the wood in, to draw water from the well. The temperature kept falling, and the sky seemed a perpetual shade of gray. And the silence— Oh, God! There was that unrelenting, terrible silence. I think—no, I know—I began to go a little mad. My hatred for Cole just grew and grew...."

She didn't speak of her terror in that awful isolation. It wasn't necessary. Morgan heard it in her voice; felt it in the tremors coursing through her body. One way or another, he vowed silently, Cole Hardin was a dead man!

"My thoughts became obsessed with plans to hurt him. But how does one hurt a man who is without heart or soul? Then I remembered the money. Cole had such big plans for spending that money. He was only waiting for the law to forget, for his crime to be minimized by time and something bigger, more recent. And because he hadn't trusted his prized whore, Cole had left all that money behind, thinking it safe from his stupid cow of a wife! But he was wrong. He didn't count on my hatred or my determination. As swollen with pregnancy as I was, I dragged myself up that loft ladder in the barn and moved those heavy bales of hay to find the saddlebags he'd stashed up there. It never occurred to me I was doing myself any harm. After all, I'd been hauling wood and heavy buckets of water for weeks. In fact, I felt positively euphoric while I sat warming myself in front of the fire, watching Cole Hardin's stolen dreams go up in smoke...." There was a brief and poignant pause before she said, "The pain took me by surprise. And then there was this flood of water as if I'd wet myself. I...I didn't know what was happening...."

"Dear Lord," Morgan rasped harshly while his stomach churned sickly. He ached for that sixteen-year-old girl who'd suffered the travail of childbirth all alone, abandoned and as good as left to die. Morgan had little doubt in his mind that was what Hardin had intended. He'd left her there knowing fully she might go into labor and bleed to death, thereby ridding himself of an unwanted wife and child in one fell swoop. "The baby?" he finally asked, drawing her even closer yet feeling so inadequate in his attempt to comfort and solace where there could be none.

"Stillborn," Jessica told him very quietly. "He came too soon. But he was beautiful, so perfect in every way that I wouldn't accept—" She swallowed convulsively. "I don't remember very much after that. The wife of the Creek rancher who found me told me I'd been very, very ill. She said her husband had buried my little boy beneath a tree just beyond the house. I wasn't very pleasant to those good, kind people. They'd saved me when I cursed anything and everyone, including God, for letting me live and taking my baby."

Morgan pressed her head down more firmly against his shoulder. "Go ahead and cry it out, Jess," he said tenderly. "Let it go."

But Jessica wasn't nearly ready for tears yet. Her head popped up and she looked at him with eyes burning hotly with a hatred for Cole Hardin that had not abated even slightly in all these years. "That Creek family's ranch was little more than five miles from the farm. Five miles, Morgan!" she hissed. "Help was within walking distance...if I'd but known! But Cole knew! He'd visited the Grayburns several times—undoubtedly to discover if the law was sniffing around the area. And when...when Mrs. Grayburn expressed an interest in making the acquaintance of his wife, that bastard told her I'd not welcome the company because I carried a prejudice against Indians! Hannah Grayburn was an experienced midwife!"

He reached for her again; Jessica wanted no part of his comfort. Before he could stop her, she'd scrambled off the bed and whirled out of reach. The turban slid from her head, and her damp hair went spilling down her back and over her shoulders. She was magnificent in her fury, even if it was directed at him now.

"And you would accuse me of playing some kind of sick game?" Jessica raged at him. "That you're the only person on this earth who suffered a grievous loss because of Cole Hardin! That *bastard* intended I should die along with our baby...alone and without a single person living to give a damn—"

And Morgan didn't give a damn if she wanted him or not. He went to her and wrapped her up in his arms, ignoring her struggles, accepting the punishment she unleashed with her curses and the pounding of her small fists. And when she exhausted herself and slumped against him, he was there to support her while she sobbed out her anguish against his bare chest. When the storm finally passed, he tilted her chin up and looked into her tear-ravaged face. "I was wrong, Jessica. More wrong than I've ever been about anything in my life. I won't ask your forgiveness. I haven't the right to expect—"

"Oh, Morgan," Jessica breathed as her arms went around his neck and she raised up on tiptoe to press her cheek to his own. "It doesn't matter. I should have tried harder to tell you. Oramay told me you would understand if I'd swallow my pride and force you to listen."

Morgan closed his eyes and thought of the advice that wise woman had given him. *Look into your own heart*... Unfortunately, he'd obstinately ignored both Mrs. Seibert's wisdom and what his heart had been telling him all along. "I'm sorry, Jess. So damned sorry...."

Both of them became aware that Jessica's quilt had long since slipped from her shoulders. Her body was no longer chilled, and his was getting hotter by the minute. Morgan wanted to kiss and love her so badly it hurt. And he saw in her face a welcome to that loving he no longer felt he deserved. Not after all he had said and done. No, he had a great deal to atone for before he earned the right to touch this beautiful, courageous and exceptional woman again. If she would even have him after she'd had time to think things through.

Tenderly, he brushed a tear from her cheek with his thumb. "It's very late and we both desperately need some rest."

In spite of the gentle manner in which he withdrew from her, Jessica felt the sting of rejection nonetheless. Morgan might understand and believe in her now, but that would not alter the reality of who and what she was. The past stood between them like a huge, impenetrable wall. Morgan would never be able to look at her and just see her for herself. Not with the specter of Cole Hardin forever hovering over her head.

She accepted the shirt he offered and covered her nakedness, noting he'd done the same by pulling on a pair of dry trousers. Still, since she had no pride left to swallow... "Would you stay with me... please?"

Without a word, Morgan extinguished the light and crawled into bed beside her, offering his shoulder for a pillow without hesitation. "Jessica, I should have told you before—there are a few things you should know about your father." The immediate rigidity of her body was not unexpected.

"Not tonight, Morgan. I'm—"

"More than a little afraid of what you might hear, not to mention madder than hell at him for the way he failed you. I don't blame you for those feelings. And you wouldn't get any argument from him, either, Jess. But it's only fair you should know he didn't just suddenly, conveniently, straighten himself out after managing to ruin your life with his drinking and neglect. I'm the one who dragged him out of that shack and sobered him up, purely for the selfish reason of getting information about you and whatever family you might have. But once his brain was no longer fogged with whiskey, Jack Cameron quickly realized I meant you harm. I threatened to beat the information out of him, and he gave me permission to do my worst. Then I bribed him with a full jug of whiskey. He poured it over my feet.

"Jess, I can't explain or excuse what he did to you, but I can tell you that you're the primary reason he straightened himself out. He once told me it would be a mercy to return to the oblivion whiskey brought him, but that it was his penance to live sober—with the horrible guilt of what he'd done to his daughter and the daily hell of not knowing if you were dead or alive. He's grieved terribly over his weaknesses and mistakes, Jessica. If that's any comfort to you at all...."

Jessica remained silent, and Morgan wisely did not press the subject. "I just thought it was something you needed to hear," he finished softly. Her slight nod against his shoulder told him she had at least heard him out. Perhaps she might begin thinking about her father in a kinder, if not entirely forgiving, light. For her own sake, he hoped so.

Lately, Morgan had been doing some thinking of his own about his relationship with his older brother. Some of the revelations had been painful and hard to accept. It was difficult to admit that Zach had been merely a human being, basically decent, loving in his own way, but also somewhat autocratic and definitely single-minded in his ambitions. Zach had trouble taking people as they were, not as he would have them be, and that failing particularly applied to his younger brother. Unfortunately, Morgan had viewed Zachary as someone exemplary, by whose yardstick he measured himself and invariably came up short. Undoubtedly, time and maturity would have either resolved their differences or encouraged an amicable parting of the ways. Instead, Zach's death at a time when they'd been at cross-purposes had only reinforced Morgan's guilt over not living up to Zach's expectations of him. As fate would have it, Zachary had controlled and manipulated Morgan far more successfully from the grave than he ever would have managed if he'd lived.

Sadly, thanks to the woman now sleeping deeply and peacefully in his arms, Morgan had come to the disquieting realization that he shared some of Zach's less-admirable traits. In particular, Zachary held no corner on being obsessively single-minded and excessively judgmental. Morgan could give big brother a run for his money in those areas and probably come away with the prize.

After the first sound and uninterrupted night's rest she'd enjoyed in more than a week, Jessica awakened with some difficulty. When she remembered they were to depart for Fort Smith this morning she felt an even greater reluctance to leave the haven of the bed. Nonetheless, the events of the previous night had given her renewed determination; subsequently, she forced her head up off the pillow—only to gasp with alarm and scramble upright, drawing the sheet high, as she came face-to-face with the strange man seated in a chair across the room. Except that he wasn't really a stranger at all.

The russet hair had faded and was abundantly shot with silver. His ruddy complexion was heavily lined, making him appear much older than his forty-five years. But there was no mistaking the identity of the man slowly rising from the chair, his throat working convulsively while he nervously twisted the hat in his hands. After clearing his throat several times, Jack Cameron finally croaked, "Hello, Jessie."

Chapter Eighteen

The first few days of the Cameron family reunion was proving to be anything but a resounding, heartwarming success. Oh, it wasn't that anyone was exhibiting hostility. In fact, all parties were bending over backward to maintain a warm and pleasant atmosphere. Trying too hard, perhaps. Because underlying all the pleasantries was a tension so palpable everyone was beginning to show the strain, Jessica most of all.

After excusing herself from Pamela Cameron's well-intentioned but awkward attempts to make small talk, Jessica was taking refuge beneath a big shady maple tree and cursing Morgan Rossiter for this nasty trick he'd played. Not only was she confused and worried over his abrupt and unexplained decision to travel ahead of her to Fort Smith, Jessica was also furious with him for the high-handed manner in which he'd thrust her upon her father and his new family. Morgan had severely overstepped himself in this matter. Then again, how like him to *assume*—

"Jessie! Hey, Jessie! Look what I found in the barn."

Loping toward her was seven-year-old David, his young face glowing with excitement. This time David was without his younger shadow. At five, Warren was still required to take afternoon naps. She smiled up at David with genuine affection. "And what have you found?"

With his dark brown eyes glowing, David gently placed a tiny ball of fur into Jessica's lap and flopped down on the ground beside her. "There's five of 'em—I counted—in that ol' grain bin. I heard 'em mewin'."

"Oh, how adorable," Jessica cried at the sight of a very young kitten. She touched the silky fur with a single finger. David followed her lead.

"Soft, ain't he?" the boy whispered almost reverently.

"Very," Jessica agreed, then frowned slightly. "But I'm surprised the mama cat let you take her baby, David. Not one this young. She might have scratched you badly."

David shrugged. "Weren't no mama cat around. You think I could keep him, Jessie? He wouldn't take up no space, and he could stay in me and Warren's room. And I'd—"

"Whoa there," Jessica cautioned. "This baby's too young to leave her mama just yet." Patiently she explained how fragile and in need of her mother the kitten was. "Plus, she's just too small to be handled right now, David. Though I know you or Warren would never mean to, it's possible you could *accidentally* hurt the kitty."

David listened with an unusual patience and solemnity. Where Warren seemed naturally quiet and shy, David was a small package of gregarious perpetual motion. Worriedly, he said, "I'd better take kitty right back then. I didn't mean it no hurt, Jessie."

Obviously, she'd overstated her case. "Oh, I'm sure she'll be just fine, David. And in a few weeks those kittens will be chasing after you on their own, eager to play." David brightened instantly, but when he took the kitten from her lap, his touch was so achingly gentle Jessica felt her heart swell. Neither did he bound across the yard this time, but walked very slowly and cautiously.

"You're very good with children, Jessica. Both the boys are very taken with you—and you with them, I think."

Jessica twisted and looked up at the woman who'd approached unnoticed. Pamela Cameron was small, slightly plump and dark-haired and brown-eyed like her sons. She was a little older than Jessica had expected, being in her mid-thirties, and attractive in a quiet and understated way.

"I brought you some lemonade," Pamela said. "It gets pretty hot in these parts this time of day."

"Thank you, Pamela," Jessica said with equal politeness as she accepted the glass, knowing that Pamela was trying again to offer more than refreshment. She was offering friendship, as well. "The boys are very sweet and well behaved. It would be impossible not to like them."

"I hope someday you'll come to love them as they clearly already love you," Pamela returned somewhat sadly. "Supper will be ready soon, and I expect your father back from town at any moment. It's a rare day when Jack is late for a meal. His stomach keeps better time than any watch or clock."

Jessica had to look away. She remembered a time when her father never bothered to come home at all. "Can I be of any help in the kitchen?"

Pamela's heart ached for this young woman. How many times a day, she wondered, did they unintentionally reopen old wounds and revive bitter memories? Jack couldn't tell her much about those terrible times in Missouri and here in Ellsworth; quite frankly, he had very little recollection of those years. Which, of course, told Pamela a great deal about what Jessica had suffered.

"No, thank you, dear," she said kindly to Jessica's offer of help. "You just enjoy the lemonade and this nice breeze...."

When Pamela was gone, Jessica rolled her head back against the tree trunk and muttered, "Damn!" Would it have choked her to admit how much she already adored and loved her younger half brothers? She was acting like a bratty, sullen child instead of a grown woman. God! She felt like a child much of the time, jealous of the obvious love her father had for his new family, while at the same time rejecting every overture of affection he made toward her. She envied the loving bond witnessed every single day in this household. Memories of her own happy childhood made her wistful as she watched her father gently tussle with his sons. Then there would come this hard knot of fear inside her chest as she looked at David and Warren, seeing their absolute trust as they gazed at their father, believing completely in the security of his love and protection. In those moments it took all her will not to scream out warnings, to caution them that, in an instant, everything could change....

Thankfully, the sound of the wagon rattling down the lane gave Jessica a reprieve from her agonizingly ambivalent feelings. As his wife had so confidently predicted, Jack Cameron was home just in time for supper. She stood and straightened the ruffled back of the ridiculous atrocity of spotted pink cotton. Perhaps she would accept that length of pretty blue calico Pamela had so generously offered. Making the dress would give her something to do while she waited for word from Morgan. And certainly having something to wear other than the outrageous costumes he'd purchased for her would be a blessing in itself.

As she glanced toward the lane, Jessica's gaze passed over the field of wheat growing beyond. An involuntary shudder quaked through her. The nightmare of abandonment still lived vividly within her. And like the little girl in her dreams, Jessica wanted very much to run toward her papa and leap into his arms, but the fear of rejection was still too great. Nevertheless, when he climbed down from the wagon, she was there to greet him.

Jack hoped the welcome he was getting indicated a mellowing. He was beginning to despair she would ever be able to forgive him, though he couldn't truly blame her. "No word from Rossiter yet," he told her without preamble. "But then he's probably only been in Fort Smith a day or two...." The disappointment he saw on her face brought a frown. "Jessie, you can't honestly be that anxious—"

"I want to get this over with, Papa. The sooner the better."

"And the possibility of a jail cell is more appealing than being here with us?" He regretted the words the minute they left his mouth. "Jessie, I'm sorry...."

"It's all right, Papa," Jessica told him softly as she moved to the back of the wagon and began gathering the items he'd purchased for Pamela.

"Or is it Rossiter you're so anxious to see again?" Jack pressed, not sure how he should feel when she didn't argue his supposition. He didn't know what the relationship between those two had been, but the way Jessica looked at every mention of the man's name went a long way in arousing his protective instincts. Sadly, Jack had given up the right to fatherly concerns such as worrying over some handsome rogue breaking his daughter's heart. At least Rossiter no longer had Jessica targeted in his zealous pursuit for vengeance. For that Jack felt a father's gratitude. He just wished he'd not given Rossiter his pledge to keep Jessica ignorant of what he was up to down there in Arkansas. Then again, it probably was best not to get her hopes up. Even making his best effort, Rossiter might not be able to sway Judge Parker into granting Jessica the full immunity he planned to demand. Still, not telling her, seeing how she fretted, was getting harder and harder....

With the last wrapped bundle collected, Jessica turned back to her father. "I think Pamela has supper about ready."

"Well then, we'd best get ourselves to the table. She just might get impatient with our dawdling and decide to toss our portions to the hogs."

Jessica's gaze dropped to her father's thickening waistline before her eyebrows lifted on a chuckle. "Then you surely must have the skinniest hogs in the entire county, Papa." On that she turned and started toward the house.

Jack stared after her, dumbfounded for several minutes by her teasing quip. Then he began to smile, really smile as he hadn't done in years. If Morgan Rossiter had ever seen Jack Cameron do anything other than scowl at him, he would have instantly recognized Jessica as this man's daughter by the breathtaking power and beauty of the smile she'd inherited.

* * *

After yet another of Pamela's delicious meals, Jessica insisted upon doing the dishes. Maybe if she started acting like a member of the family instead of a guest, some of the awkwardness would begin to ease. Somehow sensing Jessica's motive, Pamela only made a halfhearted protest, her brown eyes shining with approval.

Unfortunately, Jessica's sincere good intentions didn't survive Jack Cameron's surprise treats for his children. She had just rejoined them in the parlor when her father began the familiar and well-remembered game of "See if you can guess what's in Papa's pockets."

An old hand at this game, David yelled "Licorice sticks!" Warren chimed in, jumping up and down and clapping his hands. Suddenly, Jessica saw her brother Daniel and herself in another parlor not so very different from this one. With tears flooding her eyes, she quietly backed out of the room. She didn't stop running from that nostalgic scene until she'd reached the pasture fence. How long she stood there, staring up at the night sky, fighting to get control of her emotions, she didn't know. Neither was she certain how long her father had been standing behind her before she became aware of his presence.

"The moon's nearly full," she said inanely, wondering how much of her distress he'd witnessed and if he could guess the cause.

Jack stepped up beside her and removed something from his pocket. "I seem to remember you had a preference for rock candy."

Seeing what he held in the palm of his hand, Jessica made a choking sound and covered her face with her hands. "I can't take any more. Oh, God . . . I'm sorry, but—"

"Being here with us—with me—is tearing you apart inside. It's been gnawing at you ever since Morgan told you I was alive. When you believed me dead it was less painful, because then it was all right to remember the good times fondly and forgive me, at least a little bit, for the suffering and horror. We always somehow manage to make peace with the dead. But I'm alive, Jessie. And for your own sake, you're going to have to find some way to make peace with that, as well."

"My sake, Papa?" Jessica cried, her hands gripping the fence now. "Isn't it absolution for yourself you need?"

Jack shook his head sadly. "You don't have that power, daughter. Only God can grant me that kind of release. It's my punishment to live with the guilt of my sins. Mine, Jessie, not yours. The fault was within me...not you, my sweet daughter."

"But I'm not...I don't..."

"Yes, you do, honey. You blame yourself. Deep down you're convinced that something must have been lacking within you or I'd not have turned to the drink for my comfort when Nora and Danny died. There had to be something wrong with Jessica Cameron for her father to reject her so cruelly when she needed him most. Obviously I didn't love you enough, which probably means you just weren't lovable."

Jack reached out to touch her, then drew back his hand. "Jessie, I know *exactly* what you're feeling, because I went through it all myself when my own father turned his back on me and my mama the very same way." Jack had her full and very startled attention now. "Yes, daughter. Your Grandpa Cameron drank himself to death when I was just a boy of twelve. Oh, officially his death was called an accident. He wasn't lucky like me. My papa took a tumble from a horse and broke his neck one night coming home from the saloon where he spent most of his time and all his money. And though it shamed me for years to admit it, even to myself, his dying was a relief.

"You see, I remember well all those times I cried and pleaded with him, promising I'd be a better boy if only he'd put away the jug. I watched my mama pray, night after night, asking God to make her a stronger person, a better wife, to give her the strength and power to save her husband from the devils within him. As if it were her responsibility to make him a better man." Jack spat angrily, then raked his hand through hair graying years too soon because the sins of the father had visited themselves upon the son. "And then, after all that, I turned right around and inflicted the same terrible misery upon my own wife and children."

"But you never...not before Mama and Danny died."

"Not so that you suffered from it, but that's only because Nora was clever in covering up my excesses. Though I'm sure you remember Papa's sick headaches and all those times she'd bustle you and Danny off to this neighbor or that for a few days' visit. I think some folks suspected there was more to Jack's headaches than your mama ever let on, but since I wasn't entirely like my pa, drunk all the time, nobody could say for certain. That's one of the reasons we were moving to Oregon. Your mama thought a change of scenery, a new start and getting away from painful old memories would break the pattern I was getting into. I began to believe it, too. But when Nora and Danny died—" Jack struggled with his own tears "—I blamed myself, Jessie. Rightly or wrongly, I can't say. A lot of other people lost loved ones in that same epidemic, which either means there were one helluva lot of sinners headed for Oregon needing punishment, or we were all the victims of just plain bad luck and a fate that defies explanation. But it seemed to me that once again I'd proved myself undeserving of love or happiness. If I'd been a better husband, a stronger person— I was a failure just like my father. No damn good inside and out. And then I set about proving what I believed of myself to be true."

He turned to Jessica then ana took her firmly by the shoulders. "I'm not making excuses, daughter. I am explaining the curse my father passed down to me, because I'm terrified I have tainted you with it, as well. Oh, not in the same way, perhaps. God knows, after what Morgan has told me, you've proved yourself to be a survivor. But though most of my memory is fogged, I can't get the image of a frightened little girl, looking forlorn and unloved, out of my head.

"Hate me, Jessie," he said gently. "Pity me. Deny I ever existed. Feel toward me whatever is necessary to find contentment within yourself. But for God's sake...and your own...don't harbor the unnecessary guilt that if you'd somehow been a better daughter, a stronger and more worthy person, I'd have loved you more and failed you less. Because if you do carry even the smallest of those feelings inside, they'll eat at you all the days of your life. Down deep you'll believe yourself undeserving of love or happiness. If your own father couldn't love you, how would it be possible for anyone else? And in time, you'll start seeing every disappointment, every loss, as confirmation of that worthlessness. It will destroy you, Jessie, one way or another."

Tears were rolling down Jessica's face now, and Jack gave in to the urge to put his arms around her. He rocked her to and fro as he said, "I love you, my Jessica. With all my heart. You were...and are...the best and finest daughter a man could be blessed with. I was proud of you back then, and I'm even prouder of the beautiful, courageous woman you've become. And I thank a merciful God for the privilege of being able to tell you what my father never got the opportunity to tell me. It was never your failing, child. The weakness existed within me."

Jessica resisted as long as she could, still afraid. But beyond her father's shoulder a field of wheat shimmered beneath a moonlit sky filled with crystal stars and danced on the warm summer breezes. The chilling gray fog of her nightmare began to lift from Jessica's soul as it yielded to the greater power of a father's love.

With a glad cry, she flung her arms around Jack Cameron's neck, and they clung to each other, taking the first step in laying the Cameron family curse to its final rest.

Three more days—happier days—passed before Morgan's telegram arrived. Jessica knew by the expression on her father's face that something was either very right or very wrong before he'd even climbed down off the wagon.

"You're free, Jessie. Really and truly free," he said even as he handed her Morgan's message. She nearly tore the paper in half in her urgency to get it out of the envelope.

HARDIN KILLED IN PRISON FIRE AND RIOT STOP DEATH CONFIRMED BY LEAVENWORTH OFFICIALS STOP JESSICA FREE TO DO AS SHE WISHES STOP

Jessica's knees went weak. "I...can't believe... Are they sure...? When did it happen?"

Jack slid an arm around his daughter's waist. "I had some of the same questions when I read— Lord, I hope you'll forgive me for reading..." Jessica waved off his apology, so Jack continued as he led her back to the house. "Anyway, I took the liberty of stopping by our local newspaper office. The editor was in the process of setting type on the story for tomorrow's paper."

They'd reached the front porch of the farmhouse, and Jack urged Jessica down onto one of the two rocking chairs. He didn't tell her how Zeke Layton had held out on him until Jack reminded him of his daughter's personal connection to Zach Rossiter's murderer.

"Well, in a nutshell, a small group of Leavenworth inmates set fire to the hospital facility a few days ago. Their plan, according to Zeke Layton, was to create confusion and distract the guards long enough to cover an escape attempt. There were only two patients occupying beds in the medical area. Cole Hardin had the misfortune of being one of those two men—though I'll be damned if I don't think he got just what was deserved! Guess with all them linens and chemicals that hospital facility went up like a raging inferno. And with bars on the windows, neither man had a chance to escape the flames. I won't distress you with the grisly details. Just suffice it to say it was lucky the prison knew who was occupying the place. Otherwise, identification would have been impossible.

"Only two of the six men responsible for setting the fire managed to get away clean. The others were recaptured within a day. Personally, I've a notion to head up to Leavenworth and shake a few hands." When he noticed Jessica was still exceptionally pale, Jack reached over and captured her hands. "Honey, you *can't* be feeling remorse for that bastard's death?"

Jessica shook her head. "No, Papa. In fact, I couldn't agree more that it was indeed a fitting and deserved ending for Cole Hardin. But feeling that way..." She looked up at him beseechingly. "What kind of person am I that I could admit such a terrible thing? To actually feel gratification over the death of another human being..."

Jack squeezed her fingers reassuringly. "Only the human kind, sweetheart. Flaws and all. One who's suffered greatly because of that man's evil. And also someone who is better than most, because I don't know too many folks who'd even give those feelings a second thought, including your old papa here."

When Jessica nodded and gave him a weak smile, Jack tweaked her tip-tilted nose. "I'd better find Pamela and give her the news. She's been real worried over this thing, Jessie. I hope you know that Pamela cares a great deal—"

"Yes, I do know, Papa. She's a wonderful person. You're a very lucky man to have found her. And I have been blessed in turn by your good fortune. I've not only acquired a loving stepmother, but also a treasured friend."

Moisture suddenly blurred Jack Cameron's vision. He found it necessary to clear his throat before he was able to speak again. "I don't know about you, but I sure could use a good cup of coffee about now. Think I'll talk Pamela into making us a fresh pot. Come in and join us when you're ready."

Jessica was blinking back tears of her own as her father slipped into the house, but she smiled when she heard him bellow Pamela's name, only to be quickly admonished by the weary mother. Pamela had only recently convinced two very cranky and quarrelsome little boys that an afternoon nap was preferable to the spanking they were very close to getting. And since big sister had been at the center of their bickering as both boys competed for her undivided attention, Jessica had been ordered—kindly and diplomatically, but ordered nonetheless—to wait for her father outside.

Jessica let the warmth of belonging, really belonging, to a family again creep over her and begin to banish the terrible, unfeeling chill that had stolen over her soul since learning of Cole Hardin's death. She owed Morgan such an enormous debt of gratitude for forcing this healing reunion with her father.

"Oh, Morgan." She sighed. "How are you feeling right now? Relieved? Or cheated because fate has denied you the satisfaction and justice of seeing Cole Hardin hang for Zachary's murder?" Knowing Morgan, Jessica strongly suspected the latter.

Smoothing the telegram she'd crumpled in her hands, Jessica read the tersely worded message again...and again, concentrating upon the last line: *free to do as she wishes.*

"But what does that mean, Morgan? That I'm free to go...or stay? Or that it doesn't matter to you either way? Dear God, my love, just exactly what do you mean...?"

During the first days following the arrival of Morgan's telegram, Jessica didn't allow herself to speculate and worry too much over his decidedly cryptic message. Instead, she concentrated on enjoying being with her family, getting to know her father all over again and opening her heart fully to Pamela. From the start she'd loved David and Warren to distraction, but now she didn't hesitate to express her feelings openly, unreservedly. And when Jessica stopped getting in her own way and stopped throwing up shields to protect herself, she received in return tenfold of all the love and affection a once-desperately needy heart could hold. But even with all these wonderful blessings, there remained an emptiness, a place within her that family could not reach or occupy. There was a rather significant chunk of her heart and soul that only Morgan could fill, and one she began to fear would forever remain barren as the days stretched into weeks. The last days of July flew by. August arrived, blistering hot, and still Morgan had not returned or sent word of any kind....

"You look troubled, Jessica. Was there something in Oramay's letter to distress you?"

Jessica's gaze went to the woman sharing the front porch with her, both of them having come out here in hopes of catching whatever stingy breeze could be found on this sweltering afternoon. "Not at all. Everything in Moonshadow is just as it should be, actually."

"But I imagine your friends are starting to wonder when you plan to return?" Pamela leaned over and patted Jessica's hand. "Your father and I would keep you here with us forever if we could, Jessica. I hope you know that. But we also realize you have responsibilities and people who love you in Moonshadow, as well. People who are as important to you as we are. Jack knows you can't stay here indefinitely, and he understands. We both do. Perhaps even more than you realize...."

Pamela hadn't meant to be intentionally ambiguous with the last statement. In fact, she'd not planned to say anything at all. But now, with Jessica looking at her in bewildered consternation, she opened the topic that had been discussed almost nightly between Jack and herself as they snuggled together in bed.

"Honey, we've seen how anxiously you watch the road, noticed your confusion and despondency when Jack brings home the mail. Today, when he handed you Oramay Seibert's letter, your face lighted up...until you recognized the handwriting. It's Morgan Rossiter you're waiting to hear from, isn't it? Morgan Rossiter you hope to see riding down our lane?"

Pamela held her breath, fearful Jessica would resent a stepmother's intrusion into her privacy. And when Jessica moved from the chair and walked to the porch railing, it appeared her fears were being realized. "Jessica, I—"

"I'm really not sure what I've been hoping for from Morgan. Probably a great deal more than it's possible for him to grant, considering our history." She turned back to

Pamela, actually glad, painful though it was, to stop pretending Morgan was nothing more to her than an unfortunate catalyst for bridging her past with her present. "That he no longer despises me and believes me innocent of Cole's crimes may be the most he can possibly give."

Jessica sat down on the low rail, bracketing her hips with the hands she curled tightly around the wood. "For Morgan's sake, I almost wish that fire in the prison infirmary had never happened. He *needed* to confront Cole Hardin face-to-face. Needed the satisfaction of being the instrument that brought Cole to justice. Fate robbed him, stepped in and yanked victory right out of his hands just when he finally had it within his grasp. I don't imagine he's feeling too kindly toward much of anything right now. Unfortunately, I'm part of all that. A big part. Because if he'd found me sooner..."

She looked over her shoulder toward the empty lane beyond. In the process, her gaze passed over her father's wheat field. "I'm more fortunate, Pamela," she went on thoughtfully. "All my ghosts have been laid to rest. I'm free of the past."

"But will you be able to free yourself from Morgan, Jessica?"

No, she would never be free of Morgan Rossiter, in more ways than just the love that would always be with her. Because Jessica's body was giving her every reason to believe she was carrying Morgan's child.

"It's time I went home, Pamela. There's a future to get on with. One I hope you and Papa and the boys will be a very big part of. But I can't stay here and keep looking down a road and waiting for someone who won't ever be coming...."

Two days after her talk with Pamela, Jessica was saying goodbye to her father at the Ellsworth train station.

"God, Jessie! I hate like the devil to let you go!"

"You will keep your promise to come out next March, won't you, Papa?" Jessica's voice was thick with emotion, as his had been. And they clutched hands so tightly both their fingers were going numb. "I'm counting on seeing all of you in March." If she was right in her suspicions, the baby would be born sometime in late March. She might very much need the support of a loving family around her then. Sadly, not all the nightmares from the past could be entirely banished.

Jack wasn't sure why she was so specific and insistent about the particular month, but he would have gladly promised her the moon and the sky if that's what she asked of him. "We'll be there, sweetheart. With bells on if that's the way you want us," he added huskily, pulling her into his arms. "Honey, if I see Morgan . . . is there anything in particular you want me to say?"

Stepping back, Jessica smiled wanly. "If he asks, tell him how grateful I am that he made it possible for me to have my father back in my life again. And tell him I wish him every happiness. But only if he asks, Papa. Only then. . . ."

Chapter Nineteen

Jessica's cheeks were colored by more than the unseasonably cool weather. On this damp and blustery Sunday in late September, Jessica was also seething with a fiery-hot case of indignation.

"How could you have done that without consulting me, Earl Taylor?" she spat, breaking the angry silence she'd clung to ever since they'd walked out of church. If it wasn't for her stiff-necked pride, not to mention the sake of appearances, she would never have allowed Earl to drive her home. "My God! I still can't believe it!"

Earl Taylor was hesitant to open his mouth again. She sure did have herself a temper, though this was the first time he'd ever seen Jessie Miller in an uproar. It surprised him. But then a whole lot of things about Jessie were surprising these days. He glanced up at the gray, cloudy sky, wincing at the thought of a long, wet ride back to town after he delivered Jessie and her buggy to the Eldorado. Because sure as shootin' it was going to come a downpour within the next hour. Making a clicking noise with his mouth, Earl snapped the reins and urged Jessie's piebald mare to a swift trot and hoped the nag tied behind the buggy could keep up.

When the wind picked up and began to blow with more force, Earl decided it might be a good idea to make peace. He for sure wasn't looking forward to that ride back. A nice warm parlor, some female companionship and maybe a home-cooked meal sounded far more appealing.

"Jessie," he began cautiously, "if I did wrong, I'm real sorry. . . ." Her shrill *"If!"* wasn't encouraging. And when he chanced a glance her way, Earl decided her pinched expression and the way her blue velvet cloak was flapping and billowing up around her made it appear as if she were going to fly at his head any second now. "Well, I guess maybe I got carried away just a little, but—"

"'If'? You 'guess'? 'Maybe'? Well, let me tell you, Sheriff Taylor! There's no question about it. That windy speech you made in front of the congregation this morning will never be equaled in our lifetimes. And it won't be forgotten, either."

Jessica's voice dropped an octave as she went from strident outrage to irate grumbling. "Going on and on like that about my virtues. Making a vociferous public announcement . . . when you knew very well I wanted to spare us embarrassment later by keeping as low a profile as possible now. And if all that wasn't bad enough, Oramay and Stan were planning to make their own announcement today. Or did you forget that? Oramay had even bought a special dress. It was supposed to be their special day, and you ruined it for them."

Earl Taylor had a real long fuse, especially when exercising patience was to his benefit, but Jessie Miller was beginning to cause him to burn just a little. "Matter of fact, I did forget. But after all the years those two have been dancin' around each other, I don't imagine it'll kill them to have to wait another week or two to announce their wedding plans. And as far as you and me are concerned— Jessie, for somebody as much in need of a husband and wedding as you are, you sure as heck have been draggin' your feet about us gettin' hitched.

"Now, I know I ain't no prize, but ain't too many men I know who'd be willin', under any circumstances, to accept and raise another man's child up as their very own. And if you need remindin', it was you who came to me offerin' a bargain. Which I gladly accepted, and for some selfish reasons of my own, I'll admit, like providin' a real good home and future for my own boy. Now, I'm content and consider swappin' a ma for a pa, and vice versy, a fair exchange. I also know it ain't gonna be no love match between us, and I can live with that, too. But I don't see the harm in makin' things look better than they really are to our friends and neighbors. In the long run it'll also make acceptin' that baby as mine more a natural thing."

Jessica was in no mood to be reasonable. However, she did have to concede that Earl scored some valid points. She *had* been dragging her feet, putting him off and making one silly, empty excuse after another to keep from committing to an actual wedding date. Of course, she knew why she'd been stalling. She suspected Earl knew, also, though he couldn't put a name or a face to the knight in shining armor she still foolishly hoped would ride in and save her from this unwanted marriage. "You should have at least warned me of your plans, Earl."

And she'd have just found another reason why he shouldn't speak up, Earl knew. Which was exactly why he'd intentionally sprung it on her...and just about every other living soul in this valley in the bargain. And he hadn't done it to force her hand, just in case she *was* having second thoughts. Not entirely, anyhow. It was for Jessie's sake, too. Because she certainly wasn't getting any less pregnant as time went on. That sky wasn't looking any less threatening, neither.

Earl changed his tune somewhat. "I'm real sorry to have embarrassed you, Jessie," he said just as the house and buildings of the Eldorado came into view. "And I apologize for the way I went about it. Especially for forgetting Stan and Oramay's plans. I'll make my regrets to them first chance I get. So say you'll forgive me. Please...." he added as he brought the horse and buggy to a stop in front of that big, comfortable old log house, with its cozy parlor and huge fireplace.

"Perhaps I did overreact some," she granted while Earl climbed down and walked around to her side of the buggy.

Earl placed his hands on either side of her waist and hoisted her down, not even aware of the little grunting sound he made that evidenced his unfamiliarity with physical exertion. "Guess in your condition, a little crankiness now and then just goes with the territory."

He spoiled her determination to be gracious with his patronizing. And also with the liberties he took when he squeezed her waist several times in a manner she associated with testing the ripeness of fruit. She put a reasonable distance between them and drew the warm velvet cloak around her more securely.

"It was your effusive praise of my high moral fiber and virtuous nature I found so distressing, Earl. My God! People will remember those statements to the letter, and six months from now they will also have a heyday with the obvious evidence refuting every word you uttered."

"Then we'd best not dawdle anymore on settin' that date, had we? Otherwise, folks will be needing fewer fingers to do their counting."

Jessica nodded. How could she do otherwise? Earl's logic was infallible. Plus, snicker though people might, there was no comparison to what she'd hear if she gave birth to an illegitimate child. For her baby's sake, she would finally give Earl what he'd been harping for. "Speak to Reverend Martin. If his schedule is free, we can have a quiet ceremony the week after next. Please note I said *quiet,*" Jessica added firmly.

"Why not next week?" Earl was anxious to get himself and Lonnie settled in here. Being lord and master over a place like this was all he'd ever dreamed of and never thought to have.

"Because next week Oramay and Stan are going to be given the opportunity to announce their upcoming nuptials without anyone else stealing their thunder." When a large droplet of rain splatted the ground at Jessica's feet, she looked at Earl and said, "It's starting to rain, Earl. You'd better start back for town before it really opens up."

"I was thinking I could maybe come in and sit a spell until it blows over?" Earl said hopefully. "Otherwise, I'll get soaked...."

"I'm sorry, but I just don't feel up to being sociable today. My condition, you know..." she added with a hint of a sarcastic note in her voice that it was doubtful he noticed. "And it could very well storm into tomorrow. Your best chance of making it home dry is to leave this very minute. Maybe you'll be lucky enough to outrace those incoming clouds."

Since Earl had been on shaky ground with her since morning, and because it was obvious she wasn't entirely over her snit yet, he decided a drenching was better than pushing Jessie too far today. Besides, she'd given him a firm date for the wedding. He didn't want to risk losing ground there. "I'll ride out after I've talked to the reverend."

Untying his mount and swinging into the saddle with all the grace his paunchy form would allow, Earl took his leave with one final speech. "You won't regret coming to me for help, Jessie. I'll be a good pa to your baby, I swear. Plus, we've got no foolish, romantic notions about what we're gettin' ourselves into. We've been right honest about what each of us expects outa this bargain. It'll be just fine, you'll see."

"Be careful," Jessica managed as he spurred his mount and trotted off.

Watching him, she was forced to admit Earl Taylor deserved better than a shrewish wife, which she was already rehearsing to become. Actually, Earl deserved her undying gratitude. So what if his real interest was the Eldorado, with a mother for his son thrown in as a bonus? He was certainly right about one thing. She wasn't going to find any other men lining up at her door offering to raise another man's child. Nor did she have many options. None that were acceptable, in any case.

Certainly, she couldn't do what Oramay wanted. Tracking down and notifying Morgan of his impending fatherhood wasn't even to be considered. And she'd forced

Oramay to take a Bible oath that she would not, directly or indirectly, make such an attempt. No, getting Morgan that way was unthinkable. The loveless, businesslike arrangement she'd made with Earl Taylor was more palatable. Primarily because it was loveless. A one-sided love would eventually, essentially, tear her heart right out. Yes, she owed Earl Taylor much. She was very grateful. She was!

Jessica couldn't hold back a sob of despair before she cried, "Dear Lord in heaven! Am I doing the right thing by marrying Earl Taylor?"

"Good question, Jess. However, maybe you should consult the father of your child first...instead of going over his head to a higher authority."

"Morgan," Jessica gasped, whirling around just as he was stepping out of her front door. She registered the unrelieved blackness of his clothing, a smooth-shaved, angrily set jaw, the shape of his scowling mouth and smoky gray eyes that were burning hotly. And then the ground began to tilt.

"But if you want my opinion, lady, bartering yourself off to the first lazy, no-good jackass who comes along—"

Jessica never heard what was left of Morgan's opinion. She hit the ground in a faint.

"What the damn hell did you do to her?"

"Not a blasted thing...."

"Well, you musta said or done something!"

"Only what I thought of her marrying a lazy jackass like Earl Taylor."

"Since she's gotta know Taylor's a jackass, that ain't cause enough to swoon. So it musta been your doin', some way or another, to put her down hard like that. Has to be some reason, dammit!"

"Maybe it's her condition. Did you ever think of that? Pregnant women are given to fainting spells."

"And no doubt you're an expert on that subject! Tell me, Rossiter, just how many good, decent women have you—"

Jessica groaned. She had actually been trying to shriek that the two men arguing over her should shut up! They were disturbing her peace. Jessica didn't want to be dragged out of the agreeable void. She wanted nothing to do with what was awaiting her out there. For insurance, she squinched her eyelids tightly shut.

"I think she's coming around."

"Why is she grimacin' like that? Jessie! Jessie, it's Boone. Are you hurtin' someplace?"

"Maybe her head struck the ground harder than I thought."

"And maybe a strong, agile young buck like yourself should have found a way to catch her before she hit the ground at all!"

Jessica did a little better on her shriek this time before she ground the heels of her hands into her eyes. "If you two cackling roosters are determined to argue, I do wish you'd go and peck at each other somewhere else!"

"I think I see some color in her cheeks now."

"Her tongue is apparently unimpaired. I've never heard one with a healthier bite."

"Maybe if we can get her sittin' up on the sofa here, the blood will start flowin' faster."

"Sounds logical."

Jessica was gently lifted and helped into a sitting position. But it wasn't being upright that started the blood surging through her body; it was those strong hands, Morgan's hands, on her shoulders, cupping her hips and lingering beneath her knees that were reviving more than circulation. Neither did Jessica need to open her eyes to know his touch. Her body knew him with a welcoming beyond her control or will. And it was also telling her it would betray her, eagerly and wantonly, at the first given opportunity. The realization brought an involuntary sob. Immediately the hands beneath her knees tightened.

"Are you in pain, Jess? Do you need David Griffith?"

This time Jessica heard genuine worry in his deep, soft voice. But then he would be concerned, wouldn't he? The health and safety of his unborn child was at stake. Jessica didn't delude herself regarding the source of his distress. From the first she'd known Morgan would want his son or daughter. Unfortunately, mother and baby were a set, indivisible. To have one necessitated taking the pair. But could she live with being the booby prize he'd been forced to accept in order to lay claim to the treasure? It was a question she'd tormented herself with since David had confirmed her pregnancy. And one she had answered when making the decision to keep Morgan in ignorance of his impending fatherhood. It was also a decision Oramay disagreed with vehemently. Obviously even more vehemently than Jessica had realized.

"Jess...?"

She opened her eyes slowly, glad of the momentary blurred vision that spared her from seeing too clearly those perfectly chiseled, achingly handsome features. "I'm fine," she croaked, needing to swallow back the threat of tears before she could repeat the reassurance convincingly.

"Are you certain?"

"Very," she insisted firmly, squaring her shoulders and preparing to do battle. Despite Oramay's meddling, Jessica had not changed her mind. Morgan Rossiter could take his sense of duty and obligation...and go straight to hades! Looking directly into the dark gray eyes boring into her own, Jessica demanded, "Why are you here?" As she'd hoped, the frosty tone was sufficient to get him to back off. He rose to his feet and stepped back even as the ever-hovering Boone Larsen edged closer.

"He's here because I sent for him," Boone announced in a tone that fell somewhere between boastful and combative, as if he were proud of his meddling and was daring either party in this room to challenge what he'd done. Ignoring Rossiter's muttered but vividly expressive curse, Boone jammed his hands into his pockets and took on the young woman who'd thought him too dumb, too old or too something to figure out what the hell had been going on around here. "Figured *somebody* better step in and keep you from makin' a god-awful mess of things."

"You? But how did you— I never..." Jessica's idiotic sputtering stopped when it all became very clear just how Boone had been let in on the secret of her pregnancy...and why. "Oh, yes. I see Oramay's clever hand in this. Her vow of secrecy only extended to not notifying Morgan. But in telling you—"

"Nobody told me nothin', missy! Didn't have to! It's just lucky for you I happen to be the oldest of my ma's brood of eight. Growin' up I got real familiar with the signs there was a new brother or sister on the way. And you, my girl, was showin' most of 'em...and a few extra of your own, besides. It was pretty damned certain that you was either in the family way or you'd up and lost your everlastin' mind. Had to be one or the other, or why else would you even consider marryin' Earl Taylor? Unless you were pregnant and scared and too goddamn proud to send for Rossiter here and make him own up to his responsibility. So I fetched him for you!"

"Now wait just a minute," Morgan began, wanting to correct the assumption that *anyone* had needed to fetch him here for any reason other than this was exactly where he wanted to be right now. But neither Jessica nor Boone seemed to have any interest in his presence or anything he had to say at the moment.

"I can't believe this!" Jessica bristled, absolutely livid over what Boone had done to her. "And just who, Boone Larsen, gave you the authority to interfere—"

"Took it upon myself, by God!" Boone shouted right back. "And I ain't sorry for it, neither! Now maybe if you'd picked somebody halfway decent to play pappy to that babe, I'd have stayed out of things. But Earl Taylor? Lord, Jessie! All that lazy so-and-so's good for is to take up space. Don't think he knows what it is to work up a decent sweat, let alone take on the runnin' of a place this size. Though I'll bet he'd be real expert at watchin' you do all the work, sittin' around on his lazy butt and gettin' fatter while you're becomin' nothin' but skin and bones.

"Ah, Jessie," he went on, his manner gentling when she turned her face away from the hard truths he was tossing at her. "I love you like you was my own. I couldn't let you go through with this crazy notion to marry Earl. Oh, I know he ain't no abusive monster or nothin'. But that don't change the fact that you'd soon be soul-deep in misery living with Earl day in and day out. And that ain't countin' all the nights. Hellfire, girl! That dumb jackass don't even have the sense to see that you're the real prize of the Eldorado. I reckoned Rossiter at least had some appreciation for the woman you are. Otherwise, you wouldn't be in this fix, now would you? Also figured there had to be some feelin's on your part, too. Or you'd not have let him . . ."

Morgan cleared his throat. Loudly. "Larsen, I imagine Jessica would appreciate a glass of water about now." Couldn't that misguided old cowhand see he was just furnishing stone and mortar for the wall Jessica was busily building up around herself? God! He should have muzzled that old buzzard the minute those jaws started flapping. Now he was going to play hell even getting Jessica to listen to him. Already, without Larsen's help, she had more than sufficient cause to kick him out of here on his stupid ass. "Larsen? The water?"

Only a fool could have missed the real message being communicated by those gunmetal-colored eyes. Boone saw right away he was being given a choice between quietly slipping out the back or being grabbed up and tossed out on his ear in the next second or two.

"Yeah," he agreed with the wisdom granted by age and a strong instinct for self-preservation. "I'll get that water right now." With a parting glance at Jessie's frozen profile, Boone indulged a secret grin. When Jessie set her chin at that particular angle, it meant she'd set her mind, as well. He wondered if Rossiter had any idea what he was in for with that contrary and sometimes fiercely obstinate female. Somehow that quiet little place in Wyoming Territory was rapidly losing its appeal.

Boone's departure was marked by the sound of his boots clomping across her hardwood floor, while Jessica was trying to decide whether to rejoice or lament this temporary reprieve. True, she was spared that mortifyingly brutal candor. On the other hand, she was also now completely alone with Morgan, who'd heard every word of Boone's so very accurate speech. And if that wasn't enough, she could just imagine the phrasing and bluntly colorful terms Boone had used in executing his summons.

Accepting that she couldn't avoid facing Morgan indefinitely, Jessica took a deep breath. So deep a breath, in fact, that the binder she still wore beneath her somewhat improved wardrobe should have pressed uncomfortably against her slightly tender, highly sensitive breasts. But there was no such discomfort. Fearfully, Jessica glanced down for the first time since reawakening to this impossible fiasco. A horrified shriek soon followed the rather belated discovery that the bodice of her blue silk was unbuttoned to the waist.

"Is this what you're missing, Jess?"

Morgan had strolled over and scooped something off the floor—a strip of cut linen he was now dangling before her face.

"Damn you for having the gall of ten men," Jessica rasped as she snatched the cloth out of his hands and immediately stuffed it beneath her skirts. "And don't tell me you're not responsible for this!"

Morgan wouldn't dream of denying the charge. "On the contrary, I read somewhere that loosening restrictive clothing is advised for someone in an unconscious state. And I couldn't think of anything more restrictive or unhealthy than that damned thing!"

Anger and embarrassment brought healthy, flaming color to Jessica's formerly pale cheeks as she frantically, futilely attempted to reaffix buttons and cloth over a great deal more womanly flesh than they'd needed to cover before. It didn't help to know Morgan was looming over her, enjoying a bird's-eye view.

When the button set directly between Jessica's breasts proved unworthy of the demand by popping off in her hand, Jessica gave in to impulse and threw it across the room.

"Damn!" she growled, giving up the battle and clutching the edges of her bodice, instead, to preserve whatever modesty and dignity had been left to her. "I suppose you took a great deal of sadistic pleasure exposing me—the queen of fraud—to Boone."

Having his own past mistakes thrown up at him should have encouraged Morgan to exercise a tight rein on his tongue. But the nastiness she used in making the unjust accusation brought about a lapse in judgment. "Surely you weren't expecting to maintain that little secret after your marriage to Sheriff Taylor? Or that he'd be able to keep such a delightful surprise to himself?" Contributing to Morgan's incautious observation was a still-vivid and infuriating recollection of the evening he'd spent pumping Earl Taylor full of liquor at the Golden Rose saloon. One day very soon that son of a bitch would have cause to regret the sport he'd made of Jessica that night....

Morgan's hatefulness brought hot tears to Jessica's eyes and immediate contrition from Morgan.

"Jess... I'm sorry...."

She shook off his apology and the helping hand he offered as she got up from the sofa and walked stiffly over to the large latticed window Uncle John had painstakingly crafted and installed. Only today there was no warming flood of light, just the appropriate gloom of a miserable, stormy day.

"Damn!" Morgan muttered viciously, wishing now he hadn't sent Larsen off—if only so the old man could kick his butt around the room a few times. Zach had been right. All those years of schooling had been wasted. Because he sure as hell was one dumb bastard. God knew he'd proved that often enough these past months. Maybe once too often as far as the woman staring out the window was concerned. It was a sobering realization. Better than a good kick in the ass, actually. Because the mere thought of a future without

Jessica and their child carried the guarantee of everlasting purgatory. Undoubtedly deserved, but a fate he had no intention of suffering without one helluva battle. And battles weren't won in retreat or by taking the path of least resistance....

But it wasn't going to be easy, Morgan accepted as he joined her at the window, half expecting her to move away from him again. It didn't take him long to figure out why she didn't. She had no need to run. Not when she was so well guarded. Suddenly that protective wall of hers didn't seem quite so figurative. Morgan could almost believe that if he reached over and touched her, his fingers would encounter cold stone instead of soft, warm flesh. However, it was a commonly known fact that defenses were always fortified where they were most vulnerable.

Morgan turned slightly and braced his hip against the lower part of the window frame. "Did you really never intend to tell me about our child, Jess?"

Typically, Morgan got straight to the point: the baby. His only reason for being here. Not the baby's mother. It was a bitter pill to swallow when a woman had to acknowledge a sharp pang of jealousy toward her unborn child. But it was a welcome momentary aberration, because it gave her the strength to disregard the compelling hurt and sadness she'd heard in his voice.

"No, Morgan. I didn't want you to know," Jessica admitted. "And I regret with every fiber of my being that you were enlightened against my wishes."

"Why?"

His simple and straightforward question deserved a like response, and Jessica had one prepared and ready for him. One that was no more or less the unadulterated truth. "Because we both know that without Boone's interference you would have gone through the remainder of your life blissfully content, none the wiser and completely unconcerned about the very real possibility we might have created a child together. Now, however, it's impossible for you to ignore the reality. Honor and manly pride demands, as Boone so bluntly stated, that 'you own up to your responsibility.'

"Well, Morgan," she rushed on, wanting to get this over with before the tremors inside became quakes and the man standing beside her recognized what a god-awful actress she truly was, "consider your obligations fully met. You came. You saw. And you were honorably prepared to acknowledge responsibility. Only I sent you packing, instead. Absolved you of duty. So you're off the hook, Morgan. Thank you for coming. The door—" she directed with an expressive nod of her head "—is right over there. Please close it securely on your way out."

"Lord, Jess!" Morgan rasped as he grabbed her by the shoulders and drew her around to face him. His confidence got a mighty shaking when he caught the first terrifying glimpse of purgatory in the depths of her feverishly determined eyes. "Have you come to hate me so much?"

Hate him? Dear heaven, if only she could. "Not hate, Morgan," she answered with difficulty, twisting out of his grasp because she couldn't bear his touch another second. How easy it would be to convince herself that his distress was caused by something deeper than wounded ego.

"If not hate, then what would you call it, Jess?"

"Acceptance," she answered quietly.

"Acceptance?" Morgan frowned. "What the hell is that supposed to mean? That you accept I'm such a low-down skunk I'll gladly take you up on your offer of absolution? Hollering 'yippee' and skipping off without a backward glance like some devil-may-care youngster...?"

"All this indignant outrage is very impressive, Morgan," Jessica shot right back at him. "However, by your own words in your telegram you granted me the freedom to do as I please. I accepted you meant them. And right now it would please me very much if you would just leave as I've asked. Otherwise, I'm quite certain I can find *someone* in the bunkhouse sufficiently loyal to my wishes who will put you out." The thin stridency of her voice warned Jessica she was fast reaching the breaking point. On legs that were quivering violently, she turned, walked to the door and opened it wide. "I hope you won't make trouble, Morgan."

After what seemed an aeon or two of waiting, Morgan surrendered. Or so Jessica believed until he slowly sauntered up, gently removed her hand from the doorknob and pointedly reclosed the door.

"You would have caught your death standing in that damp draft, Jess," he observed matter-of-factly while looking down into hazel eyes that were as big as saucers. They got even bigger when he took her by the waist and swung her around so that her back was up against the closed door and he was planted solidly in front of her. Then he quickly braced one hand upon the door just to the left of her head, while the other threaded itself through the thick skein of auburn silk lying heavily against the nape of her neck.

"All right, Jess," he began before she could gather her stunned wits and start squawking protests. "We've established the fact I'm a son of a bitch. A low-down, contemptible bastard who sends thoughtlessly worded telegrams when it would have been wiser instead just to ram my stupid, aching head through the nearest wall. So maybe you're right. Considering all the misery I've inflicted upon you in one way or another since the day we met, perhaps the most decent, honorable thing would be for me to march out that door and keep on going, right out of the valley, California and your life. Just forget about you and the baby. Get on with living my life, so you can get on with your own." When she would have averted her face, Morgan exerted just enough gentle pressure on her neck to force those beautiful, suspiciously overbright eyes to meet his own. "Is that about it, Jess? Have I summed up your thoughts pretty accurately?"

Jessica was too close to sobbing for more than a very slight nod and a barely audible "Yes."

"Well, then. Now that we're clear on what you're thinking, let's move on to exploring how you feel. . . ."

The defeated sob she'd been holding broke free when she saw his intent burning out of the storm-gray depths of his eyes.

"No...don't...."

Morgan couldn't allow himself to be swayed by that anguished sound she made. This was too important; it was everything. He angled his head and bent his knees so no strain was put upon her neck as he claimed her soft, trembling mouth. He kissed her until the rigidity went out of her neck and kept on kissing her until her lips parted of their own accord and the sweet, moist depths of her mouth were being offered up to him. "Ah...honey. You taste so good...so damned good...."

The devil was back to reclaim what belonged to him, Jessica thought hazily. Her heart and her soul, her mind and her body. He possessed her with the hot, liquid strokes of his tongue, and damned her for all time when he slipped his hands beneath the open bodice of her dress. A helpless moan escaped her throat when the soft cotton chemise proved an unworthy sentinel, giving way and surrendering her eager breasts up to him without even a token protest. His stroking, rotating thumbs on her sensitive nipples were a sweet torment. Liquid fire flowed until her limbs were fluid.

He swept her boneless body up into his arms and carried her back to the sofa, setting her down gently. He knelt before her and again his hands slid beneath cloth, only this time he pushed blue silk and white cotton off her shoulders, drawing both garments down to just above her elbows, effectively trapping her arms and baring her breasts to his pleasure in one easy, unhampered move.

Too easy! But she came to that realization far too late. And when he captured both hands, even the defense of drawing her arms out of her sleeves was denied. "Damn you," she groaned as his eyes feasted unapologetically while her skin heated beneath his bold gaze.

Finally, Morgan looked up, squeezing her fingers tightly as he said, "I'm not an honorable or particularly decent man, Jess. Otherwise, I'd have kept my hands off you on the train and later in Ellsworth. Otherwise, I would have walked out that door a little while ago...."

With some modicum of sanity restored, Jessica was able to remember all the reasons why this was wrong for them both. "Please, Morgan. It would be a terrible mistake—"

"Sugar, take it from an expert...this is no mistake."

"But you're only here because Boone—"

"Wrong!" Morgan stated forcefully. "Boone's letter only hurried me along a little. I was coming regardless."

Jessica wanted so desperately to believe him, but she was still afraid to trust completely. Morgan had given her hope before and then snatched it brutally away. "But the telegram...and then there was nothing...."

"I plead guilty of stupidity. Oh, Jess, it never would have been so long, but—"

"Too long, Morgan," she rasped vehemently, thinking of Earl Taylor's announcement in church this morning. Damn the man, anyway! But she was committed, had given her word....

"Unacceptable," Morgan growled, giving up his grip on her hands to capture her face for a hard, quick kiss that was fiercely possessive and a little desperate. And as he had before, Morgan again took advantage of her stunned surprise to swing her legs up and swivel her around. Then he eased her down until she was lying full length upon the sofa.

"Ah, Jessie...Jessie," he said huskily while his lips trailed over her face and neck. "We've just got to stop saying things we don't mean."

Jessica's heartbeat raced as his tongue found the pulse point at the hollow of her throat, bathing it with gentle strokes. Her breasts began to ache and swell, the nipples tingling and tautening with an anticipation she couldn't control. If only for the sake of her conscience, Jessica made one last halfhearted attempt to stop this glorious madness. "But I'm going to be married...."

"Damn right you are," Morgan stated against the rising swell of her breasts. "As soon as it can be arranged. Today, if possible."

"B-but...you don't...understand...." Jessica's eyes drifted shut, and she bit her lip hard to keep from crying out when his heated breath fanned across one of her pouting nipples.

Morgan took just a little taste and felt her hard shudder. "See how honestly we communicate when we stay away from words, Jess?" His tongue swirled again. This time she moaned and arched her back, forcing her nipple into his waiting, open mouth. He took his time with her, drawing on her gently, nipping lightly, until the restless movements of her legs drew his attention.

Grabbing a fistful of skirt and petticoats, Morgan began to ease the fabric upward until it was bunched around her waist. Then there were only her thin cotton drawers to contend with, and they proved no obstacle to reaching the warm, dewy flesh he sought.

"Oh, you feel so good there...."

It was heaven...it was hell. Time and time again Morgan's stroking, gliding fingers brought her to the brink of fulfillment, then denied her the release her pulsing, throbbing body demanded. Small pleading noises began to emerge from her throat. Silently she cursed the arms still bound by her dress but had no strength to free them so she could either force him away or make him finish this torment.

"Oh, please," she begged softly, then sobbed again with relief when he moved and began drawing her cotton drawers down over her hips, legs and feet. She expected him to come into her then, hard and full, to assuage her now-desperate need. Her breath caught when she felt his hands on the inner part of her thighs, adjusting...lifting...separating...stroking...and kissing. Oh, god! He couldn't want to kiss her there....

But Morgan did want. He wanted to show her how special she was to him, how rare and precious. This loving was a gift. It was a pledge. And it was a tribute. Because he'd never touched another woman in this so very intimate, unselfish manner. Neither would he have believed the sweetness . . . or the deep satisfaction when he heard her cry out and felt the powerful, quaking spasms of her release against his mouth and tongue.

Jessica felt as if she had died and then been reborn. Her eyelids fluttered open, focusing slowly upon the man floating above her. Oh, yes, this was heaven, all right. Because Morgan was watching her with such an expression of loving tenderness on his face that her heart began to soar even before he spoke.

"I love you, Jessica. With all my heart, soul and body, I love you . . . love you . . . love you. . . ."

Chapter Twenty

Morgan tossed another damp log on the fire and waited until he was sure it would ignite. The tiny flicks of flame licking up over the smoky wood made him think of Jessica sitting before another hearth and slowly feeding money from a saddlebag into the flames. If it hadn't been for the high price she'd paid for her revenge against Hardin, the image would have been a pleasant one. As it was, Morgan used it to serve as a reminder of how precious the child she carried was. Too precious. He wouldn't risk Jessica or the baby merely to relieve his loins from the uncomfortable pressure of unslaked desire.

"You'll have it hot as a bake oven in here soon, Morgan," Jessica complained softly, stalling him when he would have reached for another log. "Of course, *I'm* not walking around in wet clothing, either, with my hair dripping rivulets...." She arched a brow at him. "Was it really a fire you wanted so badly—or did you stop by the bunkhouse to do more plotting with Boone? You know, it's a very good thing I didn't truly want that glass of water you sent him to fetch."

Morgan heard the teasing lilt in her voice and turned to favor her with one of his bad-boy and proud-of-it grins. "Oh, I sent Larsen to get you some water, all right. I just neglected to mention at the time that he'd be riding all the way into Moonshadow for the particular flavor I wanted."

Seated upon the floor, her back braced against the sofa and her hugged knees tucked tightly beneath her chin, Jessica looked no older than a schoolgirl. Which made him feel a lecherous old man—a very horny, lecherous old man. So much for the negligible benefits of a cold rain shower.

"Water's water, Rossiter. But it's nice to know that if I get thirsty anytime soon, all I'll need is to lick up what's dripping off you...."

The wayward image that innocent remark conjured up in Morgan sent shudders through him that were anything but chilly.

Seeing the tremor and not realizing the true cause, Jessica became genuinely concerned. "Borrowing your line, Morgan, you are going to catch your death if you don't get dry." Since he'd already vehemently refused to strip down and wrap himself in one of the blankets she'd offered, Jessica tried for a compromise. "At least take off that shirt and dry your hair. Please, Morgan," she added imploringly. "If you let anything happen to you now... I'll kill you."

Morgan acquiesced, stripping off the admittedly uncomfortable shirt and spreading it out on the floor before the fireplace. "What should I dry my hair with?"

Jessica balled up and tossed him the white cotton drawers she'd never quite gotten around to putting back on. "Will this do?"

Oh, hell, yes! Morgan thought ruefully. All he needed was reminding that she was beautifully, vulnerably naked beneath her skirts. Especially with her looking at his bare chest and torso as if he were good enough to... eat. Damn!

Lord, but he was magnificent, though leaner than she remembered. Still there was enough hard-muscled flesh to make her palms itch with the desire to feel that warm, golden skin beneath her hands. And her mouth. Oh, yes, her mouth longed to know his taste. Licking the moisture off his body would satisfy a need greater than simple thirst. Unfortunately, that gallant, surprisingly sweet, beautifully made and obstinately wrongheaded man had vowed there would be no further lovemaking between them until David Griffith personally assured him such activities were safe.

"Why the sour expression, Jess?"

He'd come to stand directly over her, and Jessica took her time as she lifted her gaze to his face, letting her eyes linger on the very visible, significantly impressive bulge straining against damp, clinging trousers. Then his chest received a more thorough survey before she finally looked directly into eyes that warned as well as burned hotly. "I was thinking what a wrongheaded, stubborn—"

"You'll get no argument from me on that score," Morgan said as he dropped down beside her, purposely choosing to misunderstand just as he purposely kept several inches' distance between them. "I am admittedly one wrongheaded, stubborn and slightly stupid man."

"Morgan, I didn't mean..." Jessica protested apologetically.

"I know that, Jess," he reassured her with a soft smile, reaching over to tuck a strand of auburn hair behind her ear. She'd unpinned the chignon he'd ravaged, and her unbound hair fell like fiery silk over her back and shoulders. Morgan would never forget the first time he'd seen her like this...and the black fury that had been driving him then. Oh, yes, he had a lifetime worth of sins to atone for. But the older ones she knew about all too well and could be dealt with later. Right now it was more important they clear the air about the past two months.

Morgan crossed his legs and leaned forward. "Jess, when I left you that last morning in Ellsworth, I honestly didn't expect to be gone more than a week, two at the most. That's why I sent for your father—"

"Thank you for that," Jessica interrupted, turning slightly so she could look at him easier. "For forcing me to make up with my father, I mean. I was being the wrongheaded one there. And you don't have to explain—"

"Yes, I do. If only to minimally improve my disagreeable image." He grinned before growing serious again. "I planned to come right back to you, Jess. I never had any doubts that Judge Parker would readily agree to granting you immunity from prosecution in exchange for your cooperation and testimony, but I was afraid you wouldn't be able to share my confidence in Parker. I didn't want you pacing in a lonely hotel room, worried and anxious, while I was busy bargaining with your life. I knew you'd be better off with your family and hoped things would turn out just as they did."

Morgan wanted very much to hold her right now, but she might not welcome his arms in a minute or two. "You see, I already knew I loved you. But after all I'd done to you...the timing wasn't exactly right for a declaration. I thought after the trial we'd both feel freer, that sharing the experience might bring us closer together, be healing, somehow. Once the past was truly resolved, we could put it behind us...."

"But the past didn't get the resolution you needed, did it, Morgan? Instead, a greater force stepped in and yanked away any chance you had of making peace with your brother's memory...and yourself. All that hatred you had stored up inside for Cole, all the need for revenge you'd carried and all the blame for failure had to be placed somewhere. And I was chosen the sacrificial lamb," she said with simple, brutal honesty. "If I'd been easier to find, less the clever actress, wasting all those years, Cole Hardin's destiny would have been *yours* to command."

Her accurate insight brought a pained wince. "God Jess! I'm not proud of that. It seems so damned insane to me now. Hell! I think I did go insane for a while. In fact, I'm sure I did." He twisted around so they were face-to-face, and his expression asked for an understanding and forgiveness he had no right to expect. "One good thing came out of this, though. During the past couple of months, I've had plenty of time to take a good hard look at myself and the kind of man I'd become since Zach's death. What I discovered wasn't pleasant, Jess. In fact, I was so appalled and disgusted that I convinced myself I didn't deserve any happiness...or a woman to love me. God knows, I was damned certain I didn't deserve you. Not after all I'd done."

"You call that a good thing, Morgan?" Jessica queried quietly. "I'm sorry, but I find it downright selfish and—

forgive me if this is unfair—typically arrogant. Who gave you authority to play God over other people's lives and decide what is or isn't best for them? I loved you, Morgan. Surely you had to know that."

Her controlled and quiet condemnation did not minimize the punch she'd landed. It was a verbal wallop he deserved and oddly enough had heard before. "You are your father's daughter," he observed with a wry grin. "Only Jack Cameron wasn't nearly so diplomatic when he stormed over to the Triple R and took me to task for breaking his daughter's heart. Of course, I defended myself admirably with an accounting of my faults and subsequent unworthiness. And then Jack proceeded to inform me that there was nothing more contemptible than a man who so enjoys wallowing in his own guilt that he destroys everyone and everything precious to him in the process. Said he was an authority on that particular subject. Of course, Jack made a number of other decidedly unpleasant observations regarding my character, but I'll spare myself the repeating of them, if you don't mind. He sends his love, by the way."

When Jessica only nodded in response, Morgan turned his attention to the fire and stared silently for several minutes. When he spoke again, his voice was thin with anxiety and not entirely steady. "Your father also said he had a daughter who possessed a rare loving and forgiving heart. I'm praying he was right, Jess." He looked at her then, not even attempting to hide the fear twisting his guts. "He was, wasn't he?"

Jessica could no more have denied him than she could have stopped breathing. She reached for his hand, brought it to her and pressed a loving kiss into the palm. It was then she noticed the thick, still angry-looking scar tissue that had formed there. "My God, Morgan. Your hand...." Alarmed eyes flew to his face.

"Now's your chance to say 'I told you so.' It festered just as you said it would, because I was too damn stubborn to have a doctor check it for wood slivers. Ah, Jess," Morgan breathed, pulling her into his arms and across his lap. "Even with everything I've told you, it would never have taken me two damn long months to come to my senses. A good amount of that time was spent flat on my back, out of my head with fever."

Jessica looked at his palm again. "The infection was that bad?"

"Almost." He would never tell her how close he'd come to losing his hand to an overeager surgeon's scalpel. Or that without the diligence and nursing of a certain lady in Kansas City, he might not be alive today. "Two weeks of non-stop drinking, very little food and a constitution already weakened from lack of sleep all contributed. I developed lung fever as a little aside to the other problem. It put me down hard and kept me down for quite a while."

Wrapping her arms around his neck, Jessica pressed a kiss to the end of his nose. "I thought you looked thinner. Are you completely recovered? Oh, Lord! You've no business at all sitting around in those—"

"Jess...Jess," he said with a chuckle. "I'm as healthy as a horse now." With some parts a little healthier than was comfortable, particularly with Jessica firmly, tantalizingly astraddle his lap. "And you are *not* getting me out of these trousers. So stop trying!"

"Morgan! I'll have you know getting you naked was the furthest thing from my mind," Jessica objected with feigned indignation. "Just what kind of woman do you think I am?"

"Beautiful, passionate, loving, innately sensual— Shall I go on?"

"Most definitely, Mr. Rossiter. Do go on...and on...."

"Difficult, sassy—"

"That's enough, thank you!"

"Loving and beloved. My love. And soon to be my wife, if she'll have me."

Jessica smiled at him tenderly. "Oh, she'll have you. Because she can't imagine life without you. And if you don't kiss her very soon—" Her voice broke at the threat of glad tears.

There was really no resisting those gently quivering lips. God, but she had the most wonderful mouth: soft, full and so sweetly responsive that one taste wasn't enough. Morgan had to go back for seconds...and thirds. Somewhere along the way, what had begun harmlessly enough escalated into a dangerously carnal mating of tongues, with bodies pressing and rocking, hands groping and desperate hearts pounding. When it finally ended, with Morgan wrenching his mouth away on an anguished groan, there was no avoiding that staying here with Jessica was impossible. He could not trust himself.

As gently as he could, he put Jessica away from him, away from the furiously demanding hardness clamoring to be freed from his trousers and buried deep inside the woman he loved. Letting his head fall forward onto his knees, Morgan drew one deep, shuddering breath after another.

Jessica, similarly curled and wrapped around her knees, was shaking with only slightly less frustration than Morgan. But only slightly. Though his loving earlier had brought her immense pleasure and soul-shaking fulfillment, it had been a solitary gratification, one that left her feeling strangely separate from Morgan, still apart, somehow. And a little afraid and unsure, her confidence wavering on her ability to satisfy and content such an unapologetically sexual man. What if his concerns were valid and David forbade them lovemaking for the entire term of her pregnancy? Would he seek satisfaction elsewhere? Even if no such restriction was placed on them, would Morgan still want her body when it was no longer the perfect thing he now praised so adoringly?

"I've got to get out of here, Jess," he breathed raggedly. "That was too damn close. I'll ride into town and talk with David today...."

"No!" Jessica cried, all but leaping at him when he would have attempted to rise. "I won't let you go out in this storm, Morgan. With our luck, you'd sicken and it would be months until we could be married, and I'd be walking around town still just a bride-to-be, with my belly out to here—" Her extended arms made a circle so ludicrously huge that it won her a chuckle.

"Honey, you get that big and we'll be cleaning out a special stall in the barn for that colt you're having." Morgan's hand maneuvered beyond her exaggerated gesture to find the real thing. His fingers spread gently over the barely perceptible mound of her stomach. "Our baby," he said with feeling, "is going to be born healthy and strong, Jess. Nothing—absolutely nothing—is going to jeopardize his well-being, or yours. I'm going to pamper you in every possible way, even if the form of that pampering means denying myself."

Jessica clasped her hands over his, deeply touched by his protectiveness. Still, there was that tiny echo of fear whispering in her ear. "You may not think it such a sacrifice in a few months."

"Dammit!" Morgan came up on his knees and took firm hold of her shoulders. "Don't you go confusing me with Hardin. Ninety-nine percent of my desire comes from loving you. *You,* Jessica! The person you are. I can't imagine you less beautiful in my eyes under any circumstances. Your body will be even more beautiful as it blossoms and ripens with our child. And I hope to God I get ample opportunity to prove just how desirable you'll be to me, as well." Morgan lifted her chin and frowned at the uncertainty still in her eyes. Damn Cole Hardin! He hoped the fires of hell were as hot as the one that had carried him there! "Come here, Jess." The need to comfort and reassure made worrying about his desires secondary.

Jessica flowed into his arms. "Oh, Morgan. I believe you love me and will love our baby. That you won't stop loving me just because I'm temporarily not as physically appealing as you find me now. When...if...that day comes, I want you to promise you'll not distance yourself physically or emotionally. I need to express as well as receive love, Morgan. Like now, for instance. I can't even touch you because...because..."

"I'm hard as a brick and frustrated as hell?" Morgan

supplied when she stumbled shyly over describing his obvious difficulty.

Actually, Morgan's crude candor didn't bother Jessica at all, which she proved by pulling back and dropping her gaze straight to his crotch. "Yes, exactly. Oh, Morgan, what will we do if David makes me an untouchable? Spend half the first year of our marriage staying at arm's length? Because you can't touch me, I can't touch you...."

Morgan's delighted laughter rang in Jessica's ears as she was yanked hard against his chest and hugged until an involuntary grunt of protest escaped.

"Honey," his deep voice rumbled, "you give me far too much credit. I'm not that damned self-sacrificing. Neither is my control that trustworthy, as you'll learn over the next fifty years or so. I never had any intention of becoming a chaste monk, particularly not with my wife. The restraint I've been attempting today would never have lasted more than a day, at best."

Jessica was admittedly confused. "But you said you had to talk to David first. That we wouldn't...couldn't..."

"And we won't until I'm sure it's safe." He saw that she still wasn't comprehending. But then showing was always better than telling in matters such as this, anyhow. Morgan brought her arms from around his neck. "You can touch, Jess. All you like...."

He was guiding Jessica's hands across his chest and down his belly, then back up again. "Anywhere and anytime. And in any manner that pleases us both." The journey of encouraged exploration ended at the waistband of Morgan's trousers. There he left the decision of taking the next step entirely and quite literally in Jessica's hands. When she looked up from where he'd tucked her fingers, Morgan drew his breath in harshly. For while her complexion was a telling shade of beet red, there was nothing but shining anticipation glowing out of her adoring eyes.

"May I?" she implored throatily.

Morgan's slow smile went past bad boy, all the way to absolutely wicked. "Honey, do your worst...your best...

and anything else that happens to strike your fancy in between." The way her fingers were already busy toying with the buttons—and the straining flesh beneath—was driving him crazy. "Just do it soon . . . please."

Cloth parted and Jessica was touching his heated shaft, tracing her fingers up and down, over and around, letting Morgan's sighs and groans of pleasure guide her. "It's so hard . . . and soft. How can it be both at once? And so hot. It's really a miracle, the way God made us. And He must have been feeling very generous when creating you, Morgan."

The words "miracle" and "generous" were how Morgan would have described the beautiful woman who was giving him such stirring pleasure with her untutored yet surprisingly clever hands. In fact, it was her very naïveté, the expressions of wonder and delight at each discovery, that pleased him more than any expert technique might have done.

And he told her so silently when he drew her mouth up to be kissed, lavishing her lips with moist strokes of his tongue. Told her again aloud, extolling her in rasping whispers when her caresses became surer, bolder. "Ah, Jess...my Jess, that feels so good. You're so good. . . ."

As any good teacher knows, even the most inexperienced of pupils when praised for effort, strives that much harder for approval, never contented until good becomes great and accolades turn into shouted hosannas. . . .

Epilogue

"This was not exactly your conventional wedding, wouldn't you agree, Mrs. Rossiter?" Morgan chuckled as he came up behind his wife and drew her back against him, his arms wrapping around a blue-calico-covered waist. "Whoever would have thought of being married in an old abandoned mining camp, adjacent to a graveyard, with a picnic on the grass serving as a reception?"

"Why, I believe it was the bride's unconventional bridegroom," Jessica returned saucily, plucking the skirt of her simple but very pretty dress. It was the one Pamela had given her the fabric for, and together they'd sewn and fashioned the calico, which made it very special to Jessica. Special enough to serve as her wedding dress.

Morgan's embrace tightened. "You really don't regret not doing this in the church?"

She turned in his arms and looked up into his face, letting him see the truth in her eyes. "Oh, Morgan. I regret nothing. How could I possibly? I'm sorry Papa, Pamela and the boys aren't here. I wish Shorty wasn't arriving two days late. But I have the rest of my family—" She glanced down at the marble gravestone nearby and then over to where the others were seated upon grass and quilts, eating, laughing and arguing. Jessica smiled at the sight of Oramay waving a chicken leg in Stan's grinning face as she took him to task for something or other. "And I have you," she finished, going up on tiptoe to receive the kiss she saw coming in his eyes.

"And baby makes three," Morgan murmured, pressing himself more firmly against her belly.

"Four if you consider that insistent intruder coming between us. Morgan! You're insatiable," she chided softly.

"Where you're concerned—damn right!"

Mouths met for a long, wet kiss that would have led only heaven knew where if it hadn't been for the very loud "Humph!" that broke them apart.

Oramay Seibert stood just a few feet away, smiling. "Lordamercy, you two. You'll ignite this whole valley with sparks like that flying around." Despite her candor, there was warm color on Oramay's cheeks, which deepened when the bridegroom took immediate shelter behind his bride. And since Morgan wasn't going to be able to rejoin them anytime soon, it was just as well everyone had decided to pack up and leave.

So amused was Oramay about Morgan's discomfiture, she hadn't noticed how her innocent, teasing comment about the valley had distressed Jessica. But when she did notice, Oramay wasn't the least bit hesitant to address the subject hanging between them like a ready fist. "Jessie, most folks got memories this long—" She put her thumb and index finger together until only a thin thread could have passed between them. "Give them a little time, and they won't hardly be able to remember what the Widow Miller once looked like, except to state how she blossomed into a beautiful woman after finding the love of a good man. As far as poor Earl's concerned—well, now that he's bought that little place down Stockton way, he's content enough. This ballyhoo won't last more than a minute...."

No one but Morgan and Jessica knew that Earl's jilted feelings and disgruntled squawking had been bought off and assuaged with that small ranch far enough away from Moonshadow to guarantee Morgan wouldn't someday knock his block off.

."And you don't need to worry about Mabel Harrison's big mouth anymore, either." Oramay chortled. "I've taken care of Mabel. She'll be throwing you nothing but roses from now on. That I can promise for certain." Oramay's grin became downright victorious. The best cure for a mudslinger was somebody willing and able to sling it right back. She leaned forward and said conspiratorially, "I'll leave you the secret of controlling Mabel in my will." With a wink, she straightened. "Came up here to tell you we're all about to leave. The sun will be setting shortly. Kathleen and Luke need to get home to the babies. Their Uncle Patrick gets a might fretful himself when they start fussing to be fed."

Jessica saw then that blankets were being folded and baskets reloaded into buggies and wagon. Boone and the men from the Eldorado were already standing by their horses. The Griffiths were nowhere in sight. "Oh, dear. I didn't realize we'd been up here so long. We didn't even say goodbye to David and Melanie."

"They're pretty near newlyweds themselves still. They understand," Oramay reassured. "Besides, David said he wanted to stop by the Layton place on their way back to collect some corn relish Millie owes him."

A shrill whistle had Oramay looking over her shoulder. "Damn that man. I've told him before I'm no dog to be fetched by a whistle. Plus, it's just not dignified for an attorney to go around sticking his fingers in his mouth!"

Morgan's breath tickled in Jessica's ear as he whispered, "Do they grumble at each other all the time?"

She laughed softly, nodded and whispered back, "Except when they're kissing. Then they get along just dandy."

"It's not polite to whisper behind folks' backs, but I'll forgive you. Especially for the treat of this wonderful wedding. I may drag Stan and the preacher up here for our shindig. Though I was thinking the hotel would be— Oh, never mind. Give me a hug so I can get back to that infernal, impatient man who's—"

Jessica hugged Oramay hard. "Going to make you the happiest woman on earth. Next to me, of course," she finished, and then drew back. "We'll come down with you and say our farewells." She'd hardly taken a step before Morgan yanked her back.

"Uh...I don't think anyone would mind if we waved goodbye from here," he insisted.

With his arm a steel band around her waist, Jessica couldn't help but take notice of his difficulty. "Oh! Well...I guess..."

Oramay was quick to assure there would be no hurt feelings, and with parting good wishes, she walked to where Stan was waiting beside his buggy. Whatever Oramay said to Stan earned her first a kiss and then a swat on her behind. But both were smiling when they drove away.

Morgan's other arm came around Jessica. "Sorry about that. But farewells are hard for me."

"So I noticed."

"Very, very hard."

"Like as in a rock...or a board...."

"Something like that." Morgan chuckled. "Let's take a walk."

He led her by the hand through the old town and up to the ridge to take in the magnificent view. The sun was a huge orange ball, dipping toward the western horizon. Spidery clouds hung over the distant mountains and were washed in hues of red and purple. The valley floor was a patchwork of shadows and light.

"The first time you brought me here," Morgan said softly as he stood just behind his wife, his hands gently resting upon her shoulders, "it was as if some force I couldn't see was wrapping itself around me. Not threateningly, but as if in welcome. Dreams, goals, yearnings I hadn't thought of in years all started speaking to me again, reminding me of what might have been if..." His fingers tightened fractionally. "I wanted to be part of this, Jess. From the minute I saw the valley, I felt I belonged here, somehow. Of course, being the hardheaded fool, I refused to accept any of it."

His arms slid around Jessica's shoulders. "I'm a rich man, honey. I could purchase a ranch anywhere...."

Jessica angled her head so she could gaze at the man she loved and needed with every part of her being. Tears were falling freely down her face as she whispered, "Welcome home, Morgan. Welcome home, my love."

* * * * *